# FRACTUM OSTIUM

A SHORT STORY COLLECTION

**MARK SOWERS**

KDP ISBN 9798332530074



Cover design by: Marcy Sowers

Created in the United States of America

# DEDICATION

*For Bernadine and Henle - generations apart but both always full of smiles.*

# TABLE OF CONTENTS

# ACKNOWLEDGEMENTS

The publication of this book would not have been possible without the incredible support and tireless work of the most wonderful wife a man could ask for – Marcy. She not only reads everything I write, but edits, formats, and has created cover art for some of my books. Without her I'd be just another writer with manuscripts clogging up the hard drive of his computer. Thank you babe!

Thanks must also be given to the writers who have inspired me to write: Stephen King, Terry Goodkind, Dean Koontz, Robert Jordan, Peter Bacho, Primo Levi, Dan Simmons, Dickens, Celine, Solzhenitsyn, Dumas, and so, so many others.

Cover art by Marcy Sowers

# ANOMALIES

"Elon-7 Remote Space Observatory reports no unusual activity over the last galactic cycle," the digital but human-sounding voice from the onboard navigation and integrated systems management computer, or ISM as it was often called, said.

"Roger," the human sitting in the command chair muttered. The bulletin had been sent out galaxy-wide through a network of subspace comms satellites. The Cosmic Science Foundation did love their data accumulators and to announce what their network of them found. Even when they didn't find anything at all. "I don't know why they keep scanning," he said to himself. "Nothing's happened in this zone in over two hundred cycles. The last interesting thing was just a comet." The man looked at the holographic display in front of him. It showed hundreds of irregularly shaped objects; most were smaller than the spacecraft he was aboard, and which he was the owner and operator of, while some were very large, nearly planetoid size. This asteroid field featured some of the biggest chunks of rock he'd ever seen, but they were still so much smaller than some of the truly enormous planets and other celestial bodies he'd seen throughout his life. The outlines of the asteroids were rendered on the display in white, while crawling over them were hundreds of small red dots and a far fewer number of blue ones. The red dots represented his mining automata – the machines that made his living for him. The blue dots were the brains of the operation – they were the delver units, responsible for surveying and mapping the asteroids, analyzing and cataloguing any mineral finds, and using their myriad drills and sensors to determine the deposit size and location of anything worth excavating.

Rex T. Chalut had owned his spacecraft for the last thirty-two cycles, after inheriting it upon the death of his father Morris. Rex's mother passed away shortly after his birth, and he'd been reared by his domineering drunk of a father. The man hadn't taught him much about life or how to deal with its ups and downs, but he had taught him how to find minerals on asteroids using this very ship and its array of machines. "Rexty," his father was fond of calling him (the nickname the old man had bestowed on him was an amalgam of his first name and middle initial, an unwelcome appellation Rex hated to this day) "if you don't learn anything else from me learn this – a good employee is fuckin' hard to find. You find a good one, you keep the sonofabitch around. Even if you can't stand the prick."

The ship had a crew of twelve, not including Rex, and every one of them had been with him at least fifteen galactic cycles. Rex paid well, even if he had been known to exhibit unreasonable bouts of rage. It was not uncommon for Rex to demolish small objects that were close to hand when a fit took him, which was usually when one of his employees displeased him. He simply hated finding new people, training them, and then listening to them bitch and moan about the long hours the job demanded. It was so much easier to find competent people, pay them what they were worth, and keep them around than it was to replace them every couple cycles. His father had been right about that at least, even if he'd been wrong about almost everything else.

"Automaton unit S-81 isn't responding," a voice said through the communications gear. The voice belonged to Santos from Engineering. It was Santos', and his partner Yevgeniy's job to monitor the automata and to repair them when they malfunctioned. Another engineer, Oscar, monitored the delvers. The three men had a workshop on the lower deck of the craft where they could dismantle and repair almost anything, and from which they monitored the robots.

This far out from Sigma Draconis and the massive city that had been constructed in its orbit over eight hundred galactic cycles ago, they had space to themselves. The city had started as a simple outpost for refueling and refitting the early cosmic explorers who'd fanned out from Earth and across the galaxy in the late twenty-second century, once the ability to move faster than the speed of light had been developed. Over time thousands of additional modules had been added to the original structure in an unplanned and haphazard fashion until it stretched out to dimensions unknown anywhere in the galaxy. Someone claimed to have measured it once and said that it was six thousand kilometers long by four thousand deep and two thousand tall. The city orbiting Sigma Draconis did have an official name, one that could be found on all galactic star charts – Locus 394, but no one ever called it that. Its inhabitants and visitors called it Hades, and not without good reason. The place was lousy with fugitives, criminals, and all-around unsavory characters. It was a great place to find all manner of illicit substances and pastimes. Or, if you weren't careful, where you could wind up on the pointy end of a proton blade.

The earliest explorers in this region of the galaxy had known nothing about the asteroids that Rex was at that moment mining; they had been more interested in mapping stars and investigating planets. Asteroid fields were things to be noted on galactic charts and avoided. Since that time the galaxy had been explored and divided into nine hundred and eight different zones. Most of them contained nothing of any real value, like the one where Hades floated – Zone 429. The adjacent Zone 430 was where Rex and his team were doing their best to mine Manginium – a mineral that had been unknown to human science until the early twenty second century. Its discovery finally provided the fuel source that allowed humans to achieve faster-than-light travel. Rex was hazy on the details, but he remembered hearing somewhere that Manginium had been named in honor of some musician from the late twentieth and early twenty-first centuries. He knew little about the mineral's history, how it formed, or what its atomic weight was and didn't care about any of that technical garbage. All that mattered to him was that it was rare, expensive, and generally found on asteroids. That's why he'd come to this remote region of the galaxy – to get rich. He'd had enough of mining for gold or copper, thulium or ytterbium, important and sought-after minerals to be sure, but they barely earned him enough coin to keep his ship operating and his crew happy. When he'd overheard a conversation at a refueling station near Tau Ceti about an unexplored asteroid field in Zone 430, he'd informed his crew where they were going, given them three galactic sols to get themselves ready, and aimed his ship toward this place. The crew had pushed back at first, reminding him that Zone 430 was avoided by most spacefarers. Several ships had disappeared there over the cycles, and the zone had developed a reputation for being dangerous, deadly. Rex had even heard it referred to as space's Bermuda Triangle, whatever that meant. When he'd told them what they were going to be mining, and more importantly how much money they'd all make, they'd rethought their reservations and agreed to the expedition.

So here he was with his crew, in the cosmic equivalent of the middle of nowhere, watching his automatons crawl around on asteroids looking for the mineral that would provide the means for him to retire to the strange reverse gravity of the fourth planet out from Procyon A where you could literally sleep on a cloud. That's how he wanted to spend the rest of his days – in leisure, with a bottle of Altair brandy close to hand.

They'd been moderately successful so far. His cargo hold contained enough Manginium to nearly buy a new spacecraft. He wanted enough to buy a planet. They were for sale if you had the money.

Lost in his thoughts of cloudy beds and exquisite drink, Rex didn't notice the small flashing green dot on his holograph until the audible alarm sounded. Jolted from his reverie, the captain peered at the screen. Something was wrong with one of his automatons. That wasn't unusual. Most of the machines were old, and malfunctions were frequent. New ones were expensive and while he wasn't against replacing his outdated equipment, he preferred to wait until it became more costly to repair an old one than to just scrap it and buy a new one.

"What's wrong now?" he muttered angrily. A touch of his finger on the hologram called up the unit's vital statistics. He read aloud: "Celestial Mining Products model THX 1139. Huh. Their stuff was usually pretty solid. Looks like an anchor fault. No, two anchor faults." The anchors were actually barbed spikes that drove themselves into the surface of whatever the automaton was operating on. In zero gravity it kept them from floating off into space. This particular model had six anchors. It wasn't uncommon to have one anchor fault, but two was unusual. "What would cause two faults? Santos!"

"Yeah chief?" the automata engineer replied.

"You see the two faults on that machine?"

"Yep. Trying to figure out what's going on right now. Might have to send down a peeper. And I'm still working on that other one."

"Alright. Let me know what happens." A peeper was slang for a drone that was outfitted with an array of cameras and sensors, and which was used for diagnosing problems with the other mining machines. It could also latch onto a malfunctioning automaton or delver and return it to the engineering bay for repairs. Rarely did one of the crew ever have to leave the ship.

There were columns of icons on the edges of the hologram which allowed Rex to perform a host of functions. Just by touching a button, he could run a complete diagnostic scan of his ship, pilot it through space, or even order dinner from the craft's 3-D food printer. He poked an icon and a window opened on the holograph. The image that appeared in it was from one of the peepers; it was just leaving the ship. In front of it was the asteroid field, the huge chunks of space rock little more than shadows in the faint light from the closest, but still very distant, star. The peeper was equipped with powerful spotlights on all sides, and one of them suddenly switched on. Santos had known his boss would be watching and had made sure to turn on the headlights.

The peeper darted through space, dodged around lazily floating and twisting asteroids, their surfaces equally dark and sparkling with ice and minerals, until it finally reached the malfunctioning automaton. The machine was on a strange-looking formation and was obviously in some distress. The two anchors were actuated by rams attached to appendages much like legs. Rex could see them retracting and thrusting back out as they vainly tried to find purchase. The other four anchors were embedded solidly in the rock of the asteroid. It was just the two on the front portion of the machine that were having trouble. Santos' voice came over the comms system.

"Looks like there's a big deposit of Manginium underneath that formation," he said. "The machine wants to get to it." The automata were programmed to move to a location the delvers pinpointed and extract whatever was there. This one was determined to get at the mineral underneath the strange formation despite the difficulty it was having. Automata could sometimes be as stubbornly stupid as humans.

"What is that?" Rex asked, knowing Santos could hear him.

"Don't know boss. The scanners aren't registering it. I'm gonna get Oscar to check out the automaton." The delver engineer was one of the smartest people Rex had ever met. By all rights the man should be working for one of the big galactic conglomerates, putting his talents to use in one of their crazy schemes to actually capture a star and use it as an energy source. Oscar was the kind of guy who could probably figure out how to do that. The problem was that he didn't play well with others. Oscar could be called prickly, mercurial, or an asshole – and any one of those terms would be appropriate. He was smart and he knew it, and he had no patience for fools or anyone slower mentally than himself. Rex tried not to interact with him unless he had to, as did the rest of the crew.

"Let me know what he says," Rex replied. "And hey Santos!" he called. "Get a delver over here and analyze that formation."

"Roger that chief."

Rex stared at the image on the screen. The strange formation looked only a little like rock. It was a pile about fifteen feet tall and approximately the same in diameter. The formation was conical, tapering up the sides to a point at the top. He watched as the peeper rotated slowly around the pile, its lights playing over the surface. No, it certainly wasn't rock. It looked more like mud.

One of the blue dots began moving toward the peeper. Rex watched until it appeared in his view screen. The machine landed delicately on the pile and several appendages appeared. Some of them drove into the surface while others hovered over it. These were the sensors and scanners that determined what things were made of. Ordinarily the delvers were quick at returning results of their investigations. This one appeared to be having some trouble. Seconds turned into minutes as it tested and analyzed. Rex was about to ask if there was a problem with this delver too when Oscar's voice came over the comms.

"This is the weirdest fucking thing I've ever seen chief," he said, "the test results are crazy."

Ordinarily Rex would have been pissed at Oscar. He'd specifically told Santos to have him look at the automaton, but Oscar had looked at the delver's test results instead. It was yet another instance of the mercurial man doing whatever he wanted instead of what he was told. He decided not to push the issue today. "What do they say?" he asked. Rex could have looked at them himself, but he didn't know much about chemical compositions and all the other technical jargon the reports displayed. It was just easier to let someone like Oscar interpret them and then tell him what they said in layman's terms.

"There's all kinds of shit in that formation – organics, weird chemical compounds I've never seen before, even what looks like scraps of metal. I have no idea what this is, but it's a scientific find. I'm gonna send the test results to someone I know at the Cosmic Science Foundation. Maybe she can figure it out."

"So, what do we do in the meantime?" Rex asked. "The automaton can't seem to get through it, and I want the Manginium its sitting on."

"It won't take long to hear back from her," Oscar said, "we'll have an answer within the hour. I say we pause the automaton and leave it there as a marker until then."

Rex didn't like his automatons idle. They had to be working in order for him to make money, and the deposit under that formation was the biggest one he'd found yet. He sighed in frustration. Maybe an hour wasn't the end of the universe. "Alright but keep me informed."

"Yep," Oscar said and disconnected. He wasn't one for following proper communications protocol; you'd never hear Oscar say 'Roger'.

Rex sat back in his command chair and watched the dots on his holograph crawl across asteroids. He dozed off and only woke when Oscar's voice blared from the comms system.

"Chief! You're not going to believe this!"

Rex shook his head and sat up in his chair. "What?" he asked drowsily.

"I heard back from my contact." Oscar was silent for several seconds.

"What Oscar?! What the fuck did she say?!"

"It's gonna be easier for you to just watch the video file she sent."

Rex touched an icon on his holograph and a window opened. He was looking at the face of a woman probably in her sixties, with close cropped salt and pepper hair and a pinched face that looked like it spent more time scowling than it did smiling. Much like Oscar. The woman started speaking and Rex listened intently.

"Oscar, I don't know what the hell you found out there, but it's nothing I've ever seen, and I couldn't find any records of a comparable substance anywhere in our databases. The closest I got was…" the woman paused, and her face crumpled up even more, an extraordinary feat Rex would have thought nearly impossible had he not just watched it happen. "This is going to sound weird because it is. A paleontologist from Old Earth found some fossilized dinosaur droppings that he analyzed chemically. Those results are in our databases, but they were so obscure it took me forever to locate them. Your find, while still dramatically different, is closest to that substance in composition." The woman attempted what Rex thought was a smile, but that looked far more like a grimace prompted by extreme discomfort, and the video ended. He sat back in his chair and stared at the holograph.

"Get that chief?" Oscar asked.

"Yeah. But what the fuck does it mean?"

"It means our little automaton is sitting on a huge pile of shit."

"How in the good goddamn is that even possible?!"

"I don't fuckin know!" Oscar said testily. "If I knew I would have told you already. Christ on a popsicle!"

"You're telling me we found a giant turd? On a fuckin asteroid? In the middle of a galactic zone where nothing ever happens?"

"That's exactly what I'm telling you," Oscar replied. "If you don't like it, well there ain't fuck-all I can do about it."

"I'm not even going to bother asking you what the fuck could have made a turd that size. Maybe some ship flew past here and dumped its shit tanks?" Emptying the sewage collection system into space was common practice among most interstellar craft. Only the big passenger and cargo ships had systems to process sewage that did not involve just venting the stuff out a port in the hull.

Oscar was incensed. "If it had just been some random ship, dumping human waste, don't you think I would have figured that out? Besides, if that actually had happened, it would all be floating around in small icy chunks. Not even landing on that asteroid and dumping the tanks would have caused a formation like that. For fuck's sake chief, think!"

Rex didn't bite on the barb, although if it had been any other crewmember except Oscar who'd talked to him like that, he'd have fired the person on the spot, ejected them from his ship in a stasis pod and let them get picked up by the next passing spacecraft. And he had already come to the same conclusion that Oscar just voiced. That turd had not been made by a ship dumping its sewage – it had been made by a single… thing. Whatever that thing was.

Rex sat back in his chair and regarded the holograph. This zone had never really been mapped like most of the others had. It had been determined early in the days of galactic travel that there was nothing of any real interest or importance here. That knowledge, when combined with the fact that ships were known to disappear in this zone, kept most spacefarers away. The charts Rex had perused before coming here showed him this asteroid field, a few rogue planets drifting alone in space, and little else.

Rex touched an icon on the holograph and listened for the ping he knew would follow. Getting up from his chair, he walked to the food printer and extracted his dinner – a large pizza with Sirius A pepperoni and Old Earth mozzarella. He returned to his chair and devoured a slice. How long had it been since he'd eaten? He couldn't remember. Time didn't really matter out here in space. It wasn't like being on a planet, with day and night cycles to regulate the circadian rhythms. Here you ate when you were hungry and slept when you were tired. Rex didn't have set hours for his crew to work, although some of them lived on schedules they set for themselves. The crew did their jobs when they were awake, slept when they wanted to, and visited the reality replication and relaxation room when they felt like it. That room was the only recreation available on the ship, and it was all the crew needed. Anything imaginable could happen in the real-rep, as it was called. When a person walked in, they were encased in a feather soft cocoon of foam polymer that could mimic any possible sensation. The material also acted as a neural interface that planted images directly into one's mind. Imagine you were a cowboy back on Earth in the old West, and you'd smell the dust, feel the horse beneath you, and experience the pain of a gunshot wound, all while embarking on whatever adventure you chose. Want to be an insect, you could do that. Miss your loved ones back home? The real-rep put you right there with them. And if you were imaginative enough, a world of your own creation was possible. Rex himself didn't visit the real-rep, but it was something his crew had insisted on, so he'd grudgingly ponied up the considerable amount of coin it had cost to have it installed. The morale of the crew had been fair to good ever since. In retrospect it had been worth the expenditure.

His pizza was nearly gone, and he was about to get a beer and go to bed when a delver unit on the hologram began blinking. What now? He peered at the blinking delver and saw that it was near the farthest known extremity of the asteroid field. What was it doing way out there? "Oscar! What the fuck is that delver doing?"

"What are you talking about?!" Oscar replied testily.

"The goddamn delver that's about to fly off into space, that's what I'm talking about! Aren't you watching it?"

"Yeah, I'm fucking watching it. And I've got it under control too. I sent it out there to investigate a weird reading I got from deeper in the zone."

"What reading?"

"One of the ship's deep space scanners picked up an anomaly so I sent the delver out to take a look. Got a problem with that?!"

Rex ignored the challenge. "What anomaly?"

"I don't know yet. That's why I sent the delver." Oscar's tone was patronizing, superior, and Rex was tempted to remind him who was in charge. The rest of the crew knew, and they also knew that Rex tolerated Oscar's insubordination even when he didn't tolerate theirs. Instead of getting into a pissing match with Oscar that neither one of them would win, Rex instead accepted the draw. "Keep me updated."

"Yeah. Sure," came the flippant response.

The delver was not a machine that was capable of deep space flight autonomously. But its scanners and sensors were superb. The little machines could detect all sorts of things from great distances. This one was hovering at the edge of the asteroid field, and Rex watched as columns of data scrolled across the holograph. He had no idea what it all meant, so he waited until the ship's integrated systems management computer, or ISM as most of the crew called it, finished its analysis. He couldn't believe the result.

"Oscar! Does that say what I think it says?!" he nearly screamed.

"Yeah chief. It does." Oscar's voice was quiet, almost reverential. Rex couldn't recall ever hearing his engineer speak in a tone even remotely like it. "It's a fucking Black Dwarf." These celestial bodies had been, up to this moment, purely theoretical. They were thought to be remnants of stars, White Dwarfs actually, that no longer had the fuel for nuclear fusion like a normal star. It was also believed that it took longer for them to cool down than the universe had existed, therefore making it impossible for one to even exist. But their little delver had just returned data that refuted that long-held astronomical belief. There were still many mysteries in the galaxy and the universe beyond, and Rex was jubilant that he might have just solved one. If the theory about them was correct, the Black Dwarf would be composed of highly compressed iron, which was not something Rex had any interest in mining. But he did want to verify their find.

"Call back all the automatons and delvers," he said over the comms system. "We're going for a ride."

An hour later the ship was hurtling through the void of space toward the Black Dwarf. The onboard sensor array was sending back reams of data while also updating their charts of Zone 430. Rex sat in his captain's chair daydreaming. If nothing else, he'd be able to upload the new charts to the Cosmic Science Foundation and get credit for exploring a largely unknown region of the galaxy. But he wanted more than that – he wanted notoriety on top of riches. Oscar and the rest of the crew had been quiet since he'd given the order to head for the Black Dwarf. They were busy making preparations for investigating the discovery. Or they'd better be. The ISM was tracking the ship's progress, and the display showed that they had about two more hours before arriving in the vicinity of the Black Dwarf. Rex slouched in his chair and stared at the holograph. Their destination appeared as a yellow dot on a three-dimensional chart display he'd called up, while the ship was depicted by a clearly identifiable outline of its actual shape in white. A line in red stretched between the two points, and Rex watched calmly as the line shrunk the further the ship traveled.

"Reading some weird anomalies around the Black Dwarf chief," Yevgeniy's voice said. The sound startled Rex, and he sat up in his chair.

"What kind of anomalies?"

"Strange gravitational and magnetic fields. Never seen anything like it. They seem to be moving. Like a ship under way but faster."

"Impossible," Oscar's voice interjected, his tone patronizing and dismissive.

"It's right fucking there Oscar," Yevgeniy replied testily. "Look at your holo!"

Rex touched an icon and his own holo changed. Yevgeniy was right. The display showed at least seven different instances of intertwined magnetic and gravitational fields. They were small, not much bigger than his ship, and they were flying erratically around the Black Dwarf. There was no pattern to their movements; they reminded Rex of how birds flew, and Yevgeniy was right – they were very fast. What the hell was that? Before he could ask the question aloud, Oscar did.

"What the fuck?!" the engineer said. "That's simply not possible."

"Well, it's happening." Yevgeniy said drily, and with not a little satisfaction. "Got an explanation?"

Oscar didn't reply. Good, Rex thought. He was rapidly losing his patience with Oscar's attitude. One of the anomalies suddenly broke away from its chaotic orbit. It zigged and zagged haphazardly for a few short moments then, as if called, flew directly toward the ship.

"What's going on?" Rex asked no one in particular. "Why's that thing coming right at us?" The ISM calculated that the anomaly would reach them in less than seven minutes. Damn that thing was fast! Even the fastest galactic conglomerate warships couldn't move like that. Rex's little mining ship had no weapons at all, and its only defensive capability was the electromagnetic repellent field that protected it from space debris. It would do nothing against something that size hitting them at that speed. He briefly considered abandoning ship, but as yet the anomaly was not a threat, just an object moving toward them very, very fast.

Uh, chief," Santos said with trepidation, "should we maybe do something? Change course or evasive action, or whatever those conglomerate soldiers say?"

"No, not yet," Rex replied. "Let's just see what that thing is." He touched an icon on the holograph and powerful searchlights mounted to the hull blazed to life, their beams pierced the darkness in front of the ship. His crew were no doubt watching the approach of the object and were surely feeling as apprehensive as Santos. The only calm one was probably Oscar. He'd be using every sensor and scanner the ship had to try and figure out what the thing was.

"Got anything Oscar?" Rex asked. He knew his crew; the response from Oscar was exactly what he'd expected.

"No," the engineer replied. "The scanners can't penetrate the fields. All I can really tell is that they're ovoid shaped. And bigger than the ship. If there's something inside, I can't tell what it is."

The holo showed the object to be less than a minute away from reaching them. Rex touched another icon which activated an array of motion-sensitive cameras on the ship's hull. Movement from any quadrant around the craft would result in the image from the camera that detected it being displayed on the holograph. Rex's eyes flicked between the approaching object and the window that displayed the camera feeds. Something flashed past one of them. The object had passed the ship, turned suddenly and sharply, and was now directly above it, their speeds of movement perfectly matched.

"Reverse video and advance at half speed," Rex said. The image the camera had captured grew to fill the holo screen. He watched as something came into the camera's field and sped by. It was hard to make out, but it looked like some kind of hand. "Repeat previous action, replay at one-eighth speed. Pause on contact. And clean up the image." His eyes flicked to the anomaly. It was still there, just out of the camera's view, matching course and speed with his ship. Rex noticed his heart was beating a little faster, and small droplets of sweat were forming on his brow. He returned his gaze to the recording of the thing's initial pass and was stunned to see what it showed. The ISM had cleaned up the blurriness of the original image nicely, and it clearly showed a four-fingered hand tipped with massive claws and which resembled the talons of a bird. A scale-covered leg ran from the talons up into the darkness beyond the reach of the spotlights.

"What the fuck is that?!" someone screamed. It sounded like Smitty the payload master. He'd been with Rex for over twenty cycles, and if anyone could have been said to be the salty old captain's friend, it was Smitty. The comms were suddenly awash in screaming and epithets, questions and speculation. It was a maelstrom of voices.

"Everyone SHUT UP!!!" Rex roared. The voices quieted. "Whatever that… thing… is, it hasn't attacked us. Now let's all just calm down and figure out what the fuck we're dealing with. Alright?!" Muted and indistinct muttering was the only response he heard. "Oscar? Got anything?"

"No," the engineer said. His voice sounded distracted, detached, distant, and totally un-Oscar like. "Still trying to… figure… it out."

Rex very much wanted to reach the Black Dwarf and get some hard data and possibly a few samples, but right now this thing above them was more important. He slowed the ship's speed by a quarter and watched as the object matched the deceleration.

"See that chief?" Santos' voice asked.

"See what?" Rex was busy watching the thing and hadn't been paying attention to much else.

"Three more have broken away from the Dwarf and are coming this way."

Rex looked quickly at another segment of the holo and saw that Santos was right – three more were coming. He slowed the ship to nearly a crawl in spacefaring terms and watched the objects approach. They were more than three-quarters of the way to the Black Dwarf now, and his sensors and scanners were recording all kinds of data. The thing wasn't large as astral bodies went. In fact, it was only fifty kilometers or so in diameter. If he could get just a little closer, he could send out a couple delvers to get samples. The Dwarf itself was totally black, a void in a void. He wasn't sure what he'd expected it to look like, but not that.

It had once been a star after all. The fact that it didn't emit any light was just… weird.

The other three objects had arrived; they were slowly circling the ship as if looking for something. Or maybe waiting for an order.

"Is the repellent field active?" he asked. His voice sounded just a little too shrill, he thought.

"Yeah, chief, it's working," Santos replied.

"Divert all non-essential power to it."

"Roger that."

Rex knew that their repellent shield was ineffective against anything larger than a human head. It was designed to deflect the little things floating around in space that were too small for most scanning devices to track. Against something the size of these things, it was as good as toilet paper against an axe. But he'd told Santos to beef it up not only for the crew's benefit, but (dare he admit it?) his own. If the ship had been outfitted with weapons, they'd have been locked and loaded, and firing solutions plotted. He'd had a chance a few cycles back to obtain some outdated conglomerate gear. It was just a couple of lightweight conductive-plasma cannons and a few atomic torpedoes, all very illegal, which didn't matter much to him, but he'd skipped it. His preference at that time was to mine and make money, not go blasting other ships to cosmic dust. Rex regretted that missed opportunity now.

The four objects had stationed themselves around the ship in precisely spaced intervals – one to the fore, one aft, and one on either side. Rex watched the holo as they began in unison to move toward his ship. He'd taken the liberty of broadcasting all their data about the Black Dwarf and the subsequent arrival of these things out on the subspace comms network. Everything he'd found would be analyzed by the Cosmic Science Foundation, and surely an expedition would be underway to Zone 430 within days, perhaps hours, and probably accompanied by a fleet of conglomerate warships carrying battle drones and the latest interstellar weaponry. They'd also see what was about to happen to his ship and what these things were.

The first camera to pick up anything was one mounted at the fore. Rex still thought it strange that Old Earth maritime terms were used for space vehicles. They'd figured out how to travel faster than light. Couldn't they come up with original names for space travel too? The image showed a hand-like appendage like the one he'd seen earlier. No, there were two of them. Fingers open and tipped with those hideous talons. They descended slowly, revealing the legs they were attached to, which were covered in silver and black scales like one would find on a fish. The legs ended at a flat surface covered in the same scales. Another camera showed the claws punch right through the flimsy deflection shield and directly into the hull. Alarms started screaming throughout the ship as other cameras showed Rex the same thing from three other points on his ship. The hiss of air leaking into space from the punctured hull was quickly cut off by automatic bulkhead doors closing, sealing off compromised areas and preventing more oxygen from escaping. Rex was mildly amazed at how quickly those failsafe measures had worked. But what was really on his mind now was what to do. He frantically scanned the holo, trying to assess the damage to the ship and find some way out of this. A scream echoed through the ship, broadcast over its comms.

"What the fuck?!" someone yelled.

"We've got to abandon ship!" someone else cried.

An image appeared on the holo and Rex stared at it in shock. One of the claws had driven through the hull and directly into Smitty's back, pinning him to the wall of his cabin. The poor man was wriggling like a bug impaled on a pin and screaming in what was surely agony and terror. Rex felt an unfamiliar stab of pain in his chest as he watched the man die. He was shocked to realize that he was sad, devastated actually, that his old payload master was meeting his end this way. Rex shook off the terrible and unwelcome feeling and refocused his attention on his predicament. The air in his compartment quickly leaked out through the ruptured hull, and in seconds Smitty had mercifully fallen silent.

Rex did the only thing he could think to do – he pushed his ship's engines to full throttle and spoke into the comms system. "Oscar, Santos, Yevgeniy – send out all the automatons and delvers. Their instructions are to attack those things. Drill, poke, stab, shoot, whatever they can do to them. Everyone stay at your post until we're clear of these things. I'm going to -" The ship wasn't moving. He checked the holograph quickly. Engines were still working fine, thrust was at maximum. They should be hurtling through space right now, nearing the speed of light and about to exceed it. Except that they weren't going anywhere. What the fuck?!

The first of his robots had escaped the hull and were sending back images of the things clinging to his ship. Audible gasps were heard as members of his crew saw the images on their own holos. Massive black and silver… wings, that's the best word he could find for them, were wrapped around his ship. There was no doubt now that these were not machines but living creatures that had somehow adapted themselves to exist in space.

More images were coming in from the automatons and rovers. The creatures fore and aft had not wrapped their wings around the ship like the two on the port and starboard sides. These two had their claws through the hull, but their long, sinuous bodies stretched out away from the ship. They had long necks topped with elongated wide heads, and their wings were open and beating hard, creating a force which was countering the thrust of his engines. Automatons were landing on them, but their anchors weren't penetrating the scales. The creature on the prow suddenly shifted. Its head dove toward the ship and a massive mouth opened, revealing rows of huge, pointed teeth which crashed into the hull with tremendous force. Rex was thrown to the floor by the impact, and he watched in horror as one row of the teeth punched into the very room he occupied. How was that even possible? This room was three levels below the top deck of the ship! The creature's jaws must have exerted incredible force and collapsed the decks above in order for the teeth to penetrate this far into the ship.

It was over. The only thing left was for everyone who was still alive to get to stasis pods and abandon ship. The oxygen in the room was quickly leaking out through the punctured hull, and if that creature opened its mouth, Rex would be sucked out into space. He had only moments left to act. "Everyone to stasis pods NOW!" he screamed, hoping as he did so that the comms system was still operational. A few voices responded in the affirmative, but too few for his liking. How many of his crew were dead or incapacitated? Rex was surprised to find the holo was still working, and he quickly sent out a galaxy-wide distress signal. Now he just had to hope that the subspace transmitter still worked. He'd already sent all the data he could to the Cosmic Science Foundation. There was nothing left to do but get to a stasis pod and eject from the ship.

The craft was creaking and cracking as Rex ran toward the single door into the room and the hallway beyond. Just as he reached it a terrible groaning and shrieking sound began. He glanced over his shoulder just in time to see those massive teeth sink further into his ship, crushing the ceiling down toward the floor. He hit the emergency close button on the door just as oxygen began to really rush from the room and was relieved to see the big metal panel slide down its track and seal in what oxygen was left. Rex dashed down the hall and was not surprised to find himself laboring for breath. The ship's oxygen generators may have been damaged, and even if they weren't, the hull was compromised in so many places that there was no way they could replace what was leaking out quickly enough to sustain life.

He reached a utility room at the end of the hall and was again relieved when he saw it contained an intact stasis pod. This room actually held four stasis pods and a number of panels and controls for some of the ship's myriad systems. Rex opened the door of the pod and climbed in. The pods were tiny, just big enough for a person to fit inside. Some of his crew liked to call them coffins since they weren't much bigger than those old wooden boxes people used to be buried in back on Old Earth. But these pods were designed to preserve life, not to be simply a vessel for conducting the already dead to whatever realm lay beyond this one.

The pod detected Rex's presence and the door closed automatically. A voice spoke to him from the pod's central computer, "Human life form detected. Initiating preservation protocol. Do you wish to record a message?"

"Yes," Rex replied. A few moments of silence followed, then the voice spoke again.

"Prepare for ejection, countdown sequence begun."

Rex waited impatiently as a digital display in front of his face blinked on and showed him that he had fifteen seconds until his pod was launched into space. He hoped that the spot on the hull this pod would eject from wasn't covered by one of those creatures' wings. It would be a short trip if it was. Or if one of them saw the pod and thought it might make a tasty snack. The countdown hit ten and Rex saw movement through a small glass window in the lid of the pod. Santos ran into the room followed by Yevgeniy. Both men made eye contact with Rex as they got into two of the other pods. He was glad they'd made it. What about Oscar? Where was he? The countdown hit four… three… two… one. Small thrusters on the bottom of the pod ignited and Rex felt the little cylindrical lifeboat begin to move. Its ejection mechanism was a tube that ran from this room, through the two decks above it, to a hatch on the hull that should be open now. The thrusters were effective, and he watched out the small window as the little pod blasted out of his ship and flew swiftly away from it. One of the wings covered the hull a few short meters from the open launch tube. If that thing had been just a little farther aft…

He watched with sadness as the craft that had been his home nearly all his life disintegrated. The creatures were tearing it to shreds with their teeth and claws. The one on the prow, the one whose teeth had punctured his control room, suddenly wrenched its head to the side and tore off a huge piece of the ship. It tilted its head back, chewed twice, and swallowed the twisted metal like a dog would a hunk of meat. It glanced briefly in his direction, and the eyes of the thing were black, utterly without pupil or iris, but somehow full of malicious intent. The creature on the stern tore off another piece of his ship and it too swallowed the ragged metal. The two that had wrapped their wings around it were crushing and compacting what was left of the hull into a crumpled little ball.

Just before it collapsed in on itself, Rex saw two other pods eject from the ship. Yevgeniy and Santos. He didn't see any other pods, but maybe some of his crew had escaped. If only these pods had comms systems so they could communicate. He desperately wanted to know how many of them had survived. Then he remembered the clustering feature. Each stasis pod held only one person. In the event of a catastrophe in space, the engineers had built in a feature that would cause all ejected pods to use their thrusters to congregate together in one spot. Their hulls were equipped with strong magnets that would automatically engage when two pods got close enough together. The overall effect was to collect as many survivors as possible into one place and hold them all together in a single mass in order to make finding and rescuing them easier for any vessel responding to the distress signal. The voice spoke again as Rex watched the two other pods move toward his. That was reassuring.

"You may begin recording." He'd forgotten about his message.

"This is Rex. I'm an asteroid miner. My ship was attacked by some kind of… creature, four of them actually, in Zone 430. I've sent all my data to the Cosmic Science

Foundation. These things are huge and incredibly dangerous. I -"

The voice spoke again: "Recording terminated. Initiating stasis in thirty seconds."

He knew what was coming next. A gas would fill the interior of the pod and put him to sleep. Next a series of automated needles would penetrate his skin and find major blood vessels. A solution would be injected into his body that would keep him alive but in suspended animation for upwards of a thousand galactic cycles.

Something occurred to Rex as he waited to fall asleep. In all the madness he'd completely forgotten the Black Dwarf. It was still out there. The pod rotated slowly, and Rex watched as his ship and the creatures disappeared from view leaving only the blackness of space visible through the window. He was getting drowsy; the gas was doing its job, but he just wanted to see it – that mythical object that had brought him here in the first place. His eyes fluttered and nearly closed. Not yet! He forced them open just as something flashed into view from his left. Two of the creatures were flying toward where the Black Dwarf should be. Between them, held in their clawed hands, was the remnant of his ship. It was nothing now but crushed metal, except for one searchlight that was miraculously still functioning and just happened to be angled in such a way that it illuminated the scene. The creatures had compressed it into something less than a quarter of the size it had been. The strength it must have taken to do that! They sped through space, their great wings flapping like birds. No, not like birds – like dragons! That was it! Something in the back of his mind had been nagging him since he'd first seen these things. He'd been unconsciously trying to figure out what they were, where he'd seen them before, and now he had it. They looked just like dragons out of some child's fairytale from Old Earth.

One of them opened its mouth and a beam of silvery light shot out, piercing space until it impacted with an object in the distance. That was it – the Black Dwarf. Its surface looked smooth and shiny in the silver light from the dragon's (why call it a creature anymore?) mouth, more like glass than compressed iron, or whatever it actually was. His eyes fluttered again, and he had a very hard time opening them. No matter what he wanted to see the final act of this tragedy.

The other dragon opened its mouth and another beam of silver light shot out toward the Black Dwarf. Rex watched groggily as the surface of the Dwarf began to vibrate, then to fracture. Just before he lost consciousness completely, he saw the two dragons throw their wings back, nearly stopping their movement, while simultaneously swinging their legs forward and throwing the remains of his ship toward the cracking Black Dwarf. The crumpled metal sped toward the disintegrating body. Just before it impacted the surface, the Dwarf exploded into countless fragments, exposing a massive silver dragon, its body curled into a ball. The huge creature appeared to be at least five times bigger than the ones that had attacked his ship. It stretched its wings out to the side, uncoiled its long neck, and shook its head like it had just woken from a nap. Rex's jaw dropped open in astonishment as the remains of his ship shot through space right toward the gargantuan silver dragon. It noticed the speeding hunk of metal just as it neared, and the dragon dropped its head, opened its mouth, and swallowed the last piece of Rex's former life.

"Locus 394 to Cosmic Science Foundation," the man said.

"Go for CSF," the woman's voice replied.

"We're picking up some strange data transmissions from Zone 430. Have you seen this?"

"Standby." The channel went dead for several seconds. The man in the control room of Locus 430, otherwise known as Hades, took a drag off his Arcturian cigarette and flicked the ashes onto the filthy floor. He was about to take a big drink of his seventy-cycle-aged bourbon (imported from Rigel and aged in Canopus casks!) when the woman spoke again.

"We've seen those transmissions. Ignore the data. It's likely a hoax. Black Dwarfs don't exist, and neither do these creatures the video purports to show. We've enlisted the assistance of the conglomerates and their security apparatus to find and prosecute the perpetrators. There's nothing to worry about." The transmission ended.

Well, that was great news! The authorities had proclaimed everything A-Ok! He should celebrate with that bourbon! Except that his eyes kept coming back to the deep space scanner screen, and he wondered what the five objects, one big one and four small ones, were that had just started moving in his direction.

# FIVE MINUTES FROM NOW

"I don't know when it started," Jo said, "I remember being at the mall one day with my mom, and I knew some lady walking just ahead of us was about to die."

"Did you see like a skull instead of her face or some shit?" a twenty-something kid with greasy hair and a moderate case of acne asked sarcastically. Several faces turned to look at him.

"You know we don't ridicule people here Stuart," the facilitator said. "If you're going to treat others in the group like that, I'm going to have to ask you to leave."

"Alright, dude. Whatever." the kid said flippantly with a toss of his oily hair.

The facilitator glared at Stuart for a moment. His frown of disapproval was replicated by everyone else sitting around the circle of folding chairs in the church basement. This was not an AA or NA meeting. It was a support group for people with problems other than substance abuse. The majority of them were here for self-esteem issues, problems in social settings, or just because they felt different from their peers. The group met once per week in this church, and the facilitator was a balding and portly middle-aged social worker who donated his time out of a deep and innate sense of societal altruism. The group was as diverse as it could get. It was comprised of men and women of every skin color under the rainbow, and widely disparate economic backgrounds. In short, America itself was represented here among the seventeen people, facilitator included, in the room.

"Go ahead Jo," he said. "I don't think our young friend here is going to make any more snide comments." The young man scowled at the room. His acne spots flared red, and he hoped his expression looked like defiance, but to those watching, it really just looked chastened and pathetically ornery. The other attendees ignored him and returned their attention to the speaker, a conservatively dressed woman in her mid-thirties.

She cleared her throat before resuming her story. "I must have been about eight or nine," she said. "And to answer your question," she said directly to Stuart, "no, I did not see a skull. I didn't see anything. I just knew she was going to die. Very soon."

The room was silent as Jo spoke; all eyes were on her, listening intently. This was a story no one here had ever heard. Most of the stories people told in this room had similar themes, similar sequences of events and experiences that had led their tellers here, but this one was unlike the others. There was no abusive parent, no school bully, no failure in jobs or relationships. They were hearing something entirely new. This lady knew when people were about to die. If she was telling the truth. And the audience wanted to hear all about it.

"I grabbed my mom's hand and pointed to the lady and told her I knew she was about to die. My mother gave me a dirty look and said it wasn't nice to talk about people like that. She thought I was making it up. Of course, what parent wouldn't? Kids make up stories all the time. If a kid told you something like that, your first thought would probably be to dismiss it as an overactive imagination. I didn't understand that then, but I do now, and I don't blame my mom for not doing anything, not saying anything to the lady, and not believing me. She didn't know, and it was the first time I'd ever said anything like that."

Some of the other participants were nodding, others were frowning slightly as if in disbelief, and one Asian woman was staring at Jo with something like fear. "Did you see her ghost?" she asked tentatively.

"No. It wasn't like that. I don't see things, just get feelings."

"I saw a ghost once. I was little too, and my brother didn't believe me. It was standing next to his bed staring at him. Then it disappeared. I told him and he called me names, so I never told my parents. I think I might be able to do what you do. Eight years later he was killed in a drive by shooting. He'd gotten into this gang and-"

"It's Jo's turn to speak right now Dina," the facilitator said gently, cutting her off before she could hijack the meeting. "You'll have your turn, but we need to let her finish."

"Yeah," said Stuart, "I wanna hear how this shit ends." The facilitator shot the young man a look but didn't pursue the matter. He would never have admitted it to the group, especially with Stuart present, but he wanted to hear the story just as much as them.

"Well, after I told my mom," Jo continued, "and she didn't believe me, I just shut up. We were walking by

Nordstrom's and there was a candy store next to it, on the far side. Right as the lady got to the entrance to that store, she collapsed. Just fell right there in the middle of the mall. Some other lady was with her, a sister or friend, something. She was screaming and yelling for help, people were walking by gawking at her just like they do on the freeway when there are flashing lights on the side of the road. Pretty soon a little crowd had gathered around. No one was doing anything that I could see, until a man came running from somewhere, said he was a doctor and started checking the lady. Someone in the candy store came out and said they'd called 911, but the doctor shook his head and took the lady's friend, or whoever she was, aside and was talking to her quietly. I could tell by everyone's faces that the lady was gone. When I looked at my mom, she was staring at me like I'd suddenly turned into mushroom or something. She took me to the far side of the causeway across from the candy store and asked how I'd known… what I knew. I told her I had no idea. It just came to me that that lady was going to die."

"That's some heavy shit," an elderly black man named Ernest said softly. "I used to feel that way in 'Nam, but it was just a feeling, never actually worked out that it happened. You still do that? Know?"

Jo nodded. "Yes. And it's made my life hell."

"Why would it make your life hell?" asked a fortyish man in a rumpled business suit.

"How would you like to know that someone is going to die and not be able to do a damned thing about it?" asked a twentyish young woman with several facial piercings and multi-colored dreadlocks. Her tone was acid, berating.

"It was just a question," business suit man muttered.

"She's right though," Jo said with a nod toward the dreadlocked girl. "When it happens, I can't do anything about it."

"Wait," said a slightly pudgy woman with a Russian accent. "You mean it still happen?"

"Yes."

"When was the last time?" Stuart asked. His eyes gleamed unsettlingly with an interest that hadn't been there before.

"How about we let her tell the story, shall we?" the facilitator said.

"It's ok," Jo said mollifyingly. "Answering their questions will tell some of the story anyway. And I get it. This is some weird shit I'm telling you. It's hard to believe. I mean, if you do believe me, then you also have to believe that I'm psychic or something, right? Well, I'm not. I can't read minds or tell you who's going to win the next World Series or anything like that. I just know when people are going to die five minutes before they do."

"That's got to be tough, no matter what way you slice it," said Ernest. Jo gave him a small smile.

"What happened the next time you knew?" Dina asked. She was frowning slightly, but her eyes were clear and focused.

"It was several years later, in the hospital." Brows around the room creased in concern, and Jo hurried to explain further. "I wasn't, I mean – I was just – my grandmother – she was in the hospital. I was just visiting,"

"Take your time," the facilitator said. "We've got this room for…" He looked up at the cheap clock on the wall. "Another hour and twenty-three minutes. And somehow, I don't think anyone here tonight will mind if their story gets postponed a week." He looked around the room; no one argued. Everyone appeared to be more interested in hearing this story than in telling their own.

"My grandmother was sick. Kidney failure or something. I don't remember. But my dad took me to see her one day. My mom must have been at work. I'd never told my dad about the mall, and I don't know if my mom did either. Anyway, we were walking down the hall, and as we passed one room, I knew the person inside was going to die. I stopped walking and looked in. My dad turned around and was frowning at me. He must have thought I was some kind of medical voyeur or something. I heard him whisper at me to move, but all I could do was stare. The person in the bed wasn't old. It was a man who probably wasn't much older than thirty, but it was hard to tell with all the tubes and wires hooked up to him. To this day I don't know what was wrong with him, but they had all kinds of things plugged into that poor guy."

"When I didn't start walking, my dad came back to me, and I could tell he was a little pissed. He wanted me to go see my grandmother, his mom, but I couldn't look away from that guy in the bed. I remember telling him that man was about to die and how sad it was that he was alone in the room. If he had family that visited him, no one was there at that moment. My dad stopped trying to get me to move and just stared at me. He didn't say anything, but he did look into the room. I clearly remember a nurse walked by right at that moment. She smiled at us, but she was in a hurry to get somewhere. You know how nurses move. I wanted to tell her, but I couldn't speak. It was like my mouth had been screwed shut and padlocked. The only thing I could do was look into that room at that poor man.

My dad and I stood there in complete silence until I saw his chest rise and fall one more time, then all the alarms started going off. Nurses and doctors came running, and we went to see my grandmother. She was doing better by then, and they let her go home a couple days later. But on the way out of the hospital, my dad and I saw them wheeling that man out of that room. They'd taken all the tubes and wires off, and he was covered with a sheet."

"When we got to the car my dad didn't start it right away. We just sat there for... I don't know how long, several minutes it felt like, before he said anything. All he asked was how long I'd been able to do that. I told him that was the second time in my life. He nodded and started the car, and we drove home. He never asked me about it again."

"So, man die just like you think?" the Russian woman asked. Jo didn't remember her name but thought it might be Svetlana.

"Yes. I thought it, and it happened."

"That makes it sound like you did it, like you killed him," Stuart said in an accusatory tone.

"Well, that's not how I meant it," Jo said testily. "It's not like I can think I want someone dead, and they die. It doesn't work that way."

The facilitator opened his mouth to speak, probably to admonish Stuart again, but someone else beat him to it.

"How does it work?" Ernest asked quietly. "I think I believe you, but you have to understand if some of us are... skeptical."

Jo nodded. "Of course; I get it. Look, I know how crazy this sounds. If it hadn't happened to me, I'd have a hard time believing it too, and I'm a pretty trusting person." She paused for a moment as she looked at the worn tiles on the floor; her audience remained silent for once while she collected her thoughts.

"I don't hear voices, if that's what you're thinking," she began. "There's no big sound or flash of light, or anything like that. It's just… me with my thoughts, then all of them get pushed out and a single thought replaces them. But it's really more of a feeling than a thought. How do I explain it? You know when you look out the window and it's raining? Somewhere inside you, you just know that if you walk outside right at that moment, you're going to get wet. You know it completely. It's an… absolute. Incontrovertible. You will get wet if you walk out in the rain. But you don't consciously think of it in those terms. You just know it. That's how it is for me. I know someone is going to die in five minutes. And let me clarify that – it's always five minutes until… you know, they die. This probably sounds like one of those 'Final Destination' movies or something. It's not."

"Our feelings shouldn't be ignored," the facilitator said. "Remember, that's why we're all here."

"The feeling I get isn't an emotion like anger or happiness," Jo said. "It's a certainty. There isn't any emotion tied to it at all, except what it makes me feel, but that's all from me, not from… wherever the message comes from."

"Let's unpack that a little," the facilitator said. "Do you have any idea where these feelings originate? Another dimension maybe? God?"

"Probably from the Martians," Stuart said with undisguised sarcasm.

"One more comment like that and I'm going to ask you to leave," the facilitator said. Jo thought he'd given his name as Randall, but she couldn't remember; she was terrible with names. The others were glaring at Stuart, but their disapproval didn't seem to affect him. He was staring at her with a smug expression.

Jo ignored Stuart as she pondered the question for at least the eleventymillionth time. "I don't know. It could be from anywhere. Or nowhere. I believe there is a God, or at least something after this life, some higher level of consciousness or whatever, but where these feelings I get come from, I couldn't say." She turned and looked directly into Stuart's eyes. "Who knows? Maybe it does come from Mars." There was a challenge in her voice, but Stuart didn't rise to it. He didn't drop his gaze either.

"Do you always know who is going to die?" Dina asked quietly.

"Most of the time, yes, but not always. I was on a sidewalk once after a concert, and there were a lot of other people around, and I got a feeling, but I couldn't tell who it applied to. I was looking around all over the place trying to figure out who it was. The group of friends I was with thought I'd lost my mind. It wasn't until I heard a car horn… then the… thump. A drunk guy had walked out into the street in front of a pickup truck. I didn't see his face until it was… over."

"Serves him right, the dumbass," Stuart said.

"Alright, that's it," the facilitator said with unveiled irritation. "You need to leave. Now. If you can behave yourself, I'll let you come back next week, but if this is how you're going to be, don't bother showing up. And I will definitely be reporting this to your probation officer. You wouldn't be here if you could learn to behave."

Stuart smirked as he grabbed his jacket from the back of his chair and practically sauntered out of the room.

"Punk," Ernest said quietly to his retreating back.

"I'm sorry about that folks," the facilitator said. Jo was mildly irritated with herself that she couldn't be sure of his name. Was it Randall? "We try to screen people before we let them attend these meetings, but he was mandated by a judge to attend. We didn't have much choice on whether or not to let him be here."

"His daddy probably paid his probation officer to pull some strings and keep him out of the clink," said the business suit guy. The group smiled at the jibe, breaking the tension created by both the confrontation and the subject matter of the conversation.

"Have you ever been able to stop it from happening?" asked the dreadlocked girl when the mirth had died down.

Jo smiled sadly. "No, but I've only had one real opportunity."

"And what was that?" Ernest asked. "If you don't mind sharing," he added hurriedly when he realized how invasive the question might have seemed.

"No, it's fine. It's a sad story though."

"Most of our stories are," dreadlocks said.

Jo nodded. "I used to like running. I'd jog all over. One of my favorite places to go was that bridge south of downtown. You know, the one that goes up over all the railroad tracks? The view of the city from there is fantastic. I'd run to the middle of it and stop for a few moments just to look, catch my breath, then run back home. One day, this was just a couple years ago, I was doing exactly that, and I got a feeling. The problem was that I was the only pedestrian on the bridge. There were lots of cars driving by, but there always are on that road. I was maybe halfway to the place where I usually stopped when it hit me. The feelings aren't ever more or less intense; they're always the same. This one didn't feel any different, but I couldn't understand how I could get one with all the cars whizzing by. Then I started thinking that maybe there was going to be a car crash, or an earthquake. Just so you know, I've never gotten a feeling about a… mass death. They're always only about a single person."

"You seem to have to be close, I mean physically in the proximity of whomever is going to pass," the facilitator said. "Is that always true?"

"Yes," Jo said. "The person is always nearby. I don't know if the feelings have physical limits, like maybe they won't come if the person is a certain distance from me, but my experiences have always been when the person is close. And that's what was strange about this one. Everyone close to me was driving. I wondered again about a car accident, or maybe someone having a heart attack while driving. It was making me crazy. I must have looked like a lunatic to anyone driving by. Some sweaty woman in jogging clothes frantically looking around like she'd just lost her kid. Or her mind."

"I was starting to think the feeling was wrong, for the first time in my life, when a car near the middle of the bridge, right by where I liked to look at the city, suddenly stopped and a kid got out. He couldn't have been more than nineteen or twenty. He just stopped right in the middle of the road, got out and walked over to the sidewalk maybe thirty yards away from me. If any of you have been across that bridge, then you know there's a concrete railing that runs along the side of it. It's pretty wide, at least ten or twelve inches, plenty of room to stand on. And that's just what this kid did – he climbed right up on it. I knew then that my feeling had been right, and I started running toward him, yelling at him to stop. Other cars had stopped on the bridge by then, some were honking, people were getting out of others, and the kid ignored them all. I was sprinting up the bridge, waving my arms and yelling, really trying hard to get his attention. He was ignoring everyone, just staring down. When I was almost to him, people that had gotten out of their cars were yelling too, but he didn't pay any attention to them. I was surprised when he looked up at me and smiled. It was the saddest, most... forlorn look I've ever seen on a human face. Then he pulled a gun out of the back of his pants, put it to his head, pulled the trigger, and fell off the railing."

The room was silent as the impact of Jo's story sank into each person.

"Very terrible," the Russian woman said softly.

"That's some shit," Ernest agreed.

"I think we've all been there, where that kid was, to one degree or another," business suit added.

The dreadlocked girl was crying quietly.

Jo waited a few moments before continuing. "I waited for the police to get there, told them what I'd seen, then walked home. I never did find out the kid's name."

"I know it," dreadlocks said. "It was Daniel, and he was my brother." Her tears were flowing freely, and she let them. "That day is the main reason I'm even here."

"I'm so sorry," Jo said.

"Damn, girl," Ernest whispered.

The Russian woman was sitting next to dreadlocks, and she took her hand in both of hers. The room was silent for a long time before the facilitator finally spoke. "This has been one hell of a meeting. I don't want to rain on anyone's parade, but we're almost out of time for tonight. Would anyone like to share anything else before we break?"

Jo looked at dreadlocks. The girl's tears had mostly abated, and she blew her nose into a tissue. "I really did try to get his attention," she said softly. "And I would have tried to grab him or something if I'd been closer. I was just too far away. I'm sorry I told that story and that it upset you."

"It's alright," dreadlocks sniffed. "You didn't know. I'd never heard that much… detail about it before. And I'm glad he at least smiled at you before…" she left the rest unsaid.

The two women stood from their chairs and shared a long hug. Others stood and murmured words of condolence and a few rested sympathetic hands on their shoulders.

"I'd like to thank everyone for coming," the facilitator said, "and to invite you all to come next week if you'd like to."

People were gathering coats and belongings, preparing to leave, when Jo stopped in the middle of donning her jacket. "Uh… I need to say something. I just got a feeling." Confused eyes turned toward her.

"You mean…?" Dina asked.

"Yes. Just now."

"What? How can that-" the facilitator said when the door to the room opened, and Stuart walked in. "What are you doing back here?" he asked. "The meeting is over for today."

"Not quite yet it isn't," Stuart said. He reached to the small of his back and pulled out a small black pistol. "I want to test the theory." He pointed the gun at Jo and grinned. "Tell me who's going to die," he said.

"I don't know," Jo replied in a pleading tone. "I can't always tell."

"I think you're full of shit," Stuart said smugly. "You're just here to play games with us. Maybe you get off on other people's pain or something, but you're a fraud."

"Stuart, I don't know what you hope to accomplish here, but you need to put that gun down right now," the facilitator said.

"Shut up Randall," Stuart replied. "You don't even know what the fuck you're talking about. You sit in your chair and pretend like you're some kind of expert in people because you went and got a fancy college degree. You don't know shit."

"I know something about people," Ernest said. "And I'll tell your punk ass that everybody in this room right now wants you to put that stupid gun away and just go home before someone gets hurt."

"She just had a feeling," Dina said. "Someone is going to die in a minute."

"Then she should know it's her," Stuart said. "Or she's just bullshitting everyone."

"I don't always know who's going to die," Jo said to Stuart. He hadn't lowered the gun. "But I did just have a feeling, which means someone is going to die. Please put the gun down. Maybe this time I can make it… wrong. This doesn't have to happen."

"Yes, it does," Stuart said. "I don't believe a fucking word you said, so if you really do have this… magic power, then you should be able to tell us all who's going to bite it the minute I pull this trigger. Go on – tell us."

"I can't," Jo pleaded. "I really don't know. What I do know is that there isn't much time left to stop it. Please don't make it happen. Every time in my life that I've ever had one of these feelings, someone has died. It doesn't have to be that way this time. That part is completely up to you."

"That's right, it is. It's all up to me. I can pull this trigger or not, but I think I want to just so I can prove you wrong. Fucking fraud."

Someone's shoe squeaked on the floor behind Stuart, and he jumped, startled at the sound. His arm jerked a little with the motion, and his finger inadvertently pulled the trigger. The gunshot momentarily deafened everyone in the room and caused most of them to duck. Jo stood stoically as the bullet whizzed past her head and embedded itself in the wall behind her.

The second gunshot shattered everyone's frayed nerves and further decimated their diminished hearing. Stuart slumped to the ground, and his pistol clattered away across the tile floor. It took several moments for the people in the room to regain their composure, and when they finally began to uncover their eyes and look around, they were shocked to see the smoking gun in Ernest's left hand. He was gazing sadly but with determination at the unmoving body of Stuart. "I didn't live through the civil rights bullshit of the 50's and 60's, Vietnam, and crack cocaine, just to let some joker like that kill an innocent woman."

Everyone was standing now, a few of them, eyes wide and still fearful, were checking Stuart's body while Randall was dialing the police on his phone. Jo was irrationally relieved to actually know his name, thanks to Stuart. The man in the rumpled business suit nodded at

Ernest who returned the gesture. Jo walked over to the wall and looked at the hole the bullet had made in the cheap wooden paneling. She poked her finger into it and touched the warm slug beyond; it had embedded itself in what felt like cinderblock. A presence behind her drew her attention away from the hole just as the first siren rang out in the distance. She turned to find Ernest peering at the hole her finger had just been in.

"I saw too many people die in 'Nam, too many die in the streets from drugs and senseless violence," he said. His voice was low and quiet, his tone almost apologetic.

"I'm not angry with you; you saved my life at minimum, and maybe more."

"Still. I never wanted to do that. Kill someone. Again. I've had enough of it for one lifetime."

Jo spontaneously hugged Ernest who returned the embrace. She wiped a tear away as they parted.

Randall was speaking into his phone, telling the 911 dispatcher that no one was in danger anymore; the threat had been neutralized. No, they didn't need a SWAT team. Everyone was fine.

A pair of police burst into the room a few moments later, guns drawn and ordering everyone to raise their hands. When they realized there was no threat, they holstered their weapons and began asking questions. Paramedics arrived shortly afterward and after a quick examination of Stuart's body, covered him with a sheet and called the coroner's office. More police had arrived, including a pair of detectives, and all of the witnesses in the room were being questioned singly and in groups. A uniformed line officer took the man in the rumpled business suit aside and asked him what happened.

"Well, have I got a story for you!" he said.

# REPURPOSED

Geoffrey and Agatha walked across the muddy ground toward the dilapidated barns across from the house. The grey sky threatened to spill more rain, but for the moment the air was raindrop-free.

"I'd really like to find some old wood," Geoffrey said as he stepped around a puddle. "I think I could make a beautiful top for that table base."

Agatha stopped to watch a flock of sheep grazing in a pasture a short distance away. That land had once belonged to her family. She smiled wistfully and turned to look for her husband. He'd disappeared into one of the barns. It didn't take her long to find him; his shout of glee revealed his location as surely as a GPS signal. She found him staring at a grime covered chunk of… something.

"Ags – this is it!" Geoffrey exclaimed. "This is what I was looking for!" His childlike joy was one of the qualities that had attracted her to him when they'd first met. It was also somewhat irritating when he got notions in his head that, like a stubborn child, he held onto no matter how hard she worked to dislodge them.

"You actually want to turn that into a table?" Agatha replied.

The barn was on what had been her family's farm just outside the village of Bibury in Gloucestershire, UK. The farm had once covered nearly a hundred acres. But time and changing fortunes had forced Agatha's father, then after he died, her mother, to sell off bits and pieces of it. All that was left now was a twenty-five-acre parcel hard by the river Coln that held the main house, a small caretaker's cottage that had served as her mother's sewing studio for the last several years of her life, and two barns full of bric-a-brac and a broken-beyond-salvation Farmall tractor. Agatha's mother had died of complications from Diabetes a little over a month before, and they were going through her things, deciding what to keep, what to sell, and what to bin. Most things had so far fallen into the third category. Neither Agatha nor Geoffrey had any interest in farming, and once everything had been gone through, the farm would be put up for sale, the proceeds used to pay off her mother's debts, and whatever was left would go into a full remodel of their own home in Swindon where Agatha was a work-from-home graphics artist and Geoffrey a case manager for the National Health Service. He also fancied himself a craftsman and loved spending time in the small shed behind their house building things out of wood.

Agatha regarded the table base in question with a deprecating eye. It was old, but that was about the only positive characteristic it possessed. Gouges and nicks marred the pedestal and decades, maybe centuries, of grit and grime caked its surface so heavily that it was difficult to tell it was even wood. Agatha thought that if something hadn't very recently rubbed against it, exposing some of the wood grain, that it would have been quite possible, maybe even likely, to have mistaken it for painted concrete.

"It'll clean up nice," Geoffrey said. "See that there?" He pointed to the spot Agatha had just noticed. "That's good old English oak, that is. Solid as the Tower of London. Who knows how old this is? If I can find the right salvage wood, I'll build you a table that you'll not believe!"

"I'm not believing you actually want to do this," she muttered under her breath. Geoffrey was diligent and passionate about his hobby. He was just… a terrible carpenter. It seemed impossible for him to cut a straight line, even with the portable table saw he'd bought last year at great expense. And she didn't want to think about his finishes. He seemed to get more stain on himself than on his finished products and always used far too much glue when just a little would have worked. But he was a good man, woodworking flaws aside, and she loved him dearly.

"What did you say darling?" he asked absentmindedly as he perused what was about to become his latest reclamation project.

"I said wouldn't a coffee be nice?"

"Yes, of course, that would be lovely, wouldn't it?" he replied, his eyes never leaving the table base. Agatha turned away to walk back to the car but realized Geoff wasn't following her. She looked back over her shoulder, and he was still staring at the table base. His lips were moving as if he were speaking to someone, but no sound escaped his mouth.

"Are you coming?" she called.

Geoffrey finally looked up; his eyes were distant, his expression distractedly blank. "Hmm? Oh, yes. Of course. I was just thinking about the planks," he said as he blinked at Agatha.

"What planks? What are you talking about?"

"I'll need some. Planks. To build the table."

"Yes, well, you get your planks later. Right now, I'd like a coffee. Shall we?"

Two months later the farm sold. After her parents' old debts were paid, Agatha received a check for just over £450,000.

"Well, we're rich!" Geoffrey said when they'd deposited the check in their bank. "Shall we take a holiday?"

Agatha glanced at him with playful scorn. "I thought you wanted to find wood for your table?" He hadn't stopped talking about it since they'd brought that filthy old pedestal home from the barn.

"I do, love. I found a place near London that has some of the best and oldest reclaimed wood in the UK. Maybe we pop on down for a bit? Have a look? Maybe stay a few days and try some of those fancy restaurants?"

They had been talking about going on holiday for a few years now but hadn't because of their jobs and the imperative of raising two children. Those children were gone now though. Grant was at the University of Leicester, taking courses in maths, and Zoe was an exchange student living with a family in North Carolina in America. They were alone, had money to burn, and annual leave from work, so why not?

"Oh, all right," she said, pretending to give in reluctantly. Geoffrey smiled at her. They both knew she wanted a holiday as much as he did.

The following week they loaded a few pieces of luggage into their car and drove toward London. They'd both been to the big city numerous times, but only for work, never as tourists, and they found the change refreshing and exciting.

"I want to dine in a Michelin starred restaurant," Geoffrey said as he drove eastward along the M4 toward the city."

"We'll probably need a reservation," Agatha replied. "And what do you want, your lordship – one, two, or three stars?"

Geoffrey glanced at her with a mock frown of disgust and said in an overly exaggerated and patronizing tone, "Three of course. Don't be daft!" As Agatha shifted her gaze to her phone, she didn't see his eyes lose focus or his lips begin moving.

Their hotel was one of the nicer examples in a city replete with them, and they enjoyed their stay very much. It was fun to splurge on luxury and fine dining when one had the means. They visited all the big tourist destinations – Piccadilly Circus, the Tower of London, the British Museum, Trafalgar Square – and generally had as much fun as anyone on holiday could expect.

On their last day in London, after checking out of their hotel, Geoffrey pointed their car in the direction of a salvage business he'd found online. The place was on the outskirts of London's western edge just a few miles north of Heathrow Airport. Geoffrey had corresponded with the owner prior to their trip, and the man was expecting them when they pulled into the car park next to the main building.

"Hullo!" a deep baritone voice boomed from an open roll up garage door. "I see you've made it out of London in one piece!" A tall and very rotund man with beady eyes and a huge, bushy salt and pepper beard walked out into the overcast afternoon sunlight.

"Well, hello there," Geoffrey replied. "You must be Maurice."

"In the flesh," the man said with an elaborate bow, sweeping his arm from one side to the other and doffing a porkpie hat that was a hideous but attention-grabbing shade of fuchsia, and which was overtaken in its garishness only by the bright orange and forest green suit the man wore on his massive frame. "Welcome to my humble proprietorship."

"Very glad to be here," Geoffrey replied as Agatha rolled her eyes at the pomp and bombast of their welcome. Her husband fancied himself a bargainer, a real hard-charging negotiator of the first order. In truth, he folded like a threadbare suit more often than not. But he enjoyed the game, and she didn't want to disabuse him of his notions, so she watched amusedly as he fell headlong into haggling.

"Right this way," Maurice said, gesturing toward the open door. "I've got just the product you're looking for." Geoffrey smiled at his wife who couldn't help but return it. He did love all this, and she loved seeing him having so much fun.

The inside of the building was filled with all manner of wood products. Boards and planks of countless sizes, shapes and colors stood on end in rows of racks. There were even antique architectural pieces that most likely came from old manor homes. Over there was what looked like wainscoting, that stack looked like pilasters, while heaped on a pallet were massive, thick planks that had once surely been mantles. There was even a statue sort of thing depicting a majestic-looking man with long flowing hair pointing out in front of him, and which must have been an ornament off the prow of a ship. Maurice saw Agatha looking at the statue and smiled.

"That one there, sad to say, isn't for sale. But it did witness the action at the Battle of Trafalgar! See just there, on the side of that chap's head?" He pointed toward a gouge about an inch tall and three long. "It's said that an errant musket ball made that little trench."

"Yes, that's very interesting," Agatha replied. She was skeptical about the provenance he just provided.

"Fascinating!" Geoffrey said as he examined the statue. "To think that Lord Nelson himself may have looked this gent in the eye at some point on that fateful day. Which side did he fight on?"

Maurice fixed him with a withering look. "Ours of course. Do you really believe I'd have some French or Spanish artifact from the losing side reposing in my proprietorship? The horror!" The big man threw his head back, clapped a hand to his forehead, and feigned a swoon. Geoffrey laughed out loud at the melodramatic display. Agatha knew in that moment that Maurice would be able to swindle anything he liked from her husband.

"Alright – enough of that! What say I show you our collection of ancient timber? That's really what you're after, right?" Geoffrey nodded.

"Indeed, it is. Lead on good sir!"

The men were having fun with their game, and Agatha was amused at how each was playing his role, but she wasn't about to let her husband be taken advantage of, regardless of what their bank account looked like after the inheritance. If she needed to speak up, she would. Until then their game was harmless, and she was content to let them play it.

As Maurice led them up one aisle and down another, she was amazed to see how dirty the place was. Sawdust and grime covered everything, and Agatha was mildly shocked to see that their guide seemed to be able to walk through the entire place, touching everything, and not get a speck of dirt on his atrocious but immaculately tailored and sparklingly clean suit. That in itself was a minor miracle, and one which she pondered in silence as the men walked before her, hemming and hawing over everything.

At last Maurice, nodding to two men in dirty coveralls who'd just finished stacking a number of long, thick planks on some sort of rack, stopped in a corner of the building and pointed to a selection of extremely aged boards leaning against a wall. "This is what you're looking for. It was a table you said you wanted to construct? These planks will make an excellent top. Geoffrey pulled one out and looked it over. The board was dark, almost black, with age, and was covered in nicks and gouges. Agatha thought it a hideous example, but her husband seemed rather taken with it, and looked carefully along its length.

"Yes," he muttered. "I think I could do something rather wonderful with this. Is it cherry? Elm?"

"That good sir is Yew."

"Fascinating," Geoffrey muttered.

"It looks rather rough," Agatha said.

"Madam," Maurice began, "That wood is over six hundred years old. Who knows what it's been through."

"How do you know its age?" she asked. Geoffrey was turning the plank this way and that, eying it down its length, running his hands across its surface, and generally trying to look like he knew what he was doing. She ignored him for the moment.

"When I get a salvage job, I do my research on the structure my crew will be dismantling. I've found that my customers prefer to know two things: how old the wood they buy from me is, and where it originated. These planks were removed from an old inn near Aylesford that, before its deconstruction and demolition, dated from the seventeenth century."

"That's only four hundred years, isn't it?" Agatha said smartly.

"Quite right madam," Maurice replied as if he'd expected her to point out the discrepancy in his story. "But I sent a sample to a local laboratory for testing. Radiocarbon dating. I'm sure you've heard of it; it's something I do for most of my products. The results indicate that the tree was two hundred years old at the time it was cut. So, you see, madam, this wood possesses over six hundred years of history."

"So, it's old wood. Alright then," Agatha replied. She glanced at Geoffrey who was still examining planks and talking to himself under his breath. His eyes were, strangely, not focused on the wood, but were distant, like his mind was somewhere else. He was probably just deciding how he was going to build his table.

"There is one other small detail relating to these planks," Maurice said, drawing her attention away from her distracted husband.

"Yes?"

"When the inn was being dismantled, workers found some documents, invoices actually, that indicate this wood was purchased in London in 1608. It was subsequently transported to Aylesford where it was used in constructing the inn."

"Do you know what it was used for in London?" she asked.

"I'm afraid not. Alas, that information has been lost in the fog of history."

"What's the cost?" Geoffrey asked, finally rejoining the conversation.

"For you sir," Maurice replied as he tipped his cap to Agatha, "and of course to you as well, madam, the price today will be £3.75 per linear inch."

"Oh my," Geoffrey said. "That's rather steep, don't you think?"

"My good fellow, this is six-hundred-year-old wood. Seasoned and shaped by time and the elements, with a character and charm that simply cannot be replicated or fabricated. Wood like this must pass through the crucible of the ages in order to reach this refined state. Planks such as these do not, if you'll forgive the obviousness of the expression, grow on trees."

"No, they do not." Geoffrey looked at Agatha. He was hooked like a brook trout; she could see it in his eyes. Even now, at this moment, they were not as focused as she was used to seeing. There was a strange combination of glint and vacancy that was most unusual for Geoffrey. Well, he was quite smitten with his table idea, and they had stopped at this place to shop for materials. She resigned herself to it; they would be buying a selection of this wood. The only thing left to be decided was the price. "Surely you can do better than that," Geoffrey said as he turned back to Maurice.

The big man sighed, a sound of defeat and resignation, but Agatha saw the sparkle in his eyes that indicated he knew he'd won. "Since you've come such a long way, and have tolerated my oftentimes overbearing nature, not to mention my sartorial choices, I'll reduce the price, for you sir – just this once, to £3.50 per linear inch."

"Surely you can come down to £2.70," Geoffrey said.

"Impossible, sir, quite impossible. No, I must remain firm at my last price. I do, after all, have a crew to pay, insurance, mortgages on both my home and this building, the utilities," he said as he swept his arms around. "And taxes, sir. Always more taxes for this and that, climate here, the NHS there, a new road, the Chunnel, whatever pet project the politicians dream up, they've got to have a tax for it. They'll bleed me dry one day, I swear. If I didn't have so many clients here, I'd pack right up and move to America – to Texas or Florida where the taxes are so much lower and the weather so much warmer."

"Hmmph," Geoffrey intoned. "But you're still here, in the UK, and we have a price to decide on."

Agatha was mildly surprised at the determination in her husband's voice. Ordinarily he would have caved by now, and they would be in the office paying far too much money for something they could have gotten cheaper. Maybe he had learned something after the last time a smooth talker had swindled him. Even Maurice seemed a bit surprised. The glint of victory was gone from his eyes, replaced by a hint of confusion and trepidation, as if he was watching all those pounds sterling flying right out the window before he could get them firmly into his pocket.

"Yes, of course sir. Let's come to an agreement, shall we?" Geoffrey nodded.

"Then I'll tell you my final price and you can decide if it's high enough for you."

"I wait with bated breath, sir."

"I will pay you…"

Agatha watched the battle of wills with a feeling of incredulity. Had her Geoffrey finally grown a backbone? It wasn't that he was cowardly, he was just too nice, too easy to manipulate. He was holding his ground, and it was a little unnerving.

"£3.35 per linear inch!" he said triumphantly.

"Done sir!" Maurice exclaimed. "We have a deal!" He extended one meaty hand, a pinky ring of gold and adorned with a large and brilliant green stone that Agatha hadn't noticed before glinted as he shook with Geoffrey. She found herself strangely mesmerized by it. "Let's go in the office and I'll get Wilhelmina to write up a bill of sale. There is just one last detail. Will you be collecting your purchases today, or shall I have our delivery lorry bring them round?"

"I think the delivery will be fine," Agatha said before Geoffrey could try to talk her into tying a pile of wood to the top of their car.

The planks arrived at their house a week later. Both of them were at work when the truck arrived, but the delivery crew had instructions on where to put the planks. When Geoffrey got home he went straight to them without even bothering to drop off his coat and satchel in the house. Agatha arrived shortly after him and was puzzled when he wasn't in his armchair watching the BBC news like he normally was. "Geoffrey?" she called out. There was no answer. "Where is he?" she muttered under her breath as she searched the house. He wasn't in the bedroom or the loo, but his car was parked in front of the house. They didn't have a dog, nor was he particularly fond of walks, so that really only left two places to search – the pub down the street, or his workshop in the backyard. Geoffrey was fond of a pint now and again, but not generally on a weekday, and never without telling her where he was going.

Agatha opened the sliding glass door that led to the small deck off the back of their house and peered at the shed her husband used for his workshop. It was small, not much bigger than one of the bedrooms in their modest semi-detached home. There was a window next to the door, and through its raindrop-spotted glass pane she could see the light fixture on the ceiling glowing warmly. The top of Geoffrey's head was just visible. It was hard to tell from where she stood, but it looked like he was hunched over, maybe looking down at his workbench. It was just a plastic folding table that was liberally covered in dried droplets of glue, sawdust, and tools he'd never put away, but she didn't correct him when he mentioned it. "Geoffrey!" she called. He didn't seem to hear her. "Geoff!" she said a bit more loudly. His head remained motionless. With a mildly aggravated sigh Agatha stepped down off the deck and walked across the flagstone path to the door of the workshop.

The small building was built on columns that lifted it off the ground, and there were two steps to get up to the threshold. Agatha wasn't tall enough to see through the window from the ground, so she climbed to the top step and glanced inside. Geoffrey was sitting on a stool staring down at his beloved 'workbench'. For once it was clean – all the tools had been put away, the sawdust and other debris swept up and deposited in the bin, and in their place on the bench were the planks they'd bought from the salvage company on their London trip. She'd forgotten they were being delivered that day. The old pedestal table base sat on the floor against the far wall, ignored by her husband as he stared at the dark wooden boards. His hands were running slowly across them, stopping here and there to rub at some irregularity in the wood, or to brush off a bit of dust. It was all quite strange. She'd seen Geoffrey get caught up and utterly absorbed in any number of things, but this was altogether different. His face was just visible in profile, and his only visible eye, the left, was staring at the wood, unblinking. It was almost like he was hypnotized. Then she noticed his lips moving. Agatha had raised a hand to knock on the door but stopped when her husband's strange behavior registered on her. Was he talking to the wood? She'd seen enough and rapped sharply on the door.

"Geoffrey! What are you doing in there?"

There was a scuffle and a thud as he jerked back to reality, knocking over his stool in the process.

"Yes, darling! Coming!"

The door opened and a sheepish face regarded her from inside.

"Whatever are you doing with that wood?" she asked.

"Oh, nothing. Just trying to figure out how to cut it. It's all in the cut, you know. A good sawyer can make or break a piece. This one has got to be just right."

"Yes, well, alright then. Would you like to eat dinner, or are you going to stare at your planks all night?"

"Coming, I'm coming!" Geoffrey said as he left the workshop and closed the door behind him. Agatha walked back toward the house, her mind mulling over what they had in the kitchen that could be thrown together for a quick meal. She didn't see Geoffrey glance back over his shoulder at the workshop, or the look of agonized longing on his face.

Geoffrey spent most of his spare time over the next few weeks in the workshop. Agatha was content to let him have his fun. She had her own interests and hobbies and found the extra time to indulge them to be quite pleasant. Their normal routine of work, come home, engage in their hobbies and pastimes continued mostly uninterrupted. He was spending more time than usual in the workshop, but that was because he had a project he was passionate about, and Agatha only asked him how it was going, never venturing further than the deck to see for herself how far along the table was. "It's great, really great," Geoffrey would reply when asked about it. "Finally sorted how I want to cut the planks, so that will be the next step. I might need to buy some new clamps. The ones I've got aren't quite long enough. Maybe I'll head round the hardware store and have a look."

A little over a month after their trip and the purchase of the planks, their son Grant called to say he'd be coming home for a holiday from university. "We'll be ever so glad to see you," Agatha said with the excitement only a mother could feel who was about to be reunited with her child.

"Tell him to bring me a block of that Stilton cheese," Geoffrey called from his armchair where, for the first time in days, he was watching BBC on the telly instead of mucking about in his workshop.

"He will," Agatha called to him from the kitchen where she was stirring a pot of boiling pasta. She said goodbye to her son and hung up.

Something woke her in the small hours. Agatha rolled over and looked at the clock on the bedside table. It read 2:17 am. Geoffrey was not in bed. She got up slowly and peered out the window that looked down from their second-floor bedroom into the backyard. It was dark but enough light from streetlamps broke the screen of houses and greenery for her to just make out a form in the middle of the garden. It looked like a person squatting down near to the shed. The figure had its back to her but seemed to be working on something on the ground in front of it. Was that Geoffrey out there? What on earth was he doing? Had he gone mental?

Agatha walked slowly and sleepily down the creaky stairs to the ground floor and into the kitchen. Geoffrey was standing at the sink wearing naught but his boxer shorts and washing his hands when she turned on the light.

"Geoffrey! What are you doing? It's the middle of the night!"

He kept his eyes on his hands as he scrubbed them vigorously with soap. "I woke up and couldn't sleep, so I thought I'd get a breath of fresh air." There was a quiver in his voice that reminded her of how a person might speak who had just finished some sort of physically demanding activity. Or was overcome with excitement.

Geoffrey rinsed his hands and dried them on a dishtowel which he tossed on the sideboard next to the sink before finally turning to face her. She was surprised at his appearance. His face was red as if he were too warm, and there was a glint in his eyes that was only there when he was at his most intensely focused.

"Are you alright?" Agatha asked apprehensively.

"Of course, dear! Never better!" The redness in his cheeks was fading, but that strange gleam was still there. It was unsettling.

"You sure? I could drive you to the all-night surgery if you feel off."

Geoffrey enveloped her in a hug and kissed the top of her head. "No need, love. I'm right as rain." He released her and walked toward the stairs. "Feeling much better now. I'm going back to bed. You coming?"

"No, not just yet. I'm awake now. Think I might read a bit. That will make me sleepy again."

"Alright then. Night."

She listened to him climb the stairs, heard the floor creak as he got into bed, then she listened up the stairwell for the sound of his soft snoring. It only took moments before she was sure Geoffrey was asleep. He never had been much of a reader.

Going back to the kitchen, she extracted a torch from a drawer and walked slowly into the backyard. She shined the light across the wet grass, searching until she found the spot where she thought she'd seen Geoffrey kneeling. The dew was brushed off the grass and blades were pushed down where his knees had met the ground. She swept the light around the spot looking for something that would explain what he'd been doing out here. Agatha glanced back at the house. The upstairs light was off, and the curtains were drawn across the window. She turned back to the spot where he'd knelt and bent over to peer more closely at the ground. The torch beam moved slowly from side to side as she searched for… what? Agatha had no idea. Whatever she was looking for, if there was anything to find, it was going to be very small. There was nothing there.

Frustrated and more perplexed than ever, she was just about to turn back to the house when the beam of the light glanced off something. Agatha went to one knee, not caring if her nightgown got a little wet from the dew and looked closer. There was something down deep in the grass blades near to the topsoil. She poked her finger at the spot and held it up in front of her face, shining the torch on it as she did. A red drip fell from her fingernail. Agatha knelt in the grass for a long time, her heart pounding, before she finally stood and walked toward the shed. The door was unlocked. That was most un-Geoffreylike. He was manic about securing his tools. She would have sworn the man saw phantom burglars behind every shrub and lurking in every shadow. Watching the BBC like he did with all their scaremongering would do that to you, make you paranoid.

Agatha stepped softly into the shed but did not turn on the light. Instead, she swept the light around. The workshop was much as she'd last seen it, with the exception of a few new items. Somewhere Geoff had acquired an old steamer trunk. It's battered form rested conspicuously in the far corner. She tried to open it, but the lock was engaged. So, he wouldn't lock the door into the shed, but he would lock this trunk? What in the world was in it? She quickly scanned the workshop for a key. There wasn't one immediately visible.

The next object was a short pole of some kind. It was leaning against the chest and, judging by the sawdust and wooden remnants scattered about, had been fashioned from at least one of the planks. It was perhaps a meter long, maybe a bit shorter, and reminded Agatha of the handle one might find on a shovel or other garden implement. Was one of their shovels or rakes broken? Neither of them were keen on yardwork, and preferred to hire boys from the neighborhood to maintain their yard. She had no idea if Geoff was trying to repair something or not. And if he was, why would he use that wood? She'd seen replacement handles in the hardware stores. It made much more sense to buy one of those than to use those expensive planks for the task.

The last, and strangest item was the open envelope on the workbench. It was of the padded variety one might use to ship a small and slightly fragile item. She looked quickly at the return address. It was from the reclamation shop. Agatha opened the torn end and extracted a single folded sheet of paper and a small cloth drawstring bag. This was turning into one of the strangest nights of her life. She unfolded the letter and read the text by the light of the torch.

I trust you are making grand progress on your project, and I sincerely hope our planks are suiting your needs beautifully. I wanted to send you a small token of appreciation for your patronage; you'll find it in the enclosed bag. Happy woodworking and cheerio,

Maurice

Agatha, utterly befuddled, swept her eyes around the small room one last time and was just about to switch off the torch when a tiny object caught her eye. She could just see the end of it poking out from behind an empty bottle of Fuller's London Porter. Agatha moved the bottle slowly and nodded to herself as she confirmed what she'd first thought. It was a sewing needle. Had Geoffrey taken up needlepoint? A short length of black thread hung from the eye. Geoffrey had twisted and tied it into a noose.

Grant arrived a week later for his holiday. Their son had changed in the months he'd been gone. The last time he'd been home he was clean-shaven. Now he had the scraggly tuftings of a nascent beard.

"What is that small furry creature doing attached to your face?" Geoffrey asked his son good-naturedly.

"Rooting for grubs," Grant grinned in response.

"Why don't we have a dinner party to celebrate you coming home?" Agatha suggested after she'd hugged her son.

"Great idea, mum," he said. "I'll invite all my old mates. They'll all come round for your cookin'."

"Too bad your sister can't be here," Geoffrey said. "But I'm sure she's having a splendid time in the States."

"She put some pictures on Facebook the other day. Did you see them?"

"I don't use that rubbish," Geoffrey replied tartly.

"Pictures? I didn't see them," Agatha said excitedly. "Show me."

Grant pulled his phone from a pocket and swiped the screen. Moments later his mother was giggling with glee.

"Geoff," she said, "she's in Florida – at Disneyworld! Have a look with us!"

"I'll look next time. If we're having a bloody dinner party, then I need to finish the new table."

"What table?" Grant asked.

"It's just your father's latest project. All very hush-hush. Don't bother asking him to show you – he won't. We'll have to wait for the big reveal, like on DIY SOS."

"Oh. Right, then. I'm off. Gonna meet a few of the lads down the pub. Be back later. Bye mum. Bye dad!" And with that Grant was gone. Geoffrey went back to his workshop and left Agatha alone in the kitchen to try and decide what to cook for the party.

Three days later, on a cloudy Saturday evening, people began arriving for the celebratory dinner. Grant, the guest of honor, would be leaving the next day, back to Leicester to resume his studies, but tonight was an opportunity for his old schoolmates and a few family members to congregate and reminisce about when they'd all been younger. Agatha's sister Evelyn was coming with her daughter, ten-year-old Elizabeth, as was Geoffrey's mother June. His brother and sister-in-law lived in Spain where George was an executive with a utility company, but he'd sent his regards and regrets that they couldn't be there.

Geoffrey had been working feverishly to finish the table, which he now not-so-jokingly called his masterpiece. "Ags," he said to her the night before the party, using his pet name for his wife, "everyone is going to be shocked when they see it."

"If it's finished, why don't you bring it in?" she asked.

"I will, I will. Tomorrow."

Agatha sighed. He'd hardly been in the house but to eat and sleep since buying those planks. Before the table project he'd spent the odd evening in his workshop, but most were spent in the house. It had been the complete opposite since. At first, she'd been happy for him to have a project he was so passionate about. Now she was beginning to hate that table, those planks, and the workshop itself. Maybe once the table was in, the big reveal finished, it would be out of his system, and they could get on with their lives. She chuckled out loud at this piece of wishful thinking. Geoffrey was a good man but given to fanciful notions. Some might even call them bollocks, call him a tosser, and maybe both were true from a certain perspective. But he was her tosser and she wanted him back. After the dinner party, after his command performance during the revealing of his majestic new table, maybe things would go back to normal.

The first guest to arrive was a mate of Grant's named Robert. Shortly after Isaac, whom Grant had been friends with since they were small children, and his date, a young lady Agatha recognized as being from their neighborhood, knocked at the door. She offered the girl a cup of tea while she tried to remember her name, and was relieved when she heard Isaac call her Rebecca. Grant was outgoing and funny, and quickly became the focal point of the party, entertaining the guests with stories of university life and shenanigans he got up to in Leicester. Geoffrey was nowhere to be seen.

He'd brought his table in and set it up in the dining room, but it was covered with bedsheets that hung all the way to the floor hiding every inch of it until he was ready for his triumphant moment of revelation. Agatha hoped he wouldn't upstage her son. Geoff could be charming and hilariously funny, but he could also be overbearing and annoyingly peculiar.

Their house wasn't large, and the table just fit into the dining room. Agatha thought she could squeeze all the guests in, but they might bump elbows a bit in the doing. Most everyone had been in the more spacious living room that was adjacent to the dining room while they at hors d'oeuvres and chatted. Evelyn was helping her sister in the kitchen while Elizabeth listened to her cousin's stories in the living room. The laughter of the guests made them both smile while they finished off the cooking.

Geoffrey finally made his appearance about a half hour after the guests arrived. He'd been out in his workshop but was immaculately dressed for dinner. Agatha was happy about that. If he'd come in filthy, she'd have made him shower and change clothes, which would have delayed the meal. The Stilton cheese Grant brought home was nearly gone, as was the cream cheese dip and the sausage. Everyone had arrived hungry. Good. Geoffrey could be counted on to help with dishes, but he was useless when it came to putting leftovers away. He just couldn't seem to find lids for the plastic containers, nor could he ever get food from the pan into the storage container without slopping it all about the place.

"Everyone," Geoffrey said to the group in a loud, commanding voice. All heads turned toward him as conversation died. "As you all know I'm a bit of a hobbyist woodworker, and tonight I'm going to present my latest creation. I think it might possibly be the best work I've ever done." His eyes lost focus for a moment and his lips moved. Agatha couldn't be sure, but she thought she heard him mutter something that sounded like 'gator' or 'raider'. That was strange. Was he alright? She was about to touch his elbow when he perked back up and resumed addressing his expectant but slightly mystified audience.

"You may or may not have heard the story of how this table came into being," he said, gesturing toward the sheet covered piece. He briefly recounted the story of the pedestal and the trip to London which had been punctuated by the visit to Maurice and his reclamation business that resulted in the purchase of the old planks. "I really talked him down in price, utterly beat him up!" Geoffrey said triumphantly. Agatha was tempted to roll her eyes at this bit of embellishment but resisted the impulse. Instead, she reached for a cracker and one of the few remaining slices of Stilton. Geoffrey paused in his story, allowing the tension to build to just the right level before sweeping his arm across the tabletop in a grand gesture of presentation. "So here it is – my masterpiece!" He took hold of the sheets in the center and lifted them straight up like removing a blanket from a bird cage.

The guests stared silently at the table, and Agatha was completely confused. What had he been doing out in his workshop all this time? He'd definitely built a top for the pedestal, but all he appeared to have done was arrange them into the roughly rectangular mass they were all looking at, and nail them together. He hadn't planed them, sanded them, trimmed them, or stained them. They were the same planks that had been delivered to their house all those weeks ago. The table looked like it should have been either in a museum or for sale in a junk shop for £10. The guests weren't sure what to do, so a couple people started clapping politely but hesitantly. Grant saved the moment.

"Bravo, dad! Well done! It'll become a family heirloom, this one!" The other guests smiled uncertainly but following the son's lead began congratulating the father on creating such a fine piece of furniture. Agatha was mystified and more than a little anxious about what he'd been doing out in the workshop. He obviously hadn't spent much time working on the table. Geoff was smiling and shaking hands, basking in the adulation of his adoring fans, like some pop star on a red carpet somewhere. Except that these fans were not fawning, and their congratulations were strained, forced, their eyes hesitant and perplexed. He didn't seem to notice. When the last hand had been shaken Agatha touched his shoulder.

"We should set the table so we can serve dinner now," she said quietly. His eyes went blank again, and he muttered something. It sounded like 'repentance' or 'penitence'. What in the world was wrong with him tonight? No, not just tonight – since they'd gone to that cursed reclamation and repurpose store on the way back from London. He hadn't been right since.

The table took only a few moments to set, and soon everyone was seated and eating. The jovial tone had returned to the conversation after the discomfort of the table reveal, and Agatha was glad for it. She raised her fork to take a bite when suddenly her lips began tingling. One of Grant's friends grimaced and dropped a hand to his stomach. June was talking about some funny incident that happened when Grant was a small boy, and out of nowhere she began slurring her speech. Within moments everyone at the table was experiencing some variety of distress. Agatha looked at Geoffrey who hadn't said anything in the last several minutes. His eyes were vacant but his lips were moving again. The tingling had spread to her arms and was quickly traveling down to her hands. She found it very difficult to move. Elizabeth was doubled over in her chair, both arms wrapped around her midsection. "My tummy hurts mummy," the little girl said.

"Whuh ish thish?" Isaac slurred. The young man's eyes were wide and terrified, and before he could stop it, he leaned over and vomited in the lap of the person next to him.

Geoffrey stood from his chair at the head of his table, placed both his hands on its rough surface, leaned forward, and regarded the guests with an imperious look. "This is it," he said in a voice Agatha had never heard from him before. "Your hangman's meal. The executioner is at hand." The voice was simultaneously deep and high-pitched. It sounded like multiple people were saying the exact same words at the exact same time, only the sound was coming from her husband.

"What… do…?" she managed to ask through now completely numb lips. Geoffrey turned his hawkish gaze to her. His eyes were fierce, intensely bright, full of anger, malice, intent. Agatha was terrified. Who was this man who'd just minutes ago been her Geoffrey?

"The blood court has passed its sentence," he said in that hideous voice. It was like something out of The Exorcist, she thought. Agatha couldn't move now; her entire body was paralyzed except for her eyes which darted around the room. All of the guests were suffering from intense, debilitating abdominal pain or were, like her, completely immobile. A stench reached her nose; someone's bowels had voided, and the room now reeked of shit and vomit. Still Geoffrey surveyed the room.

"The accused have been convicted of treason against The Crown, which being against the laws of the Holy Roman Empire, my Lords have decreed and given sentence that all shall be condemned from life to death by axe." Geoffrey left the room but was back in moments carrying a massive axe with a jet-black blade. Only the sharpened edge displayed the silver of steel. Agatha recognized the handle. It had been leaning against the old steamer trunk in the shed the night she'd seen him kneeling in the backyard. The night she'd found the letter from Maurice. Was this what he'd been doing in his workshop – making this hideous weapon that looked like it had come straight from Tower Hill circa 1605? He began muttering to himself and his eyes lost their intensity for a moment.

"The planks talked to me," he said quietly. The strange multiple-speaker quality in his voice was gone, replaced by the voice of the old Geoffrey. "I didn't have a choice. They made me." He looked around at the room with a haunted and pleading stare. "Please don't be angry. It's the planks. They're from a scaffold. From long ago. People were… Executed on them. They need… Blood. I have to give it to them. They told me to do it." He shook his head as if to clear it, and when he raised his gaze, that intensity was back. And so were the voices.

"What is legal and just pleases me," Geoffrey said in a single voice this time. This voice was not his, but it was alone. It had a strange accent, and the timbre was completely alien. Then another voice spoke. "What is legal and just pleases me," it said. This voice was as different from the first as that one had been from Geoffrey's. The mantra was repeated nine more times, each time in a distinctly different voice. Agatha and the other guests who weren't incapacitated by pain, were staring at Geoffrey with a mixture of awe and sheer terror. The axe was laying on the table; light glinted on the sharpened edge. Geoffrey's hand was caressing it as though he were petting a cat. Then his eyes lost their fierceness, and the old Geoff was back again.

"Do you know where I got this?" he asked as he ran his fingers along the axe. "It was in your mother's barn, Ags. I found it the day we got the table base. It was under a pile of rubbish. The handle was broken. I fixed it. With the planks." His eyes lost focus as he pondered something, then lit up as if he'd had an epiphany. "I haven't told you yet!" he exclaimed. The glee in his voice was utterly incongruous given the situation. Evelyn vomited on the table, splattering the other guests with emesis, as a wide-eyed and ghoulishly grinning Geoffrey watched. "The table base. It was made from the same planks! They've been apart for so long." His voice had suddenly gotten sad, melancholy, then just as quickly morphed to elation. "I reunited them! They were so pleased with me." He looked around the table at the guests. Isaac and Rebecca were tapping on their phones, while Grant struggled to get his from the back pocket of his jeans. Geoffrey stalked over to them and snatched the devices away. "We'll have none of that," he said forcefully, "no nine-nine-nine calls." He quickly took the phones from the rest of the guests. Grant and June tried to stand, but Geoffrey gripped them by the shoulders and forced them back into their seats.

"What are you doing dad? What is this?" Grant asked. The pain in his voice was obvious, his words coming between gasps.

"It's shellfish toxin. That's what I've fed you. They said to do it. So, you can all face your judgment. It was easy. Put it on the Stilton. I work for the NHS. I know people and how to get things. Maybe you won't... feel it. But maybe... not. Aaaahhhh..." The last sound trailed off as if Geoffrey himself was in pain but slowly losing consciousness. Then the look returned to his face and all of the voices began speaking at once again. "Executioner, I command you in the name of the Holy Roman Empire, that you carry these poor sinners to the place of execution and carry out the aforesaid punishment." Geoffrey disappeared into the kitchen, and Agatha heard the back door open. Grant looked at her pleadingly through now paralyzed features, and Agatha felt a tear run down her cheek.

Geoffrey returned with a dolly on which rested a massive square block of wood. He'd clearly constructed this from the planks. The dark timber seemed to emit an otherworldly menace. Geoffrey suddenly pulled his shirt off, revealing his pale torso and thin but sinewy arms. Then he reached into a pocket of his pants and removed a black fabric hood which he placed over his head. It covered his entire face with holes only for his eyes. It was crudely made from a type of cloth anyone could buy in a sewing shop and was clearly something he'd made himself. That's what he'd been sewing out there. Agatha remembered the needle she'd found behind the beer bottle. And the noose he'd fashioned from the black thread.

Geoffrey, now looking very much the part of an executioner, snatched up the shirt of the person to his left –

Evelyn, his wife's sister. He dragged the immobile but clearly terrified woman from her chair and forced her to her knees with her head laying squarely on the block. Then he simply stared down at the unfortunate woman as her tears splashed on the dark wood, darkening it even more with their salty wetness. Was he really going to do this? It had to be some kind of prank, a sick game, didn't it? Could her Geoffrey actually kill someone? Execute them as if this was all some trial from the Gunpowder Plot or the English Revolution? How could he do this?

Grant was struggling to move, but the paralysis had so affected his limbs that it looked like he was having a series of muscle spasms. Some of the other guests had toppled out of their chairs from the intense pain and were on the floor lying in puddles of emesis and urine, heedless of the mess. The only person who seemed to have any semblance of control at all was Isaac. He'd been one of Grant's closest mates and was a big lad who played rugby. He was obviously in pain, but didn't seem to be fully afflicted with paralysis, and he was trying to stand, a carving knife in his hand. Isaac managed to get up from his chair but knocked it over as he stood causing a clatter that attracted Geoffrey's attention. The erstwhile host spun around at the noise and saw his enemy moving toward him. He immediately picked up the axe and taking a single confident step forward, smacked the lad in the side of the head with the flat of the blade. It dropped him, unconscious, to the floor, and the knife clattered away. That, Agatha realized, had been their last best hope to stop what she was now sure was about to happen. If only he hadn't knocked over the chair!

Geoffrey silently regarded the prone form of his son's friend, then turned back to Evelyn. She hadn't moved. Her face was stuck in a grimace, but her eyes were shining wetly and full of more terror than Agatha thought it possible for a person to exhibit. Geoffrey hefted the axe, testing its weight. Then he did something strange: he raised it straight up toward the ceiling until it bumped into the plastered wallboard. She understood. He was determining how to swing the axe. Raise it too high and it would crash into the ceiling. Too low and it wouldn't have enough force, enough momentum, to do the job in a single stroke. This hideous thought flashed through Agatha's mind just as Geoffrey made his decision. He swung the axe in a looping motion that brought it around behind his back, over his right shoulder, and ended with it whistling through the air and embedding itself with a solid thunk in her sister's neck. Blood sprayed from the grievous wound, but it did not sever her head. The sound everyone in the room had heard was the blade making contact with one of her vertebrae. Geoffrey grunted and pulled the axe free. Agatha was staring at her sister in horror and disbelief. The impact of the blade seemed to have rendered her unconscious; her eyes were closed, which was itself a small relief. But she was obviously still alive if the enormous flow of blood from her damaged neck was any indication. Geoffrey raised the axe and swung it again, modifying the angle slightly.

This time it worked.

Her sister's head, separated from her body, rolled off the block and thumped across the dining room floor. A great gout of blood sprayed from her torso, covering the far wall and much of the floor. Geoffrey, calmly and as if he had all eternity, picked up the severed head and placed it on his table directly in front of and facing his wife. Agatha stared at her sister's dead face. Her eyes were still closed, but her mouth was slightly open, and her skin was splattered with blood. She could almost have been sleeping. Red liquid seeped from the ragged flesh where the axe had struck and began to pool on the dark wood of the table. Had those planks really caused all this? If what Geoffrey had said was to be believed, then they were somehow… possessed? Was that the right word? It was as good as any. But how could wood absorb… spirits? Demons? Bloodthirst? Whatever the entities were that had been speaking through his mouth and animating his actions? Or had Geoffrey just suffered some kind of mental breakdown? Maybe he'd had an illness all along and no one noticed it until he finally snapped. The reasons and motivations seemed trivial at the moment.

Geoffrey looked slowly around the room until he seemed to remember Isaac. The lad was flat on his back, unconscious, and the executioner wasted no time. He picked up a carving knife from the table and cut the shirt Isaac was wearing right up the front, exposing his chest. Geoffrey perused the flesh for what felt like an hour to Agatha, then slowly made an incision horizontally across the stomach. He dropped the knife and pulled the edges of the cut apart, opening a hole in Isaac's stomach just above the waistline. Then he plunged both hands into the opening and began removing the boy's entrails. Agatha was horrified to see Isaac's chest rising and falling as he breathed. He was still alive! While being disemboweled! The poor lad! The only consolation was that he was still knocked out from the blow of the axe. This entire event was impossible to believe, to reconcile, to comprehend. How had her dear eccentric husband turned into such a murderous monster?

When he had an impossibly large pile of viscera on the ground next to Isaac's motionless but still living body, Geoffrey reached his hand into the chest cavity, forced it up inside the rib cage, and after a moment's searching, gave a tremendous pull. Agatha was stunned to see him holding a small, fist-sized organ in his blood-drenched hand. "Behold! The heart of a traitor!" he cried triumphantly in that hideous multi-person voice. Geoffrey surveyed the room, the condemned, before slowly placing the stilled heart directly on the wood of his table. A small pool of blood leaked from one of the torn vessels. His eyes were shining with victory, and something else. Madness, Agatha thought. She dropped her eyes from his face and regarded the eviscerated corpse of what had been Isaac, a nice and proper young man whom she'd liked very much. He hadn't deserved to die like this. A rustling sound called her attention back to…him, and she was shocked and terrified to the core of her being at what she saw.

Geoffrey had snatched up another person – her ten-year-old niece this time – and forced the girl's head onto the block. Just before Agatha lost consciousness, she saw the girl's phone on the table. Most of the screen was covered in vomit, but she thought she could see light emanating from it. She passed out when Geoffrey raised the axe again.

"What an awful thing that was," the elderly woman said to the other elderly woman across the fence from her.

"I've never heard of it! Seven people! Who could do such a thing?"

"The police said he went mental. Of course, one would have to be, wouldn't he?"

"I thought he'd started acting strange," the other woman said. "Why just a few weeks ago, I was out tending my peonies when I found a dead cat behind the lilac. It had been there a few days and smelled awful. I called Edward and he took care of it. He said later it looked like its neck had been broken. I didn't think much of it then, figured maybe it had fallen and landed wrong somehow. I mean, it was just a cat, after all. Now I wonder."

The other old woman shook her head. "It's a tragedy, it is. All those people dead. And for what? Because some bloke went all pear shaped?"

"Mildred down the street said that her nephew, who is a copper, told her that they have surveillance video of him walking away from the house afterward. She said he was wearing pants and an executioner's hood, no shirt, and carrying a bloody axe. Can you believe it? An axe! As if he'd just finished off Cromwell or something."

"Did you hear about the recording?"

"What recording?"

"I have it on good authority that one of the victims managed to start a… What do they call it? Brook stream or something?"

"Live stream I think."

"Yes, that's it. The little girl had it on phone while it was all going on. Apparently, the last thing he said, after he finished the final victim, was something like, 'Lord judge, have I executed well?' And then he actually replied to himself! Said, 'You have executed as judgment and law have required.' If that doesn't make the bones quake."

The other woman shivered, although it was a sunny, warm day. "Well, I certainly hope they catch the nutter," she said. "I have to run dearie. Are we on for Bridge next week?"

"Of course!"

"Hullo!" a deep baritone voice boomed from inside the building. "I see you've made it from Birmingham in one piece!" The huge man waddled out the big roll up door to meet the young couple who'd just pulled into the parking lot. The woman extracted a child from a car seat in the back and cradled the babe against her shoulder as she and her husband walked toward him.

"Hello," the man said. He met the big man just outside the door and marveled at the suit he was wearing. It must have cost a fortune to have something that hideous – a bright shade of salmon with blue stitching, a silver tie, and a purple bowler – custom-tailored, which that suit surely was.

"Welcome to my humble proprietorship. My name is Maurice and I'll be your tour guide this afternoon."

"Pleased to meet you, Maurice. I'm James and this is my wife Lilly and our daughter Paige."

"I bid you a fond welcome! Please, right this way. I've recently acquired a piece made by a one-time customer that I believe you'll be highly enamored with," he said as he led them through the door and into the warehouse. "I sold him the planks he made it from – six-hundred-year-old wood! It's quite an item, and I believe it will fit splendidly in your new home. This unfortunate fellow ran into some legal troubles, and I was able to buy not only the wood but the table he built with it from a police auction." He stood aside to let the young couple enter. They didn't hear him muttering under his breath. "The planks… they said I had to."

Author's Note

This story was inspired by a show I watched on HBO called 'Gunpowder'. It's about the infamous Gunpowder plot of 1605. If you've never heard of it, then maybe you've seen the movie 'V'? That film was inspired by the event, and one of the two protagonists wears a mask that purportedly depicts a stylized likeness of Guy Fawkes, one of the conspirators in the original plot. The idea for this story came to me while watching a rather gruesome execution scene in 'Gunpowder' that took place on a wooden scaffold. I wondered what had become of the planks it was built out of, and away my imagination went. This story is the result of those musings. The reason for this note is to explain part of it. Most of the dialog Geoffrey utters during the dinner party scene, well, the official sounding parts of it anyway, were stolen by me from an article I found online about executions from the past. I didn't delve too deeply into the lore of executions or England; I did enough real research in college to last me for the rest of my life. I'm much more interested now in just crafting a story that I enjoy, and that hopefully others will too. But in order to have at least an aura of authenticity, sometimes it's necessary to do the bare

minimum of research. So, for this story, I did. The article I took the dialog from was published in Slate, and I found it after a very quick internet search. It's actually not precisely an article, but an excerpt from a book by an author named Joel F. Harrington, who himself references other, more archaic literary works that he used as source material to write his own book called The Faithful Executioner. I assume the lines I stole were taken from those sources and were things that the participants in those macabre proceedings would have actually said. Why in the hell have I typed all this? Because I believe firmly in attribution. I'll never intentionally plagiarize someone else's work. I don't need to; I have enough ideas of my own. But for this story I wanted to know what the judges, juries and executioners might have said, and to replicate those words in a relatively accurate fashion. And I don't know about you, but I thought it added a creepy, more sinister vibe to the scene. If you'd like to read the excerpt, and I'd highly encourage you to do so, you can find it here:
https://slate.com/news-and-politics/2013/05/executioners-in-medieval-europe-history-of-capital-punishment.html

I'd also strongly recommend you read Joel's book. I did after I found that excerpt, and it is fantastic! You can find it here:

https://www.amazon.com/Faithful-Executioner-Turbulent-Sixteenth-Century/dp/1250043611

Mark Sowers
Wasilla Alaska
August 2022

# PATCHOULI PUKE

"Zat is a myth," Archambeau said in his French accent.

"Yes, I read this somewhere," Coelho added, her native country of Brazil prominent in her enunciation. She pronounced read like reed instead of red. "Was maybe in *Frontiers in Human Neuroscience.*"

"She might have you there Randy," Mike Roberts said to his colleague. "I somehow doubt that particular journal's sitting on your nightstand."

"Yes, I think Mike is right, maybe she does," Leonid added. His accent was distinctly Ukrainian, but he'd been in America long enough to have lost some of it, and his English was excellent.

Randy looked at his audience of four, then out the round window. The earth from 220 miles up looked huge and small at the same time. The International Space Station was at that moment on the dark side of the globe, and the lights of cities across Europe, Africa and western Asia created a chaotic spiderweb of sparkling brightness across the otherwise blackened sphere.

"Well, whatever the number is, the whole point of the exercise was to try to get to the cognitive level of Einstein or above," Randy retorted.

"It did no work," Archambeau said with a mischievous smile. The others laughed out loud, finding mirth in the joke made at Randy's expense. The joke's subject smiled too. He knew the little Frenchman was just ribbing him. It was one of the ways they kept the mood light here in this tiny little series of tubes far above the world. The ISS was so cramped that the five people currently inhabiting it were constantly in each other's way. The only time they weren't bumping into each other was when they were sleeping.

The International Space Station was nearing the end of its operational life. In the next year or two, it would be decommissioned and deorbited into earth's atmosphere. Any parts of it that didn't burn up on reentry would, if all went according to plan, crash harmlessly into remote waters of the South Pacific, far from land and humans. There were only five astronauts on the station now. There had been more originally, but space exploration had moved on to other things, and budgets for sustaining personnel on the station had been cut. Governments didn't want to pay for outdated equipment. They wanted shiny new toys that looked good on the evening news and social media. The ISS was *very* old news that no one cared about anymore except scientists back on earth who still relied on the station and its staff to carry out experiments for them. This crew would be the next to last to live and work on the ISS before it was sent to its fiery and watery death sometime in the near future. It seemed such a waste. Over $150 billion dollars had been spent on the thing since its inception. It had even been called the most expensive item ever built. And they were going to just let it burn up in the atmosphere and sink to the bottom of the sea.

Randy Pello had been here six months of a scheduled eleven. He'd come from earth on a Space X vehicle launched from Florida, and at one time that company launching rockets into space had been shiny and new just like the ISS had been. Now it was routine, the luster had worn off, and people's attention had turned away. The Webb telescope was taking dazzling pictures from its home far out in space, rovers and probes were delving Mars and circling other planets in the solar system, and there were new projects in the works that would soon capture the public's interest the way Space X and the ISS once had. The memories of individual humans are short, their collective memory even shorter, and like last Christmas' broken toy, the ISS would soon be discarded in favor of something else.

"Go on with the story," Mike said when the laughter had died down. "I want to hear how it ends."

Randy looked around at his small audience. These people were not only his colleagues, but they'd become his friends over the last few months. Jacques Archambeau was here representing France, Fernanda Coelho from Brazil, Leonid Toptunov from Ukraine, and himself and Mike Roberts from the USA.

"So, like I said, I'd heard that *the number*, as I called it, was about ten percent."

"You mean that humans only use on average ten percent of their brain's capacity, right?" Mike asked.

Randy nodded and continued. "Einstein supposedly used somewhere around thirty percent of his brain. If the theory's been debunked, then it's been debunked. What's important is that my friends and I believed it when we were kids, and we wanted to do something to get access to the unused part of it, activate it, use it to come up with the next… lightbulb, or theory of relativity, or something."

"Ze folly of youth," Jacques said with mock wistfulness. The others laughed except Randy who shot him a friendly scowl.

"So, you take hallucinogens to accomplish this?" Fernanda asked. "How do you become astronaut with this activity?"

Randy grinned wickedly. "NASA never found out!" The whole group roared with laughter at this bit of obfuscation on their colleague's part. Every one of them had gone through a rigorous and extremely thorough background check, among a host of other qualifiers, prior to being admitted to the program that sent astronauts to the ISS. It was rare for someone to successfully hide something like drug use from the horde of investigators, shrinks and doctors that poked, prodded and interrogated them about their past.

"You must be very good at fool lie detector test," Leonid said proudly. "Good for you!"

"Why, thank you!" Randy said with a little bow.

"So, tell us what you did," Mike nudged in order to get the conversation back on track.

"It was my friend's cousin," he continued. "This guy was some kind of hallucinogenic guru, real Timothy Leary disciple. He'd been all over the country looking for drugs that would open doors in his mind. Peyote, LSD, mushrooms – he'd tried them all. But he'd heard of something from South America called ayahuasca that really got his balls sweaty. You know about it Fernanda?"

The Brazilian woman nodded. "It has been use for many years by Amazon peoples," she said. "Traditional medicine for century."

"That's the stuff," Randy said. "The guru thought if he could get some of it and mix it with a few other things, that he'd be able to... see God or some damned thing. He was obsessed with it. My friend and I just wanted to expand our intellects. We didn't really care about visiting alternate dimensions, or talking to the spirts, or whatever. We just wanted to turn that ten percent of our brain that we used into fifty. Or a hundred."

"How old were you when you do this?" Leonid asked.

"Seventeen."

"Young."

"Yes. But determined. I was already planning on going to college. I'd tested high in math and science, and I liked school, so I figured why not keep going. But I also wanted to be prepared when I got there. I'm competitive by nature, and I wanted to blow the doors off the other students academically. So that's the genesis of our little project."

Something began beeping in another module, causing all heads to turn toward a digital monitor on the wall.

"Is just the centrifuge finished spinning," Fernanda said. "I will handle." She pushed herself away from the wall and floated off down a narrow tube that led into other parts of the station.

"I'll finish the story at dinner," Randy said as the rest of the group broke up to go back to work.

Six hours later Randy was done with his tasks for the day and was floating comfortably next to one of the many round windows that allowed the occupants of the station to look out on their green and blue home far below. It was still surprising to see it from here. Looking at pictures of Earth taken from this vantage point was an entirely different thing than actually seeing it from space yourself. It seemed impossible for there to be so much misery and suffering on such a beautiful orb. The greens of tropical Africa gradually receded as the Sahara took over, both surrounded by the azure colors of the seas that bordered the continent, all of it overlaid with varying gradations of white and grey clouds. How many kids were down there being forced to mine blood diamonds at gunpoint? Or how many fundamentalist Islamists were plotting heinous acts in the name of their religion? There was a hurricane in the Gulf of Mexico, and he wondered how many island homes it was destroying at that moment. Then Central America came into view, and he wondered how many people were being forced, under threat of violence, to do horrible things by the ruthless drug cartels that operated with such impunity throughout the region. And there, to the north, were the US and Canada, where the hideously oppressive and destructive political ideologies had infected the minds of so many people. As the western hemisphere disappeared, the vast Pacific came into view, and Randy wondered if at that moment an earthquake or a volcano somewhere on the Ring of Fire was causing devastation. A few minutes later he saw land again – the east coast of China. How many Uighurs and Falun Gong practitioners were down there in prison camps at that exact moment being persecuted, tortured, and murdered by the Communist government for their beliefs? It was easy to ponder these things from this far above the world, from the safety and security of distance, and easy to forget about them when they weren't right in front of you.

Someone called his name down one of the tubes connecting the modules and, having put himself in a rather maudlin mood, Randy sighed and abandoned the window in exchange for dinner and company.

The crew had gathered in the tiny galley, and most of them were eating already. Randy extracted a mylar pouch containing dehydrated a Thai curry dish and rehydrated it with a dose of water from a specially designed dispenser.

"You finally made it huh?" Mike asked. Randy nodded as he cut open the pouch with scissors and ate his first spoonful.

"You know geography, yes?" Leonid asked.

"I'm ok with it," Randy replied after swallowing a second mouthful. He hadn't realized how hungry he was.

"We just talking about Luxembourg," Leonid continued. "You know this country?"

"I've heard of it, sure. It's pretty small."

"Très petit," Jacque added.

"What do call person from Luxembourg?" Fernanda asked. "This is question."

"I vote for Luxemburger," Mike interjected. "I like the way it sounds. Maybe I'll open a fast-food restaurant someday and that'll be the name of it!" Everyone laughed.

"Luxembourgeoise?" asked Jacque. "Could be Marxist Luxembourg person!"

"No. That would be rich Luxembourg person," Leonid said. "Marxist Luxembourg would Luxemproletariat."

"Hasn't someone looked it up?" Randy asked. "It's not like we don't have internet access here."

"Is more fun to make joke," Fernanda said with a smile. Randy grinned at the Brazilian woman.

The laughter died out as the astronauts ate in silence for a few moments. They all missed home, but being here was not only an incredible personal achievement, but a tremendous national honor that all of them took very seriously. No one wanted to embarrass their country, and all were diligent, hard workers who also happened to enjoy each other's company and who, fortunately for morale, were possessed of mostly compatible senses of humor.

"You never finish ze story from earlier," Jacques finally said to Randy. "We would like to hear ze end."

"Where did I leave off?" Randy asked as he finished his curry and took a long pull from a water bottle.

"College," Mike said.

"Oh yeah." Randy's eyes went vacant for a moment while he gathered his thoughts. "So that guru guy I mentioned. Wish I could remember his name. It was Devin or Kevin, something like that. Doesn't matter. I'll just call him the guru. My friend who introduced me to him, his name was Theo, convinced the guru to mix us up a batch of this concoction he'd created. We'd told him about our plan, the whole mind or consciousness expanding thing, and he was all about it, thought it was a great idea, so he made us a batch his signature… stuff. To this day I have no idea what was in it, but when he gave it to us, it was in a Mason jar and looked like greenish-black sludge. And it smelled horrid."

"So was liquid?" Fernanda asked.

Randy nodded. "Yeah, but it was really viscous, almost the consistency of cake batter."

"And you just drank it?" Mike asked with a skeptical look.

"No. Not right away. The guru told us it was going to taste as bad as it smelled, and after I'd gotten a whiff, I kinda lost my nerve a little. Theo had to cajole me for a week before I finally agreed. I could just see myself vomiting the minute the stuff hit my tongue, and I *hate* vomiting."

Leonid nodded. "Yes, at home once I drink too much vodka and blahhh!" the Ukrainian said as he mimicked the action of emesis. The crew laughed at his comically contorted features.

Randy smiled and continued. "Theo told the guru about my... reluctance, and in his wisdom concerning all things hallucinogenic, he suggested mixing it with a can of frozen orange juice. Now I have to say it wasn't a full Mason jar. There was probably only about a cup of the liquid, or maybe two hundred and fifty milliliters for you metric folks."

"Which is everyone but you and I," Mike said quickly.

"You Americans," Jacques said, "always with ze miles and ounces. Who use zese things anymore?"

"We do," Randy said with a glare of mock indignation.

"Stop now children," Fernanda said. "No international incident on ISS!" Jacques and Mike smiled as Leonid grinned and shook his head.

"When I finally decided to try the stuff, we picked a holiday weekend, I think it was Labor Day, so we had three days off in case we had to recuperate. I'd been on a few benders before, with booze, and I knew that my constitution needed a recovery period. Since we had no idea what this stuff was going to do to us, I insisted on drinking it early on in the long weekend." Randy paused for a moment to collect his thoughts before continuing. The humor among the group had dissipated and been replaced by anticipation. They wanted to hear the end of this story.

"Theo lived with his dad in a big house on the other side of town. His mom had left when he was young, and his dad owned a car dealership, so they had money. I took the bus to his place since I didn't have a car. His dad was out of town, so Theo had the house to himself. When I got there, he was all ready to go. He'd gotten the orange juice, had the Mason jar of the stuff, and was just itching to drink it. I was still kinda leery, especially when he opened the jar and I smelled it again. Almost called it off right there. But I'd told him I would, so I was sort of honor-bound to go through with it. I kept telling myself that if it worked, then it would be worth it."

"Did you drink?" Jacques asked impatiently.

"Relax," Leonid said to the excitable Frenchman. "Let him tell story."

"Yes. I drank," Randy said. "Theo used to smoke a lot of pot back then, and he always had patchouli oil around to cover up the smell. He'd practically douse himself in the stuff. It didn't bother me; in fact, I rather liked the smell of patchouli. But it was always there when you were around Theo." Randy paused and took another drink from his water bottle before continuing. His audience waited quietly, even Jacques, but the Frenchman's eyes were shining with unasked questions and unvoiced quips.

"We stood there in his kitchen for a few minutes, not really saying much, just chattering inanely about kids at school, rock and roll, and whatever else came to mind. There were two plastic glasses on the counter next to the stuff; like I said, he was ready. Theo finally got fed up with my stalling and asked if we were gonna do it or not. I said ok, and he wasted no time in mixing the orange juice in with the stuff in the jar. He poured us each a glass, we knocked them together, said 'Cheers' and pounded the stuff like a cheap beer."

Jacques couldn't stop himself. "How did it taste?!"

"Let him tell!" Fernanda admonished him. Jacque ignored her.

Randy looked directly into Jacques' eyes. "It was the worst tasting stuff I've ever tried," he said flatly. "If you mix raw sewage, sawdust, rotten fruit and rancid butter together and take a swig, that would probably be better than the god-awful shit we drank that day."

The room erupted in laughter. Jacques was folded over double and holding his stomach, Mike and Fernanda had tears pouring down their faces, and even stoic Leonid was chuckling with easy mirth. Randy couldn't help it; the laughter was infectious, and he joined them.

"I managed to get it all down," he said when everyone's composure had been regained, "but I had to hold my nose to do it. Even with the orange juice it was still the worst flavor I've ever tasted. After we drank it we went to Theo's room to hang out. He had all kinds of cool psychedelic stuff in there – lava lamps, this glass globe thing with electricity inside that lit up when you touched it, a black light, all the things you'd expect high school kids who like partying to have. And he had a phenomenal stereo system his dad had gotten him that we always turned up far too loud. His room was huge; there was even a couch in there where I always sat. He had a desk with an office chair that he sat in, and we went in there to wait for the stuff to take effect. Theo played a cd on the stereo, *Animals* from Pink Floyd, and we just kind of did nothing for the next half hour or so."

Something beeped from another module. "It's the Charged Particle Detector," Mike said. The CPD was a subcomponent of the Radiation Assessment Detector, or RAD, along with the Fast Neutron Detector, or FND. They were essential to monitoring radiation and protecting the crew. If one of them was beeping, then something was happening. "Have to put the story on hold for a minute," Mike said as he pushed off from a wall and floated off toward the sound.

"Something just hit us," Leonid said.

"Could be anything," Fernanda added.

Jacques' usually quick humor was subdued at the moment. No one liked to hear the RADs issuing warnings. Radiation was abundant in space and extremely dangerous. The ISS was shielded against it, and since it was in low Earth orbit it also received protection from Earth's magnetic field, but there was still a lot of radiation out there.

Mike returned a few moments later with a puzzled expression on his face. "We just got hit by what appears to be a pretty big wave of solar radiation."

"That make no sense," Jacques replied. "Sun activity low right now."

"I know," Mike said, "but that's what the data says."

"Where it come from then?" Fernanda asked.

"Maybe was not solar radiation but something else?" Leonid added.

"The data is pretty clear," Mike said. "If it's *not* solar radiation, then it's something that looks just like it. But where it came from... who knows."

"What was the exposure level?" Randy asked quietly.

Mike was silent as he looked at his crewmates. "Six thousand milli rads," he said gravely.

The room erupted in shouts.

Jacques was technically in command, but at the moment the Frenchman was screaming louder than anyone. The only words that were intelligible were the occasional *'sacre bleu'* scattered among the much more frequently uttered *'merde'*. Mike had to wave his arms and shout louder than everyone else to get the room back under control. The only one who didn't yell was Randy. He took the news stoically if a little nonchalantly.

"The maximum dose is fifty!" Leonid exclaimed.

"How this happen?" Fernanda asked in a tone that was near to hysterical. "My husband and I have baby in year or two. What about *that?!*"

"Everybody calm *down!*" Mike ordered. He'd been a colonel in the US Air Force and had a commanding presence about him when he wanted to use it. The crew responded by lowering the volume of their voices, which eventually trailed off into a tense silence. "Good. Thank you. Now can we have a discussion without screaming again?" They nodded. "Alright. We all know the maximum daily dose is fifty, just like Leonid said. The question we need an answer to is: what did each of us *actually* receive? Check your dosimeters." Everyone looked at the small monitors they were wearing.

"Seventy-two," Leonid said with a sigh of relief.

"Forty-three," Fernanda added.

"Twelve," Jacques said softly.

"And I got eighteen," Mike added. Everyone was so busy smiling sheepishly at their momentary loss of composure that no one noticed Randy hadn't spoken yet. Leonid was the one who finally looked in his direction.

"Randy?" he asked. Everyone's eyes turned to him. He was still looking at his dosimeter with an unreadable expression.

Mike nudged him gently with an elbow, "What's it say?"

Randy raised his head slowly, a frown creasing his forehead. "Nine thousand six hundred and five." Everyone's eyes bulged, but they kept their cool this time.

"I'm going to call mission control," Mike said quickly.

"I come too," Jacques added as the two of them floated off into another module.

Fernanda, who in addition to being a scientist was also the ISS' medical officer, immediately insisted that Randy accompany her to another module where she made him strip to his underwear. "I want to look for red skin, like sunburn," she said. After several moments of examination, she frowned at him. "You look ok," she said in a mystified tone. "That much you should be burn. But nothing."

"That's good news, right?" he asked. Randy felt the same as he had before the RAD went off. He'd read that exposure to high doses of radiation could bring about all kinds of effects, like the red, sunburned skin Fernanda had been looking for and the taste of metal in the mouth, among other things. He felt completely normal at that moment. But was he? Radiation exposure could also take a long time to manifest in the form of symptoms or ailments. Maybe ten years from now he would develop some kind of cancer.

"I do not know," the Brazilian said. "You may be ok, maybe no. But must get to Earth soon for test."

"I'm not scheduled to rotate out for five months yet, and there isn't a resupply mission for a month and a half. I think I'm stuck here for a while," he said with more cheer than he felt.

"I will talk to Archambeau," she said confidently. "He will get ship here for you to go home." Randy nodded and got dressed.

"Might as well finish my story," he said "Everyone seemed to enjoy it, and I was just getting to the good part. Shall we?" he asked as he gestured toward the tube that led back to the others and Fernanda gave him a brief smile, then pushed off and floated away.

The group, minus Mike and Jacques, was back together a few moments later, and conversation was dominated by Randy's level of exposure. He assured them that he felt fine, and Fernanda informed everyone that she hadn't found any obvious symptoms of radiation exposure. They were all shaking their heads at the anomalous nature of the event when Mike and Jacques floated back into the module.

"What they say?" Fernanda asked. Mike stared at each of them in turn for several long moments, then shook his head as if clearing it of cobwebs.

"They told me," he said very slowly, "that the radiation burst was detected by one of their satellites."

"Good. What was origin?" Leonid asked.

"That's the strange part," he said. His voice was quiet, only a little above a whisper. "They said that the origin was… *inside* the ISS." No one spoke.

"Impossible!" Jacques finally said at last. "We have no equipment on board to generate such powerful burst. I tell them zis, but zey no listen."

"He is correct," Leonid said. "My specialty is particle physics; I know this to be true."

"They were insistent and confident," Mike replied. "MC has no idea how it could have happened. They're going to ask experts from all over the world to look at the data and offer potential explanations. It's got them that baffled."

"Well!" Randy said trying to lighten the mood. "Looks like we might be in the middle of a major discovery! Maybe they'll build statues of us someday."

"We have to die to get statue," Fernanda said. "I like live too much for that."

Jacques nodded vociferously. "Oui," he said. "I no want to die yet.

"No one does," Leonid said. "And we will not. But this is mystery of physics. Nothing like it ever happen in space before."

"Well, there's nothing we can do about it now," Mike said. "All systems are functioning nominally, there are no crew injuries that we know of, and everything seems to be in good hands down below." He looked at Randy. "You might as well finish your story."

"Where was I?" he asked.

"You were in Theo bedroom, with Pink Floyd," Fernanda answered.

"Right. So, we were just sitting around, waiting for something to happen. And nothing did for what seemed like a long time, but maybe it was just the anticipation. We were really hoping that we'd found the key to unlocking the brain's potential. The guru sure made it seem like if anything could, it was his concoction. Now that I think of it, I'm not sure we ever asked him if he'd taken this stuff himself, or if he'd just randomly mixed it all together for us. And he never did tell us what was in it. Not completely. It definitely had ayahuasca and LSD, he'd told us that much, but beyond those two, who knows what the guy threw in the pot. Could have been nuclear waste, I don't know." Randy's eyes went vacant as he dug around in his memory.

"The room stunk of patchouli. I think Theo must have dumped a whole bottle out or something. I usually liked the smell, but that day it was making me feel nauseous, and I told him he'd used too much of it. Or the nausea could have been the stuff we drank. Whatever it was, I felt the nausea getting stronger and stronger. Theo had his own bathroom, and the door was open. I kept looking at it, wondering if I should go wait by the toilet. But I kept hoping it would go away. At one point Theo looked at me and asked if I felt alright. I sort of remember shaking my head, but if I'd have opened my mouth, he would have had a mess on his carpet. And that was it. I knew it was coming, so I got up really quickly and ran to his bathroom. Barely made it to the toilet. It smelled worse coming back up than it had tasted going down. I flushed the toilet and hurled again. Then again until my stomach was empty. There was a stack of Dixie cups next to the sink, and I washed my mouth out with water and Listerine before going back to Theo's room. He was looking at me strangely, like I didn't belong in his house, but then he lit up and started laughing. 'We're calling this shit Patchouli Puke!' he said. And that's what we called it from then on – Patchouli Puke. I thought it was as good a name as any, and kinda funny."

"I am going to create cologne with this name," Jacques said, "It will be like Chanel but better!" Everyone laughed as the Frenchman threw his head back and raised one clenched fist in a triumphant pose.

The stress and anxiety of the strange radiation burst had been momentarily forgotten as the audience found themselves absorbed in the story again.

Randy continued with a grin at Jacques. "I flopped down on the couch and stared at an MC Escher poster he had affixed to the ceiling."

"Who?" Leonid asked.

"MC Escher," Randy said. The blank look didn't leave Leonid's face.

"Google him," Mike said in order to keep the story flowing.

"The poster was of these crazy staircases that went up, down, and sideways, all in the same building and with people walking on them," Randy continued. "It was totally gravity-defying, anti-reality, but mesmerizing. I was staring at it intently when the people on the stairs suddenly started moving. It was a poster – of a piece of artwork. The people on it *couldn't* move. They were just ink on paper! But they were definitely walking. One of them turned and looked at me, and it was like some kind of dress form – a completely androgynous body with no face. But I'd swear I heard it say 'Join us', even though it didn't have a mouth. Next thing I knew it was like I'd levitated off the couch and was flying toward the poster. Then I was *in* it. I felt my shoes touch the stairs. The figure was next to me, and it stretched out its hand and touched my shoulder. I didn't feel threatened by it, and it didn't hurt, but there was something insistent in it, like it wanted me to do something."

The crew were all staring at Randy as he talked, their attention completely on the story as each imagined their own version of the bizarre events he was describing.

"The figure had no face; it was just a smooth oval head on top of the body. I looked behind me and I could see the spot where the picture stopped – the edges. They were like faint lines in the air and across the stairs. But I was looking around from *inside* it. And it kept going. The stairways went all over the place. More figures were walking up and down them, going I had no idea where. The one that had touched me was still there, that blank face staring at me. I tried to talk, to ask it what it wanted, but my mouth didn't work. My hands were at my sides, and I raised one to my face, to touch my mouth, but all it felt was smoothness. I had no face – just like the figure. Then I started to panic. There was no heartbeat in my chest, and if there had been it would have been pounding like a machine gun, but my thoughts were all there. Then I noticed my hand and the arm it was attached to. They looked just like the figure's. I looked down and my body looked just like it's body. I'd become one of them somehow."

The other astronauts were listening intently, their eyes narrowed and their faces rapt with attention. "Go on," Mike prodded.

Randy looked away for a moment to collect his thoughts before continuing.

"My first thought was to get the hell out of there, get back to Theo's room. So, I turned around to dive back out of the picture. I could see the room as if I was looking through a window or doorway. Theo was there, in his chair, his eyes closed and his head nodding gently to Pink Floyd. My body was *not* there. I tried to jump, but nothing happened. Then I tried to will myself back there, to imagine myself onto the couch. And again, nothing happened. I was really panicking then. All kinds of thoughts were flying through my mind. Would I ever get back? If I did, would I still be just a faceless figure? What if I was trapped here? What did these things eat if they didn't have mouths? What would my parents say? My girlfriend? I was well and royally fucked, in my own not-so-humble opinion. Then the figure touched me again. There was an urgency this time, and I managed to get myself under control enough to look the thing right in its smooth blank face. It looked right back. I was screaming inside, asking it what it wanted, but there was no sound in that place. It was the most complete silence I've ever experienced. Even sensory deprivation tanks aren't that quiet. I didn't know what else to do, and the figure seemed to want me to move, so I did the only thing I could – I started walking up the stairs. It followed me. The stairs ended a few steps up and a new staircase began that ran off to the right, but down and at an impossible angle. There didn't seem to be any gravity in that place, otherwise figures would have been falling off stairs everywhere. I should have fallen as soon as I stepped onto that new staircase, but I didn't, just kept right on walking. The figure kept following. The place went well beyond the borders of the original picture; I couldn't tell how far; the staircases went on forever, most of them with figures on them. There was even one figure – I'll never forget it – the thing was carrying a tray of empty champagne glasses. Why there would be glasses in that place when none of the inhabitants even had a mouth was just another mystery."

A repetitive beeping began in another part of the ISS. It was a different sound this time. "Mission control want to speak," Jacques said. "I will see what zey want." The Frenchman floated off toward the beeping sound, leaving the rest of Randy's audience to ponder what he'd told them.

"I have hear of these… trips, you call them, yes?" Leonid said. Randy nodded. "Sometimes a person take these drugs and poof! Mind gone forever. You did not have this problem."

"No. I was lucky. As far as I know there were no residual effects of my… trip."

"What about Theo?" Fernanda asked.

Randy's face fell. "He… discovered heroin a year or two later. The last I heard of him, he was living under a freeway overpass and selling his… body… for drugs. I haven't seen him in twenty-five years."

"So sad," Fernanda said with a shake of her head.

Jacques floated back into the module with a puzzled expression on his face. Everyone wanted to ask what MC had said but knew that when he got that look on his face, he wouldn't speak until he'd collected his thoughts. Instead of prodding him to no avail, they waited patiently while he ran through his process.

"The radiation," he at last said slowly. "Is like nothing ever see before." The other astronauts looked at each other, their faces confused.

"What you mean?" Leonid asked.

"They say radiation is new variety. No record of it ever. It is no on electromagnetic spectrum. Only way zey see it is because it disrupt seven satellites moments after detection."

"I thought they'd detected a massive burst of solar radiation," Mike said. It was more a question than a statement.

"Zey did," Archambeau replied. "Zis was different but happen at same time."

"What else they know?" Fernanda asked.

"Preliminary analysis indicate zat new radiation somehow… what is word?... piggyback? Yes – piggyback. On solar radiation."

"That's not possible," Randy said flatly.

"Zey say zat too," Jacques shot back. "But it is what data show. Wavelengths different but intertwined somehow. Is new phenomenon. Unmatched in physics history."

"There isn't squat we can do about it now. The eggheads down on earth will have to figure it out. If there's no danger to us, I suggest Randy finish his crazy story," Mike said.

Fernanda shrugged. "Why not?"

"I like this story," Leonid said. "I want to hear end."

"Where was I?" Randy asked. The discussion of this new form of radiation had derailed his train of thought, and he couldn't remember where he'd left off.

"Ze champagne glasses," Jacques prodded.

"Oh yeah. It's still a mystery to me why that… figure was carrying around champagne glasses when not one of them, or me, could drink from them. I watched until it disappeared into a doorway on one of the stairway landings, and I never saw it again." The audience exchanged glances, their raised eyebrows and questioning expressions silently asked if anyone had a hypothesis concerning the mystery of the champagne glasses, but no one did.

"I just wanted to leave," Randy said after a short pause. "The doorway or window back to Theo's room was far behind me; I'd gone deep into that... picture, place, whatever it was, and I was over it. I was a little surprised, but fatigue wasn't a problem. Going up and down all those stairs would have exhausted me in this world, but in that one I felt fine, not tired at all."

"I have no idea how long I climbed those damned stairs. It seemed like days at the time. They all looked the same, just endless stairs and landings leading into who-knows-where. There were doorways and windows, other figures walking around, it was all just insane. The figure, my figure, was still behind me, following me everywhere I went. I was ignoring it since it didn't seem to want to help or do anything other than tag along behind me."

"Finally, I reached a landing and took a step down onto the next staircase, and it touched my shoulder. I'd almost forgotten it was there, and the touch startled me. When I turned around it was standing on the landing with its arm held out towards a strange object embedded in the wall. It looked like the door to a vault – one of those huge round steel ones that you see in movies about bank robbers. Except that this one was made of something like glass. The surface was shiny, but inside it was some kind of red viscous liquid. I looked at it for a bit and could see things swirling in it, like tiny approximations of the figures that had been caught in a whirlpool. It was hard to see them;

they were deep in the… door, but they were definitely there. I was half expecting something to happen, like a scene in a horror movie where the victim is staring into a mirror and suddenly a hand smacks against it from the opposite side. I thought maybe one of those figures would spurt out of the vortex they were caught in and splatter against the inside of the glass. But it didn't happen. They actually disappeared, like water going down the drain when you pull the plug on the bathtub. The figure touched my shoulder again and gestured toward the vault door. For the first time since getting there I felt fear. Something was not right about that round red mass. The figure didn't seem to like that I wasn't moving, and it pushed me toward it, and I actually stumbled a little. When I held out my hands to stop myself, they went right into the stuff. It wasn't liquid as we know it. Well, I suppose it could be like mercury in that it didn't stick to me or get me wet. I pulled my hands out immediately, and there was nothing on them." Randy stopped speaking for a moment, his eyes vacant.

"Did you feel anything?" Leonid asked. "Heat, cold, pain?"

Randy shook his head. "No. My hands went in, and I pulled them out. Nothing else changed."

"Étrange," Jacques said.

"Oui," Randy replied. "Très."

"What happened next?" Leonid asked.

"It pushed me again, which pissed me off. I was yelling at it in my mind, calling it every name I could think of. I've no idea if it knew what I was thinking or not. The absence of mouths made it rather difficult to communicate, except through gestures like it was using. I was pretty sure it wanted me to go into that big red vault door, but I wasn't too eager to oblige. Watching those tiny little figures, if that's what they were, swirl away down the unseen drain was not at all encouraging. It was easy to imagine myself becoming one of them and ending up in that place's version of a sewer. I thought about running and even looked around for an escape route. Except that there were figures approaching from everywhere, converging on us. Getting back to the place where I'd come through, the window into Theo's room, was going to be impossible. I didn't remember the way. Even if I could have gotten away from all those figures, and there were hundreds, maybe thousands, I'd have been lost in no time. The place was the most epic, gargantuan maze ever conceived. By the time I figured all that out, every stairway I could see was covered by the figures. They walked as close to the landing I was on as they could get and just stopped. Others stacked up behind them until there were rows and rows of them, four abreast on each step and stretching away as far as I could see. For a moment I felt like a politician or a rock star on some impossible stage about to perform for an adoring audience. Then the figure pushed me again. Hard. I fell right into the red vault door and through it."

Randy took a deep breath and exhaled slowly as he looked at the faces of his colleagues. Every one of them was intent on the story but also realized that speakers needed a break from time to time. There was a bottle of water on a tether floating in the air next to his head, and Randy took a big gulp to wet his dry mouth.

"This is one of the weirdest stories I've ever heard," Mike said.

"Sim," Fernanda added. Leonid and Jacques simply waited for Randy to resume the story.

"I don't know what the substance was I'd fallen into," he said at last, "but since it behaved pretty much like water, that's what I'll call it. And there was some kind of force pulling on me. I was immediately swirling around just like I'd observed from outside. It was impossible to see; the water was almost like paint, it was so thickly colored, and I had no idea if I was alone in it or not."

"I swirled around that thing for I don't know how long. It was impossible to tell if there were boundaries there, walls, like inside a pipe or something, but I assumed there were based on how I just kept spinning and tumbling. There was a discernable pattern to the movement; I was whirling clockwise, that I could tell, but the force of the water was so strong that it kept rolling me around, up and down, all over the place like flotsam. Eventually I was able to figure out that my rate of spin, rotation, was increasing, as if the tube or funnel, or whatever vessel contained the water and me, was narrowing. And then I *was* in a pipe. I could touch the walls if I stretched out my hands. The damned figures had flushed me down the toilet!" His audience chuckled at that, and Randy joined them, continuing when the mirth abated.

"I was lucky I didn't need to breathe, or I'd have drowned long before I ever popped out of that tube, or funnel, or whatever it was. I'd tried to slow myself down by pressing my hands against the walls, but it didn't do anything. Then the walls were just gone, and the water started to dissipate, spread out, lose its force. It wasn't as dense as it had been, and I thought I could see something through it. Then everything exploded. Not like a bomb, but there was an intensely brilliant light, effulgence like I've never seen before or since. But it didn't hurt my vision. And it was the strangest shade of blue, like a cloudless sky but darker and lighter at the same time. I wish I could describe it better. There's never been a color like it anywhere on earth that I've ever seen."

"Sacre bleu! Zat is some story," Jacques said.

"Yeah. It's quite a whopper, buddy," Mike added.

"And I'm not even to the good part yet," Randy said.

"Then continue," Fernanda pressed, "ignore them."

"The blue was everywhere, all around me. It was almost like I could feel it, hear it, and I know that sounds weird. I mean, how do you *hear* a color? But that's what it felt like. There was a... tone... that I somehow knew was coming from the blue. It wasn't threatening or ominous, and in fact I remember feeling very peaceful. All the stress and anxiety I'd been under after going into the poster was gone, and I think I would have been just fine if someone had, at that moment, told me I was going to spend eternity there."

"Zis story," Jacque interjected. "It seem like you sink it was real. Not some, how did you say? Trip."

Randy was quiet for several seconds, his face thoughtful. When he finally spoke, his voice was very quiet. "I believe it *was* real. As real as this place, this moment is, for all of us."

"How you explain that?" Leonid asked skeptically. "Is not possible to go into painting. Completely against laws of physics."

Randy nodded. "I would agree," he said. "I know enough about physics to know that you're right. But wait until I finish the story until you decide what's possible or not."

Leonid nodded halfheartedly, his disbelief evident on his face.

"I floated in the blue light for a while. It really was sort of like being here, like weightlessness. The tone was there too, deep in the background but present somehow. I'd have fallen asleep if I could've. I'm not one-hundred percent positive about this, but even today I believe that food, water, sleep – things we all absolutely *have* to have in our world, oxygen, were unnecessary there. I've no idea how life was... sustained. But it was."

"I must have gone into some kind of trance without knowing it, because ordinarily I get bored easily if I don't have something to keep me occupied. But I never felt bored in the blue – not for a moment, even though I was just floating in it. The peace and calmness I felt from the tone and the light must have, I don't know, eradicated those feelings. I wasn't even thinking about going back to Theo's room, to my world. Home. It wasn't like I was indifferent, or wanted to stay where I was, I just didn't think about anything. Which for me is nearly impossible; my mind is always running. It's a perpetual motion device. Remembering it now its exceedingly bizarre, but that's what happened."

"And then I heard the voice. It wasn't much louder than the tone, but it was utterly clear, crystalline, if a voice can be that. It's the best adjective I can think of for it. I don't remember the exact words, so I can't quote it verbatim, but I can paraphrase. It welcomed me in a language new to me, and which sounded nothing like any language I'd ever heard, but I could somehow understand it. The voice said, and this will sound cliché, that they'd been waiting for me for a long time. I asked who 'they' were, and it laughed. I guess the speaker could understand me as well as I could it. How I spoke without a mouth... never did figure *that* out.

When it was done laughing at me, the voice told me it was everyone, which made no sense. So, I asked again who it was, who was everyone. It didn't laugh that time, and when it spoke it said, and this I remember clearly: 'We are everyone who has come before.' Before *what* is what I wanted to know, and instead of answering, the blue began to change, and an image appeared. It was like watching a tv screen, but more real, more present. The scene was of a caveman, a Neanderthal or something. I'm not an anthropologist so don't ask me. It was a man, covered with hair and a huge beard. He was wearing animal skins and was clearly injured; there was blood on his face and his chest. I couldn't see what was wrong, where he was hurt, but he was gasping for breath. Then he died. I could actually see the... soul... leave his body. It was only there for a millisecond, but I saw it as clearly as I see the earth out that window. It was shaped like a human, but was... liquid, watery, almost transparent." Randy gestured toward one of the viewports in the hull of the ISS. Outside and far below them, the frozen expanse of Siberia stretched away to the edge of the globe. Clouds covered most of it, and the winter snows covered the rest, slowly giving way to green in the southern latitudes.

"Zis story get more *fou* every minute," Jacques said. "How you see ze soul?"

Randy shook his head. "I don't know. But it was there."

"I believe all peoples have soul," Fernanda said. "Why this hard to believe?"

Leonid and Mike were watching their colleagues' faces dispassionately but attentively, clearly interested in the story and the mini debate but choosing not to participate.

"I don't expect you to believe in the soul, and I'm not trying to convince you," Randy said to Jacques, "But I know what I saw." Jacques shook his head dismissively.

"Fine," he said in a tone of finality. "Continue." Randy held the Frenchman's gaze for a long moment before resuming the story.

"As soon as I watched the soul, or whatever it was, leave the caveman's body, the image changed and there was another person in front of me. A child this time. It was a little girl, probably no more than four or five years old, and she was wearing a white robe or gown of some kind. Her face was covered with sores and lesions, and her eyes were closed. She was lying on what looked like sand, maybe on a beach or a riverbank, and there were shadows around her. People. They were standing around her in a circle, and I could hear them crying. Then the image changed, it was like a movie when the camera pans out and away from a closeup shot, and I could see the people. There were five of them – two adults and three more children of varying ages but all older than the little girl. They were a short distance from a town or settlement. The houses were made of a tan-colored stone, people were walking around just like they would in any city or town, but the strangest thing was what I saw looming above the town a short distance away – an enormous white pyramid. The sun was shining on it, and it was almost too bright to look at."

"Now you are at ze pyramids?! In Egypt?!" Jacques asked incredulously. "When zey were still intact?" The gnarled frown of disbelief on his face betrayed more than his tone of voice concerning what he thought about this new development.

"Look, I'm just telling you what I saw, alright?!" Randy snapped. "I really don't care if you believe it was real or not, but I'm not making any of this up!"

"I vant to hear rest," Leonid said. "Quiet French man or I take away your cheese and wine." Jacques' frown turned into a grin at the barb from the Ukrainian, and the tension was broken.

"So, no more interruptions?" Randy asked. "Let me finish the story already?" Jacques nodded.

"Yes, I'm pretty sure I was at the pyramids, in ancient times shortly after they were built. The place looked far different than it does now, as you'd expect. But I wasn't there for the pyramids; I was there to watch that little girl die. And I saw *her* soul leave her body when she did. The image changed yet again, and I was watching men in helmets fighting with swords. I'm sure they were Greeks or Romans, one of them. There were hundreds of men fighting each other in a field, and the image zoomed in on one man. I saw a sword slash his arm and another stab him in the stomach. It was horrific. He fell to the ground, ignored by the rest of his army as he died too. And yes, I watched his soul leave. Then the images started flashing in front of me, people dying everywhere, all over the world, from every era of humanity, it seemed. Some were calm and peaceful, painless, others were violent like that soldier, and others were too horrible to talk about. I had nightmares for years afterwards from some of them. It was impossible to count the deaths I witnessed, but there had to have been millions upon millions. It felt like I was watching the death of every human being who had ever lived. Maybe I was. Every race you can imagine, from every part of the earth was there. Deserts, jungles, snow, forests, villages, cities, single individuals on their own somewhere, small groups, large groups – I watched death in every form imaginable. And at every one of them – *every single one* – there was a soul that left the body. You can call it by a different name if you want to. Spirit, essence, soul – they're all the same thing as far as I'm concerned. I'm not trying to preach or proselytize, just to tell you what I saw." The crew members were looking at each other uneasily, their faces uncertain and tinged with more than a hint of gloom.

"When the slideshow of death was over, and I have no idea how much time passed while it played, it could have been a minute or a century, the voice spoke again. It told me that I was... on the other side. I asked if the place was heaven and was told no but nothing else. To this day I don't know if heaven and hell exist or not. I asked about the figures in the painting and the voice actually laughed a little. It said that they were gatekeepers to other places. It didn't explain, but I surmised that it meant that all those doorways, all those windows I saw in that place with the stairs, that beyond the boundaries of the picture Escher drew, were... portals to other planes or dimensions, whatever they were. I asked why they'd been waiting for me, and it said that it just wanted to communicate with our side, that I had some kind of latent ability that the Patchouli Puke had activated, and that was the reason I was there. Apparently, they'd been watching for eons for someone to be born with the ability I supposedly had. If I actually *did* have some kind of ability. That day was the only time it ever manifested itself, and I still don't know for certain whether or not any of that was even real or just an incredibly vivid hallucination brought on by the Patchouli Puke. The voice said it was nearly time for me to go back, but I had so many more questions. It said I would have the answers in time, but that for now it wanted me to take a message back with me."

"What message?" Fernanda asked, her eyes wide and luminous.

"That we aren't alone. They are with us all the time, watching, seeing. The last thing it said to me was that there is so much anger and hate, pain and suffering in this world, but that once we die, when we cross over to their place, that all the awful things are left behind. I could believe it based on how I'd felt in the blue. Before I saw all those deaths. Before the voice started speaking. I asked more questions, but the voice stopped answering." Leonid was frowning, and Mike was staring at the floor. Fernanda and Jacques were looking at Randy with unreadable expressions.

"A few silent moments passed where nothing happened. I had no feeling of movement, but I could sense something changing. The blue wasn't as intense as it had been, it was... darker somehow, but without actually getting dark. I know, it's really weird, but that's how I perceived it. Then there *was* movement. The blue did get darker – fast. In a very short time it was black, and I could feel myself spinning and tumbling again, like when I'd been in the funnel. It was impossible to tell where I was going, not like I knew where I was to begin with, but the feeling of calm was gone, replaced by the anxiety most anyone would feel at being carried along by some unknown force with no way to stop or control yourself, or even to know what you'd find at the end. I was completely powerless, utterly helpless, like a twig in a flash flood. And there was a roaring that came to me, a huge, powerful sound that overwhelmed every thought in my head. I thought I could see things then, in the blackness. Figures, forms, stretched out to galactic proportions, *universal* proportions, larger than anything, trillions of light years across and far deeper than any telescope has ever peered into the universe's past. And they were everywhere. It sounds impossible for something so massive to exist, let alone have company, but they did. Don't ask me where I was. These things were so huge, so vast, that I could barely comprehend their size. But the strangest thing was that I *could* comprehend it. It was like my mind expanded so far beyond anything humans have ever experienced, that it gave me the ability to see them for what they were. We've all heard that the universe is so big, the distances so enormous, that it's nearly impossible, if not *completely* impossible, for humans to envision it, to truly comprehend the *scale* of it, the sheer size and magnitude. In that moment I saw things bigger than the universe, larger than anything we've ever conceived, and I could see *all* of them in totality. And they had a sentience, intelligence, a presence almost like life but beyond it. That fact I knew absolutely. One of them turned to me and laughed, the loudest, most intensely massive sound ever created. The sound banished the roar, completely destroyed it, and for a moment I thought it would destroy my mind too, it was so loud. Then it was just… gone. The… entities were gone too, and I was back in the blackness. It could have been space, or another dimension, some dark hole in my own psyche, or a bedroom closet, I don't know, but it was completely silent yet turbulent. I felt my mind contract back to its normal bounds, which would have been the strangest thing I'd ever felt if I hadn't been through so much other strange stuff."

"The blackness didn't last as long as the red or the blue had. After the entities disappeared it was only a few moments before I saw something speeding toward me, and before I knew it, I was tumbling through an arched window into the Escher stairwell world, and I came to a stop completely unharmed and standing on the top step of a set of stairs. The figures were gone; I didn't see a single one anywhere. And I was in a different spot than where I'd been when they forced me through that vault door; it was nowhere in sight. What I did find was a window through which I could see Theo staring into space. It was my way back home. I'd never been so eager to leave somewhere in my life, and I practically flew through that window. Next thing I knew I was on the couch in Theo's room, and he was mumbling something about SpongeBob and an axe. I didn't ask what that was about. He seemed ok, other than the blank look on his face, and I felt fine. Whatever the Patchouli Puke had done to me, the effects were gone, and I was sober as a Puritan. I hung around for an hour to make sure Theo really was ok, and when he started to come around, to recognize the world around him again, I said goodbye and I left. He never mentioned that day or the Patchouli Puke again. Maybe he had a bad trip and wanted to forget it, who knows, but we drifted apart after that. I focused on my schoolwork, and he on… drugs. And here we are," Randy said as he finished the story.

Mike let out a low whistle, Leonid simply stared, Fernanda was looking out the window at Earth, and Jacques was examining his hands. Fernanda spoke first.

"I think you went beyond. To other side where dead live," she said quietly.

"Maybe," Randy replied. "I still don't know what happened."

"I go check instruments," Jacques said as he floated away into another module.

"He having trouble believing," Leonid said. "Jacques is man of science. You just tell story about something he no understands, cannot quantify or study."

"I didn't mean to upset him," Randy said. "But aren't we all scientists?"

"Yes, we are – that's why we're all here," Mike replied. "Leonid is right. Jacques just can't fathom what you've experienced. To him everything is observable, has qualities that can be measured, exhibits predictable behaviors. If your story is true, if what you described *actually happened,* then his entire world just shifted cataclysmically, and he doesn't know how to deal with it. Your experience shouldn't be possible, but I think he believes you, which means he has to reevaluate his entire system of belief and understanding. It's a lot for a man like him."

"Do you believe me?" Randy asked with sudden earnestness. He'd never told that entire story before to anyone, and it suddenly mattered a great deal to him that these people, his friends and colleagues, believe it.

"I believe you," Fernanda said with a smile and without hesitation.

"I too," Leonid answered, "even though I no understand physics of it."

"I believe you saw what you described. Whether it was real or just a hallucination, I don't know," Mike said slowly. Jacques floated back into the module at just that moment.

"I hear from MC," he said gravely. "Zey concerned about radiation exposure, especially you," the Frenchman said as he gestured toward Randy. "Zey sending ship to evacuate you for medical study. Space X will launch tomorrow, ship here next day, you leave day after."

"I'm leaving?" Randy asked, obviously incensed. "But my rotation isn't finished!"

"No argue," Jacques said sternly. "Ship come, you go." He made a chopping motion with his hand to indicate the finality of the statement.

Three days later Randy left the ISS. His colleagues wished him well and waved from the windows as the Space X capsule decoupled from the ISS and floated off. They sent additional supplies up in the craft, and a few new experiments, but no crew member replaced Randy.

He looked out the window at the slowly shrinking station as the capsule dropped away. In a short time, he would be reentering Earth's atmosphere. It was a bittersweet moment. He loved being in space, on the ISS, and had truly wanted to finish his residency before going home. It felt like he was letting the rest of the crew down. They would now have to perform all the tasks that had been assigned to him, and although he knew intellectually that leaving was the right thing to do, his sense of duty and responsibility didn't make it easy. No one would fault him or call him a shirker for leaving; he was only following orders from his superiors on Earth. Still, as he watched the ISS grow smaller and smaller through the viewport, he felt intense regret over his truncated mission.

There was very little for him to do once the craft had decoupled from the ISS. Most of its systems were monitored and operated by mission control, and although he had a screen in front of him that displayed enormous amounts of data, and which would allow him to operate the craft himself in the event of some catastrophe on Earth, he was really just a passenger in this celestial taxicab. Randy was fine with that. He'd been trained and could operate the craft as well as anyone, but recent events made him ambivalent about it, and he was glad someone else was driving.

Alone with his thoughts, Randy's mind drifted aimlessly as he awaited reentry. He thought of his colleagues left behind on the ISS, of the story he'd told them about Patchouli Puke and his experiences in the Escher poster, of his modest house on the Gulf of Mexico in Texas, of the problems in the world that he was going back to, and of how they all seemed so insoluble. Up in space there wasn't much time for news or the troubles of the planet below. The days were filled with duties and functions, and free time for reading or watching television was limited. The astronauts were informed by MC of major social and political developments, but more in-depth reading of the news was very low on their list of priorities. Randy was a bit of a news junkie, and he would have a lot of catching up to do once he got home.

A voice chirped in his ear telling him that reentry was about to begin. This was Randy's second trip to space, and he'd very much disliked reentry the first time. He was truly dreading it this time, especially the six-minute-long communications blackout that would happen sometime around twenty-five minutes before the capsule splashed down in the waters off Florida. There was nothing anyone could do if the ship experienced some kind of problem or incident during reentry. The craft was completely at the mercy of gravity and the Earth's atmosphere. The fear of being cut off from mission control was psychological more than practical. Randy hadn't told anyone about it, but he'd experienced what was for him pretty severe anxiety the first time he'd gone through the blackout. If he had mentioned it, they might not have let him fly again, and he'd been determined to return to space after his first time away from Earth. A little anxiety for six minutes was a miniscule price to pay for being able to see the globe from a vantage point very few ever attained.

The craft began to shudder as it fell into the atmosphere. Soon the blaze of reentry would scorch the heat shield on the bottom of the capsule. It was strange to think that such a relatively small thing could withstand the intense heat created by the craft traveling through the upper atmosphere, and it was terrifying to think about what would happen if it failed. The people who'd built this craft were among the smartest in the world, and Randy was eminently confident in their abilities. Still, they were humans. And humans sometimes made mistakes.

A voice was saying something; the sound reached him from the speakers in his helmet. What was that? Radiation? Again? "Say again mission control," Randy said into the microphone that was built into the helmet.

*"We've detected a massive spike in radiation levels. How does your system display look? Everything ok?"*

Randy looked at the screen in front of him. "All systems nominal," he said.

*"Roger that. How are* you *feeling?"*

"I'm fine."

*"Check your dosimeter please. Spaceflight doc is insisting on it."*

Randy glanced at the indicator he wore on his belt and his heart started pounding. When he didn't reply for several seconds, his contact at mission control prodded him. *"You still there?"*

"Yeah." Randy said slowly. "I'm here."

*"What does your dosimeter say?"*

"Uh, it's fine," he said. "I'm under acceptable levels."

*"Yeah,"* the voice said with obvious skepticism *"Roger that. Instructions from flight doc are to monitor and advise if there is any change."*

He glanced at the dosimeter again. The level of radiation exposure it indicated was far above acceptable. It was the highest reading he'd ever heard of and could possibly be the highest ever recorded. It read twenty-seven-thousand-four-hundred-and-eight. Randy gulped. His lie would be discovered the moment NASA downloaded the data from the dosimeter, which they would most definitely do. After the Challenger and Columbia disasters, those folks (mostly) had gotten their scat together. He was relatively sure this would be his last flight, so he wasn't afraid of the lie jeopardizing some future mission to space, but there would be questions he'd have to answer. Randy was formulating answers to hypothetical questions when the most intense pain he'd ever felt stabbed him directly in the brain. If he hadn't been buckled into his seat, he would have toppled out of it. The capsule was really vibrating with the turbulence of reentry now, and he heard the voice from mission control again.

*"Communication blackout in two minutes."*

The pain was so excruciating he couldn't speak. Somewhere in the recesses of his mind where the pain hadn't quite reached yet, he realized that might have been a good thing. If he had tried to say something, all he would have done was groan, which would further inflame the suspicions of mission control. The whole splashdown and subsequent retrieval could turn into a circus P.D.Q. if they found out what had happened in the last few minutes. If they knew the level of radiation he and the capsule had been exposed to, it was not out of the realm of possibility to think that they might just let him sink into the Gulf of Mexico. But knowing them they'd want to study the capsule. And its occupant. They would figure out a way to get both to a lab where he would be poked and observed for weeks on end, while the capsule, instead of going to a museum where it belonged, would end up being sliced to ribbons and subjected to all manner of tests. And who knew? Maybe they would slice *him* to ribbons too in the interest of science.

The pain hit again, and he almost passed out.

*"One minute to blackout. Acknowledge."*

Randy couldn't speak if he'd wanted to.

*"Acknowledge!"*

He managed to mutter something that sounded like an affirmative, but it wasn't good enough for his interlocutor.

*"Say again. Acknowledge. Thirty seconds to blackout."*

"Yeah. I got it," Randy forced himself to say through clenched teeth. "Acknowledged."

*"Roger that,"* the voice said.

If that guy said 'roger that' one more time Randy was going to find out who he was and strangle him with a bungee cord at his first available opportunity while crazily and repeatedly screaming the man's favorite phrase throughout the operation. The thought almost made him laugh despite the intensity of the pain.

*"Ten seconds to blackout."*

Wonders would never cease. He'd not have to hear the guy say 'roger that' for six whole minutes.

Nothing changed discernably when he entered the dead zone in the atmosphere. There was a roar from outside, and he could feel the ship changing attitude as thrusters fired to keep it on the correct trajectory, but that was the only difference. The pain in his head had abated a little, and he was just about to applaud that fact, when the strongest spike yet happened and he passed out.

Randy had no idea where he was. It was utterly dark and eerily silent. Was he dead? No, he could feel his body, so he probably wasn't dead. Then again, he'd never been dead before. Did dead people feel the limbs of their… souls? Essences? Whatever left this world and went to the next one? Did a soul have limbs? He started to chuckle as he imagined himself in the next life as an octopus, tentacles flailing around and trying to find purchase on a cloud while angels strummed harps and flitted around like fairies. The chuckle grew into a full-throated laugh tinged with more than a little hysteria, and Randy decided that since he could hear his own voice, it was quite likely that he was still alive. Now where in the hell was he?

Being in such complete darkness confused one's senses, but he was quite certain he was standing. Randy slowly stretched out his arms and was surprised when his hands touched something solid. He felt around for several moments until his hands detected a seam. Randy pushed and shoved against the barrier with increasing force until at last something gave and a door swung open.

He was stunned to find himself back on the Escher stairway. One of the faceless figures stood in front of him holding a tray of empty champagne glasses. Randy looked down at himself and was not shocked to see that his body was the same as the figure. He was one of them. Again. The figure with the tray turned and walked up a set of stairs to the right. When Randy didn't immediately follow, it turned and looked back at him, that faceless face somehow was able to convey the question, *Well? Are you coming or not?* He was still in a state of shock, but it was dissipating as he adjusted to the unexpected development. Randy reminded himself that he'd been here before and been able to get home, so this time should be the same. Then he thought about the blue and the overwhelming sense of peace he'd felt there. Maybe he'd get to go there again. This time without having to watch all that death.

Once his anxiety and shock had abated, Randy moved toward the figure with the tray, and it turned away to resume its journey. He could have sworn that blank face had an expression of smug satisfaction on it.

They walked up and down stairwells, past countless doors and windows, and Randy was beginning to wonder if they were going to wander in here forever when the figure finally turned toward a closed door and stopped in front of it. There was nothing unusual about the door. It was made of wooden planks held together by simple metal bands and looked like a door in a castle or maybe an English manor house. The figure stood to the side and Randy approached the door slowly. He had enough experience here to know that the figure wanted him to open the door, but he wasn't sure he wanted to find out what was on the other side. The last time he'd been in this place, he'd had to play along with the figures. If he hadn't, he probably wouldn't have gotten home. That was likely the case this time too. So there really wasn't any choice but to open the door. Why did he feel such a sense of anxiety? Nothing had harmed him the last time, and nothing had so far this time either, so what the hell? He just couldn't shake the sense of doom that kept reappearing.

He would have sighed if he'd had lungs and a mouth, but instead Randy pushed down on the handle and opened the door. Beyond was a massive room. He'd been in some large rooms in his time – banquet halls, theaters, stadiums – but this place dwarfed them all. It was difficult to judge the distance, but Randy was fairly certain this place was at least two miles across. The room was round and featured a huge dome for a ceiling. He was reminded of the US capitol building in DC or Brunelleschi's Dome in Florence, Italy. Except that this dome was far larger. For such a huge place, it was also very plain. There were no ornate finishing, murals or sculptures. Just huge walls rising around the room and tapering to the point of the dome far above. There also didn't appear to be any windows or other doors in the place other than the one he'd just opened. Randy stood on the threshold and stared into the void of a room. It was empty. He would have thought that fact a bit strange if this place wasn't completely strange to begin with. But, he reminded himself, everything new and unknown is strange until it becomes familiar.

He glanced at the figure with the tray, but it was no help. The thing just stood like a mannequin where it had stopped. Randy turned away and walked into the room. His footsteps made no sound, and he thought idly that if they had, the echoes in this cavern would have been fun to listen to. He had no idea what he was supposed to do, so he just wandered around for a time. Randy looked at the floor, the walls, the ceiling so high above, but it all looked the same. Whatever the material was that this place was constructed from, he couldn't identify it. Stone, plastic, concrete – it could have been any of them, or something else completely. There were no seams like in block construction, no joints or mortar, and it was all the same uniform cream color. Smooth and unblemished. Randy was slightly impressed and a little disturbed at the sameness of it.

He'd reached a point near to the center of the huge round room when he finally looked back toward the door. Figures were filing in one after another and were making their way to the far side of the room. It was so silent here that he'd had no idea he was no longer alone until he'd looked. The figures ignored him as they walked in single file across the vast space. Randy had nothing else to do, so he watched as they reached the far side and began lining up. There was a definite pattern that he quickly discerned was a spiral. The figures were lining up shoulder to shoulder in neat rows, but with gaps at regular intervals that he could tell would eventually resolve into a spiral with a gap that would leave just enough space for a figure to walk between the rings, around and around, and which would eventually lead to the center of the room like a concentric maze.

Time passed in the warped and nearly imperceptible way that it did here, and soon the spiral was complete. An ultra-precise machine could not have created a more perfect shape, Randy thought as he looked at the form the figures had created. All of them were facing inward toward the center where there was a small open space large enough for perhaps five or six figures to stand comfortably. He was a head taller than all the other figures here which allowed him to see over them, and a glance toward the door showed him the figure with the tray of glasses making its way toward the center followed by three others. They reached him faster than he'd expected, and soon all four stood facing him in silence. The one with the tray proffered it to him, and not knowing what else to do, Randy picked up one of the empty champagne flutes. It stuck to his fingerless round ball of a hand as if by velcro. The other three each took one as well, and they, as a tripartite unit, threw their heads back and looked directly up at the center of the dome. He gazed around and noticed every other figure except the servant with the tray was doing the same. Randy looked up too, and was confused when there was nothing there but the cone-shaped interior of the dome.

He stared with the others for a moment, then dropped his head and looked at the room again. The scene reminded him of a sci-fi movie where everyone is taken over by some alien entity and becomes part of a hive mind, all doing the same thing at the same time. It was eerie.

The figures stood motionless for what seemed to Randy to be a very long time. He was about to try to find a way out of the room when they started moving again. Slowly and in complete unison, the group took a single step to the right. Then they took another, and another, until every figure was moving sideways around the room. The overall motion was circular, and Randy realized that if he was viewing this scene from above, it would be like looking down on a whirlpool or a tornado. Himself, the waiter with the tray, and the other three figures were still in the opening in the middle as the rest spun around them with increasing velocity. They were already moving faster than any humans ever could, and if he'd held a scarf up, Randy was sure it would be fluttering in a breeze created by the rapid passage of so many bodies.

He'd dropped his gaze from the ceiling to watch the spiral shape of figures around him as it spun faster and faster, like a fan winding up to full speed, and he glanced back up when he saw the others in the center were ignoring the activity on the floor. The ceiling, much to his surprise, was moving. Lines had appeared in its surface that ran from the apex down to where the dome ended and the walls began. As he watched they peeled back like a flower bud opening, and revealed blackness beyond. It was impossible to tell if he was looking at sky or that limitless and impenetrable dark he'd seen the last time he was here.

The figures were spinning so fast now that he could barely discern their individual bodies as they sped past him. The waiter and the other three still stood in the middle, heads turned toward the blackness above, and Randy suddenly realized he was moving. There was no sensation of motion. One minute he was looking over their heads, then next he had to bend his neck down to see them. He was floating up toward the opening and whatever there was beyond it. Randy didn't feel fear, but he didn't feel that sense of tremendous calm he'd felt before either. This was just another curiosity in a place filled with them. He looked up at the blackness, back at the whirling figures below, now quite far below, and up again. The darkness seemed to descend to meet him, and a long moment later it enveloped him.

Randy had no idea if he was flying at light speed or was utterly motionless, so complete was the black around him. He had no sense of anything but his own mind, a realization that made him think of those sensory deprivation chambers some people entered in a quest for personal enlightenment or whatever. The worst part about this place was the complete disconnect from time. It had no meaning here. If it was a fourth dimension as some scientists believed, then he thought he most likely wasn't in it, or at least was not susceptible to its effects. And there was no roar. He remembered distinctly that the last time he'd been here, in this darkness, there was an enormous, unimaginable roar that had nearly driven him insane. That sound was not present. So maybe this wasn't the same place. And the entities, those beings, if that's what they were, that had somehow been massive beyond the universe, weren't here either. He wondered how his crewmates were back on the ISS. Was Jacques getting over his hissy fit about the story? Had Leonid talked to him? Was there any news about the new type of radiation they'd detected? That still seemed impossible.

Randy's thoughts drifted as his… body? Consciousness? Essence? Soul? What part of him was actually here? And where was his corporeal human body? Was it still in the capsule descending through the atmosphere? Had it landed in the Gulf of Mexico yet? How long was this going to go on? It was a good thing time had no influence on this place, no meaning or force here, or it was quite possible he would go insane alone in this absolute blackness with nothing but his own thoughts.

Something was different. Or maybe it wasn't. He thought he'd seen a light. Just a flash of yellow gold far in the depths of the dark. This could all be a dream or an hallucination. Randy remembered the spikes of pain that had stabbed his head just before blacking out and coming here. Maybe he had a brain tumor that was causing all this like that John Travolta movie. Would it make him a genius like it had Travolta's character? Probably not. Most likely it would just kill him. Or leave him senseless and incapacitated. A hysterical thought occurred to him – Randy the vegetable. Once a great astronaut, now a cauliflower! He heard a carnival barker's voice announcing the exhibit. "Step right up here everyone and see the modern miracle! A man who ascended to the highest heights of his profession, and we're not just talking turkey here folks – this guy really *did* go way up high – all the way into space! And now because of an uncooperative little ball of cells in his brain, he's no different than that head of broccoli you steamed to go with last night's meatloaf! So pay your money and take your gander, cause when this show is over, so is harvest time! Right this way young lady, the human rutabaga is just beyond that curtain…" The voice trailed off, and Randy thought of John Merrick, better known as the Elephant Man and whose actual name was Joseph. Would he end up like that poor man had? A circus sideshow freak people paid money to gawk at?

What the hell was happening to him? He was thinking about *the Elephant Man?* Maybe he really was cracking up.

There it was again, then gone. Just the tiniest impression of light. Or maybe it was just color. Randy watched the spot intently, all thoughts of carnivals and elephant men banished. He was just starting to convince himself that it had all been in his mind, when a pinprick of yellow appeared. This time it didn't disappear. Was that the way out? Randy imagined himself moving toward it. Or maybe it toward him. It didn't matter which, but somehow, he knew he needed to get to it. The gulf between them was enormous though. Galactic perhaps. Could he even get there? Or was it right in front of him but so tiny that it looked to be light years away?

Randy stretched out his hand toward the point and immediately felt himself stretched beyond imagination. He felt like one of those entities, pulled like taffy until he was longer than the galaxy was wide. Maybe this was a singularity, a black hole. Oh, piss on it. He was done trying to figure out what this place was, why he was here, and focused all his energy on leaving. Randy sent his thoughts out along his impossibly stretched body and told it to collapse back to its natural size. Remarkably it did. He felt a sensation that made him think of a rubber band being pulled taut and released, and in a blink he was back to normal. Or, he reminded himself, as close to normal as he could be in this place. The light had changed. It was larger now. Maybe half the size of a dime, although it was hard to judge size. He yelled at it, screamed at it, to grow, to come get him, to take him home. And it listened. He watched it get larger and larger, like the end of a train tunnel approaching. What was that song? Was it Metallica? Some heavy metal band. He remembered the lyrics: *Then it comes to be that the soothing light at the end of your tunnel, was just a freight train comin' your way.* Music! He was thinking about music and song lyrics in here. Insane. Then he stretched again, but toward the growing spot of light. He felt its pull, like the tractor beam in Star Wars pulling the Millennium Falcon into the Death Star.

The light grew and grew, gold and yellow, warm. Little sparks shot off from it like fireworks that blazed for a moment and died in the darkness around it. Randy was mesmerized by the sight and watched until the light dragged him over its threshold.

Someone was talking. What were they saying? Fried? What was fried? Chicken? French Fries? There was a rumble in his stomach. He was famished. The voices again. Everything? What did that mean? There was no more fried chicken? He was moving. On his back. Light. It hurt his eyes. There was something on him. A blanket. Warm. Like the light in that darkness had been warm. And bright. Such pretty little fireworks. He wanted to see them again. They'd been like a Fourth of July sparkler, but better. Far better. Prettier. The blanket was gone. Cold. Still hungry. Were there any French fries left?

"Are you ok?" someone said. A man's voice. "Can you hear me?"

He didn't want to talk. His head hurt. There was light that hurt his eyes. Couldn't they make that light stop? Someone else was speaking. A woman's voice this time.

"Yes, that's what I said. The entire machine is fried." So, no chicken or French fries then. Disappointing. They'd been talking about a machine. What machine? The capsule?

"How can that be?" a different man's voice asked. "This is a one point three-million dollar MRI machine. It can't just be… fried."

"Well… it is."

The other man's voice spoke again. "Come on buddy, you have to sit up."

Hands were behind his back forcing him upright. The motion made his head hurt for a brief moment, then the pain abated to an ache. He opened his eyes slowly and saw that he was in a room. There were people in hospital scrubs standing around looking at him and the tray he was sitting on. Behind him was the donut shape of an MRI machine. A man in a suit was arguing with two women in hospital scrubs about the machine and how it simply *couldn't* be broken. The women were trying to tell the unbeliever that it was. Randy ignored him. The man who'd helped him sit up, also wearing scrubs, was still there next to him. He was speaking.

"You feeling ok? Need a drink of water?" Randy shook his head. How had he gotten here? He was about to ask the man if there was anything to eat, when a young woman in casual business clothes burst into the room.

"You have to come look outside *right now!*" She exclaimed. Everyone stopped talking and turned toward her.

"We'll be there in a minute," the man in the suit said.

"No!" the young woman nearly screamed. "Right now! You *have* to come look!" She turned and dashed out of the room. The people remaining looked at each other in confusion.

"I'm going to go look," one of the women in scrubs said, leaving the suit and the other woman to stare at her back. As she disappeared around a corner, a chorus of shouts and screams echoed through the building. Randy swung his legs over the side of the tray and stood unsteadily. The suit and the other woman in scrubs dashed out of the room. The man was still there, but he was looking anxiously toward the door.

"Think you can walk?" he asked.

Randy nodded. "Go ahead," he said. "I'll be right behind you." The man smiled grimly and darted from the room.

The shouts and screams were louder as Randy made his way through the hallways. This was obviously a clinic or a hospital, but he still didn't know where he was. Or why he was in here. He rounded a corner and was greeted by a wall of floor to ceiling windows. People were lined up in front of them, their faces pressed to the glass as they peered out at something. Others were running for what looked like a bank of elevators and a door with a sign that read Emergency Stairwell. Many were screaming. Randy found an empty spot at one of the windows and looked out. He was three or four stories up, and when he looked down, he saw what everyone was screaming at. The faceless figures were here. Hordes of them were walking across the grounds of what was surely the campus of a medical complex, albeit one that Randy didn't recognize. Their hands were rotating at the ends of their wrists, and in front of them was a swirling round vortex, like a miniature tornado, but instead of grey and black, it was blue. The figures were walking toward running humans who were being pulled into those vortices where they disappeared as if they'd never been. The blue. It was that same shade of impossible sky blue he'd seen all those years ago. Randy watched as person after person – young or old, man or woman – disappeared into the blue tornados. He was not afraid; he'd been in that color before and knew what was waiting there.

The people at the windows were frantically trying to make calls on their cell phones, to text, to check social media or news, but none of their electronic devices worked. Randy noticed then that the lights in the building were out and it was a brilliantly clear and sunny day. A good day for this, he thought. Yes. A very good day.

Someone screamed from the vicinity of the stairway and Randy turned toward the sound. He watched calmly as one of the figures emerged from the door, vortex spinning in front of it, and saw a woman get pulled across the tiled floor from ten feet away and into the blue. He stood still and silent as more of the figures appeared from the stairway and fanned out across what he now recognized as a lobby or waiting room. People were running and screaming, frantically trying to get away from the figures, but the force of their vortices was inescapable. In a few moments every person save Randy had disappeared into the blue. Two of the figures stopped a short distance from him and dropped their hands, the vortices fading away to nothing as they did. One turned toward the stairway and Randy glanced that direction. He was not surprised to see the butler appear with its tray. A single champagne flute stood on it, but this time it was not empty. The butler moved deliberately toward Randy and stopped directly in front of him. It stretched out its arm, offering him the glass on the tray. He looked at the glass curiously. Inside it was a substance he couldn't identify. It was the same color as the blue, but was moving slightly, as if an unseen force was stirring it from within. Randy didn't hesitate. He took the offered glass and raised it as if in a toast. "Cheers," he said as he tipped the glass to his mouth and drank. Whatever the blue substance was, he didn't feel it slide down his throat, but he did feel it explode in his stomach. Instantly the blue was all around again, and with it that sense of complete calm and peace. Randy floated for a time, unconcerned about anything. Then the voice spoke again as he'd known it would.

"We tried to tell them, but they wouldn't listen," it said. Randy thought back to all those scenes of death that he'd been forced to watch, and he knew what was coming next. "So, we had to show them."

*A few brief notes on* Patchouli Puke*:*

*Some of the scientific elements are probably not, at least according to current knowledge, feasible. It's a story, not an academic paper, and I took some liberties.*

*The actual ISS orbits the earth from west to east. In this story it orbits from east to west. I'd already written the passage where Randy is mulling over all the ills that afflict earth when I discovered that inconvenient little fact, and I liked it the way it was. I was also too lazy to rewrite it to represent the actual orbit of the station. Oh well. Liberties and all that.*

# THE HORIZON BEHIND

"Come on over here boy," the old man said, "got a story I want to tell ye." The boy, no older than fourteen or so, dutifully obeyed the old man. "Yer ma told me 'bout what you done at school. You know it ain't ok, don't ye?" the boy nodded. "I was a mite the same as you when I was a young'n," he continued. "Nobody could tell me nothin'. I knew better'n all them adults. They was just a bunch o' ninnies, whinin' and cryin' 'bout me and how's I did things. But it cost me somethin' later. Turns out I didn' know half what I thought I did."

The boy was perched on the edge of an armchair next to the hospital bed where the old man lay. A plastic tube ran from a tall metal bottle to a small device under his nostrils that pumped oxygen into his cancer-ridden body. A slew of orange and white prescription bottles stood like captured chess pieces on a nightstand between the bed and the chair. The boy looked at the bottles, then at the tube, and finally at the withered form of the old man. His grandfather. A doctor had been to their house the day before. Well, if a single-wide mobile home in a dilapidated trailer park could be considered a house. The doctor had been a nice man, but distant. He came, examined the old man, spoke quietly to the boy's mother, and left.

"What did he say?" the old man called from his bed.

"Nothing different, it's all the same," the mother replied from the kitchen where she was cursing over the malfunctioning propane-powered stove. She worked as a waitress at a diner about a mile from the park. They had no car, so she walked to and from work regardless of the weather. It was summer right now, so the walking was easy. But winter and the deep snows that fell in this part of the country were hard on her. There was something wrong with her knee. She'd never told her son the story, what had happened, and suffered her pain silently, but he could tell it hurt. That's why he'd done what he did. To get some money so they could buy a car for her to drive to work in. Except that he'd been caught and suspended from school. After a visit with two police officers.

"I didn' do what you done 'til I was in my twenties," the old man said. "Fore that I jus' liked to fight. Wasn't nobody that could take me neither. Leas' not when I was a young'n. Once I got older, I met a few who was more'n a match fer me." The boy listened silently. "But lemme start at the beginnin'."

"My daddy weren't a good man. He liked a drink. More'n a drink, he liked a whole bottle. Sometimes he'd be the nicest guy – take me fishin' or shootin' out t' the woods. But most times he'd jus' get mean. Sometimes real mean. Them times my momma'n me'd try t' leave fore he could get to wallopin' on us. Yep, he liked t' do that. When he was drunk, wasn't nuthin' you could do t' make 'im happy. Momma tried, bless her heart, but there was a hate in that man that nuthin' was ever gonna git rid of. Wish I knew where it'd come from. Maybe I coulda helped 'im wit it."

The boy stared at his grandfather. He'd never heard him talk like this before, telling stories about *his* parents. Most of what the old man talked about, when he talked, was how his favorite baseball team was doing, and fretting about how to find a bookie from his bed so he could bet on the ponies.

"School didn' mean diddly t' me," the old man said. "Prob'ly like it don' mean diddly t' you. Ye ought t' change that way o' thinkin'. School is the way out, the path I wish now I'd a took all them years ago." A wistful look came into his eyes as he saw something in his past, some memory that belonged now only to him. "There was a girl," he said quietly. "Miss Sadie from down the road. We know'd each other from the time we was little uns. Used to play t'gether at the park. Went to the same elementary school, diff'rent middle schools, then back t'gether fer high school. She'd moved to a diff'rent part o' town by then, and my old man had lef' Ma an' me. We wasn't sad t' see him go. But it made things hard on her. Jus' like it's hard on yer ma. She never tell ye th' story 'bout her knee did she?" The boy shook his head. "An that's jus' right. It's her story t' tell. Not mine. Why don' ye ask her 'bout it sometime? I reckon she'll tell ye." The boy nodded.

"Back t' Miss Sadie. She were good in school, studied an all jus' like the teacher said t' do. I didn' tho. Lots o' stuff goin' through my head back then. School jus' didn' seem like sumthin' worth doin'. Miss Sadie tried t' get me t' study with her, but I had other things t' do. Like eat. My Ma had a hard time after Pa left. She struggled t' keep a roof over our heads an food on the table. She did try. I didn' know how hard til I grew up. By then it was too late t' say thank ye. She'd already passed. Never did see my Pa again. He could be alive right now, I don' know. If he is, t' hell wid 'im. The bastard kin rot wherever he is."

The boy's mouth was slightly agape at these revelations, and at the vehemence with which his grandfather condemned the man he'd called Pa. It was so out of character that the boy knew he was hearing the truth, and it fascinated him.

"So, Miss Sadie, she had it right. Study and stay in school if ye want t' succeed. Not too many drop out and do well later. Some, but not many. Course her life was diff'rent than mine. Her Pa didn't wallop her or her ma. He was some kinda business man, wore suits and such. Her Ma did things for the church. That's one other thing – get ye some churchin' up. They's mostly good folks go t' church. Like anywhere there's some bad uns, but most is good. And they'll help ye when ye need it. Wish I'd a knowed that back when too. There's so much I wish I'd knowed. Maybe me tellin' ye can help ye not wish so much when ye gits t' my age. So, me an' Sadie, we was from diff'rent types o' lives. Maybe I woulda turnt out diff'rent if I'd had her Ma and Pa instead o' the ones I had. Who knows?"

His mother cursed from somewhere in the living room. The walls of the single-wide were very thin, and the words were as clear as if they were in the same room. It was nothing new. His mother cursed all the time. But for some reason she didn't like him using the very words she used. He thought it didn't matter since he used them at school and when he was with his friends anyway. It didn't really bother him that he couldn't use them at home, even if she did.

"You listnin' boy, or jus' thinkin' bout yer ma cussin?"

"I'm listnin'."

"Good. Cause here comes the important part. By high school I'd decided I knew enuff. What th' hell did I want with Hist'ry and Math? Meant a hill o' beans t' me. Only thing I liked 'bout school was the girls. But most o' them didn' like me much. So I lef' not long after I started tenth grade. My Ma was sick by then, but she wouldn' pass for another ten year. I wanted t' do somethin' t' help her out. So I started doin' what you did – sold some stuff. Back then mos' folks called it reefer. I'm sure you kids got yer own name fer it now. Maybe more'n one. Don' matter. It's the same stuff. Turns out I was pretty good at sellin' it. Guy I got it from used t' love t' give it t' me cause he knew I'd move it all in a matter o' days. And I never cheated 'im. That's 'bout th' only thing Pa ever taught me – ye don' steal. And I never have. Not once. Not even when the hole in my belly felt like th' Grand damn Canyon."

The boy stared at his grandfather. He knew! Knew he'd been caught selling gooloo at school! Mom must have told him. But why?

"Don' ye worry 'bout why she told me," his grandfather said as if he'd read his grandson's mind. "It's enuff that I know. Ye don' really unnerstand right now, but ye will in time. Especially if ye ever has kids o' yer own. All this'll make a ton more sense than it does right now." He paused and met the boy's eyes for a long moment. "Ye ready t' lissen some more?" The boy nodded.

"Like I was sayin' I sold reefer after I lef' school. Saw Sadie one day at the mall and tried t' say hi. She was with some boy in fancy clothes. He looked at me like I was a piece o' what ye might scrape off yer shoe. She looked at me for a second, then looked away real fast. The look on her face… I'll ne'er forgit it. She looked like I'd kilt her fav'rite puppy or somethin'. Wasn't til years later I unnerstood what that look meant."

"What did it mean?" the boy interjected.

"Good – ye *are* lissenin! She liked me, ye see. I didn' know it then, but she did. And not jus' as a friend neither, but more than that. She was sad t' see what I'd become. Maybe she wondered what mighta been if I'd had a better pa, or if I'd studied wit her when she ask't. I don' know her exact thoughts, but that's what it was."

"How do you know that?" the boy asked.

"Well, why don' ye shut that trap o' yers and I'll tell ye the rest o' the story?" The boy nodded. "Alright then. I was real sad Miss Sadie didn' wanna talk t' me, and I was near comin' t' blows wit that boy she was wit. No one ever got t' look at me that way without gettin' a knuckle sandwich. He was th' only one, and that's jus' cause he was wit her that day. I seen him again a few years later, and he and I had more'n a few words. I didn' forget and didn' forgive. And I'll tell ye' this – that ol' boy'll ne'er forgit *me.*"

"I did ok sellin' reefer for a couple year until I got caught the firs time. Cop saw me sell some to a kid in a parkin' lot and he took me down sumthin' fierce. This was the 70's and cops was diff'rent. Now they gots t' be all touchy feely what wit them body cameras they all gots t' wear an phones wit cameras all o'er the place. But back then they'd thump ye good if ye decided ye wanted t' mouth off t' them, or fight. I didn' do neither, but he slammed me 'round jus' the same. Prob'ly t' teach me a lesson. Lemme know who was in charge. I didn' care. I'd been beat up by my Pa plenty o' times. That cop weren't gonna make me scared or hurt me worse'n Pa did. The bastard broke my jaw once. Ma took me t' the doc, said I'd fallen on the playground. They never said nuthin' bout it, jus' patched me up and sent me on my way. Back t' that cop. He cuffed me up and took me t' jail. Firs' time I ever been there. Seen a few fellas I knowed, couple I'd had beef with too, but they let me alone. I was there thirty-six days. Got convicted o' distribution, as them law-yers call it."

"When I got home from jail Ma was pukin' in th' toilet. I didn' know what was wrong, and she didn' wanna tell me, jus' said she was fine. I had too many other things on my mind t' worry too much 'bout it. If Ma said she was fine, well then that's how it was. I didn' argue wit her. Went right back t' my old ways too. Next day I was back sellin' reefer. By this time we was livin' in a crappy lil apartment on the other side o' the town. That was down Texas where I grew up. Weren't til some years after that when I moved up north here and met yer grandma."

The boy was surprised. He'd known his grandfather was from the south, but not where. Hearing the old man put a name to the place of his birth made him feel a little more complete, like a part of him he hadn't known was missing suddenly came back from wherever it had been hiding and clicked into place with the rest of the puzzle pieces that made up his person, his history.

"Things went on like that fer a while. I sol' my reefer and tried t' take care o' my Ma. Cept she got worse n' worse. Doc said it was Hepatitis. We didn' have no money or insurance, so she got that gov'ment health care. Bastards don' pay fer squat. Doc said there was a treatment, but we couldn' afford it, and the gov'ment wouldn' pay fer it."

The old man was silent for several moments as he watched his memories scroll by like a stock ticker on tv. At last he spoke again. "Sumthin' new had just showed up in

Texas by then – cocaine. Blow. Ye've heard of it. I started sellin' it too. Made more money'n I'd ever made offa reefer. Got in lots more trouble too."

"The treatment fer the hepatitis cost a bundle. I was savin' ever'thin' I made from sellin', kep' it in a plastic tackle box in my closet. Only good thing that ever come o' that gov'ment health care nonsense is that Ma got into low rent housin'. I couldn' live there wit her cause I was too old by then, but I found me a place wit a couple other fellas I knew from sellin' and we was roomies fer a spell."

"I got my product from a fella who drove it up from Florida. I'd meet 'im ever couple weeks and he'd gimme a big ol' bag or three o' blow. I'd do my thing – break it up into small packets t' sell. An' sell it I did! Its prob'ly the thing I was best at in life. Sad to say, but true. So one day I'm out on the street sellin', supposed to meet my guy that day t' git more. It all happens jus' like its supposed to. He pulls up in his car. Not too fancy so's he don' attract attention. He jumps out, opens the trunk, I walk over and peek in, sure enuff it's in there – my bags. I drop his money in the trunk, pick up the stuff and start walkin' away, jus' like always. Nex' thing I know there's cops ever'where. Lights and sirens, guns and dogs. They had us but good. Got slammed around again, but not so bad this time. These guys was feds – FBI, DEA, some such. They took us both t' jail. I got convicted. Again. Did seven year in a federal pen that time. And my money I'd stashed fer Ma's treatment? Who knows. The cops didn' lemme go home and git it. One o' my roomies prob'ly took it. I never saw either of 'em again. Couldn't prove nuthin' anyway. Only thing that matters is it never got t' my Ma. She died a year 'fore I got out. I didn' see her once the whole time I was inside. She was too sick t' travel."

A single tear rolled down the old man's cheek. He didn't wipe it away.

"That there is what I regret mos' of all," he said quietly. "That I ne'er got t' tell her goodbye."

The boy was stunned at this display of raw emotion from his grandfather. He'd thought the old man invincible, at least until the cancer started eating away at him. Even then he seemed like such a powerful man, diminished as he was. Nothing could hurt grandpa, he'd thought. But now, he saw, he'd been wrong about that. Grandpa was... just a man. Maybe he'd been wrong about some other things too.

"No use cryin' over what I cain't change," he said softly as a second tear followed the first.

"Once I got out o' that fed pen, I didn' know what t' do. Ma was gone, my money was gone, 'cept for the fitty dollars the feds give me the day I got released. I had nuthin but that fitty and the clothes I was wearin'. I stood outside the gate o' the prison for a good long while, jus' starin'. There weren't much aroun' them parts, jus' flat ground and a couple o' ranches a ways off. I didn' know what to do, where t' go. What the hell was I gonna do wit the rest o' my life? I had no relatives I knew of, no place t' go. I'll tell ya boy, that's the mos' alone I e'er felt in my entire life, standin' outside them prison walls wit nowhere t' go. Ye don' e'er wanna feel that – unnerstand?" There was a vehemence in the old man's voice, an insistence that demanded attention, acknowledgement. The boy, wide eyed, gulped and nodded. His grandpa held his eyes for a long moment before giving him a return nod, a silent acceptance of an unspoken pact just made.

"So I jus' started walkin'. Had no particular place in mind, jus' wanted t' be away from that prison. It were a hot day, and I took my jacket off, slung it o'er my shoulder. Didn' have no hat and the sun was beatin' on me sumthin' fierce. I got maybe a mile or so down the road when an old pickup pulled alongside me. Old timer inside askt if I needed a ride. I said I'd be much obliged fer one and he tol' me t' hop on in. He drove me t' the highway a few miles from the prison and dropped me off. But the ride weren't th' important part o' meetin' him, it was what he tol' me. We was chattin' about nuthin' when he said he'd always wanted t' see snow. Had been in those parts all his life and ne'er made his way north in winter. That planted an idea in my mind. I'd go see snow. If that old boy couldn' cause he had fam'ly, or a job, or whate'er, well, I'd jus' go see it fer him. So that's how I come here."

"Not long after I git here, to this big 'ol city, I met yer grandma. She was workin' as a waitress at a place ye got t' be eighteen t' git into. I didn' know that at first, jus' met her at a bus stop. It was pourin' rain and we both was soakin' wet. We run into the bus stop t' git out o' the rain, not t' catch a bus. That time o' year ye git lots o' little thunderstorms that dump rain for a few minutes, then move on. Ye've seen 'em. Anyway, we's under the cover o' the bus stop an' she's shiverin', jus' wearin' a thin little sweater that was done soaked through. I give her my jacket jus' t' be nice t' a lady. It was wet on th' outside, but still dry inside. She at first said no, then I darn near made her take it. The smile she give me when she felt it dry and warm, well that made me ask if she might like t' git a cup o' coffee with me at the diner down the street. She said she had t' git t' work, but that maybe day after tomorrow we could meet. Then she took a pen and paper from her purse and wrote down her phone number fer me. Jus' like that, a pretty young lady give ol' *me* her phone number! I ne'er seen the like!"

"We meet a few days later, jus' like we planned, and wasn't she jus' as cute as a bug in a rug? I tol' her right then that I'd been in prison. She didn' ask why or for what. Surprised the hell out o' me. Mos' folks that's the first question they ask when they fin' out you been inside. Next question is what it's like. I don't answer those. Watch a movie, you wanna know that. Mos' the ones I seen ain't too far off."

"Me an' yer grandma dated fer a couple months fore I ask't her t' marry me. She said yes, and we got hitched by a judge at city hall. See, yer grandma didn' have no fam'ly either. She'd left home about the same age I was when I quit school. Her ma was gone, run off somewhere, and her pa… well, he wanted her t' do things her ma shoulda been doin'. I ain't sayin' no more'n that."

"I wasn't sellin' at that time. I'd had my fill o' that life and was tryin' t' go straight, as us ex-cons like t' say. I'd seen an ad in the newspaper lookin' fer construction laborers, and they hired me. I wasn't makin' much money, but it were enuff t' pay fer a small room in a boardin' house. They don' have too many o' those around these days, but back then they was common. Yer grandma and I, we found us a lil' apartment once we was hitched and moved in. Life was good fer a spell. Until I los' my job. The projec' was finished, and they didn' need me no more. I knowed that from the start, but the big boss, he tol' me he might have more work after if I was a good 'un and showed up e'er day. I did, but he didn' have no more work. A restaurant hired me on as a dishwasher, but I didn' like the boss there. He and I near come to fists more'n once. Last day I worked for 'im, I knocked out two of his teeth on my way out th' door. Don' you EVER do that, y' hear me?" he said as he pointed to his grandson. The boy gulped and nodded. "Good. That ain't the way, no matter what yer friends might tell ye. There's a time and place fer that kind o' thing, but that's only when someone is threatenin' you and yers, not jus' when someone's done made ye mad."

The old man paused and took a long drink from a glass of water on his nightstand. Then he emptied a small container of pills into his frail and shaking hand, threw them all into his mouth, and swallowed the lot with another gulp of water.

"Damn pills make me feel pret'near worse than the damn cancer," he muttered. The old man lay his head back on the pillow and stared at the ceiling for several long moments. At last, he dropped his eyes to meet the gaze of the boy and resumed his story.

"Yer grandma and me, we was happy. It was definit'ly the happiest time in *my* life, and I think it was in hers too. She'd quit workin' at that other place, and had a job as a seamstress with a lady who made weddin' dresses. She loved to sew, yer grandma. And she was good at it. The lady paid her pretty good, and I did some odd jobs here and there. We wasn't rich, but we was makin' it. Then she got pregnant. She worked right up until she jus' couldn't anymore. The boss lady had t' let her go, said she unnerstood, but needed someone who could make it t' work e'er day. Cain't blame her. She had a business t' run. Cept that put yer grandma an' me in a hard spot. I had me a wife and soon a baby t' look after. How was I supposed t' do that wit no job? So I went back t' sellin'. It was easy in the big city. There was plenty o' folks walkin' aroun' lookin' fer sumthin. Alls I had t' do was find a fella t' gimme me some stuff an' go sell it. So that's what I done."

"I need t' tell ye sumthin else 'bout me from them times. I used t' smoke my own product. And drink some too. Yep, I drank e'en tho my daddy had been such a mean ol' bastard when he drank. I wasn' mean, leas' ways I don' think I was, but I sure wouldn' back down from no fight neither. I will say this too: I ne'er once hit yer grandma. Ne'er e'en raised a hand to her. I'd seen enuff o' that from my Pa and swore when I was a wee tyke that I'd not do th' same come my turn as a man. There's sumthin' cowardly 'bout a man who hits a woman. It's like he's got hisself a enemy he cain't see or fight direct, so he takes it out on those who are weaker'n him. He feels better for a spell, then starts right in again. Leas' that's how it was with my Pa. Cain't say for sure 'bout other folks. So, you listen good here boy. If ye e'er drink, don't ye *dare* hit a woman. Ye git me?" The boy nodded vigorously. "Alright then. I'll keep on wit my story. Ain't too much left, but its import'nt."

"One day not long after yer ma was born, I was out doin' my sellin. Yer grandma knew what I was up to fer t' pay the bills, and she didn' like it none, but what else was we gonna do? I couldn' find no job, weren't nothin' comin' in from her, an' three mouths t' feed. I did what I had to. That day I was jus' 'bout sold out o' my stuff and fancied myself a beer. There was a lil' tavern not far away, and I walked o'er to it. Bartender knew me a lil', knew who I was at least, and he poured me a cold one. It was nigh on three o'clock or so. I had one, then another one, then another one. I look at the clock at one point an it's near on seven! I was feelin' pretty saucy round 'bout that time and thought I might take a cab home. Bartender calls me one an' a few minutes later I'm home with my missus and yer ma. Now I had a way when I was sellin' o' keepin' spendin' money separate from what I had t' pay my guy for the stuff. My money went in a back pocket, his money went in the front one. I give yer grandma my money fer she can git groceries and such, then I fall dead asleep on the bed. Next mornin' I wake up wit a turrible hangover. You ever git one, ye'll know it. My missus is feedin' the baby in the kitchen. She ain't none too pleased wit me, but I know we'll be ok. I jus' got t' git my guy his cut o' the money, he'll git me more stuff, I'll sell it, and we'll git outta this town, go somewhere warm. Maybe back to Texas where I knows more folks and has more chances t' make things happen. Who knows? We'd done talked 'bout it a bit, and she didn' seem t' mind."

"I get my hungover carcass up outta bed and start riflin' through my pants fer the money. Cept it ain't there. I stop, take a deep breath, and look again. No money. What in the red-forked hell?

The bar.

I git dressed faster'n I e'er have in m'life, and run all the way there. Course it's too early in the mornin'. Weren't but a lil after 8 when I git there. Place don' e'en open til noon. I's gittin' frantic now. My guy made it real clear firs' time I done bidness wit him – no money, no stuff. But I still owes him. I don' pay… Well, e'erybody pays one way or t'other."

"I paced up 'n down in fronta that bar fer hours til the barkeep showed up t' open it. He let me in but said nobody turnt in no money day before. I figured as much. He let me look 'fore the place opened, but it weren't there. I either los' it, or someone stole it outta my pocket. I think I reached in the wrong pocket t' pay fer a beer an' it fell out on the floor. Someone saw it an' picked it up thinkin' they hit the jackpot. An' they did. That was near four thousand dollars. In those days, that were a small fortune. I didn' know what I was gonna do, but I knew me an yer grandma had t' leave. Soon. My guy was supposed t' meet me that afternoon, and if I didn' have his money... I didn' know what'd happen, but it wouldn' be good."

"I ran back t' our place and tole yer grandma t' git packin'. She wanted t' know why, an I said I'd tell her later, but we had t' go right then. Yer ma was asleep in our bed cause we couldn' afford a crib, and me comin' in like I done, caterwaulin' and all, well it plum woke her up. I didn' care. We had t' go right then. Yer grandma got all kinds o' upset at me, but I jus' kep' on her t' move. It didn' take long t' pack since we didn' have much. And in jus' a few minutes we was runnin' down the stairs o' our apartment buildin' and out in t' the street. She didn' have much o' the money I give her left cause she bought groceries an paid the rent. But I reckoned there was enuff for two bus tickets to Oklahoma, maybe to Texas, so I said we needed t' get t' the Greyhound station. It were a couple mile away and we started walkin'. No money t' spare fer a cab, and it was gonna be too long a wait fer the city bus."

"We'd gone 'bout six blocks when he found us. My guy. They wasn't even lookin' fer me yet, just happened to be drivin' by and seen me an yer granma walkin'. He had other guys wit 'im in his big ol' car. Four big fellas. Prob'ly had guns too. See I weren't sellin' reefer fer him. I was sellin' blow agin. And those boys didn' play aroun'. My guy know sumthin' was wrong right away. Weren't that hard to figure out, I s'pose. Man and his wife 'n baby walkin' real fast down the street carryin' suitcases? Pretty suspicious, that. He says he wants his money right then, e'en though we wasn't supposed t' meet til later that day. I tell him I ain't got it, but that I kin git it. He don' like that much. Tells my missus t' git in the car. People walkin' past us on the sidewalk there, not a one o' them stopped or said nuthin'. Jus' kep' on 'bout their business. They knowed what was happenin'. Ye walk the streets fer a spell, ye'll learn what's what. Their eyes'll tell ye they know. I s'pose I woulda kep' walkin' too. Folks don' like t' git involved. Might git themselves hurt. So they jus' keep walkin' right past ye, maybe give ye a sidelong look as they pass. Ain't that way out the country where I come from. Out there folks'll mos' likely stop an help ye. But not in the big city where we was."

"Well, I weren't about t' let my wife get tookin' from me wit'out a fight. I went right at the sonofabitch. Cept one o' his guys was faster. Sucker cold-cocked me an' it was lights out. I woke up t' someone shakin' my shoulder an askin' me if I was alright. Turns out it was one o' my customers, a lady who lived in an alley. My wife an' baby was gone. I didn' know what t' do, so I did the only thing I could, e'en tho I hated ever minute of it: I went t' the p'lice."

"They didn' care nothin' bout my wife an little girl. They figured I was jus' another drug dealer gittin' his comeuppance. Sure, they took a report, said they'd 'investigate', but nuthin' e'er came o' it. They was diff'rent in those days, like I tol' ye before. Cops these days is more like social workers than cops in my day. They was brutes then. Now they's all gone soft, like this whole damn country."

"I didn' know what t' do. Thought about robbin' a bank, but didn' have no gun. Didn' wanna get more federal time neither. Woulda done twenty year on that beef. Maye more since I was a con. Stealin' was about the only way I could git money quick enuff t' pay. C'ept I wasn't no thief. Sure I'd sell stuff t' people who wanted it, but so do the folks who work in stores. Only diff'rence is the product. My mind was so tore up from yer granma bein' taken from me that I didn' know what t' do. E'en went t' my ol' construction boss t' see if he'd loan me some money. C'ept he was movin' outta his house. Got foreclosed on and was takin' his fam'ly t' Florida or some such place t' start o'er. He didn' have nothin' t' loan me. Alls I could do was try t' find my guy and beg fer more stuff t' sell. But I couldn' find 'im. Looked e'erywhere too. Talked t' e'eryone I knowed.

I wandered around fer two days lookin' fer my guy and waitin' on word about my wife an' baby. Then one day I happened by a tv store. They used t' have them in those days. Big ol' window with a bunch o' tvs in it, all fer sale, all on the same channel. Ye could stop and watch and no one cared. I seen one an' on the screen was a pitcher o' yer grandma. Words under it said sumthin' like 'Local woman found dead. Baby in hospital while investigation continues' or some such. I los' it right then. Jus' broke down sobbin' right there on the street. Folks what walked by looked at me kinda funny, but I didn' care. My missus was gone and my baby in the hospital. Thinkin' bout that got me t' movin' I hightailed it away from that damn tv store straight t' the hospital."

The boy was staring at his grandfather with incredulity. Why hadn't he heard this story before? Why hadn't his mother told him any of this?

"Don' believe me?" the old man asked.

"I believe you," the boy replied. "I just…"

"I know," his grandfather said quietly. "Hard t' digest ain't it? I'm puttin' a lot on ye today. But ye can handle it. I know ye can. An it's time ye learnt a bit about what life kin be like. Ye ready t' hear the res'?" The boy nodded. "Alright then. Good."

"When I got t' the hospital, the nurses didn' believe I was yer ma's pa. Ye gots t' remember – I'd been sleepin' rough like. Hadn' had a shower in days, wearin' the same clothes. I was a sight! Prob'ly smelt sumthin' fierce too. The apartment was still there. I coulda gone an cleaned up. Jus' didn' think o' it. My mind was too tore up o'er my missus. I finally got a boss o' some kind, tol' him what happened, and he call someone on the phone. Fella tol' me t' wait a spell, that someone would be there t' talk t' me. An' a few minutes later, here come the cops. Those bastards arrested *me!* They thought I done kilt yer grandma! I know ye watches some o' those cop tv shows, but back then they didn' have things like DNA or security cameras, cell phones and such. It was jus' my word agains' theirs. An' I was a convicted drug dealer. The pros'cutor cooked up some kinda nonsense about a 'marital dispute' between us, e'en had a couple witnesses said they seen us arguin' the day she gone missin'. I ne'er seen any o' them folks before or since. Don' know where they come from or where they got off to. Didn' take a jury long t' convict me o' murderin' yer grandma. They sent me up fer forty year. Back t' prison I went. Yer ma went in the foster system. That kin be a bad place fer little 'uns. Some folks is good people, others jus' want the state money they git fer taking care o' the kids. But they don' give a damn 'bout the kids at all, jus' ignore 'em and collect the checks. An' some is worse than that. They hurt the kids. Those folks… I hope they all burn in hell."

"So, there I am, back in prison again, my missus gone, yer ma gone t' god knows where, an' nuthin' I kin do but sit an' wait til I get out. Forty year is a long time."

"Bout ten year after I go in, I meet a new fella. He got hisself sent up fer some kinda bank nonsense, embezzlin' or sumthin'. Man had hisself a education, smart as a whip, he were. He an' I git t' talkin', an' he says t' me that he'll help git me my high school deeploma. I heard ye can git that in prison, but I ne'er cared much t' work at it. This fella though, he changed my mind. I ne'er did read much, but he git me t' read a couple books that it turnt out I liked a bit. No, I liked a LOT. Fore I knew it, he had me studyin' fer the test, and I past it. Got me my deeploma a buncha year late, but better'n ne'er. Damned thing is, I dun it myself. He jus' nudged me in the right direction. Sometimes that's all it takes t' git goin' is a nudge."

The boy was utterly confounded. So many of his notions about his grandfather had been blown to smithereens on this chilly autumn afternoon. He hadn't consciously formed them, observed, recorded and catalogued various data points, then processed them all to reach a conclusion. They'd just sort of… grown. Sprouted. Like grass in a crack in the sidewalk. If you looked at it, really paid attention, it seemed as though it shouldn't even be there. Yet there it was, nonetheless. How did that grass get in there? Had someone planted it? No. Some other force, some method unseen by human eye, ignored by all but the bugs who feasted on or lived in it, had caused it to grow in that most unlikely of places. His grandfather had been a giant to him, as close to a god as anything he'd ever known. Yet here he was admitting to shortcomings, flaws, problems. The only problem he'd ever known his grandfather to have was the cancer. And where had it come from? Had it just grown inside him like that grass in the sidewalk crack?

"I did twenty-seven year o' my sentence fore some outfit started t' lookin' into my case. They's good folks who try t' help innocent people git outta jail. They found all kinds o' stuff the cops done wrong back when I was firs' arrested. They e'en found a witness who seen those men take yer grandma that day. Even'chully a judge gimme a new trial, and they found me innocent. By that time they e'en had DNA evidence agains' the men that dun fer yer grandma. Three of 'em was dead, includin' the man I'd got my stuff from. Turns out he'd made some other fella plenty mad 'bout sumthin', and got hisself kilt a couple year after I went in. They found one o' the two other SOB's who was wit him that day, an' he went up fer murder and kidnappin' a couple year after I git out. Course by that time he was nearin' an old man like I am now, an' it didn' mean nuthin' t' him. He'd been in and out plenty o' times. Once you been inside ye can tell someone else who been in too wit jus' a look. There's a way they looks at things 'roun them. It's a dead giveaway e'er time."

"So when I git out, the firs' thing I wants t' do is find yer ma. I reckoned we had us a lot o' catchin' up t' do, an' I wanted t' git started. She weren't too easy t' find though. See by that time she'd already been married t' yer pa an' changed her las' name. It took me near on two year 'fore I found her. And she didn' want much t' do wit me at firs'. I think she blamed me fer all that happen t' her. An maybe she were right. Lots o' it were my fault. Mostly cause I weren't there t' take care o' her, and cause o' that she ended up in some bad places. But even'chully she come roun' and lemme see ye. Remember that firs' time we met? Ye was jus' a lil' 'un back then."

The boy looked over his shoulder to find his mother standing in the doorway, leaning against the jam and smiling faintly. Her eyes lit up when he saw her, and her faint smile turned radiant.

"Mom?" the boy asked. "Grandpa said I should ask you about what happened to your knee."

Her smile turned sad, and her eyes dropped to the floor. "Your father did it to me," she said quietly. The boy turned to face his grandfather in shock, but the old man simply looked back at him. There would be no explanation from him; this was her story to tell, but he could tell his grandfather knew what had happened.

"We were just kids when we got together. You came along a couple years after. Your dad liked to drink… and do… other things. And like your grandfather's dad, he could get… mean… when he drank. But I drank right along with him. We were both a mess back then. One night we'd been out at a bar, both drunk, and when we got home he got mad about something. It doesn't matter what, and I don't remember, but the point is we started fighting. At first it was just words. Then he… hit me. In the stomach. He'd done that enough times by then, and I wasn't going to take it anymore, so I hit him back, slapped him across the face. He'd taken some martial arts classes or something when he was younger and still knew some of those moves, so when

I slapped him, he kicked out at me. Hit me right on the knee. I couldn't walk for days. He wouldn't let me go to the hospital. It finally healed. Sort of."

The boy had only very vague memories of his father. He'd been there one day, then the next day he was gone. Neither he nor his mother had seen the man since. His mother had been vague about why his father had gone, and now he thought he understood why.

"Ye see?" his grandfather said, "I tole ye she'd tell ye if ye ask't."

"You're old enough now to know the truth, as sad as it is," she said quietly.

The old man coughed, a dry, rasping sound that left him wheezing afterwards. He took a small sip of water from a glass on the nightstand, then held it out to the boy who ran to fill it from the kitchen faucet.

"You think he's getting it?" the mother asked quietly.

"I 'spect so. Maybe not all o' it, but enuff. He's a good boy; he'll be ok." She smiled and stepped to the side as her son came back with the fresh glass of water.

"Alright. You ready t' hear the rest?" The boy nodded enthusiastically.

"So, like I said, yer ma weren't easy t' find, once I got out. It took me a spell, and at first she didn' want nuthin' t' do wit me. But finally she let me come by and see ye both. She was still wit yer pa then, an he an I didn' like each other right from the start. I could see in his eyes he was an angry man, like *my* pa were. Yer ma didn' tell me much 'bout him at first. But as time went by, she start t' say lil' things. I unnerstood well enuff. She wanted 'im gone. Away from the both of ye. So one day I show up when I knowed you an her was out, and yer pa and I, well, we had us a lil' chat. He didn' quite know what t' make o' me, old con that I am, but I could see he was afeared o' me. An he were right t' be. Bein' in prison'll learn ye a lot o' things ye wouldn' learn on the outside. Ye ain't careful, it'll turn ye into someone else too. Someone ye don' like. Who other people don' like." The old man paused and looked down at the thin blanket that covered his withered legs and lower torso. The boy stared at his face, trying without knowing he was doing it, to read the emotions etched on his wrinkled and pensive countenance. "This is the part I don' like," he said quietly. "It's the part makes me... not like myself none. Yer pa had t' go. It were that simple. If he didn', then either he or I were gonna end up in the grave. He knowed it too, like I did. So the day we had us a talk, he decided it were time t' be on his way. Packed his stuff an lef'. Yer ma come home a couple hour later and she knowed what happen."

The boy turned to look at his mother who was smiling at him sadly. "It's true," she said. "Your father was going to kill one of us if we'd stayed. But he wouldn't let me leave with you. Oh, I could have left by myself, but I refused to leave you with that terrible man. You don't remember but he beat you nearly as bad as he did me. Once when you were not even two, you spilled something, or broke something, I don't remember which, and he paddled you with a wooden spoon until you were... bloody. I tried to stop him, but he hit me so hard I blacked out. When I woke up, he was outside smoking a cigarette. He saw me and acted like nothing had ever happened. In that moment I decided to leave. But it wasn't until your grandpa found me that I was able to do something about it."

The boy was shocked. His mother rarely mentioned his father, and when she did it was always something vague and innocuous like telling him he had his father's eyes. She'd never told him these stories before, and he didn't know whether to love her more for getting them away from his father, or hate the absent man for being the monster he was. Maybe he could do both.

"So, I run him off," the old man said. "And yer ma ne'er seen him since."

"And I don't ever *want* to," she said with more force than she'd said anything up to that point.

"After that yer ma and I, well, we got close. Maybe not as close as we coulda been if I'd never got sent up, but close as I coulda hoped fer. Course she knowed by then that I hadn' kilt her ma, that someone else'd done it, but I'd still lef' her alone all those years. It sure musta been hard on her." Two tears ran down the old man's face, one from each eye. The boy turned and looked at his mother and was surprised to see her weeping openly.

"You came along at just the right time dad," she said. "It all happened the way it was supposed to.

"Maybe so, but I cain't hep thinkin' you'da been in a better place if I'da never got sent up."

"You're here now, with us, and that's all that matters."

The raw emotion on display in the room shocked the boy, and made him feel just a little left out. His mother and grandfather were having a moment between them that didn't involve him, and he wasn't sure how to handle it. Then a thought occurred to him – maybe he didn't have to handle anything. It was their moment, their feelings on display, not his. He could just watch and appreciate without being involved.

"I'm gonna go make some tea," his mother said. She smiled at him before walking away, and the boy turned back to his grandfather. The old man wiped his eyes and blew his nose into a Kleenex filched from a box on the nightstand. It was rather amazing, the boy thought, just how many items one could fit on the top of an ordinary nightstand if some thought was given to their arrangement.

"We're almos' at the end," the old man said. "Not much more t' tell that ye don' know. After yer pa lef', it were just the three o' us. I helped yer ma as I could wit money or watchin' o'er you when she had t' work an there weren't no one else t' watch ye. Remember them times? We'd do puzzles on the kitchen table, or ye'd have me read ye them lil' books ye used t' like. I ne'er was happier than when I read t' ye. That ol' boy I met in prison what got me t' gettin' my deeploma sure helped out when it come t' readin'. I 'spect witout that I'da ne'er been able t' read t' ye. That woulda been a cryin' shame. See I love books now. When I was a young 'un, I ne'er had time fer 'em. Now I wished I'da read lots more'n I have. Still, wit the time I got left, I'm gonna read as many books as I can. Ye oughta read more yerself while ye gots the time and youth fer it." The boy nodded again, thinking of the small shelf of books in his tiny bedroom. He was going to start one as soon as this conversation was over.

"I found me a job, which is hard t' do when yer a felon. No, I didn' kill yer grandma, but I did get convicted o' sellin' a few times. Course that were a lot o' years ago, and I ain't the same man I was then. The car dealership hired me t' answer the phones and say 'how do' t' anyone come through the door. I liked the job. It didn' pay much, but it were fun and I got t' talk t' some nice folk. Some not nice ones too, but ain't it always that way? Then the cancer come callin' an' here we are. Now I'll not lie t' ye – that doc was here earlier said my time's runnin' out. He don' know how long I gots lef', but it ain't much. That's ok. I'll git t' see yer grandma again soon, and I'll always look in on you and yer ma from the nex' place, if'n they'll let me, whoe'er the warden is up 'ere." The old man was silent for several long moments, his eyes far away, his breathing shallow and forced. Finally, his eyes focused in on the boy's and in them was a presence, an intensity, a fire, he'd never seen there before. "Now ye promise yer grandpappy sumthin' will ye?" he asked in a sandpapery but still forceful voice. The boy nodded. "Don' ye do no more what ye done at school here recent. That ain't the way. If'n ye need more proof than me and what I jus' tole ye, well yer as hardheaded as a fire plug and ain't nuthin' gonna hep ye. Now if yer as smart as I think ye are, ye'll not keep on wit that nonsense. If'n ye need some money, they's plenty o' folks out there'd like t' hire a young man wit a head on his shoulders and some fire in his blood t' get the work done. Ye go find them, show that yer reliable, honest, and willin' t' handle yer bidness. The rest'll come natural enuff. Ye unnerstand?" The boy nodded.

"I promise Grandpa. I won't do that no more."

"Well, I reckon that's jus' right. Now go on, git yer butt on up outta here. I'm tired an I need th' rest. We'll talk agin later."

The young man walked onto the stage gingerly, like it might collapse under his weight if he didn't step carefully.

That was absurd of course, but it's how he felt at that moment. The tassel on his cap hung to one side, and he watched as the person in front of him, a young lady he'd had a few classes with, shifted the one on her cap to the other side after she'd shaken the hand of the man with the silver hair and accepted the small document case he'd given her. Then it was his turn to shake the man's hand and receive the little case. He heard his name come over the PA system. It was loud and sounded strange, echoey and hollow. From somewhere far to the back of the huge open-air arena where the event was taking place, he heard a woman's voice cheering. Mom. It was soon drowned out by the PA announcing another name, and several voices cheering for that person. Whoever it was had a big family; they'd been nearly as loud as the PA. His mother's single cheering voice must have seemed small in comparison to anyone else who might have been listening, but it was louder than anything to him. He walked to the far end of the stage where a set of steps led down to the ground. His right hand found the handrail, and as he descended, he glanced toward the sky. "I hope you're proud Grandpa," he said softly.

# STUCK ON FAIRVIEW LOOP

"Jim hated this road. Fairview Loop was absolutely horrible. The lanes were too narrow, the corners too sharp, there were no shoulders, and the edge of the asphalt was far too close to the ditches that lined either side of it. In summer it was fun to drive because of those features, provided some dickhead-in-a-hurry wasn't riding your ass all the way. But it was winter now, and the road was covered in snow and ice, and here he was again, stuck behind another accident. At least it was still light out. In the dark it was nearly impossible to determine where the lanes were. The ditches were full of snow right up to the level of the blacktop and above, so it became very hard to tell where the road dropped off. The double yellow line down the middle separating the lanes of travel was more often than not totally covered with compacted and frozen precipitation. It was the worst when another car was coming toward you, especially if it was equipped with those bright white headlights that started showing up on cars and trucks a few years ago. They were utterly blinding; the glare from them effectively obliterated your ability to tell where the road was. If one could judge the drivability of a road by how many accidents it experienced, Fairview Loop was rivaled only by the Glenn between the Palmer Fairgrounds and where it split off from the Parks at the edge of the Palmer Hay Flats. Ok, maybe he was feeling a little dramatic. There were a couple others in the region that were just as bad.

Jim had lived in Wasilla for the last fifteen years, twelve of those at his house off Fairview Loop. When he'd bought the place, his neighborhood had been small and relatively undeveloped. But as home prices in Anchorage and Eagle River had soared, people had moved out here to the Mat-Su Valley where land was still plentiful, homes affordable, and the government, or more accurately the lack of it, hadn't turned a vibrant region into an outhouse. His house was a ranch style offering on a three-acre lot with a well and septic, and large detached garage. He'd paid one hundred and forty thousand for the place, and according to an appraisal he'd had done for a refinance the year before, it was now worth three hundred and twelve. Jim didn't care what it was worth because he planned on living there the rest of his life.

Alaska was not Jim's state of birth; he'd actually been born in Oklahoma in 1983 to a military father and stay-at-home mother. They'd moved around a lot when he was young but had eventually settled in Colorado Springs where his father had worked at the Air Force Academy. After high school Jim had held several different jobs, most of which were low-skilled and low-paying like cashiering and construction laborer. He considered joining the service like his dad, but the military life held no allure. He didn't have anything against it, he just preferred to be able to do what he wanted, when he wanted. His parents were kind, caring people, and his father had never pushed him toward a specific vocation, unlike some of his friends whose parents had dragged them into sports or forced them to attend college. Jim had been allowed to make his own choices. So, when he saw the ad on a social media site for seasonal workers needed at a lodge in Southeast Alaska, he figured that was worth a try. He worked at the lodge four summers in a row and loved it. The owners asked him to come back for a fifth, and when he accepted, he also decided to make the great northern state his permanent home. So, in the late spring of 2006 he packed everything he owned into his little Toyota Camry and began the long drive north into Canada, across the Al-Can highway and on to the small town of Skagway. A short airplane ride later he was at the lodge.

The summer passed quickly, and when it was over Jim got into his car and headed for the population center of Alaska – Anchorage. He didn't much care for the city; it was like most others of a similar size – crime, strip malls, traffic lights that were way too long – everything he disliked about cities. The one thing Anchorage had that he did like was its proximity to so many outdoor adventure opportunities. Jim found a job quickly, stocking shelves in a grocery store, but when he heard about the Arctic oilfields and the lucrative jobs available there, he was intrigued.

The North Slope, as the region is known, or colloquially just The Slope, contains vast deposits of oil and gas. Jim knew nothing about oil and gas extraction or the Arctic, but some online research piqued his interest. In a matter of weeks Jim had found a job and was on his way north. Since the oilfields are so remote, one does not just drive to work like most people do; oilfield workers in Alaska are flown to their jobs in passenger planes, a commuting method Jim found most enjoyable, especially on clear days when the sheer size and beauty of his adopted state was on full display out the small window in the plane's fuselage. The schedule of a sloper is pretty straightforward – you work twelve hours every day you're there, no days off (not even major holidays), then you leave. If you're on a two and two rotation, then you work two weeks and have two weeks off at home before you have to go back to work again. Jim loved it. He'd work his hitch, as stints in the oil patches are known, then go home and have two weeks of free time to do whatever he wanted.

Within a year of going to work on the slope, he'd bought his house. Oil companies paid well, much better than any other job he'd ever had. And the negative things he'd heard about them, about how they utterly decimated the environment in their greedy and insatiable search for profits, were not true at all. The oil companies working in the arctic were the most environmentally conscious outfits he'd ever seen. They'd installed miles and miles of pipelines to carry oil and other fluids to and from the wells. Those pipelines had to be built above ground on steel supports to keep the freeze/thaw cycles of the tundra from causing them to sag and rupture, and they'd actually built them high enough from the ground to allow caribou and other animals to pass freely underneath them during the snow-free summer months. And animals *always* have the right-of-way. If an arctic fox is laying in the middle of the road, drivers just stop and wait until it moves. No one will question or berate them for it. If a piece of equipment leaks a bit of oil or hydraulic fluid, anything more than a cup – as in a measuring cup like you would find in a kitchen – then a spill response team is brought in and the fluid and any contaminated materials are collected and disposed of in an appropriate manner at a hazardous waste facility. Jim had to chuckle and shake his head at the environmentalists who so loved to protest against the oil companies while drinking from their reusable plastic water bottles, or paddling around protesting the offshore drilling rigs in their plastic kayaks, or buying groceries from their local farmer's market and never once wondering how those luscious cantaloupes and fantastically green kale leaves got from the farms to the parking lot where the market was. Most of them probably never wondered either just how many things in their lives were made from oil. And all the people who were so vociferously calling for oil production to be shut down on the slope because of some amorphous environmental threat it supposedly posed had obviously never been there. The Arctic is vast; the places where oil is extracted are tiny, a few hundred acres in an area of nearly one hundred and fifty thousand square miles. There are dozens of *countries* that aren't that big. For someone to say that a ruptured pipeline spilling even a few thousand gallons of oil is going to kill off all the polar bears or create an environmental catastrophe so profound that the area will never recover, has absolutely no idea what they're talking about. Once Jim saw the region for himself, he understood how completely absurd the claims of the environmentalists were. If they wanted to live like it was 5781 B.C. again, well, more power to them. They could all go live in a mud hut somewhere and use their own shit to fertilize their organic vegetables. But much of the rest of the country and the world beyond enjoyed life the way it was, with its modern amenities and conveniences, most of which had at least some connection to oil.

Jim did not consider himself overly political, but he did know what he believed in, and he was savvy enough to know that actions taken by local and state governments had, generally speaking, a more direct impact on his life than what the feds did. For that reason, he tried to keep abreast of things locally. He read the initiatives and propositions, researched candidates for office, and voted his values. So, when he saw somewhere online that the Mat-Su Borough was trying to get voters to approve a new tax package to pay for road improvements, he read through the press release and was pleased when he saw that Fairview Loop was one of the roads designated for upgrades. It was about time! He hadn't given much thought to roads when he'd bought his house, but now that he lived here, he sometimes wished he'd bought a place in Meadow Lakes, Big Lake, or Houston, especially since the area was growing, and the roads were becoming both more congested and dangerous. Development can be positive and negative. There were more restaurant options now than there had been, for example, but there had also been an increase in crime. A neighborhood close to Jim's had seen so many burglaries and catalytic converter thefts, that it had been nicknamed the Rodent Highway in honor of its non-law-abiding denizens.

Jim lived alone, and when he went to work a neighbor kept an eye on his house. He'd installed a security camera system, which he could access from an app on his phone, but it helped to have an actual person watching too. Pam was a divorced mother of two who loved horses; she had three on her property. Her kids were both grown and on their own, so Pam had time on her hands and was happy to watch his house. Jim had never asked her what she did for money, but she didn't work. Maybe she'd gotten a big divorce settlement. It didn't matter, and it was her business anyway. Jim was just happy that she was friendly and was willing to watch his place when he was on the slope. In return he helped her with her horses when she needed it. In fact, he was supposed to help her today; she had a delivery of hay bales coming sometime this afternoon, and Jim had offered to help her stack them in her barn. Except that he was stuck behind whatever was blocking the road up there.

He'd gone to the grocery store and was on his way home when he ran into the back of the traffic jam. The incident was too far around the next turn in the road for him to see what was happening, and he didn't really care. It was certainly just another accident, and one which no doubt everyone had slowed down to look at. The strange looky-loo phenomenon that afflicted most people when they saw flashing lights on the road was perplexing to Jim. Everyone simply *had* to dynamite their brakes and look when they passed a cop with someone pulled over for a traffic violation, or a tow truck trying to hook up to a disabled vehicle. Slowing down to be safe and not hit some person working on the shoulder of the road was one thing. Slowing down just because you saw flashing lights was another. What did people expect to see? A mangled car? Blood? A dead body? Most people would be highly disturbed by seeing someone dead in a car wreck; it would be an image they'd never forget, never unsee. So why slow down? Why look at all? Drive carefully, but drive on by. What the majority of people probably didn't realize was that by slowing down to look at a traffic accident, and one that they probably wouldn't really want to see the outcome of anyway, they were actually creating a hazard for drivers coming up behind them. It was short-sighted, self-indulgent and utterly unnecessary.

He didn't know if the event holding him up right now was an accident or something else, but it was getting late, and he was anxious about letting Pam down. A glance at his truck's dashboard told him the ambient temperature outside was 7 degrees Fahrenheit. Chilly but not horribly cold for this place at this time of year. He was wearing a warm coat and knit beanie and had a pair of gloves on the passenger seat. The truck's fuel tank was almost full, and the heater worked well. He could sit here for hours and be fine. Jim briefly considered turning around using the oncoming lane and taking a different route home but rejected the idea. It was a long way around, and his house was less than a mile from here. Most of the time these traffic jams only lasted a few minutes. No, he'd wait his turn. Eventually cars would start moving and he'd get home.

His cell phone was on a little mount on the dashboard, and he plucked it off, opened the message app and sent a text to Pam, letting her know he was stuck in traffic. She replied almost immediately saying it was fine, and that the truck delivering the hay hadn't arrived yet. It was probably stuck in the same traffic jam he was. That made him feel a little better, although he was getting hungry and felt the mild urge to take a leak. Hopefully it wouldn't be too much longer before things cleared up.

He must have dozed a little in the warmth of the truck, because when the horn of the vehicle behind him blew, it jolted him. Jim rubbed his eyes and looked at the road in front of him. Cars were still stacked up like cord wood. Nobody had moved. That was good and bad. Good in that he hadn't held up traffic by falling asleep, bad because the traffic jam was still there. How long had he been out? He looked at his phone and noticed the time said 4:28.

His text to Pam had been at 4:24. So he'd been asleep three or four minutes. Why was the person behind him honking? Impatience? Turn around and take another route buddy – everyone's stuck in the same shit and honking wasn't going to make it any better. It was like creepers at traffic lights. Why was it that some people, when stopped at a red light, insisted on inching forward every time the car in front of them did? It wasn't going to make the light change any faster, and just put more wear and tear on your brakes. Now he had some jackwad behind him honking the horn as if that would make the traffic magically disappear and allow the prick to continue to his destination unimpeded. Jim looked in his side mirror but couldn't see the car. It was a little black compact thing, and his truck was too wide. He checked the rearview mirror and could just see the roof of the little car; it had pulled up too close to his rear bumper for him to see into the interior.

He sighed and looked out the windshield at the line of cars in front of him. Movement right at the curve in the road caught his eye. Were people fighting up there? It was getting hard to see in the gloom of twilight and the glare of headlights on snow and ice, but he was pretty sure he'd just seen two figures wrestling on the ground. They'd moved out of his line of sight, so he waited a few moments to see if they'd come back into it. When nothing happened he shook his head and reached for the stereo controls.

Jim didn't like music radio; they played the same songs over, and over, and over until one could barely listen to them anymore. He was a big rock and roll fan, and his favorite band was AC/DC. How many albums had they released in their storied career? Twenty? Twenty-five? Each one had probably between eight and twelve songs on it, which gave a conservative total of let's just say one hundred and sixty songs by that band. Radio stations played ten of them. Maybe fourteen or fifteen if they were feeling particularly adventurous. That worked out to roughly between six and nine percent of AC/DC's entire catalog. The other ninety-one to ninety-four percent went completely unplayed on radio. No wonder it was a dying medium. How many artists were that that got no radio play at all? Thousands probably. Jim enjoyed a few podcasts and sometimes listened to internet radio stations where you could hear more obscure music, so he turned off the radio which had been tuned to a nationally syndicated sports talk show on the AM band and unlocked his cell phone. There was a podcast he liked about Alaska, and the hosts were a husband and wife who gave all kinds of good advice about camping and obscure places to go that were away from tourists. Jim turned it on and began listening.

"And we're live from Hatcher's Pass today, where we're going to tell you about Bomber Glacier and how to get there. We know it's not of the truly unknown places in our lovely state, but it is worth the hike. Uhh, hang on a second. We're getting some instant messages here… Something weird's going on… What is that?" Jim frowned at the announcer's tone of voice. It was the husband. He was usually completely cool and even keeled, but not now. There was a shrillness to his voice that smacked of fear. "Uhh, folks," the man said, "I'm not one for conspiracies or anything, but I've just been sent a video from one of our viewers that I think you should see. This was from a livestream event that happened a few minutes ago. It's up on all our social media platforms now. If this is a hoax, it's a good one."

Jim opened an app on his phone and scrolled until he found the podcast people. Right there at the top of their page was the video the guy had mentioned. The time stamp said it had been posted three minutes ago. Jim clicked the play button and watched closely.

The video started with a woman's heavily made-up face. She was wearing a pink knitted pullover hat with a magenta tufted ball on top of it and was obviously inside a car when she began speaking in an annoyingly bubbly and squeaky voice into the phone. "So here I am stuck in traffic, waiting for I don't know what the problem is to go away, and I thought why not put out another video for all my followers. I'm so mad right now! This is just bullshit! This traffic jam has been going on for like, at least fifteen minutes and all I want to do is get home so I can feed my little snuggledybear. She's got to be *so* hungry!" The woman held up a bag of dog treats so the camera could see them. "She just *loves* this brand. If you've got a little snuggledybear of your own, give them these. I promise they're going to *love* them!" Jim was starting to feel the urge to vomit along with his growing need to piss. "So now I just wanted to say one more thing. If the people who make these are interested, I'd love to do a video for them. If the price is right! When you're as good as me, you don't come free!" Jim felt like smashing his phone, but instead he kept watching. "I would have brought my little angel with me, but chihuahuas have *such* short fur and it's *so* cold outside." The woman turned her phone toward the window of her car. Wherever she was, it gloomy and snowy outside, like where he was on Fairview Loop. She'd just started speaking again about some utterly mindless topic when suddenly the driver's side window of her car shattered. The woman screamed in terror, and Jim watched in amazement as a huge hairy arm reached in. The phone fell out the window and tumbled to the ground, landing face down and cutting off any further video. But the audio was still recording. A guttural snarling and snapping sound could be heard, then a pain-filled wail from the woman which cut off suddenly. It was silent for a moment, then a car horn sounded, and the video ended.

"Folks," the podcast man was saying back on his live broadcast, "that's not the only video we have. We've just posted another from Fairbanks, two from Juneau, and several from the Anchorage/Mat-Su areas. Some of them are very graphic. Please use your discretion around children, and if you have guns, get them. We don't know what's happening yet, but it's nothing good. We're going to end our live broadcast and head home. Sorry for the short one today, but we hope you all understand. See you next time," the man said, and the feed cut out.

Jim had forgotten about the fight, or whatever it was, that he'd seen a few minutes ago. He scrolled through the other videos the podcast people had posted and clicked one at random. It showed the back deck of a house, with a snow-covered yard, a shed and a small chicken coop. The video began playing and for the first few seconds the only movement was trees swaying in a breeze. Then from the left side of the screen a hulking figure came into view. Jim unconsciously brought his phone closer to his face as he stared at the unbelievable image. It was huge and covered in hair. The video was in black and white, so it was impossible to tell what color it was, but he could tell it was dark. The thing was facing away from the camera, but its back was extremely broad, its arms unnaturally long, and muscles rippled and bulged under the hair. It walked toward the house and casually smashed its fist through the sliding glass door. The creature had to bend down dramatically to get into the house, and Jim guessed it was well over seven feet tall, and maybe closer to eight. Nothing happened for several seconds, then he watched in dismay as the creature emerged from the house. Its face was covered in hair like the rest of its body, and it had a wide mouth, blunt nose, and eyes that must have been glowing, they were so bright in the black and white video. The thing was dragging something behind it – a woman, Jim was shocked to see. It had her by the hair, and her hands were trying vainly to pry the thing's fingers loose. Her legs were kicking wildly, and her mouth was open in what was surely a scream of terror, and Jim was glad the video had no accompanying audio. The creature stopped in the middle of the snow-covered deck and furiously slammed the woman's head down. She stopped struggling, obviously dazed or possibly unconscious from the force of the blow which the snow didn't seem to have cushioned in the slightest. The thing stared down at the still form of the woman for a moment, then crouched down and began tearing at her torso with its hands. In moments the snow around her body was dark with blood and chunks of flesh. The rib cage had been exposed, and the creature thrust its fingers between the bones and ripped, exposing the organs beneath. Jim nearly vomited and almost turned the video off, but a morbid fascination kept his eyes focused on the screen. He took hold of the door handle just in case. The creature regarded the obviously now dead woman for a moment, then punched one hand into the open chest cavity and tore out her heart. It raised the grisly trophy to its face and bit into the no-longer-pumping organ.

His gorge rose quickly, and Jim barely got the door open before emptying his stomach onto the frozen roadway. The podcast people had been right about the video being graphic. There were several more, but he didn't want to watch them. The other video of the annoying woman in the car came to mind. Had the same kind of creature attacked her? Being home suddenly seemed like the most important thing in the world. He closed the video, which had mercifully ended and checked his text messages to see if there was anything from Pam; there wasn't. In fact, he didn't have any new messages from anyone. Maybe these videos, and word of them, hadn't yet spread throughout his group of friends. A question popped into his mind, and he reopened the app where he'd found the videos. Jim didn't play any of them, there were now over fifty, but instead looked at the captions and titles. A quick survey of a dozen told him that they'd all been filmed in Alaska which supported what the podcast guy had said, and as far as he could tell, within the last hour. What the hell was going on?!

Alaska was a state known for its friendliness toward firearms, and Jim owned several. Most were hunting rifles and shotguns, but he also owned an AR-15, an AK-47, and several pistols. One of those pistols was in the console between the front seats. He took it out and removed it from the holster he kept it in. The Sig Sauer 1911 Emperor Scorpion fired .45 caliber ammunition, and with the jacketed hollow points in the magazine, it possessed plenty of stopping power. It was also a very reliable and comfortable pistol, and worth the price. A quick check showed him a round in the chamber and an engaged safety. The holster featured a small side pouch that held a second magazine, and he checked it as well, even though he knew it was full.

He put the holstered pistol into an inside pocket of his jacket and looked out the windshield. Jim was startled to see cars turning around ahead of him. One drove past and he clearly saw the faces of a terrified woman and two kids. One of them was staring at a cell phone. A kid with a cell phone pressed to his face was nothing new, but something told Jim they'd seen one of the videos and had decided to try to get home another way. Cars up ahead were turning around in droves now, their tires slipping on the ice. One of them tried to accelerate far too quickly for the conditions, and its nose slid off the road, leaving the back end blocking half the lane. More vehicles quickly stacked up behind it, unable to get around, and horns began blaring. A man got out of a pickup and stalked toward the stuck car, screaming profanities. Everyone had now heard of or seen the videos of what was happening, and panic was setting in. Jim glanced at the rearview mirror and watched as a compact car, several spots behind his truck, decided to turn around and pulled out right in front of a one-ton work truck that had been fortunate enough to not get stuck behind the car that was off the road, and they collided with a metal-tearing crash. Glass, plastic and hot fluids sprayed across the ice. Now he was stuck in front and behind. The man who'd been screaming had returned to his truck and was driving it like he was in a demolition derby, pushing other vehicles hither and thither with his front bumper. In a few seconds he'd cleared himself a path, even pushing the car that was half off the road the rest of the way down into the ditch. The man gunned the throttle as he sped past Jim's truck and only slowed enough to push the one-ton out of his way in defiance of the loud admonishments of that truck's driver. The last Jim saw of him was steam rising from what was surely a punctured radiator as he sped off down Fairview Loop. That guy's engine would overheat soon, and he'd be walking.

Miraculously the road ahead of him was now open, and Jim put his truck in gear, letting it creep slowly down the road. The car behind him, seeing that things were moving, suddenly pulled out into the oncoming lane and sped past him. Jim shook his head as the car approached the twenty-five mile per hour curve and didn't slow for it. The car slid off the road and rolled several times, coming to rest on its passenger side against the thick trunk of a birch tree. A young man was climbing out of the driver's side window, which was facing the sky, and glared at Jim as he drove slowly by.

As he got to the corner, he noticed spots of red on the ground where he thought he'd seen the fight. A pink knitted cap with a magenta tufted ball on it lay at the edge of the road. Drag marks and generous streaks of blood led off into the trees. The incident with the annoying woman had happened right here. The wrestling figures had most likely been her and whatever the thing was that had dragged her out of her car. Where *was* her car? There. Just off the road was a small SUV with a shattered driver's side window. Blood was splattered on the door. Jim looked around but nothing moved. The attack on the woman had happened several minutes ago, yet only one horn had sounded when it was actually happening. Hadn't anyone in other cars seen it? Was everyone's attention so riveted on the little electronic devices in their hands that they'd completely missed seeing some massive… thing… smash that woman's car window and pull her out? Was humanity so distracted that they'd missed what was right in front of them, only to later see it happen on their phone through some social media app? The answer, apparently, was yes.

Rounding the corner beyond the scene of the attack, he saw what had caused the traffic jam in the first place – a grader had slid sideways and was blocking the entire road. Road graders in Alaska weren't just used for construction – in winter they were used to plow snowy roads. Three tow trucks were hooked up to the big machine and were still working to straighten it out. Jim had to stop behind four cars that apparently hadn't gotten the word about the goings on, or their drivers had realized that the blockage was nearly cleared and had decided to wait a few more moments. It didn't take long for the tow trucks to get the road grader sorted out, and the line of cars began moving. These drivers, even if they'd heard the news, were being more cautious than most of the others, and Jim was thankful for that. Now that he was free from the traffic jam, the last thing he wanted was for some idiot in a hurry to run him off the road, although he did feel a sense of urgency to get home.

His house wasn't far from the road grader, and in a few moments, Jim was pulling into his driveway. Pam's house was next to his, and her lights were on. He didn't see the hay delivery truck, but that seemed very unimportant considering what was happening around the state. Jim took his groceries into his house, dropped them on the kitchen counter, and retrieved his AK-47 and three loaded magazines from his gun safe. He pulled the Sig Sauer from his jacket and clipped its holster on his belt as he walked back out of his house and through the snow toward Pam's place. He wanted to check on her since she lived alone and find out if she had heard anything about the creatures. What the hell were they? He didn't believe in UFOs, the Loch Ness

Monster, or Chupacabra, those things were for obscure, seldom-visited websites and late-night radio shows. But damned if the creature he'd seen in that video didn't look a whole lot like a sasquatch. Could it *actually be* one?

Jim was halfway to Pam's place when he saw the shadows emerge from the trees at the far edge of her property. It was fully dark now; the day having died while he waited in the traffic jam. The shadows were moving quickly toward Pam's front door. There were four of them, Jim saw to his chagrin, and they were huge. He chambered a round in the AK and raised the rifle to his shoulder but didn't fire. The shadows were too far away and too close to Pam's house. Jim started running as fast as he could in the knee-deep snow, but it was hard slogging, and he fell several times. There was no fence between their lots, but Pam did have a large corral behind her house for her horses. The animals must have sensed danger because they were whinnying loudly enough to be heard through the walls of the barn where they lived when not outside.

As they neared the house a motion light came on, and the shadows resolved into four of the creatures Jim had seen in the horrific videos. He was shocked to see them in person, the fur on their hands and faces was red with blood and their eyes glowed a strange silver color. One of them looked his way and stopped; the other three smashed through the front door and into the house beyond. Jim mentally kicked himself. He should have just called Pam from his house. She might have had a chance to… do what? She had guns just like almost everyone else in this state, but would she have been able to get to them? Would she even have believed what he'd have told her about these things? It was immaterial now; all he could do was deal with the creatures the best he could, and hope Pam was ok.

The creature that had not entered the house was now moving toward him, its long legs carving through the deep snow with ease. It was about seventy yards away, and he could tell his initial estimate of its height was pretty close – the thing was well over seven feet tall. It must have thought he'd be easy prey because it started running. Jim shouldered the rifle again and waited until it was about fifty yards out. The big silhouette was hard to miss, even now that it was outside the glare of the motion light, and when he touched off a round, he was rewarded with seeing it jerk. Except that it didn't slow down, and if anything, moved faster. He could now hear a low growl, a guttural sound, like rocks banging on metal far down a deep shaft. It was unnerving. He fired again but couldn't tell if his round hit the target or not; it didn't jerk that time. Jim pulled the trigger four times rapidly and the thing slowed a little. It was now less than thirty yards away and still approaching. The 7.62mm rounds were not BBs. If he'd shot a human with them, that person would be dead on the ground, or very near to death. This thing though, it barely seemed to feel them. He fired again, making sure to take careful aim directly at center mass, and was gratified to see the fur on the thing's chest puff a little, accompanied by a spray of red. Surely that direct hit would put it down? No such luck. It opened its mouth and displayed a set of wickedly hideous fangs on both the upper and lower jaws. A snarl of aggression and rage burst from its throat, and it lunged forward into the closest thing to an all-out run that Jim had seen it make yet. He began pulling the trigger as fast as he could, the crack of the rifle shots echoing through the cold night. Bullets impacted the creature all around its torso, but still it came. Twenty yards, fifteen, ten. It was so close he could smell it, a rancid, foul stench. Jim took a deep breath, aimed directly at the creature's head and fired three times. Each round found its mark, and he watched in relief as the back of the thing's skull exploded. It pitched backward as the last round hit and fell unmoving to the ground. Jim was about to take a closer look at the massive corpse when a scream rang out from the direction of Pam's house.

Jim looked up and saw the three other creatures drag his neighbor out of her front door. One was holding her arms; the other two each had a leg. Pam was kicking and flailing as hard as she could, but the things were far too strong. About fifteen feet from the door they stopped, holding Pam suspended in the air between them. Jim started running toward them, ejecting the magazine from the AK and doing his damnedest to get another from his pocket and into the rifle's receiver. He was maybe thirty yards away when he finally got the mag in, chambered a round, and started yelling at the things. "Hey! Over here!" he cried, but the creatures ignored him. Jim was loath to fire with Pam being in the middle of them, but he didn't think he had much time left before she ended up like that poor woman in the video. He stopped running, brought the rifle to his shoulder, and sighted on the head of one of the creatures holding her legs. The round cracked in the cold air but must have missed; the creature didn't move. Jim ran a few steps closer and was just bringing the rifle up again for another shot, when the creatures all began huffing and puffing. The sounds they made were rhythmic, metronomic, like chanting, and there almost seemed to be a sort of rudimentary language to them. He was momentarily stunned at this new development and was unprepared when the chanting stopped, and each creature began pulling with all its might and weight on Pam's limbs. There was a terrible scream, followed by a rending sound, then the poor woman's body disintegrated as her arms and legs separated from her torso. The scream reached an even higher pitch, which seemed impossible to Jim, then suddenly, mercifully stopped. He was sickened to his core as he watched the creatures begin gnawing on Pam's limbs like someone would eat a barbecued chicken drumstick. Their lips were smacking as they bit, and he could hear their teeth crunching bones.

Jim walked slowly toward the three massive sasquatches. That's what they *had* to be. There was no other explanation for their existence. Even if they weren't actual living examples of the mythical creature, that's what he was going to call them until they had a better name. He was numb from watching Pam's horrific death; the only thought he had was killing these things before they got anyone else. Jim had no regard for his own life. Dying at that moment didn't even occur to him. All he wanted was to watch their heads explode as his rifle rounds punched through them.

He raised the rifle again and was surprised to find his heart, which had been pounding, was beating almost normally. His hands had been clammy and wet with sweat but were now dry. He could have been out at the target range practicing shooting or sitting on his couch watching a documentary about the making of baby food for all the anxiety he was feeling. The creatures were too intent on their… meal… and didn't notice Jim approach within twenty yards of them. He aimed carefully at the head of the one closest to him and fired. It crumpled to the ground in a spray of blood and hair. The other two stopped eating their grisly dinner and looked at Jim. Their expressions were blank, vacant, like a junkie who'd just shot up some quality China White. The farthest one slowly lowered Pam's leg and let it fall from its fingers. It took a step toward Jim and was met by a bullet through its forehead. The other one snapped out of its trance and with a strange sound, like a lion's roar combined with a pig's squeal, it dashed toward Jim. His first two shots missed, and his heart suddenly started pounding again as his own mortality loomed before him in the shape of a huge hairy monster with bloody fangs and an enraged expression. His third shot caught the thing in the mouth, but it was moving toward him so quickly that it crashed into him, and both fell to the ground.

Jim was on his back, his wind gone, the creature lying face down on his right side and its right arm across his chest. The thing was definitely hurt and badly, but it was still alive. The arm was clutching at Jim, trying to pull him closer. The mouth was a ruined mess, the teeth broken and mangled, but those shining silver eyes were filled with a ferocity and malice Jim had never seen in any living thing. His rifle was gone, knocked out of his hands in the collision and lost somewhere in the snow. He fought against the straining sasquatch's arm, vainly trying to pull himself out from under it. Goddamn, the thing was strong!

He was losing the battle; the ragged and broken teeth were getting closer no matter how hard he fought. It was incredible – the tenacity of this thing! It had taken an AK round straight in the mouth and was still trying to kill him! What kind of monster was this?

Jim felt a searing in his right shoulder as what was left of the thing's teeth finally found purchase. The pain was exquisite, and he felt bone break under the tremendous force exerted by the jaws. Another couple seconds and those teeth would be in his throat. He didn't have a knife, or he would have driven it into the thing's eye. He needed a weapon, but what? The teeth released and he felt them bite onto his clavicle, and the fragile bone snapped. Jim almost passed out from the intensity of the pain but fought against the darkness that threatened to claim his consciousness and his life. He was just about to drive his fingers into the thing's eyes since he didn't have a knife when he remembered what he *did* have – his pistol. How could he have forgotten it? The Sig was in its holster on his waist. The only problem was that he was right-handed, so he'd put the pistol on his right side. He frantically scrabbled with his left hand, trying desperately to get hold of the grip, while his injured right arm, its strength greatly diminished by the shoulder injury, did its best to fend off that horrid mouth. His fingers, wet with melted snow, slipped around it but couldn't quite grasp the gun. The sasquatch released the remnants of his collarbone and stretched its mouth toward his neck. Jim took advantage of the opening and pushed away as hard as he could manage with his right arm. The creature's mouth latched back onto his already bitten shoulder, but it gave him the precious seconds he needed to get the pistol out of the holster.

He'd racked a round into the chamber, all he needed to do now was release the safety, point and shoot. His fingers were fumbling at the small lever; it was hard to release the safety with the left hand when the gun was not an ambidextrous model, but one made for right-handed shooters. He got the safety off but dropped the pistol as the sasquatch removed its mouth from his shoulder and lunged for his neck. It nearly got him, missing by whiskers. Thankfully this time the broken teeth latched onto only air.

Jim's left hand was scrabbling around between his body and that of the sasquatch, frantically looking for the pistol, while his right was doing all it could to keep the creature away from his neck. The pain was excruciating. There it was! His hand scraped over the slide, but it was just a little too far away for him to get a solid hold. He was rapidly tiring, his breath coming in labored gasps. It had been a horrifying afternoon, and his nerves were frayed, his energy nearly depleted. And he'd never taken a leak! Strange to think of something so routine, so mundane, at a moment like this. If he died it wouldn't matter if his bladder was full or not. If he lived then he'd piss on this fucking thing's corpse. Either way – one of them was going to die in the next few moments.

His hand swept over the pistol again, fingertips straining for purchase on the snow-slicked grip. The sasquatch was losing strength and energy too, its snapping wasn't quite as ferocious, its arm not quite as strong. But it was still stronger by far than Jim was. If he didn't get the gun soon and end this, the sasquatch would.

Pain and blood loss were making him woozy, but Jim struggled against the creature, his left hand still desperately trying to get a grip on the gun. He'd been so engaged in killing and then fighting these creatures that he'd momentarily forgotten about Pam. The memory of her death flashed into his mind and anger flared within him. The unexpected adrenaline rush gave Jim just enough energy to push the sasquatch away and quickly make a final snatch at the pistol. This time he got it. He brought it up, heedless of the snapping mouth of the sasquatch and fired.

The bullet punched through the lower jaw and continued up through the roof of its mouth, then as a final coup de grace, blew the top of the thing's skull off. It slumped into the snow and lay unmoving.

Jim lay on his back for several long moments, breathing in the cold night air and the stink of the dead creature. Somewhere in the distance dogs were barking and sirens wailed. A light breeze came up and he began to feel the cold. Odd that he hadn't felt it before. He'd read somewhere that the senses do strange things in times of extreme stress. Maybe he'd been cold the whole time and just hadn't realized it. The focus he'd felt, almost like tunnel vision, when he'd fought the sasquatch on the ground, and to a lesser degree when he'd shot the other two after they'd killed Pam, had been so intense that he couldn't remember ever experiencing anything quite like it.

He lay in the snow, the pain in his shoulder ebbing from a fierce sharpness to a throbbing ache, when another feeling began to intrude on his thoughts. Damn, did he have to piss. Jim rolled on his side, not quite ready to get up yet, opened his fly and fulfilled his promise to himself as he let loose an immensely relieving stream onto the dead sasquatch. When he was finished, he sealed his pants back up and rolled onto his back again. The sky was clear, and thousands of stars blinked above him, their glow uninfected from the glare of city lights out here in the country. Something glittered to the north and Jim raised his head just a bit. The Aurora Borealis had begun to shimmer across the sky. Waves of green ebbed and flowed like bore tides, descending in a blink from the heavens and tap dancing just above the treetops, then just as suddenly morphing into a sheet of luminescence that waved like a flag in the wind before dissipating in the space of a breath. Jim had seen the Northern Lights countless times but couldn't recall ever seeing them put on a more spectacular display. He wondered idly if the sirens were coming this way and if someone would find him. And Pam.

He had to get up, move, put something on his shoulder. It was hard to tell if the blood had stopped flowing or not; his body was feeling very cold now, but he didn't know if that was from blood loss or the temperature. Maybe both. Jim struggled mightily until he finally managed to roll over and get to his knees. A wave of dizziness threatened to topple him face first into the snow, but he fought it off. Standing was harder yet, but the desire to live propelled him up and forced him to stagger toward his house.

He made it to the front door, which he'd left unlocked and was soon in the warmth of the interior. A mirror on the living room wall showed what a bedraggled and bloody mess he was. Jim shrugged out of his coat and looked at his mangled shoulder. The blood had definitely stopped, but the bites were pretty severe, the skin torn and ragged where the sasquatch's teeth had rent his flesh. He was going to have one hell of a scar to accompany the story. The broken collarbone had swelled up dramatically until it looked like he had a balloon under his skin. He shuffled into the kitchen and turned on the hot water, then pulled a towel out of a drawer and soaked it under the tap. The heat felt wonderful on his hands as the cold started to leave his body. As it fled a slew of aches and pains rushed in to replace it. He thought wryly that maybe he should have stayed out in the snow as pain in every part of him seemed to flare up at once.

The touch of the hot towel made the bites on his shoulder blaze with fiery agony, and it was all he could do to keep cleaning the wounds. Who knew what kind of germs the sasquatch carried? Then again if it did have some kind of disease, he most likely had been completely infected by now. Fresh blood flowed as he wiped off what had clotted, and Jim kicked himself for that. Should have just called 911 and let the paramedics deal with the bites. But maybe the paramedics were busy this night. Maybe they wouldn't come at all. Maybe the 911 dispatchers were so busy fielding calls that he'd get an automated message: "Please hold for the next available representative" or some such shit. Wouldn't that be just rich – call 911 for the first time in his life and end up on hold? No, it would probably be smarter to just get in his truck and drive to the hospital, which was about twenty minutes away. Could he stay conscious that long? He thought so.

Jim drank two glasses of water from the kitchen tap, one of which washed down four ibuprofen tablets, wrapped his shoulder in clean gauze which he'd daubed liberally with Neosporin, secured the whole with an ace bandage, then found a zip up hoodie on a hook in his mud room and put it on as gently as he could. He left the house and walked to his truck, the pistol back in its holster but on his left side this time, and got in. The Aurora was still shimmering in the sky, but a few high wispy clouds had moved in, blunting its brilliance a little. The engine fired as reliably as it always did, and he got the truck turned around and pointed at the street. In moments he was on Fairview Loop heading back the way he'd come earlier. When he reached the spot where the road grader had been, there was nothing left of the traffic jam except for the cars that were off the road. He drove slowly, looking for more of the creatures, but nothing was moving in the night. Lights were on in houses, and everything looked normal. Even the wrecked cars weren't unusual for this time of year. He'd seen cars sit in medians and ditches for weeks, even months, in winter before someone finally hauled them away.

Fairview Loop was barren of cars and sasquatches. For that Jim was thankful. What it was not barren of, he discovered as he drove slowly along the icy road, was evidence of violence. Even in the dark he could see spots at intermittent and erratic intervals that were obviously blood. Strangely there were no bodies, either human or sasquatch, to be seen. He already had a pretty good idea what the creatures did to humans they killed, but what did they do with their dead comrades?

Jim didn't pass another car all the way to the Parks Highway. It was the first time in his memory *that* had happened. He drove up the on ramp toward the southbound lanes of the Parks; the hospital was just off the next exit. There were several cars on the highway, all headed the same direction. That was strange – not a single one was driving toward downtown Wasilla. As he pulled onto the off ramp at Trunk Road, he saw lines of cars coming from both directions toward the hospital. Apparently, half the Mat-Su Valley was in need of medical care. Jim soon found himself in his second traffic jam of the day, although this one was at least moving. Progress was slow, and what was normally about a two-minute drive from the off ramp to the hospital parking lot took fifteen, but he finally was able to pull his truck into one of the last available stalls. Some people, he saw, were parking their vehicles out on the shoulder of the road or pulling off the asphalt onto undeveloped parts of the huge lot. Streams of people were hurrying toward the doors of the big building, many of them bloody and moaning in pain. Jim walked slowly behind a middle-aged couple who were muttering something about wishing they'd stayed in Oregon instead of moving north. Neither one of them seemed to be injured, so Jim ignored them and focused on walking across the icy parking lot.

The long, narrow waiting room, the entire front wall of which was made of floor-to-ceiling plate glass, was full. People were standing, sitting and laying down anywhere they could find space. Groans, moans and shrieks echoed from all over the first floor, and there was a veritable flood of tears from men and women, old and young. Jim waited patiently while harried nurses tried their best to gently triage the slew of patients they found themselves facing. A woman a few feet away began sobbing, then screaming, as a man she was cradling slumped to the floor, his shirt and jacket soaked in blood. Jim watched grimly as a nurse ran over and checked the man's pulse and shook her head. He could hear her murmur softly to the wailing woman that she was sorry and that there were just too many injured and not enough doctors to treat them all. He pulled his attention away from the distraught woman and eavesdropped on a conversation a man probably in his seventies was having with one probably in his forties. "I came here when I heard the alert," the older man said.

"So did I," replied the younger man. "Why would they want us to all gather here?

"I don't know, but I've lived here a long time, and the Alaska State Troopers are about the best there are at what they do. When they say to do somethin', I listen." The younger man nodded at this trenchant piece of advice. What alert had they been talking about? Jim was just about to ask when a commotion at the door caught his attention. Several people were running from the parking lot toward the hospital. Something about them looked familiar, but he couldn't tell what through the smoked glass of the windows. Then he saw it – the familiar uniform of those same Alaska State Troopers. There were eleven of them sprinting across the parking lot. The first one to reach the automatic sliding doors made sure to activate the sensor so they opened, then turned and watched as his colleagues darted through the into the hospital. Jim wondered what was so urgent, and he gasped out loud when he checked the parking lot again. At least a hundred sasquatches were advancing toward the hospital. They were walking calmly but purposefully, their unnaturally long arms swinging at their sides. Jim still had his pistol, but it wouldn't do much against that many of the creatures.

"Everyone get away from the windows!" one of the Troopers yelled. Most of the people fled at the command through the doors separating the check-in and waiting area from the rest of the hospital; only a few too shocked or too injured to move were left.

"If anyone has a weapon, preferably a gun, get up here – we need you!" another one called out. A few people pulled handguns from inside jackets and purses, but most looked around in shock at the trooper's words. Who would have a *gun* in a hospital? That was like bringing a lit flare to a rice paper art display.

"Who would have guns here?" a haughty voice asked, giving voice to what many of the remaining people were thinking. Jim turned to look and saw the two people from Oregon whom he'd followed into the hospital. It was the woman who'd spoken. Apparently, they'd decided not to heed the Trooper's advice to leave the waiting room.

"Most everyone in this state has guns ma'am," a twenty-something kid said matter-of-factly.

"Well, I never!" the woman said. "If we'd known how gun-crazy this state was, we'd have never left Oregon. And there is simply *nowhere* to get good wheatgrass juice here either!"

The young man, without saying anything, glanced at the woman, an expression of mild disgust on his face. But he did pull a big revolver from behind his back, which caused the woman's eyes to bulge and her husband, or whoever he was, to sharply draw in a breath. The kid smirked at their reaction and turned to face the windows. Jim nudged a Trooper who was standing just ahead of him and holding an AR-15. "I've got a pistol but I'm right-handed," he said inclining his head toward his injured right shoulder. The pain was fierce, and he wanted it to stop, but he had to do his part here. "I killed four of those things tonight," he added quietly. The Trooper had ignored him up until he said that, then the person turned to face him. Jim was mildly surprised to find himself facing a woman.

"You killed… four of them?" she asked incredulously.

"Yeah. Go for the heads. I put at least seven or eight rounds from an AK into one, center mass, and it just kept coming. The head is the best way to put them down. The woman nodded.

"Ok, thanks. I haven't had to fire at one yet." She noticed his shoulder just then. "How are you going to shoot with your arm like that? Didn't you say you were right-handed?"

"I'll do what I can." The Trooper just looked at him, then turned to face the oncoming army of no-longer-mythical beasts.

"Are you *really* going to *shoot* them?" the Oregon woman asked in a shrill voice.

"If they try to breach this facility, that's exactly what we're going to do," one of the Troopers replied.

"But how can you *do* that? They're probably an endangered species! They're surely protected by the government, like polar bears." The Trooper didn't bother to respond to the woman. Instead, he flipped off the safety on the AR he was holding and pulled back the charging handle to chamber a round. "I'm going to report you if you shoot that... gun!" she screeched. "I'll call the EPA, The Department of the Interior, my congressman, my senators, the White House, the governor – anyone who will listen! I'll have your job you murderer!" The Trooper turned to look at the woman.

"Lady, if you want to report me, go right ahead. Those things out there are about to try to *kill* you. If you don't want me to protect you then just walk right on out the door, get in your car, and drive away. I'm sure those things won't mind." The woman looked out at the sasquatches, their huge forms no more than twenty yards from the building now, and many of them covered in blood, and blanched. Then she gagged when one of them raised a human arm to its mouth and started gnawing.

"Well... maybe... um..."

"Then shut the fuck up and get back," the Trooper said. Jim smiled and glanced at the kid with the revolver.

He was covering his mouth with his hand and trying to turn his guffaw of amusement into a cough. The woman's husband decided he wanted his turn too, and he rounded on the Trooper.

"You police are all the same – nothing but violence and murder! And you're a misogynist to talk to my wife that way. We left Oregon to get away from people like you, and -" his wife cut him off.

"Coriander Flynn Smythe! We both know how evil and racist these... *police* are. Let's go. Those poor creatures won't hurt us. They're just misunderstood. It's people like this who have oppressed them and forced them to hide from the world for who knows how many centuries. Hunters and killers who take life for amusement and trophies. You're all just... stormtroopers of the patriarchy. Come on! I won't spend another minute in here with these *people*!" Coriander dutifully followed the woman toward the door. Jim thought it was strange that the woman had addressed the man the way an angry parent would talk to a recalcitrant child, but whatever; they were strange people.

"I wouldn't go out there if I was you," the woman Trooper said. Coriander glared at her as he walked past.

"I'll bet you'd like nothing better than to just *shoot* every single person in this hospital!" he said. "Those creatures out there will treat us better than *you* have!" The Trooper shook her head as the doors closed behind the delusional couple. "Idiots," she muttered. One of the other Troopers flipped a switch on the wall to deactivate the automatic opening mechanism on the doors.

Jim looked around the now quiet waiting area and saw the Troopers and about ten other people, all with guns, nervously facing the windows. The sasquatches were right outside now. They'd stopped walking and were standing in a skirmish line staring at the hospital. Coriander and his wife were walking slowly toward them, their hands raised and mouths moving, but no one could hear them through the thick glass. They were probably offering the sasquatches their entire granola stash and a dog-eared copy of The Complete and Unabridged Works of Karl Marx in return for safe passage. The sasquatches seemed surprised that humans were walking toward them instead of running away, and their expressions were as close to confused as Jim had yet seen. Coriander and the woman got to within three paces of them when four of the creatures stepped forward and began tearing the two well-intentioned but incredibly misguided and naïve people to shreds. "Morons," someone said. Their screams were just audible through the glass, and Jim looked away, not wanting to watch their final moments, no matter how stupid they'd been. The carnage was over in seconds, and everyone focused on the enemy before them.

The sasquatches had finished with the Oregon people and had turned their attention back to the hospital and the richer prey within. There was a long pause, like gunfighters in the old west facing off, then the sasquatches rushed the building en masse. "Aim for the heads!" Jim yelled. "Don't bother with center mass shots!" Guns began blasting and the windows exploded in showers of glass. The sound in the wide but shallow waiting area was thunderous, deafening. Sasquatches were falling under the barrage of rounds, but there were too many; several broke through the shattered windows and set upon the hospital's defenders. Jim had his pistol in his left hand, and he fired at one that was attacking the young man with the revolver. His round found its mark and the creature's head exploded. The kid nodded his thanks and turned to blast another one that was coming for him. Jim took his time and fired at sasquatches that were getting too close to humans. He dropped five before having to reload. The woman Trooper had emptied the magazine in her AR and was frantically trying to get another one out of a pouch on her duty belt when a huge specimen stalked toward her. Jim saw it just as he released the slide on the pistol which chambered another round, raised the gun and fired. The hollow point hit the creature's head, but it was a graze, not a fatal shot. It did give the woman just enough time to get another mag into the AR. She quickly chambered a round and fired, dropping the creature less than five feet from them.

The smell of cordite, blood and sasquatch stink was heavy in the air, and Jim wished he could either get a breath of fresh air, or at least cover his mouth. Someone screamed across the room; one of the defenders had gone down. Then another, and another. "Fall back!" someone yelled.

Jim raced toward the double doors that led deeper into the hospital and held one of them open. "Over here!" he called out, and the woman Trooper joined him and held the other door. Several people and all of the Troopers heard him and immediately ran for the doors. A couple others hadn't heard over the din, and as the roar of their last shots died out, they looked around and realized their predicament. Jim and the Trooper were still at the doors, and they yelled and waved at the small group of people. "Get over here," she screamed. There were four of them, Jim counted, and all dashed from where they were and made for the doors. The sasquatches were quick though, and three of the people fell before they got halfway to their goal. The last one, a man, ran through the doors and disappeared down a hallway. Jim and the woman, he noticed her nametag said Jenkins, pulled the doors closed behind them and thrust a metal broom stick through the handles. It wouldn't hold the big creatures for long, but all they needed was a few seconds to get away from the doors. Where to go after that was the real question. "How many rounds you got left?" Jenkins asked as they dashed away from the doors

"Two or three," Jim replied.

The trooper grunted and handed him her Glock service pistol. "Make them count," she said gruffly. "Got one more mag on my duty belt. I'll give it to you in a minute." He nodded.

They slid around a corner, nearly slipping on the linoleum floor, and ran down another hall. The crash of the doors being forced open behind them echoed through the building. No one else was in sight. Maybe they'd all run out a back door and were trying to get to their cars and go somewhere else, or they'd ascended the staircases to the hospital's upper floors. Jim wondered about the announcement he'd heard someone mention earlier that had caused all these people to congregate at the hospital, but there was no time to ask Jenkins about it. Self-preservation was much more important than learning little details.

They entered a big room with a nurse's station in the middle that was surrounded by exam rooms. The lights were on in the main room, but not in any of the others. A head popped up from behind the counter – one of the other Troopers. "Over here," the man whispered. Jim didn't think it was a good idea to hide there. The sasquatches could surround it easily and whoever was inside the rectangle-shaped station was done for. Then again, they could pick off the creatures as they entered the room from the hallway, then run out the far side if they started to get through. Lacking a better plan Jim followed Jenkins into the nurse's station and dropped to a knee, his chest heaving and shoulder blazing with pain. He felt fresh blood running down his right arm but ignored it.

"You ok?" Jenkins asked as she pulled the promised extra mag for the Glock from her duty belt.

Jim nodded as he took it from her. "Yeah. One of them bit me earlier tonight. I was coming here to see a doc." A rumble sounded from back down the hall before Jenkins could reply. The sasquatches had gotten through the door and were on their way.

"Lock and load!" one of the Troopers said. Jim wondered where everyone else had gone, and he took a quick look around. Eyes peered back at him from the dark exam rooms. People were hiding in here. If the Troopers and the others with guns didn't stop the sasquatches, everyone was dead. This place was a deathtrap. Why hadn't they just run? There had to be an emergency exit at the back of the building. No time to wonder about it now; the first sasquatch burst into the room and was felled by a bullet from someone. The crack of the gunshot was even louder here than it had been out in the waiting room. Jim thought his eardrums might have ruptured, and he swore that if he lived through this, he would be far more diligent about using earplugs anytime he was around loud noises.

His first guess at how many sasquatches were outside the hospital had been about a hundred. Jim had no idea if that was anywhere near accurate, or if more had joined since the battle had begun, but he was sure they'd killed well over fifty. More were pouring out of the hallway, met by gunfire, and they were dropping under the barrage of bullets, but there were just too many. In moments they'd broken free into the room and were converging on the nurse's station. Jim shot one that was reaching over the counter toward a Trooper, then another that was trying to rush through the entryway leading to the interior of the station. "Get out! I'll cover you!" one of the Troopers yelled. The shooters realized how tenuous their position was and all except the Trooper who'd volunteered to cover the others rose from their positions and dashed for the far side of the room, leaping over the counter and running toward exam rooms. Frightened screams rang out from those who'd been hiding instead of fighting, and people started panicking.

Jim watched Jenkins as she took position in the doorway of one room, her AR barking and dropping sasquatches. He'd ended up at the entrance to a hallway; a sign pointed the way to the imaging department. There was a cart of some kind next to him, laden with all manner of medical implements. One of them caught his eye – a bottle of rubbing alcohol, and an idea formed in his imagination. He picked up the bottle and unscrewed the cap. One of the sasquatches was about ten feet from him, facing away and seemingly unsure of which human it wanted to eat next, and Jim took two quick steps toward it. A squeeze of the bottle coated the big creature's back in alcohol, and Jim pointed the bottle at the floor, making sure to create a small puddle of the liquid right below it. He didn't smoke and didn't have a lighter, so he crouched down, put the barrel of the gun against the puddle and pulled the trigger. The small gout of fire from the pistol ignited the alcohol and flames suddenly jumped up the sasquatch's back. In seconds it was burning like a torch. The big monster let out an ear-wrecking screech of fear and pain that Jim had not heard from any of them until that moment. It caused the other sasquatches to stop what they were doing and look.

The flaming creature began running around in utter terror as the long hair on its body blazed. It crashed into two others that were menacing a Trooper who was desperately trying to reload his pistol, and then three were on fire. Those two began screaming and howling like the other, and also ran crazily around the room, bumping into yet more sasquatches and in moments most of them were ablaze. Smoke from burning hair and flesh began to fill the room, and the sprinkler system suddenly came on. That seemed to further discombobulate the creatures, and those who weren't on fire suddenly ran from the room, dragging as many of the dead sasquatches as they could. That explained why he hadn't seen any dead ones laying around, Jim thought. They took their dead with them. But there were too many corpses for the living sasquatches to take them all. The sprinklers quickly extinguished the flames on those who'd caught fire, and all but one of them were on the ground writhing in pain and slowly dying. The other hadn't been burned as badly and was still standing defiantly. It opened its mouth and roared in rage, then lunged toward a Trooper who was slowly converging on it, his pistol up and aimed at the creature. The Trooper fired and the sasquatch fell.

People were coming out of the exam rooms in various states of amazement and distress. Some were crying, some laughing hysterically, and others were grim and silent. A little boy about six years old was staring at one of the dead sasquatches. A woman, presumably his mother, stood behind him with tears streaming down her face. "Why did they want to kill us?" the little boy said.

"I don't know sweetie," the woman replied in a quavering voice.

"Didn't they like us?"

Jenkins had heard the little boy, and she walked over and knelt down in front of him. Sweat beaded her brow and her hair, which had been pulled back in a bun and stuffed under a fur cap, had come loose. Jim thought for the first time that she was quite pretty. "I don't know why they attacked us," she said to the little boy, "and we may never know. But I *do* know that you're safe now." The mother smiled at Jenkins through her tears and took her son's hand. The other Troopers were guiding people out of the slaughterhouse the room had become and were taking them to another part of the hospital. Nurses and doctors were tending to the wounded, and someone had figured out how to turn off the sprinklers. Everyone was soaked, but no one seemed to care. The last two living sasquatches were still writhing weakly, the rest having died, and once the room was clear of civilians, the Troopers used their service pistols to end the creatures' suffering.

"You should get that shoulder looked at," Jenkins said to Jim.

"Yeah. Probably. I don't really feel it at the moment though."

"Once the adrenaline wears off, it's going to hurt like hell," she said.

Jim nodded. She was right of course, but he didn't care at that moment. His shoulder had been hurting for the last… how long? Hour? Hour and a half? That was probably about right. He was amazed at how much had happened, how the world had changed so dramatically in such a short time. But didn't it often happen that way? Disasters, be they natural or man-made, often took very little time, relatively speaking, to cause their chaos. It was the clean up afterwards, putting everything back together again, that was the hard part, and which took the longest. "I'll find some ibuprofen. There are lots of people here who need a doctor more than I do."

Jenkins regarded him with a quizzical look. "Tough guy, huh?" she asked.

Jim smiled and was about to make a flippant reply when a male nurse walked up. "Let me take a look at that shoulder," he said. The pain was slowly coming back, just as he'd known it would, and Jim allowed the nurse to sit him down in a chair and examine his injuries. Jenkins had wandered off and was talking to some of the other Troopers. A couple of them were on their radios and cell phones, presumably reporting the events of the last few minutes to their superiors. The kid with the revolver walked by and Jim stopped him.

"Hey, what was that about an announcement you mentioned earlier?" he asked.

"You didn't hear it?" the kid replied. Jim shook his head. "It was on the radio, one of those emergency alert things that make that terrible squealing sound. It said for people to remain in their homes and barricade the doors and windows. It also said if you were not in a safe location to come here or to a couple other places. I think it mentioned a school, but I don't remember. I live in Chugiak but out this way, so this is where I came." Jim was no military strategist, but it did seem strange to him that the authorities would tell people to seek shelter here. Hospitals weren't exactly known for being hardened redoubts. Maybe it was a question he'd never know the answer to. It didn't matter now. He was here with all these people whose lives had been saved by a small group of armed citizens and a cadre of Alaska's finest. How they'd gotten here and why seemed immaterial in light of everything else.

The nurse had finished cleaning the bites and was now fretting over the collarbone. "This might need surgery," he muttered. "Gonna need x-rays to be sure." He dressed the bites and put a sling on Jim's right arm. "Don't move around too much until we get pictures of that," he said. Jim nodded. Sirens were wailing somewhere outside, and nurses were wheeling people in on gurneys. The sasquatch threat seemed to be over, and now the big job of tending to the wounded and cleaning up the mess had begun. Based on the number of people with injuries more severe than his that he saw just in this room, it might be a while before those x-rays happened. Jim considered just getting in his truck and going home, but the thought of Pam and what had happened to her torpedoed that idea. Jenkins had finished talking to her colleagues and was walking toward him.

"Just got word from headquarters," she said with a tired sigh. "The creatures have disappeared again. No one knows where they came from or where they went, but it's over for now."

"Good. I'm done with sasquatches."

Jenkins smiled. "Me too. What I really want is to go home, take a shower, and go to bed. After a couple of really stiff drinks."

The nurse was suddenly back at Jim's side. "Come on. You're next for an x-ray." Jim grinned at Jenkins and followed the man into the imaging center. A few minutes later the x-rays were finished, and he was back at the nurse's station. The bodies of the sasquatches were gone, and a cleaning crew was methodically working on the mess. Things were getting back to normal. It was strange to see something as mundane as a person mopping a floor after all he'd just gone through. The whole situation was utterly surreal. He watched as the cleaning crew righted toppled furniture and cleaned blood from the walls. The people had been moved to another part of the hospital; this room was too damaged by the sprinklers and gunfire to be usable. Jim heard a doctor talking to a nurse about the possible pathogens the sasquatches may have deposited here. Sterility was vitally important in hospitals, and the staff in this one had been on top of things from the first moment. Jim stood alone in the room, unsure of what to do next, or where to go. The nurse had told him to wait for the results of the x-rays but had left as soon as he'd gotten to the imaging department. Now the man was nowhere to be found. Should he go to the waiting room? Wander the hospital until he found the guy? Just go home and come back tomorrow? He decided to go find the man.

Jim walked slowly down the hall the sasquatches had come through on their way to the nurse's station. Voices reached his ears from somewhere ahead, and he made his way toward the sound. Doors and hallways led off this one into other parts of the building, some of them were labelled with names, others weren't. One caught his eye – Patient Relations. What exactly did that mean? If you were grumpy at a nurse who told you something you didn't want to hear about your unhealthy lifestyle you could file a complaint or something? Didn't like the Jell-O? Fill out this form! He sighed as he walked past the door. A thumping sound from inside it stopped him. He listened closely for a few seconds, waiting for it to reoccur. Jim stepped closer to the closed door and waited. There it was again. It sounded like someone had bumped or kicked the wall. Someone could be hurt in there, unable to speak. He opened the door, revealing a tiny office with a desk and three chairs. He stuck his head in and the snapping teeth of a sasquatch just missed his cheek. Jim yelled in startlement and backed out of the little room. The sasquatch came around the corner of the doorway; it had been right next to it, hiding just out of his line of sight. The creature was injured; it was moving slowly, and blood streamed down its right leg and from multiple spots on its chest. The thing should be dead with all that blood pouring out of it. But the malice in its eyes was very much alive.

"Hey!" Jim screamed. "There's another one here!" His back thumped into the far wall of the hallway, and he was suddenly paralyzed with a fear he hadn't yet experienced on this terrible night. The sasquatch was stalking toward him; there was no doubt of its intention. The thing's jaws were snapping, and silvery ropes of drool dripped from its fangs. "Hey!" Jim screamed again. "In here!" He had no idea if anyone had heard him or not. His hand went to his gun which was back in its holster on his hip. Then he remembered he was out of ammo. And he'd given Jenkins back her Glock. Unarmed and one-armed, Jim faced the sasquatch. Less than six feet separated them. The stench of the thing was cloying, overwhelming, and he nearly vomited. The creature stretched out its hand at Jim's frozen form; its fingers were inches away from taking hold of him, when a blast rang out in the hallway. The sasquatch's head exploded, and its body crumpled to the ground. Jim, shocked, turned his head to the left and saw the kid he'd talked to about the announcement. His big revolver was still in his hand, his arm extended, the barrel smoking lazily. "Got him," the kid said calmly.

Jim's knees gave out and he sank to the floor. His vision tried to go dark, but he fought it off. Shouts and the sound of people running brought him out of his daze, and he stood slowly. Four of the Troopers, Jenkins among them, came sprinting down the hallway and stopped when they reached Jim and the dead sasquatch.

"How the hell did we miss one?" one of the Troopers asked. No one answered.

"Nice shot," Jenkins said with a grin to the kid as he smiled and walked off. She looked at Jim appraisingly. "Can't always be the hero I guess."

Jim smiled, then started laughing, and soon everyone was laughing with him. How could they laugh now? After all this? It didn't seem possible. Who would laugh at such a time? Well, they would. Why *not* laugh? There would be time enough to mourn and be sad later. Right now, laughing seemed to be the most natural and therapeutic thing in the world. Forget everything else.

"You mentioned something earlier," Jim said to Jenkins as everyone's laughter died out and the other Troopers walked away, "and I was wondering if you're still up for it?"

"What?" she replied, obviously confused.

"A stiff drink."

Special thanks to Chris Schneider for giving me the title "Stuck on Fairview Loop" from which this story emerged.

# WHO OWNS IT

"Disinfect! Reinject!" the crowd chanted in unison as it marched through the city streets.

"What are they talking about mom?" the boy asked.

"They want that island across the bay given back to the native people who lived there before our ancestors came here," the mother replied.

"So, we weren't always here?"

"No, sweetie. My great grandparents came here from Europe. Your daddy's parents brought him here from Romania when he was a baby. The native people were here a long time before us. Lots of them used to live on that island, but it was taken from them by the government a long time ago. They want it back."

"But a lot of people live there now," the boy said with an expression of confusion on his cherubic face. "What would happen to them and their houses? All their stuff?"

The mother sighed softly. "I don't know."

"The measure is passed," the politician on the raised dais said as cameras clicked and flashed. "All citizens of the island in question will be remunerated to full market value for the properties seized under eminent domain.

Ownership, including all attendant rights and legal authority to the entire landmass is now passed to the group Citizens for Repatriation of Ancestrally Possessed Properties. This council is adjourned."

The journalist in the back of the room touched the screen of his phone and held it to his ear. "They passed it!" he exclaimed. "I can't believe the motherfuckers actually did it! It's the first time in history! They actually gave back stolen land to the people it was stolen *from*!" He listened for several moments while someone on the other end of the line spoke. "Yeah, you bet I got the whole thing on video. Even livestreamed it. If something happens to my phone, we can get everything from the cloud." The other person spoke again, for longer this time. "No shit," the reporter said in a somewhat quieter and less exuberant tone. "So, I might have to stay here a little longer then because these environmental assholes are bringing suit?" He listened again. "Well, fuck me."

The small group of people sat around the dining room table in the modest house on the quiet residential street. Cups of green tea steamed into the warm air as several pairs of eyes gazed worriedly at each other. At last, a slim, grey-haired man with round rimmed glasses finally spoke. "The deer were there before anyone, before people. That island *needs* to be a wildlife refuge. No one should be allowed on it at all. It should be reserved for animals and native flora *only*."

"We all agree with you," said a dreadlocked young woman across the table from him. "But the council gave it to those people, not to the animals like they should have. And the courts will take years to decide the matter. What are we supposed to do about it *right now*?"

"Fire," someone else said.

"We got it under control chief, but everything on the island is gone. Total loss. The drought turned the entire place into a tinderbox."

"Not much we can do about it," the voice coming over the radio said. "At least it was out there and not on the mainland. The whole city would have gone up. We'd have had Maui 2.0."

"There are some rumors floating around about boats being seen near the island late at night, and I have more than one report of a fire being spotted just before the whole thing went off. Most people seem to think it was a backyard firepit that got out of control."

"Whatever it was, our investigators will figure it out soon enough.

"It is the judgment of this court that after the devastating fire which so ravaged the island in question, and after hearing expert testimony from so many august and learned experts, that we find in favor of the plaintiffs. The island will henceforth be set aside as a nature and game preserve after thorough and exhaustive archaeological and anthropological studies are concluded. All previous judgments and rulings related to the landmass in question are hereby annulled and vacated. Court is adjourned."

The man on the train opened the news app on his phone and browsed the headlines. Another seven murders. A video. Another mob ransacking a department store. Another protest that turned into a riot complete with looting and destruction because someone somewhere was pissed off that they couldn't have their way. He yawned and scrolled down, his still sleepy eyes drooping as he tried to alleviate the boredom of his daily commute. Then a headline caught his attention, and he sat up straighter in his seat. Apparently, some dinosaur bones had been found on a local island during an excavation or something. Dinosaurs? Here? That was far more interesting than a group of undisciplined, petulant, entitled punks smashing everything they could find in an orgy of self-righteous violence, or the five people who'd been murdered the other day. Or wait, hadn't the headline said seven? Who cared. Dinosaurs were *interesting*. He read through the article with a gusto generally reserved for happy hour.

A man in a tweed jacket and conspicuously thick black glasses stood rigidly at a lectern in front of a lecture hall full of mildly attentive people. "Our team of professors, doctoral candidates, and undergraduates has determined unequivocally that dinosaurs predate other life on the island. Therefore, it is the recommendation of this committee that all flora and fauna that have been reintroduced to the island since the devastating fire of a few years ago immediately be humanely eradicated, and a program to reintroduce the island's original inhabitants, to include all plant and animal life, be implemented as soon as possible."

"Does this guy think Jurassic Park was real or something?" someone in the audience whispered.

"If you believe in evolution, then you must believe that even the dinosaurs began as something like salamanders," the man in front of the government building said through his bullhorn. "If we can't bring back the dinosaurs and give them the island like they deserve, then I say give it to the salamanders!"

The crowd gathered in front of him roared its approval.

"Chutes deployed nominally, capsule touchdown confirmed. Congratulations team Demeter – the first soil samples from another world have come to Earth."

"Now comes the hard part," said a thirtyish Asian woman to a fortyish middle eastern man. "We have to analyze that stuff."

"A meteorite crashed today on our local island which has been the scene of such controversy over the last few decades," the AI newscaster said. "Preliminary analysis after recovery indicates that its origin is Mars."

"The salamander project failed because not enough was done to protect them. There was no flora for them to hide in after the island was cleared, since we couldn't resurrect the plants from the Mesozoic era, and they all fell prey to predators, starvation and exposure." The man listening to the podcast on his headphones as he jogged on the treadmill shook his head. Would people never learn to quit playing around with nature? They were humans – not gods.

"After careful and thorough analyses, we have been able to determine without doubt that the meteorite did indeed come from Mars," the scientist said. He was in front of a camera but looking down at a piece of paper and reading from it. "The soil samples the Demeter project recovered some years ago are identical in composition to those retrieved from the meteor. Further, we have been able to confirm that the dinosaur bones recovered from the island where the meteor landed, bear identical chemical and molecular signatures to both."

"Is he saying what I think he's saying?" the university administrator asked. Another administrator next to him glanced over. "Yes, I think he is," she said. "Here comes the big news."

"We can now, after many years of extensive research and analysis, say without doubt that life on this earth originated on Mars."

"They brought the dinosaurs back and put them on that island, but they all died. Why would they do that? Didn't they know what would happen?" the girl whined to her high school classmates.

"You have to understand," the AI teacher on the screen at the front of the room said, "that in those days they didn't really know what they were doing. They thought they could control everything, right every wrong that had ever been committed. Their hearts were in the right place, but their minds had been riven and warped by ideology instead of shaped and molded by logic and reason."

"But the poor dinosaurs," the girl whined again. "My dad showed me a video of one dying in the snow. It looked so sad!"

"At that time there was a widespread belief that the earth was warming up dramatically due to human activity, despite voluminous evidence to the contrary. Had the contention been true the climate would have been perfect for reptilian lifeforms such as dinosaurs. Unfortunately for those creatures, humans were incorrect. Opinions from that era regarding the climate were not materially different from the belief centuries before it that the earth was flat."

"So, all the dinosaurs they worked so hard to bring back to life all died because they were wrong about the earth warming up?"

"Yes."

"Well, everything began with the big bang," the physicist on the panel discussion said. "It's that singular moment that has given birth to everything – the cosmos, the stars and planets, life. We're all, every one of us, just cosmic dust when you reduce us to our basest elements."

"Ashes to ashes, dust to dust," the minister said over the grave of the deceased.

"All those in favor say 'aye', those opposed 'nay'." The man in the huge chamber waited several moments. "The ayes have it," he said at last. "Operation Shiva has been approved."

The airplanes flew high above earth, their contrails crisscrossing the sky like lines on an azure chalkboard. At a command from some authority, they released their payloads just as scores of missiles launched from silos all around the world.

The family sat in their living room watching on the screen mounted to the wall as the end of everything neared.

"Why are they doing this mommy?" a little girl asked.

"Because no part of this world belongs to anyone, and it's not fair for us to have more than someone else, or to own something that used to belong to a different group of people. Like that scientist said, we're not anything other than cosmic dust, so they are returning us to what we once were so that we will all be equal."

"But doesn't that mean we're going to die?" Unshed tears filled her eyes as she gazed imploringly at her mother.

"Yes."

Far out in space, beyond the moon and the orbit of Mars, a craft floated silently in the darkness. Its crew watched as the small orb so far away was transformed from a beautiful greenish-blue into a hellish fiery grey.

"Well, give it a few galactic cycles to settle down, then we'll go reseed it. Just like we did for that other planet last cycle," one small mouthless and eyeless creature said silently and telepathically to the one next to it.

"What a bunch of morons," the other creature replied. The rest of the crew began chuckling at this most unexpected development. They'd been watching that planet for thousands of cycles, waiting for the moment its inhabitants reached a certain level of technological proficiency at which time they would have peacefully introduced themselves and invited the planet and its entire population into the galactic community. But no. They'd decided to blow themselves up instead. Idiots. They deserved it.

"Hey! Anybody wanna cruise the Crab nebula?"

# ON ICE

"No, you fucking heard me right. I want them to freeze my corpse when I'm dead." He did not slur the 'g' at the end of the expletive. The people in the board room far up in the high-rise office building in the financial district of the big city stared at the older man at the head of the long conference table. It was extremely rare they heard him use profanity. When he did it usually meant someone was about to lose their job. Fall from these lofty heights if you will. With no golden parachute to slow their descent to the gutter below.

"Sir," began a middle-aged man halfway down the table. Rank in this company was everything. Those with it sat closer to the man at the head. Those without sat further away. It was sycophantic and hierarchical, but just the way the man at the head wanted it. Those below him needed to know exactly where they were in this stratified room. The man's middling rank should have precluded him from even speaking at this event, but something had gotten the best of his self-control. Ambition perhaps? Perplexity? Presumption? It didn't matter. He'd now drawn the attention of the patriarch, the lord of this fiefdom. A most unwise choice in the best of circumstances. This was not the best. "Are you sure you want to-" He didn't finish the question.

"Get out Jensen." His voice was even, measured, calm, without a hint of anger or malice. The very absence of emotion made it somehow more chilling, more impactful.

The middle-aged man peered at the older man with disbelief. His open mouth began to twist itself into a word forming shape, but he never got the chance to say what was on his mind.

"I didn't fucking stutter. I said get out." The older man's voice hadn't changed, but his right arm was raised, hand pointing toward the door. This was unprecedented. *Two* curse words during the same meeting. It had never happened. No one else spoke as Jensen stood slowly from his chair, picked up his leather binder and pen, left his half full coffee cup on the table and quietly left the room. He stared blankly at the old man's aged hand, which was still pointing toward the door, as he left. Eyes did not follow him. Watching someone who'd just been fired take their walk of shame out the door was considered bad form among this group. And bad luck. No one wanted to be next.

"I trust I don't need to reiterate." No one spoke. "Like I said a few moments ago, freeze my body when this disease has finally claimed me. That is my final directive to you. There is a company in Switzerland I've retained who will store my remains until such time as the technology exists to… resurrect me. My will has been recorded, and all my assets will be placed in trust. I will reclaim them in my… second life." His eyes scanned the room in a deliberate search for challengers. There were no takers. "You all have copies of my will and directives in the folders in front of you. Legal has assured me that all my affairs are tidied up, so there is really nothing more to say. Maybe we will see each other again, maybe not." The man stood from the plush chair at the head of the table and strode from the room without another word.

D. Pierce Bresnahan started InCopis shortly after graduating from college. The investment firm had grown over the decades to become one of the most influential and successful firms of its kind anywhere in the world, and had made him extremely wealthy in the process. His prescient knowledge of markets and finances had propelled him to mythical status among his peers, while his icy and decisive managerial style had led to comparisons with Stalin and Che Guevara among his employees. Pierce, he never went by his given first name – Dudley, had devoted his entire life to growing the behemoth that InCopis now was. His life was his work, his company. Pierce had never married, and he'd never liked or wanted children, so at twenty-six he'd had a vasectomy. His idea of legacy was reserved for where his name would be placed among the pantheon of the world's giants. Thoughts of pampered and entitled progeny appearing in the tabloids along with the salacious details of their latest scandal sickened him, and he never regretted not reproducing. Pierce had never devoted much time to thinking about when his life would end or what he would do with his wealth when that time arrived. Until he got a phone call from his doctor after a routine physical.

"Mr. Bresnahan," his secretary said when he picked up the phone, "Dr. Monroe is calling for you."

"Put him through." He waited while the call was transferred.

"You there D?" a voice asked.

"Yeah, I'm here." Paul Monroe was the only person alive he allowed to call him D. They'd met in college as freshmen and had been friends ever since. Pierce Bresnahan did not have friends. He had employees, associates, and a very few peers. Most people would have been surprised to find that there was someone in the world he actually considered a friend. Paul's life had taken him into medicine where he'd built a moderately successful private practice. Pierce wouldn't go to another doctor.

"I have… news for you. Want it in person or over the phone."

He sat perfectly still at his desk for a few silent moments. Paul was not one to gloss things over. It was the main reason they'd become friends – he was frank and direct, just like Pierce himself. "Just tell me Paul," he said. His friend sighed through the phone.

"You've got cancer."

Those three words, spoken over the phone three years ago, initiated the series of events that had inexorably led Pierce to this precise moment, and to the unpleasantness his doctors assured him was just ahead. He walked from the boardroom to his office down the hall and stood in front of the floor-to-ceiling windows. This view had greeted him every workday morning for the last thirty-three years, and had said goodbye to him every night. Now he was looking at it for the last time. With these eyes at least. His personal possessions, the ones he wanted to keep anyway, had already been packed and moved to a long-term storage facility. All that was left in here was the furniture. His prized possession, an original Peter Paul Rubens oil on canvas he'd bought from a private collector for an exorbitant sum, and which had once hung on the wall across from his desk, was on indefinite loan to a museum. Pierce glanced at the empty wall, the sprawling city below, and around the room, then spun on his heel and left his office, and his company, for the last time in this life.

A few minutes later, in the backseat of his chauffeured Bentley, Pierce reflected on the last three years. He was not prone to melancholy, and this was not a moment of sadness, but one of contemplation. After Paul had given him the cancer news, he'd done what his old friend had told him to and visited a world-renowned oncologist. He'd been mildly surprised to discover that it was a woman. From India. Pierce cared about competency rather than gender or what continent one's DNA originated on, and when she'd given him her diagnosis, he'd accepted it as he would have had it come from Paul Monroe. Three to five years, she'd told him. That was how much life he had left. At sixty-four he'd lived well, far better than most humans who had ever existed. But he still had things he wanted to do. Politics had rarely interested him unless the machinations of the mindless in that arena affected his business. He'd hired consultants and lobbyists to deal with that morass of filth. Philanthropy, he'd always thought, was for the weak and guilt-ridden. It was something trust fund kids and bleeding hearts got involved in to make themselves feel better about their wealth, earned or inherited. Pierce was interested in two things – acquisitions and domination. Worldwide. He'd bought countless companies over the years, both foreign and domestic, folding them into his own organization where they'd helped it become the juggernaut that it was. He'd purchased huge swathes of real estate that ranged from dilapidated tenements and slums to entire middle-class neighborhoods and opulent modern palaces masquerading as homes. He also owned the building where his company was headquartered. Pierce wanted to own it all, control it all. He'd even bought people. The right palm greased at the right time was an art form he'd long ago mastered. He had assets in every industry imaginable – communications, technology, medicine and biotech, mineral extraction, transportation and logistics, manufacturing, aerospace. D. Pierce Bresnahan was into all of it. He even owned a couple farms and restaurant chains.

But he wanted more. Always more. The cancer had ruined that. Cut everything off. All his plans, like some fragile icicle, had fallen off the gutter and shattered on the ground below. Then he remembered the news article about the place in Switzerland. Cryonics was nothing new. It had been talked about for years. He recalled the famous baseball player, Ted Williams, and how supposedly his head had been frozen with this method so that someday he could be brought back to life. Pierce had never paid much attention to the technology or the stories about it. The entire thing was a curiosity, nothing more than bad science fiction someone was trying to make real. Except that the Swiss company claimed to have resurrected some animal test subjects.

Pierce had forgotten about the article until after his cancer diagnosis. When it popped into his mind one day during a radiation treatment, he'd sent a contingent of his people to investigate. They'd returned with surprising news – the Swiss had done exactly what they'd claimed. That was when his ruined plans had reconstituted themselves. The technology did not yet exist to resurrect humans, but, his people assured him, the Swiss were making great progress, far more than others who were trying to do the same thing. Ted Williams could stay in the freezer in Arizona or wherever he was. Pierce was going to Europe.

The customized Boeing 737 landed in Geneva several hours after his final board meeting. He'd owned the plane for over twenty years, and it had flown to nearly every country in the world. After this, its last flight, it would be leased out. Pierce didn't like the idea of others flying around in his plane. He'd been involved in every aspect of the refurbishment after he'd bought it, right down to picking out the upholstery and the wine selection. It was, like the Rubens, one of his prized possessions. And he was leaving it for others to enjoy. He sighed in regret as he got into the Range Rover that was waiting to convey him to the country chalet with the spectacular mountain views where he would spend his last few days and weeks.

The bucolic scenery of Switzerland flashed by out the window as Pierce mulled over what would happen next. There were a number of administrative things yet to handle – forms to sign, tests to take. It was all very bureaucratic. The only thing Pierce despised more than incompetence was bureaucracy. In his mind they were nearly one and the same thing. Bureaucracy, it seemed to him, was something unimaginative and ineffective people put in place to disguise their own shortcomings and ineptitude. It was utterly unnecessary and overburdened nearly everything in civil society. Maybe when he came back from wherever he was going he would end it forever. It would be his welcome-back-to-the-world gift to humanity. That thought perked him up a bit, and he gazed in appreciation at an enormous massif in the distance. Switzerland was surely one of the loveliest countries in the world, and he was content to spend his remaining days here.

Their destination was just outside the town of Thun, and Pierce fell asleep to the hum of tires on asphalt. A hand on his shoulder gently shook him awake, and he looked out the window at the opulent chalet that was now home. It was a beautiful summer day that was stretching toward evening, and Pierce was hungry. His cancer treatments had mostly destroyed his appetite, but today was one of the good days when it had returned. What was bad was the pain. Medications did little to blunt its sharpness, and it was particularly brutal as he extricated himself from the back seat of the Range Rover. Pierce winced as he stood up. The people here had one job – to care for him until his last moment. There were nurses, chefs, cleaning staff, and a cadre of burly security guards whose jackets bulged with muscles and concealed pistols, even a husband-and-wife team of gardeners to tend the immaculate grounds. He would lack for nothing while he lived. Just like his entire adult life.

A doctor and a lawyer were waiting for him in the study. Of course there would be a lawyer. Aren't there always lawyers? Well, he was an extremely wealthy man, and large estates required a lot of planning and legal maneuvering. Lawyers were an unpleasant necessity. Like shitting. The doctor was only there to verify that he was of sound mind so he could sign the papers the lawyer had for him. Those papers were the final river to cross before going into the deep freeze. The cancer was progressing more rapidly than his oncologist was comfortable with, and they'd decided to hasten his end via assisted suicide. It would be better to leave this world early, before natural death from the disease claimed him, thereby preserving as much healthy tissue in his body as possible for the future resurrection. No one knew what medical technology would be capable of in years to come, but why take chances? The entire operation consisted of nothing more than extra bureaucracy. As Pierce signed the papers absolving anyone and anything of responsibility and culpability for his passing, he daydreamed for a moment about having taken all of this to some lawless and non-bureaucratic place where none of it would be necessary. Like Somalia.

When the papers were signed and the lawyer (thankfully!) gone, the doctor lingered behind. He was a fortyish Swiss man of slight build and with a pronounced, Pierce thought it ghastly, widow's peak. There was something in his eyes that looked like pity. He instantly hated the man but could tell he wanted to speak. "Is there something else?" he asked flatly, concealing the scorn he felt.

"Are you sure you want to do this?" the doctor asked haltingly. "I hesitate to say it, but if the soul exists, and I personally believe it does, then you will probably be in a place you won't want to come back from."

"Are you asking if I believe in God? Heaven and all that?"

"In a manner of speaking," the doctor replied. "Just for the sake of conversation, what if there is an afterlife, if those things are real? And what if it is as beautiful and peaceful as some of the world's religions have led us to believe? Would you really want to leave such a place and return here? If it even becomes possible to do so? I only ask because if we do develop the ability to resurrect you, then you may not wish to return once you're there, but also may not be able to stop it or tell us not to do it."

Pierce stared at the doctor for a long moment. He was tempted to tell the man that his question was presumptuous and invasive, but resisted the urge. "I have things I still want to do in this world. If your hypothetical situation ever becomes reality, well, I'll deal with it then. If this afterlife of yours is as pleasant as you seem to believe it is, then I can always kill myself again. Right now, I'm tired from the trip and would like a nap." He turned away from the doctor and walked upstairs to his bedroom.

Pierce hadn't decided how much longer he wanted to live before voluntarily ending his life. He'd intentionally left his self-imposed expiration date blank in case anything unexpected happened. Nothing did, and after a week he was ready. He told one of the nurses that it was time, and a few hours later a team of medical experts, including the doctor with the widow's peak, were gathered at the chalet for his last moments. The pain from the cancer had grown to the point that even the strongest drugs weren't helping, and Pierce didn't want to endure it any longer. Besides, what was he waiting for? There would be no cure coming any time soon. The cynical part of him said that there never would be a cure. There was just far too much money tied up in everything related to cancer – research, treatment, end of life care, drugs, surgeries. Cancer, and diseases in general, were multi-billion-dollar industries, not unlike the company he'd built. Too many people had too much to lose if a cure for cancer ever made its way to market. Even funeral homes would see their finances impacted negatively. That was another reason he'd decided to end his life – to pass the time until the social and economic conditions of the world changed enough to allow a cure for cancer to be widely released should one ever be developed. That time was not now, or even in the foreseeable future, so this was his only true option. He'd heard some rumors that a cure already existed and that it was being suppressed by powerful forces, but he didn't believe that. In his position, with the contacts and influence that he had, if there was a cure, he'd have heard of it.

The procedure itself was relatively simple. He'd been prescribed a lethal dose of a barbiturate called Secobarbital. All he had to do was open the capsules and dump the powder inside them into a glass of something and drink it. The doctors had recommended something with a powerful flavor to mask the bitterness of the drug. Pierce had been strangely preoccupied by what that something, that beverage, would be. It would likely be the last thing he ever drank, in this life at least, and the options had been spinning through his mind for the last two days. He was mildly annoyed at his own inability to make a decision and banish the thoughts. Indecisiveness was utterly out of character for him. He'd finally narrowed the choices down to fresh squeezed blood orange juice, or a bottle of Penfolds Grange Hermitage 1951, which at over one hundred and forty thousand dollars per bottle was more an investment item than an apéritif. Pierce finally decided on a compromise. He would take the Secobarbital mixed with orange juice, then enjoy a last glass of his favorite wine afterwards. It was unwise to mix barbiturates and alcohol, but what did he have to be afraid of? He was killing himself anyway. That was the whole point of this exercise.

It was time. The cocktail of Secobarbital and blood orange juice was mixed, and the wine was poured, the medical team was all present, and a refrigerated van from the cryo company was standing by to transport his corpse to their facility where it would immediately be processed for long term storage. All he had left to do was die. But that was the part he was now struggling with. Talking about it, planning it, had been easy. It was all just administrative and bureaucratic gobbledygook. Now he actually had to imbibe a lethal dose of drugs. He had to voluntarily end his own life – a life he loved more than anything else. Here he was, one of the wealthiest and most influential people in the world, in a hospital bed in an opulent Swiss chalet, surrounded by doctors and nurses and attendants and functionaries, about to leave, of his own free will, this life that had given him so much. No, this life that he had made, through sheer force of will, into what it was. What it had been. What he hoped it would be again in the future. It was far harder than he'd thought it would be to pick up that glass and down it. There was such a small amount of liquid in it – only about half a soda can worth, probably not more than six fluid ounces, or here in Europe where they use that god-awful metric system, one-hundred and seventy-five milliliters.

Everyone was gathered around the bed where he lay. The drinks were on a nightstand to his right. All eyes were on him. Pierce looked around at the gathered faces. They wore a range of expressions from concern and sympathy (both of which annoyed him), to boredom and even irritation and impatience (which infuriated him). He briefly entertained the idea of calling the whole thing off so he could berate everyone for their reactions to his last moments. But no. That seemed… cowardly. He'd come here to do this – this exact thing – at this exact moment. Delaying it would only exacerbate his agitation and harden the expressions of the spectators into visages that would drive him to rage. Without a word Pierce reached over and picked up the juice glass, downing the liquid in three large gulps, then sat back against the raised backrest of the hospital bed to wait for the end. The doctors had told him that within five minutes or so he would slip into a coma. Death would follow anywhere from thirty minutes to two days afterwards. The duration depended on the subject's physical condition and weight. The doctors assured him that he would probably last no more than a few hours at most and would likely leave the world within the first hour after drinking. Pierce ignored the audience and picked up the other glass, savoring the intense flavor of the red wine as it washed away the slight bitterness left from the drug's passage over his tastebuds. He sipped the wine slowly and was slightly disappointed when he swallowed the final drops.

"That bottle isn't going to finish itself," he said calmly to the room. "You all might as well polish it off. How many other times in your life will you get to drink a bottle of wine that costs more than most of you make in a year?"

He was satisfied with the reactions on the faces. Most visibly bristled at his blatant and pointed denigration of their economic status vis á vis his own. One man to his left even grumbled something under his breath. Yes, this was as it should be. People needed to know their places. The anxiety he'd felt about dying was gone, replaced by the smug satisfaction of knowing that he was still in charge, in command, above these people in every way, no matter what they might think.

Pierce was starting to feel the effect of the drug and the wine. His eyelids were drooping, and his body felt heavy. Soon he would fall asleep. Then the coma. Then death. Then he would find out what really came next. Would he be reincarnated like Hindus and Buddhists believed? Or maybe the Abrahamic religions were right, and he'd go to heaven or hell. Or maybe none of them knew anything about it and had just made things up over the centuries for one reason or another. Pierce didn't claim to know and had very little curiosity about what happened after death except academically in relation to how it would affect his potential return to his soon-to-be-dead body.

That body felt very heavy now. It was nearly impossible to keep his eyes open, and his thoughts were fuzzy, muddy, jumbled. As his eyelids closed for the last time, he heard someone in the room speak. The words were difficult to make out. His ears felt like they had cotton balls stuffed in them. He couldn't tell if it had been a man or a woman who'd spoken. What had the words been? Someone else spoke. Closer to him. Easier to make out. He understood these words. Accented. Swiss? German? Not American. "Yeah, the world will definitely be a better place when that motherfucker is gone."

The sky was that color somewhere between grey and white that one sometimes encounters on overcast days. The featurelessness of the clouds was so complete that it was impossible to tell where they began, and vacant air ended. But why was he looking at the sky? Sounds drew his attention and slowly his head tilted forward to its normal position. He was in a huge line of people. There were other equally huge lines on either side of him and more beyond them, all enclosed within twenty-foot-tall grey walls spaced about a hundred yards apart. He was reminded of crowds entering a stadium for a sporting event. (Or cattle in a chute at the slaughterhouse.) At stadium gates there were always multiple attendants checking tickets, and each one had a line of people stacked up waiting to get through just like this. Except he was not a fan of sporting events. And this was not a stadium. So, what the hell was it?

The ground was flat and comprised of a material the same grey as the walls and that looked like concrete, but which was soft like grass. There had to be thousands of people here. A woman in line directly ahead turned and looked at him. She had a face that reminded him of people from Latin America and a bright smile. "Just arrived, I see," she said.

"Who? You or me?"

"Both of us." The line moved forward a couple steps. Someone at the front had passed through whatever barricade was up there. What exactly *was* up there? He couldn't see; there were too many people in the way. But the top of another wall horizontally connecting those on either side was visible. So there had to be a gate or doorway of some kind.

"Are you alright?" the woman asked. He stared at her with a frown, still trying to work out what this place was and how he'd gotten here. What was the last thing he remembered? Yes, that voice. It had insulted him. He was going to find out who had said that and destroy their life. No. He wasn't. This was not the world he knew. It was the next place. He was dead. Understanding collapsed on him, and it must have shown on his face because the woman touched his arm as her own face adopted a look of concern.

"Did you just remember, just figure it out?"

"Yes," he managed to stammer. He was having a hard time reconciling the situation. The line shifted forward again, and he unconsciously moved with it. But why should he be having trouble accepting the fact that he himself had put in motion the very events that had deposited him here? Maybe being dead and knowing it was just too much for a person to handle. But the woman didn't seem to be having any trouble.

"It'll be fine," she said with a look of understanding. "It took me a minute to figure out where I was, then I realized that this was the start of my next adventure. Isn't it exciting?!"

He stared at the woman with an incongruous mixture of contempt, fascination and perplexity. How could she possibly think this was going to be an adventure? He was here until his body back on Earth could be resurrected. This place was a waiting room, nothing more.

"Uh, yeah, sure," he said as he looked again toward the front of the line. He still couldn't see anything. But he did notice that everyone here was wearing the same thing.

Their outfits were a hideous shade of avocado green that reminded him of kitchen countertops from the 1970's. The clothing itself was all the same style – trousers and a loose-fitting short sleeved shirt very similar to hospital scrubs. There was not a jacket or hat anywhere in sight. Shoes were the same color and were of the slip-on variety like those kids that rode skateboards wore. What were they called? Trucks or cars or something? He seemed to remember buying the company that made them, but damned if he could remember its name. Then another fact registered on his still muddled consciousness. Every conceivable type of person was here from the youngest newborn to the oldest of the old, and every skin color genetics had created.

"Yes," the woman said as if she'd read his mind, "everyone here is dead. Just like you and I are." A scream from directly behind them caused him to jump. He spun around and found himself looking at a young black man who was frantically patting his chest as if looking for something.

"You're alright," the woman said as she leaned around him to speak to the new arrival. "Whatever happened it's all over now."

"I was with my sister. We were walking to the market and a car drove up. A man with a gun leaned out and…"

"Where are you from sweetie?" she asked.

"Haiti," the young man replied. "Where am I?"

"The next place," she said. "What's your name?"

"Wilky."

"And what's yours?" she asked looking at her other conversation partner.

"Pierce," he said distractedly. He was still trying to see what was happening up ahead and still failing. The line moved forward again, several paces this time, and he thought maybe a group had gone through. The kid's scream had turned a number of heads, but they'd all turned back, their curiosity satisfied. He watched the ends of the lines. People were randomly appearing, just materializing out of the air. One moment there was nothing, the next there was a person. He watched one of the lines next to his as three people appeared simultaneously.

"Some kind of accident," the woman said quietly. Wilky was crying quietly to himself. "He'll be ok in a minute," she said to Pierce. "Something about this place makes us get over our grief pretty quickly."

"How do you know all this?" Pierce asked testily. "You're in line right in front of me, which means you couldn't have been here very long before I arrived, but you seem to know all about it. How?"

She smiled serenely. "Because I've been here before." Pierce frowned at her. "It wasn't like I died on the operating table and had one of those out-of-body experiences. I lived a completely different life once, and I remember it."

"What are you saying? That you've been…reincarnated?"

"Of course. All of us have. You too, even if you don't remember."

She sounded like one of those crackpot New Age weirdos. Next thing he knew she'd be talking about crystals, pyramids, and the ascension. Or aliens. Pierce wondered if cutting ahead in line would cause him to be sanctioned in some fashion. But who would administer it? There were no cops, no attendants like in an airport TSA line with people in uniform telling you to take everything out of your pockets and your laptop out of your bag. There wasn't even a line monitor in an orange vest with a Stop/Slow sign they would spin around like a traffic flagger. So, what was stopping him from just leaving this woman and the mewling kid and walking to the front of the line? Nothing. But that wasn't entirely right, was it? There *was* something. A feeling inside him. It would not allow him to leave his spot. Infuriating. He wanted nothing more than to just stride away toward that wall at the front of the line and demand to see someone in authority. But he couldn't. He might as well have been wearing concrete shoes like the mobsters used to put on their victims just before they dumped them into some body of water. As much as he wanted to leave, D. Pierce Bresnahan wasn't going anywhere.

The kid had finally stopped sniveling, and the woman had ceased jabbering, and Pierce, although he despised queues, had reached a form of détente with himself about being in this one. It had been decades since he'd had to wait for anything. A man in his position, with his resources and influence, simply did not wait. The line was moving steadily if more slowly than he'd have liked, and Pierce amused himself by waiting until a new person appeared and imagining the scenario in which they'd died. An elderly man appeared a few lines away who had a beatific smile on his face. He'd probably had Alzheimer's and was happy to finally remember his own name and not shit himself uncontrollably. There a fortyish woman crying her eyes out. She'd gotten drunk and driven at high speed into a highway bridge support column. A child, little boy of about seven or eight looking utterly perplexed. Little brat ran out in front of a car chasing some toy or other that had gotten away. A group of nine or ten middle eastern looking people, both men and women and of varying ages appeared within seconds of each other in the same line. Probably killed in a suicide attack by some jihadi. Pierce was just beginning to enjoy himself and his game when he realized the front of the line was very near.

The woman hadn't spoken to him in a while, but she turned and gave him a grin. "Almost there. Are you excited?"

"No. I just want to get it over with."

"Ooohhh, I can't wait!" She was practically giddy with anticipation.

"For what?" he asked. "Do you know what happens next?"

"No. I don't remember that part. But I do know that I'm going to live again. I hope this time I get to go somewhere tropical. Where would you like to be reborn?"

Pierce ignored her question, and she finally realized, after several long moments of smiling at him idiotically while she waited for his answer, that he wasn't going to give her one. The disappointment on her face as she turned away was quite satisfactory.

He ignored her and craned his neck around the line of people in order to get a view of its end. The sight was anticlimactic. Pierce didn't know what he'd expected, but it wasn't the middle-aged black woman wearing the same style of clothing as everyone else but in tones of Grey Poupon mustard and holding a clipboard. Behind her, in the face of the wall, was a plain metal door without window. It looked like the door to a janitor's closet one might find in any commercial building. Other people dressed in the same vomitous color as her stood at the head of each line and in front of an identical door. Pierce counted twenty-seven to the left and nineteen to the right of his own line. The woman was speaking to an elderly Asian man, but he couldn't hear what they were saying. She said a few words to him, he responded, and she looked at her clipboard. A moment later she looked up, said something, and gestured toward the door. The man smiled, opened the door, and disappeared inside. Pierce couldn't tell what was beyond the threshold.

Two people later it was the woman's turn. She gave him a sterile glance and stepped up to the woman with the clipboard. Pierce strained to hear what they were saying to each other, but it was as if there was a soundproof barrier between them. He could see their lips moving as they conversed, but the only noise was the murmur of conversations around him and the occasional scream or wail of a new arrival. The conversation between the women lasted longer than the others he'd seen, and Pierce was getting impatient. His former line mate was probably telling the unfortunate line monitor about how she'd been reincarnated before and wanted to go to Fiji or some damned place this time. No doubt boring the other woman's ears off like she had his. He was about to tell them to hurry it up when the clipboard holder gestured toward the door, and the other woman disappeared inside. His turn.

Pierce strode up and planted himself in front of the woman. "Name?" she asked. Her tone was not exactly bored, but not warm either. It was… official. Yes, that was the word. He'd used the same tone himself countless times when speaking to his employees.

"You don't know my name?" he asked. This was perplexing. Shouldn't these people in the mustard-colored clothes know who he was? Wasn't this the afterlife? Shouldn't they be… omnipotent or something?

"If I knew who you were, I'd have just looked at my list," she replied in the same confident tone. Pierce bristled a bit. He was the one who spoke like this, not the one spoken to.

"D. Pierce Bresnahan."

"What's the D stand for?" She glanced at the line behind him. Her expression was reminiscent of a fast-food restaurant cashier who's just seen a bus load of high school kids pull into the parking lot five minutes before closing time. Pierce was tempted to upbraid the woman for her condescension, but restrained himself just before a biting comment escaped his mouth.

"Dudley," he said through gritted teeth. He'd always hated that name. It had belonged to some ancestor of his, or so his father had told him. Pierce hadn't cared. Dudley was a horrendous name for a child, and he'd turned it into an abbreviation and adopted Pierce early in life. The teasing in school had been merciless.

The woman glanced up at him with an unreadable expression. Was she about to mock his name? He had a retort ready if she did. But she looked down at her clipboard. Pierce looked too and saw a simple piece of white paper with two columns of words on it. She ran her finger down the column on the left until she found his name. The column on the right contained a row of single words. The word next to his name was Interview. He couldn't stop himself. "What does that mean?" he asked testily.

She gave him a cool glance. "It means you've been selected for further screening. Through that door please. Someone will be with you shortly."

"Further screening? What is this? I paid an exorbitant sum to have my body cryonically frozen so that when a cure for my disease is finally discovered, I can be brought back to life."

"That's probably why you were selected," she said. Her tone was as flat as her stare. She clearly had no idea who he was.

"What does that have to do with it?"

The woman cocked her head to the side as if she were about to speak to an idiot. It made Pierce furious. "You know," she said, "most people are pretty happy when they get here. Once they get over the surprise of being dead. I haven't had to call security in three centuries, but I can if I need to. Now do you want me to do that, or do you want to just go through the door?"

"How dare you threaten me –" was all he got out. The woman twirled her finger in the air, and two huge men appeared on either side of him. They were easily seven feet tall and enormously muscled. Both were dressed in the same clothes as everyone else, but their color was an awful shade of brick red. Pierce looked from one to the other. The men were staring at him with identical expressions - like he was a grotesque bug that had just landed in their bowl of oatmeal.

Pierce stared haughtily at the goons, then at the woman with the clipboard, and silently, but in as dignified a fashion as he could manage, walked through the door.

He was in a room. The lights were bright here. They irritated and stung even though his eyes should have been used to the light. Pierce looked around in confusion. The first thing he saw were the lights themselves. They looked like any other fluorescent fixture that he'd ever seen; the kind with two long bulbs running in parallel. There were just a lot more of them mounted to the ceiling than were really necessary. White ceiling behind the lights. Light grey walls. Tiled floor made of what looked like those asbestos versions from the 50's, and they'd been installed in an alternating grid pattern of medium grey and black like a chess board. The room wasn't large, maybe twenty-five feet square. In the middle was an old metal desk which also looked like it was from the 50's. There was a single chair on either side. The chair closest to him was a larger version of the hard and uncomfortable chairs he'd sat in way back in grade school. Wooden seat, metal frame, no armrests. He'd hated those chairs. The other chair was made entirely of wood and was just like the equally uncomfortable chairs the teachers had used all those years ago. It did have armrests. He'd sat in one once when his fifth-grade teacher had left the room for some reason, and it had been just as bad as the chairs provided to the students. In fact, this room reminded him quite a lot of his fifth-grade classroom. If there were half the number of lights, three big chalkboards mounted end to end and a slew of desks (with those medieval torture devices that posed as chairs), it would have looked very much like that room. But there was no teacher nor any students. Only him. On the far side of the room was another door. Solid wood with a narrow and vertical rectangular window. The glass had that little diamond shaped wire mesh in it. Safety glass or something. He'd never really known why the wire was inside the glass. What was the point? What did the wire do? Receive radio signals? Keep someone from breaking into the classroom? Who would do that? Everyone wanted to leave school, not get in and hang around. It hadn't made sense to him then and didn't now.

Where was he? Why was he alone? The sound of the door opening drew his attention. A man walked in. He was on the younger side, perhaps thirty, lean, severe of face, and wearing yet again the same clothes but in a pleasant shade of royal blue. Why couldn't he have gotten that color? The avocado green made him want to vomit every time he looked at it. The man sat in the teacher's chair, opened a desk drawer, and withdrew a plain manila folder which he opened and began to flip through disinterestedly. "My name is Davis," he said in a bored tone.

"Is that a first name or last?" The man stared at him as if he were a mildly interesting exhibit in some obscure and sparsely visited museum but didn't answer the question.

"Are you going to sit?" he asked when Pierce didn't immediately take the other chair. "We have things to discuss. I'm sure you would be more comfortable if you sat." The man's tone was calm but patronizing. Pierce would have fired him on the spot if he'd been an employee of his.

"Alright then," the man said dismissively when Pierce neither responded nor sat. "It says here that you had your body cryonically frozen should the technology ever exist to not only cure your terminal cancer, but to resurrect you in toto if that also becomes possible." He had a vaguely British accent that Pierce found moderately annoying. He'd never liked accents from the UK. They made people sound pretentious. But then again, didn't standing there like a dolt while this guy read his file (they had a file on him!) make him look uncertain and weak? Pierce sat. Davis didn't react.

"So, is this all true?" the man asked after he'd flipped through a few more pages in the file. He was holding it up so that only he could read it. Pierce would have liked very much to have been able to see what it said.

"If you're referring to the part about my body, then yes, it is true."

"It also says here that you are… were… one of the richest and most powerful people in the world. Is that also true?"

"It is," he replied smugly. Maybe now this low-level bureaucrat would treat him with the deference he'd earned and deserved.

"That explains a lot," the man muttered without raising his eyes from the file.

"I don't believe you told me what this is all about," Pierce said in his most authoritative voice.

"Then you believe correctly. I didn't." The man never raised his eyes from whatever he was reading.

Pierce's anger was rising. This lout didn't even have the courtesy to look up when speaking to him. The dismissiveness was intolerable. "How about you let me look at that file," Pierce said. It was not a question; it was a command, and it took supreme effort to keep his voice even. He had to change the subject, regain some measure of control. This man had taken it from him effortlessly. Pierce was not used to being in a subordinate position to anyone.

"Sorry," he said without a trace of remorse. "Subjects are strictly forbidden from seeing their files."

"Then what the hell are we doing here?" It was impossible to keep the acid and venom from his voice this time, but his tone didn't faze the guy.

"Screening you," he said emotionlessly.

"Yes, that's what that woman said before I came into this room, that I'd been selected for additional screening. What are you screening me *for*?"

The man was silent as he read. Pierce was about to get out of his chair and snatch the folder from the insolent whelp when Davis unexpectedly snapped it shut and stuffed it back into the desk drawer. "You're not a nice man," he said matter-of-factly.

"Nice? Is that what I'm here for? To determine if I'm nice or not? You could have just asked me without going through all this nonsense."

"It's policy. You understand. And since you mentioned it – are you nice?"

Pierce couldn't believe what he was hearing. He'd voluntarily ended his own life and come to *this*? Some sort of afterlife inquisition that wanted to know nothing more than whether or not he was nice? Is this what passed for government here? Was this idiot just a minor part in a post-life bureaucratic machine? More interested in his phone or lunch break than in helping the customers? Like a hellish DMV? Well, that was not exactly the best example. Most DMVs were hellish. It was a key building block of their governmental DNA. Like anything to do with the EPA. Or the IRS. "Since you asked – no. I'm not nice. Now can we get on with… whatever happens next?"

"In due course. Some of the information in your file gives me cause for concern. I need to confer with some of my colleagues." The man stood from the chair and walked to the door.

"Are you just going to leave me here?" Pierce demanded as he glared at the man.

"Won't be long." The man said cheerily and left the room without another word. Pierce shook his head in disbelief. This place was like the office of some mid-level bureaucrat or the worst dentist he'd ever heard of. He sat back in the chair and folded his arms across his chest to wait. There wasn't even a magazine in the room to thumb through. Did they have magazines here? Afterlife Weekly maybe? Next World Geographic? Hereafter Review?

Then he remembered the folder. Pierce hurriedly looked around the empty space. No security cameras or two-way mirrors like some police interrogation room. He stood from the chair and hurried around to the other side of the desk. What he found wasn't possible. There were no drawers. He'd watched the man open one, had seen the actual drawer as it had protruded from the frame of the desk. All he saw now was a smooth metal surface and a hole for the legs of whomever sat here. Pierce ran his hands across the metal. It was as smooth as it looked. He felt around in other places on the desk and found nothing but more cool and featureless metal. How in the hell had that guy opened a drawer that didn't exist? The sound of the door opening made him scurry back to his chair.

"You won't be able to get into the desk," the man said as he reentered the room. "It only opens for one of us." Pierce, slightly ashamed at having been caught in his snooping, was about to ask who 'us' was when three more people walked in. Two women and one man. There was something different about how they looked compared to the other… what should he call them – Denizens? Officials? Attendants? – of this place. Their skin was smoother, healthier-looking, and had a vague yellow tint to it. Their clothes were the same shade of blue that Davis wore. Pierce dismissed their appearance. They looked like normal people, walked like normal people, and once they opened their mouths would probably speak like normal people. Just like everyone else he'd met here thus far.

His interlocuter sat back down at the desk while the three others stood shoulder-to-shoulder horizontally in a perfectly straight line a few steps behind him. Their bearing was martial, their posture rigid. All three wore completely neutral expressions and stared at a spot somewhere above his head. *Ten hut,* he thought to himself, picturing a scene from some military movie when the commander makes the troops stand at attention.

Pierce sat in his chair and waited for Davis to say something. He'd taken the file from the desk drawer again (how the hell did he do that?), and was thumbing through the pages. It was a thick file. He stopped flipping and eyed one page closely; his eyes flitted from side to side as he read what must have been text. A tremendous urge to lunge across the desk and seize the file from Davis nearly overwhelmed Pierce, and he struggled mightily to resist it. He desperately wanted to see what was in that folder.

"Yes, this item here is one we have some questions about." Davis turned to look at the three people behind him. "Your turn." One of the women spoke first.

"You never procreated. Why?" she asked in a flat and emotionless tone that reminded him of that voice that used to tell you your call couldn't be completed as dialed when you punched a wrong number on the phone. The question was direct and far more personal than he liked, and Pierce hesitated to speak.

"We can't continue until you answer," Davis prodded.

Pierce drew a slow breath and frowned with irritation. "Because I don't like children and didn't want any."

"Unsatisfactory," the other woman and the man said simultaneously. *In stereo,* Pierce thought. This was bizarre. Who the hell were these people? Synchronized speakers? Was it an Olympic event here like swimming was back on Earth?

"What do you mean unsatisfactory?" he asked, not bothering to disguise the exasperation and derision in his voice. "I answered you truthfully. What more do you want?"

"We'll come back to that," Davis said with a glance back over his shoulder at the three strange yellow people. "Moving on." He flipped a few more pages and stopped again. "So… you started your business at twenty-three years of age." It wasn't a question. Pierce nodded anyway. "In order to do that you borrowed money, I believe you'd call it start-up capital, from a family friend. It says here that this friend was an elderly woman your grandparents had known for many years."

"Yes, that's correct. What about her?"

"She died destitute a few years after advancing you the loan. We'd like you to explain the circumstances as you understand them."

"Is this a courtroom?" Pierce asked. He was incensed at the gall of these people. Digging through his past, his personal life, like it was a garden patch they were going to plant onions in or something.

"Do you see a judge or jury?"

"Well now let's just think about that shall we?" Pierce said in the tone he reserved for the densest of his employees. "The three people behind you could very well be a jury, and you might as well be a judge, or at least a prosecutor. So, from where I'm sitting this actually looks very much like a courtroom. Except that you haven't told me what I'm on trial for, nor have you indicted me or offered me counsel. You're just asking extremely inappropriate and very personal questions. And you still haven't told me why."

"It's all part of the screening process," Davis said tiredly as if he was talking to a child.

Pierce shot from his chair. "That's what you keep saying, but why? To what end? This is ridiculous! I want to speak to your supervisor, your boss, whoever is in charge here, immediately. This whole thing is a sham, and I've been jerked around enough!"

Davis exhaled loudly through his nostrils and looked at him disinterestedly. "The woman you borrowed the money from?" he asked flatly.

Pierce, breathing heavily, slowly sat back down. It was clear he wasn't going to get anywhere with the frontal attack, so he'd have to just play their game until he could pick a different one to play. Maybe he should just walk over to the door and let himself out. See what else was out there. He was clearly in some kind of building. It stood to reason that there were other rooms here, other people like these freaks. Maybe he could find someone with some authority and put an end to this farce. All he wanted to know was how long he had to wait here until he could get back to his body and resume his old life.

"Yes, I borrowed money from her. But there was never a written agreement between us, and she told me not to worry about paying it back immediately. She knew it would take some time for my business to grow and that I would need to plow almost everything I made back into it."

"Continue," Davis said. The yellow people hadn't spoken, moved or changed their expressions since the pronouncement of 'unsatisfactory' a few moments earlier.

"Well, at least you're happy with that," Pierce said testily. He folded his arms and stared at the four people in front of him.

"Continue," Davis said again with slightly more emphasis.

"Continue what?" Pierce asked.

"Your explanation of the events." There was a quality to Davis' voice that hadn't been there to this point. It was just a tiny bit edgy, anxious. Good. He was starting to turn this conversation his way.

"This is an interrogation. That's all this is. I might as well be in handcuffs in some shabby room at the local precinct. What's next? Torture? Enhanced interrogation methods like the ones that were so newsworthy a few years ago?"

"Continue," Davis said. There was no mistaking it this time – the man was getting annoyed. Pierce smiled inside and continued his recalcitrance.

"You might as well take me to the dungeon now. Just put me on the rack, get out the knives and drills and whatever else you people use, and get on with it. Or you could just send me on my way. My body is waiting for me to get back to it, and I'd rather not sit here answering your inane questions for all eternity." Davis blinked at him. It was the first physical reaction he'd gotten from the man, and Pierce was exuberant at the triumph.

"I see you don't want to continue," he said after a long moment of staring at Pierce like he was something unpleasant that had gotten stuck in a drainpipe. "That reduces our options." Davis turned to the three yellow people and nodded. In perfect unison they rolled their heads back until they were facing the ceiling, opened their mouths, and exhaled slowly. Pierce watched in confusion as their mouths closed and their heads rolled back forward. Three sets of eyes focused on his face. There was something alien in their gazes, inhuman. Or maybe *beyond* human was a better way to put it. Pierce had done battle with the best and smartest the business world had to offer, and rarely had he been beaten. Whatever the quality was that he detected in their eyes, it cowed him utterly. He felt his heart begin to beat faster. Wait. Wasn't he dead? How could he have a heartbeat? Didn't matter. It was there and hammering away inside his chest. This was not what he'd expected. He opened his mouth to quickly tell them the rest of the story about how he'd just ignored the woman when she'd asked for her money back, and how happy he'd been when she finally died and quit calling, but his mouth didn't work. No matter how hard he tried to speak, nothing happened.

"I regret that it has come to this, but you really didn't leave us any choice," Davis said. "It is your stated wish to continue the interview?"

Pierce still couldn't speak, and fear was quickly taking over his thoughts. "You can nod or shake your head no," Davis said. He obviously knew what was happening here, which rekindled the anger in Pierce and drove out the gathering fear. He nodded vigorously.

"Right. This way then. Come along." Davis stood and took a few steps toward the door. The eyes of the yellow people had left Pierce and were focused on that far away place somewhere above his head again. He would have been screaming in rage if his mouth worked. Pierce briefly considered picking up the chair and bashing Davis' head in, but ultimately decided against that course of action. If these people could freeze his mouth so effectively, it was entirely possible that they could freeze the rest of him too. Then he would be completely helpless and unable to resist whatever they might decide to do to him. A little voice in the back of his mind spoke up just then. It didn't visit very often, but when it did, he listened. He'd even named it: The Interior Monologue. Sometimes he just called it TIM. It had given him some of the best advice he'd ever gotten.

*You still think you have some measure of control, that you can make choices and effect the outcome of whatever this proceeding is. Listen here sonny boy – you control* nothing. *These… people have* all *the power. You should have just answered their questions and played ball, but no. You had to be the big shot. Mr. Large and In Charge. How'd that work out for you? Not so well, I'm thinking. Now get your ass out of that chair and follow Davis there. You've got no idea how things work here, but you're still acting like this is your boardroom or something. It ain't. Time to give up the tough guy act and go with the flow, or you know what happens? You get royally fucked.*

Pierce hated it when The Interior Monologue lectured him. But he had to admit that it was right, as much as it galled him to admit that anyone (*or any voice,* TIM reminded him) other than himself was right. He choked on his pride for a long moment, then got up from the chair and silently (*you can go quietly, but could you go loudly?*) followed Davis.

Outside the door was a sterile hallway. The same tiles as back in the room covered the floor out here, and evenly spaced doors just like the one he'd just walked through marched away into the distance to his left. The hall was long, a few hundred yards at least, with a set of double doors at the far end. It was deserted. Davis turned right and Pierce saw another set of double doors maybe twenty feet away. A door slammed behind him, and he tried to spin around to look, but his body wouldn't obey. He could walk forward and turn his head slightly to either side, but looking behind him or pivoting was impossible. The same force that had sealed his mouth had apparently done the same thing to the rest of his body. He felt like he was being funneled toward something.

*Maybe that's exactly what's happening here. You're like a cow at the slaughterhouse being forced down the chute to where the killer's waiting with the sledgehammer. Remember you thought about that back in line? Or maybe it's the compressed air thing from that movie. What was the name of it? You don't watch many movies, but you watched that one. Something about old men?*

Sometimes the voice stayed around longer than he wanted it to. Yelling and cursing at it never helped. He had to ignore it until it got bored and left on its own, back to wherever it lived. But before doing that, TIM almost never failed to irritate him immensely by spitting out whatever advice it had.

He followed Davis as he passed through the doors which opened on their own, and into another hallway. This one was much shorter and ended at a single plain wooden door. Davis stood to the side as it opened and gestured to him to keep walking. They exchanged a glance as Pierce passed him but said nothing to each other.

The door closed without a sound behind him, and Pierce looked around in bewilderment. He was on a platform of some kind. It was like a warehouse loading dock or maybe a subway station. A thick whiteness covered everything within about fifty feet, so he couldn't tell whether he was inside or outside. There was no sound or movement of air. The stillness was eerie and complete. The platform was made of plain grey concrete which dropped off a few paces from him. Pierce walked to the edge and looked down. If there was ground below, he couldn't see it; everything was covered in that strange whiteness. It didn't look like smoke or clouds, had no texture or form at all. As he frowned at it, Pierce was reminded of snow on flat ground. But that wasn't quite right either. Snow was comprised of individual flakes. This was all one mass, one piece or unit, as far as he could tell. It was more like... laminated countertops. He briefly considered stepping off the edge of the platform. Maybe that whiteness was solid, and he'd be able to stand on it, walk across it to where it rose up in front of him in a wall. The entire platform was enclosed by the stuff on all sides. Pierce looked up and saw a ceiling of the same material perhaps twenty feet above his head. It was difficult to judge distance without the contrast of shape and color though. He looked over the edge of the platform again. Would it be so bad to just let himself fall off? Wasn't he already dead? What was the worst that could happen? He'd die again?

"Dudley P. Bresnahan?" a female voice from behind him said. Pierce spun around, thankful he was suddenly able to do that again, and prepared to excoriate the cretin who'd dared to use his first name. There was no one there; the platform was empty.

"Who the hell is that?" he demanded. He could talk. The spell was broken. Whatever it had been.

"Are you Dudley P. Bresnahan?" the voice asked again. It was coming from everywhere, from the encompassing white.

"Pierce," he snarled.

"Repeat?"

"I said *Pierce*!"

"I have your name as being –"

He cut the voice off. "I do not answer to... Dudley. I go by my middle name – Pierce. Dudley is a name for horses."

"Then you *are* Dudley P. Bresnahan?"

"I just said so, didn't I?" Were all disembodied voices this dense?

"Please acknowledge with either yes or no."

Pierce snarled at nothing. "Yes! For Christ-on-the-high-dive's-sake, yes!"

"Your transportation will be arriving momentarily. Have a pleasant next life."

Next life? What did the bitch mean, next life? Was he about to be reincarnated? Or was his plan finally starting to pay dividends? Pierce looked around the strange platform at the enveloping, cloudlike nothingness and decided that it was the latter. Soon he would be back in his old body, his disease healed, and well on his way to true immortality. That's really what he'd wanted all along. It's what everyone who tried to cheat death, to lengthen the lives of humans through scientific advancement, wanted. He mulled the word over in his mind. Immortality. For something so open-ended, it had a strange finality to it that was incongruous with its larger meaning. The inability to die. If it was not possible to die, then that fact itself was as final as death. But his experiences here had proved that death was not the end. There really was something else beyond life as he'd known it. This simple discovery was utterly profound. If it could be proven back in his former world scientifically, empirically and without question or error, that an afterlife did exist, then Pierce had the antidote to most of the world's problems. He began to ask himself questions. What were the world's problems? Hunger, war, famine, social unrest and political grievances. What was at the root of them? Life. Everyone wanted their version of a better life for themselves and their families, their countries, the world. Whether that meant living in extreme luxury like some Middle Eastern oil sheik or simply having enough food to eat and relatively clean water to wash it down was immaterial. At the absolute base of everything was life. Despite most of the world's population believing in one religion or another, most people acted as if their life on earth was the only one they'd ever have and were doing their damnedest to make it as easy and comfortable as possible, even if that meant making it difficult for others. If he could prove that dying was only a conduit to something else, then the motives, the impetuses, for many of the world's problems were instantly rendered impotent. If you get to live again somewhere else, then why expend so much energy dropping bombs on each other or trying to advance the cause du jour? There was little incentive for it other than instant gratification or perhaps the settling of old grievances.

Pierce knew there were massive holes in his logic, but he was relatively sure he had the basis of what could, with a little fleshing out, become a solid plan for action. He'd never been much of a philosopher or world peace advocate, but he cared greatly about his own legacy. If he could prove to the world that the petty (and not so petty) squabbles that had proven so destructive throughout history were completely unnecessary, then he would be forever remembered as the man who had brought calm to a tremendously troubled planet. The statues they would build of him… The monuments engraved with his name… The power and influence he would instantly gain… It was time to get back into his old body and hire the best scientists in the world. He *had* to prove that the afterlife was real.

Pierce hadn't realized that he'd absentmindedly turned away from the edge of the platform, and when he turned back around, he was surprised to find himself looking at a subway car. The doors were open and there was a person sitting on the bench seat just inside and to the left. He hadn't even heard the thing arrive.

"Please enter car number seven," the woman's disembodied voice said.

Pierce stared at the bizarre and unexpected sight. If this was car seven, then six, eight and every other car in this train was obscured by the white. The person inside was facing away from him but turned and looked out the door. The face belonged to a man of Asian ancestry. Pierce could never tell what country people Asian people were from. This guy could have been Chinese, Japanese, or Hmong. He didn't care what people looked like, only what they could do to make his company more successful.

"Train's leaving. Better climb aboard," the man said. His tone was mild but slightly suggestive of impatience. Pierce almost bristled. "It won't wait forever," he added.

The woman's voice piped up again as if to reinforce what the Asian guy had just said. "Please enter car number seven. The doors will be closing momentarily." It sounded like a recording played over a PA system. Maybe it was, but he didn't see any speakers. The voice seemed to come from all around, as if the white nothing itself were speaking. Pierce strode quickly to the train car and crossed the threshold just as the doors slid closed behind him with a hiss. He sat down on the hard plastic seat across from the Asian guy and felt the train lurch forward.

"Glad you made it. This has been a pretty boring ride so far," he said.

"So far? You've been on this train a while?"

The man nodded. "This was my eighth stop." The two men regarded each other silently for a long moment. "You look familiar," the Asian guy finally said. "Do I know you from somewhere?"

"People recognize me occasionally," Pierce said dismissively.

"What's your name?"

"Pierce. And yours?"

The man smiled. "You probably wouldn't be able to pronounce it. Just call me Mike."

Pierce nodded slightly in acknowledgement. He was relieved Mike hadn't pushed to know who he was. "What happened at the other seven stops?"

Mike shrugged. "Not much. Four of them were empty. The train didn't wait long. It stopped, the doors opened for two or three seconds, then closed and away we went. Reminded me of a school bus stopping at train tracks. You ever see how they'd do that even if they were empty? They'd stop and open their doors, train or no train, students or not?"

"No, can't say that I ever saw that."

"Oh. Well, that's what they do."

"The other stops?" Pierce prodded, hoping the man wouldn't get distracted by inanities again.

"There was a lady at one of them. She was wandering around crying. Never did get on the train. She was still walking around when we left. At one there was an old guy sitting in the middle of the platform staring into space. He didn't even blink while we were there. It was kinda eerie, like Anthony Hopkins in *Silence of the Lambs*. You ever see it?"

"No. What happened at the third stop?"

"That one was at least sort of entertaining. There were two boys, teenagers, probably about sixteen or so, beating the shit out of each other. They didn't get on either, but at least I had a little fun watching the fireworks," Mike said with a grin.

"Yes, well, I'm sure that was… nice. What do you know about this place? This train?"

"Not much. I went through the line like everybody else, then they put me in this room with way too many fluorescent lights, and a lady questioned me about my life. When she was done, they took me out of the room, and I ended up on a platform like the one you were just on. Then the train came, and… you know the rest."

"How long between stops?"

Mike grinned. "I have no idea. There's no clock in here, and I was always terrible at judging time. My wife used to get so mad at me. We were late for everything."

"So, you remember your previous… life?"

"Yeah. Don't you?"

"Oh, I do, yes, I do. I remember everything." He was fantasizing about all the awards and accolades the world would bestow on him when he proved the existence of the afterlife. The Nobel Prize would be displayed conspicuously in his house. He'd have an ornate marble dais built just inside the front door where everyone who ever came in would see it before anything else. Even before meeting him.

Mike regarded him silently for several moments. "I think I remember who you are," he said at last. Pierce raised his eyebrows slightly but didn't speak. "You're that business guy. I saw you on the cover of *Forbes* or something. You were one of the richest men in the world."

"I still am," Pierce said flatly.

"I guess," Mike said with a hint of disagreement. "Money isn't helping anything in this place though." He waved his arms around and looked from side to side at the endless white nothing outside the windows.

"It will be waiting for me when I get back," Pierce said airily.

"When you… I remember now. You had yourself frozen so science could bring you back to life someday. You had cancer or something. There was an article in the newspaper about you."

Pierce perked up at this revelation. He'd died before this man, therefore Mike knew more about what had happened in the world since he himself had left it. He peered intently at Mike with sudden and acute interest. "What's happened in the world since I died?"

Mike frowned. It was not a question he'd been expecting. "Well, I died a little less than a year after you, so not much. The usual wars, famines, natural disasters, terrorist attacks, politicians getting caught doing all kinds of illegal and immoral things. Nothing really out of the ordinary. Why? Were you expecting something... momentous?"

"I'm waiting for science to develop the technology to not only bring me back to life in my own body, but to cure it of disease and make me youthful again. Do you know if there have been any developments in those areas?"

Mike grinned wryly. "No. I was a civil engineer. I designed housing developments in the suburbs. Science was never really my thing. I liked building stuff."

"Well surely you must have seen a news article. You just said you'd read about me."

"Yeah, I read about you. But that was just an article in my local newspaper. I don't even think I finished it. The journalist started listing all the things you did in your life, and I got bored, went on to something else."

Pierce was incensed at this. "You... didn't finish the article? I've led one of the most interesting lives anyone on the planet ever lived, and you couldn't be bothered to read about it for three minutes?"

Mike grinned again. He was clearly pleased with himself to have elicited such a strong reaction from Pierce. "Like I said, I got bored. I like building stuff, not reading tabloids."

"Tabloids?" Pierce nearly shrieked as he shot from his seat. "My life was not a tabloid piece!"

"You might want to sit down. This train stops –" Mike didn't get to finish his sentence. The car jerked as the brakes applied, and the rapid deceleration was unexpected. Pierce tumbled to the floor and banged his head on a handrail. "Suddenly," Mike finished when the train had ceased moving.

Pierce stood slowly, rubbing his head where it had impacted the hard steel rail. "You might have warned me earlier than that," he said with a frown.

"I was going to, but you got all bent out of shape that I didn't read about you." Mike answered. There was no apology in his voice, but there was a challenge. Pierce fixed the Asian man with a glare, then dropped his gaze and looked out the window. The platform outside was just like the one he'd been on a short time ago. There was an old woman standing on it. When the doors opened the same female voice instructed her to board car number seven. With a smile the woman waddled in and took a seat on the other side of the doors from Pierce and Mike.

"And how are you two today?" she said cheerily.

"I'm well, how are you?" Mike answered with a smile. Pierce didn't speak.

"Oh, I'm so happy!" the woman said. "They told me I'm going to see my Milton soon. He died at Hue in Vietnam. I never remarried."

"I'm so sorry, and so happy for you," Mike said with a genuine smile. Pierce stared at them both with an unreadable expression.

"Thank you dear. It was a long time ago, but I still remember him so well."

"I'm Mike. What's your name?"

"Oh, aren't you a dear. I'm Edith. It's very nice to meet you."

"You too," Mike said warmly.

Pierce grimaced at the niceties. Couldn't they just get to the point of all this? Why did they have to play this stupid get-to-know-each-other game? There were more important things than this lady's long dead husband or Mike's pleased-to-meet-you inane banter. What a colossal waste of time.

"Did you say you're going to meet him?" Pierce asked sharply. Edith turned a cool gaze toward him.

"Yes. That's what I said."

"Then you know where this train is going? What's at the end?"

She regarded him quizzically for a moment. "No. I have no idea. They told me that I'm going to see Milton. That's all I know. All I *care* to know."

"Fat lot of help you are," Pierce sniffed as he turned away.

"Hey!" Mike said. "You don't have to be an asshole about it. She doesn't know where we're going any more than you or I do."

Pierce ignored the comment and stared out the windows at the passing white nothingness. All he wanted was to get back to his body and resume his life. Was that so much to ask? His inner voice spoke up again.

*You're almost whining Dudley,* it said. TIM never used his first name unless it really wanted to get his attention. It had it. *Get yourself together. Neither of these two morons knows anything about anything. This train is going somewhere, so you'd better be ready when it gets there. You've got no idea what's waiting for you at your stop, or even which stop is yours, but based on the way things have gone so far, I'm sure you'll know it when you get there. Now, do I have to keep reminding you who you are?* Tim paused for a long moment. *I didn't think so.*

Pierce wanted nothing so much as to find the body from which that little voice emanated and give it a good, solid thrashing. Physically beat it bloody. But that would mean beating himself bloody, wouldn't it? He pushed the violent thought from his mind and focused on listening to the mindless chatter occurring between his fellow occupants of the subway car. Fellow occupants – that was rich. Those two were not his fellow *anything*. He was so far above them in every way that both of them may as well have been at the bottom of that hole the Russians drilled some years back. The deepest hole in the world, it had been called. While he floated above them somewhere in space. A galactic gulf existed between them and himself, unbridgeable and as vast as the cosmos.

"Well, that's a terribly sour look on your mug," Edith said. Pierce shot her a scowl that would have melted the face off one of his employees. The old woman simply stared at him with a neutral expression. Pierce noticed her hair at that moment. It was nearly pure white and very thin. He could see her age-mottled scalp through the thin screen of hair. The urge to retch threatened to overwhelm him. How could he vomit? He wasn't alive. The strangeness of his situation made him forget all about Edith and her hair, Mike and the train, while he pondered how all this was even possible. His body, their bodies, the train, the interrogation room, everything had substance, solidity, as if it were real. Weren't ghosts supposed to be transparent or something? *Was* he a ghost? Maybe not. But if not, then what exactly was he? A spirit? Pierce turned away from Mike and Edith who were amiably chattering away at each other and pinched the skin of his forearm as he used his torso to screen the action from the others. He felt the skin, the pain as he squeezed. Pierce didn't presume to know anything about the afterlife or ghosts, but he was relatively certain that he was as real here as he'd been in life. Life. He needed to get back to it.

He absentmindedly stood just as the train began to decelerate and was nearly thrown to the ground again by the force of the braking. Only an instinctive grab of a metal pole (probably installed exactly for situations like this one) stopped him from doing another faceplant. Pierce mentally kicked himself for not remembering how hard this thing braked.

"Please remain seated until the train has stopped moving," Mike said in an irritatingly accurate facsimile of those recorded messages that frequently played in airports and train stations.

Pierce snarled at Mike. "You can take your attitude and –"

"And what?" Mike said threateningly as he stood from the plastic bench seat. "You gonna do something?" His hands were balled into fists, his posture aggressive, an angry glare on his face.

Pierce suddenly didn't know what to do. He was no stranger to conflict. In fact, he relished it. But that was in offices and boardrooms, his messages delivered through lawyers and documents, dressings down in board rooms and offices. This was an entirely different kind of conflict. He'd been in a fistfight once as a child; he seemed to remember it happening in third grade. And he'd lost. The man in front of him was thirty, maybe forty, years younger and in shape. He also looked like he could handle himself.

"Come on then, if you think you got somethin'. Make a move." Edith's hand on his arm softened Mike's glare but didn't entirely defuse the situation.

"Leave him be dear," she said quietly. "He might have been tough when he was young, but now he's just an angry old man." Mike continued to stare at Pierce for another long moment, the challenge still in his eyes, before finally dropping them to meet Edith's calm gaze. He sat back down as the train rolled to a halt, and the doors opened with a hiss.

"This is my stop!" Edith said giddily. Pierce hadn't heard the voice of the announcer, but for some reason this woman thought she was where she needed to be. "My Milton is waiting for me!" She hurried off the train as quickly as her short legs would allow. The car's remaining occupants watched as she ambled across the platform. There was no door in the far wall, and each was wondering where she was going when Edith suddenly vanished. Pierce blinked, and Mike physically jerked in surprise. "Where the hell did she go?" the younger man asked.

"How should I know?" Pierce responded. "You saw the same thing I did." Mike glared at him but didn't reply.

The doors slid closed, and the car moved away from the platform, leaving Edith, wherever she'd gone, behind. The two passengers studiously avoided looking at each other, nor did they speak while the train rolled silently towards its next stop.

Pierce, his gaze on the white nothingness out the windows, wondered idly if he was fast enough to spring from his seat and punch Mike in the jaw before the man could react. He slowly turned his head, sweeping his gaze over Mike and quickly judging the distance. It was too far. He was too old and slow. Not that he'd ever been fast. Pierce was never interested in athletics, performed either by himself or others, and he hadn't been in a gym since high school. Mike looked like he spent a lot of time in a gym. Maybe in a boxing ring too. What was he even thinking about? Initiating a bout of fisticuffs in the afterlife? What the hell was wrong with him? His imagination wandered, and he pictured two angels with massive wings dressed in police uniforms arresting him for assault. *'You're being booked for grievous spiritual* (bodily?) *harm.'* Pierce felt the sudden urge to laugh out loud at the absurdity. Instead, he dug the fingers of his right hand into his left forearm. The pain was instant, and he let go. He peered intently at where his fingers had just been. There were clear indentations from his fingernails. Perhaps he did have a corporeal body here. Or at least the illusion of one. So punching Mike in the face just might cause the bastard some pain. He was reconsidering his earlier plan to lunge from his seat, steeling himself for the action, when the train again rolled to a stop. The doors opened, and the voice of the woman spoke again.

"Dudley P. Bresnahan please exit the car."

Mike was staring at him with a dispassionate expression. Pierce started to say something scathing to him when the voice spoke again. "Dudley P. Bresnahan. Exit the car immediately." There was an urgency in the voice and a further quality to it which Pierce recognized from his many decades of delivering the same thing – a threat.

"This isn't my stop," Mike said derisively, "so it must be yours."

Pierce rose without a word and left the car. As the doors hissed closed behind him, he clearly heard Mike say, "Later dickhead."

Incensed, Pierce spun around to spit out the comment he'd formulated a moment before, but the doors were closed, and the train was pulling away. He watched impotently through the window as a smug smile slid across Mike's face. If he ever met that man again…

"Please exit the platform through the door," the voice said again. Pierce shoved thoughts of Mike and violent retribution from his mind and looked around. This platform was just like the others he'd seen except for the door directly across from where the train had just been. It was made of wooden planks like you might see in some old English castle, and was held together with iron bands, totally out of place in this environment. Pierce walked hesitantly toward it and was surprised when it opened on its own. Beyond it was nothing but more whiteness. He stood still for several moments as he peered in vain through the door, hoping to see some indication of what was on the other side. Then the voice spoke again.

"Exit the platform through the door," it said. No 'please' this time. He looked over his shoulder and was shocked to see the white changing to a dark grey. It looked like water spreading across a floor, and it was coming quickly. The whiteness was being swallowed up, transformed, by that grey. Pierce had always been a man who trusted his instincts. There was, of course, no substitute for hard data, but gut feelings were sometimes just as important, maybe more so, and he'd always listened to his. The Interior Monologue chose that moment to pipe up. Pierce wasn't sure if TIM and his intuition were connected;

they often displayed themselves without the other. But he was fairly certain they were, at the very least, related.

*Come on D. You know that grey stuff isn't... healthy. It might even be dangerous. In fact, it is. And you* know *it is. So quit waiting around hoping someone comes out of that door and tells you what's on the other side and get your ass in gear. Remember gears? It's been so long since you've driven a car that I'll bet you don't. Sure, you know what they are, just like you know what that grey stuff is, but they're not something that enters your daily consciousness. You sure as hell haven't had to think about hammering the throttle going uphill to get your piece of shit Toyota to drop into a lower gear in order to maintain speed in a very long time. Nope, you've had* people *to think about that for you. For decades. Well guess what old buddy? It's time to start doing - and thinking - for yourself again. That grey shit is getting pretty close. You should probably nut up and just boogie on through the door over there.*

"I'll fucking kill you one of these days," Pierce muttered. The Monologue did not reply, but he thought he heard distant laughter as he stepped toward the door and through.

The room burst into applause as the man on the stage finished his speech. As the audience filed out of the room, looks of wonder and incredulity graced the faces of most people.

"Can you believe they actually figured it out?" a fortyish man said to another fortyish man.

"No. I mean, yes. Look, they've been studying this for years, so eventually someone was going to make a breakthrough. I just didn't think it would happen in my lifetime." The two men continued the discussion as they walked down the wide hallway outside the hotel conference room they'd just left. A thirtyish woman stood with her back to the wall and spoke animatedly into a phone she'd pressed to her ear.

"Yes!" she exclaimed. "It's all just data like we thought. I mean, we already knew that with DNA and everything, but to be able to prove that the data actually gets transmitted from the body to… some other place, at the moment of death, is… revolutionary!" She listened for a moment before replying. "This is one of those seminal moments in history that come along only a couple times in a century. The world just changed."

"Preparing for upload," the technician in the white lab coat said. "Systems functioning nominally."

"Is the host ready?" a professorial man with a beard and tweed suit jacket asked.

"It is," someone else said. "Bio scanners indicate all remnants of the disease have been eradicated. The host is as healthy as it can be for its age."

"Proceed," said the bearded man. He peered through a large glass window at the body lying on the table in the room beyond. It was covered with a sheet, so he couldn't see the face, but the right arm was visible. Old. Wrinkled. The beginnings of liver spots dotted the flesh. A bundle of wires and tubes ran from beneath the sheet to various machines around the room that monitored the body's biometrics, and which would act as a conduit for the imminent download. He didn't know who the host body had been before and didn't care. There was a job to do, and he would do it.

A large square machine in one corner began to emit a low hum. Rows of lights flashed and changed color as technicians monitored an array of screens in the control room. A digital clock on the wall was counting down. Under a minute to go. The man with the beard, when he was a child, had loved stories about rocket ships blasting off into space, and the countdown had always been his favorite part. Watching the numbers dwindle down still, even in this place where no rocket engine would ever ignite, gave him a small thrill.

When the numbers hit zero, the hum from the machine in the corner grew in intensity. It was accompanied by a low, deep thrumming that was felt, mostly in the bones and sinews, more than heard. The bearded man didn't like this part. He'd asked the engineers to do something about it, but they claimed the device that caused it was integral, even critical, to the machine. It simply wouldn't function without it, so unfortunately there was no way to decrease or eliminate this unpleasantness. Like many things in life, it had to be borne.

He'd done this before, dozens of times. The procedure that was at that moment happening had been refined and perfected over several decades. Some of the world's smartest people had contributed to the machine in the corner. The one he secretly hated. This was his job, and he was very well compensated for it. But that machine always left him feeling nauseous after a session. The feeling had been worse recently with the last session forcing him to take the day after the procedure off. Missing work was not something he did. The engineers had looked at the machine, and they'd assured him it was fine. Maybe he just needed some time away. A vacation. His wife would be elated. Someone spoke and jarred him out of his reverie.

"Eighty-seven percent complete," one of the technicians said.

"All systems nominal," another intoned.

A loud beep issued from the machine causing every head to turn.

"It's never done that before," the bearded man said. "Systems check."

"I just did that sir. All systems-"

"I said check them," the bearded man commanded. He was in charge, and his people knew it. The technician ran his checks again.

"Uh… there's something strange here," he muttered.

"What?"

"Ninety-four percent complete."

The technician was frowning at his screen as the bearded man looked over his shoulder. Everything looked ok. Except that thing there. What was it called again? Downstream Cerebral Interface. The DCI. Ordinarily it would be near 75-80 gbit. For some reason it was at 63. That was too low.

"Upload is frozen at ninety-seven percent. Something's wrong; this hasn't happened before."

The bearded man flew into action, issuing orders and barking commands at the technicians who were working frantically to correct the problem. Several tense minutes passed until he finally spoke quietly. "That's enough. There's nothing more we can do. Terminate session, full shutdown authorized on my authority. Preserve all logs and data before you leave the room. Call the bio-waste team to dispose of the subject." The bearded man looked around the room. The faces that looked back were frustrated, downcast, angry. His team had never failed before, but they had done their jobs; he was proud of them and told them so. "There will be an investigation of course, and we will figure out what happened, but does anyone have any preliminary thoughts? I'll put them in my report. It may save the investigators some time if they have an idea where to start."

A thirtyish woman to his left spoke. "I was watching the feed as the upload was occurring. It looked to me like the data got corrupted somehow. The servers were spinning in circles trying to maintain integrity and continuity."

"Ok, we'll look there first. Great work everyone. Go home for now. We have two more of these tomorrow."

The team shuffled slowly and quietly out the door. Two young men talked softly as they walked down the hall toward the exterior doors and the parking lot beyond.

"Who do you think he was?" one of them asked.

"No idea. Somebody rich for sure."

"Just once I'd like to know who we're bringing back from the dead."

"You know they can't tell us. If it turns out we know the person or have some kind of bias against whoever it is, we could sabotage the whole operation."

"Yeah, it makes sense, but just once I'd like to know."

There was grey. Switzerland. Grey. InCopis. What was that? Grey. Only grey? Who? Rubens. A painting, yes. Grey. Grey? No, grey. InRubens. No, not right. In-something. Grey. Penfolds Grange Hermitage. InSwitzerland? Wine? Expensive. In1951. What? Secobarbital. Grey. Why grey? InGrey? No. Yes? Old woman. Loan. Pay back? In. RubensCopis. Yes! No. Expensive? Grey.

The thoughts were so jumbled. Why couldn't he focus?

Grey.

The middle-aged man waited in the breakroom until the rest of his coworkers were gone. They'd been so disappointed in their performance. Some of them would go to their local watering hole where they would drown their dejection in drink. Not him. He had something else to do.

Back in the control room he restarted his terminal and the big machine in the corner. This wouldn't take long, and since there was no subject in the other room, it was a fairly simple operation. He turned the web cam toward him, clicked a button on his screen and spoke for a few short moments. When he was finished, he clicked a few other things on his screen, listened to the hum of the machine, and waited for the message to pop up on his screen. Less than a minute later, it did. "Upload complete," he read softly.

Grey. Why grey? Why InCopis? Where Rubens? What Rubens? Penfolds GrangeCopis. No. No! Train? InTrain. Mike. Mike Rubens? InMike? Yes! Loan.

The grey was changing. A face appeared. Unfamiliar. Never seen it before. Mike? No. Mike was Asian. This was Caucasian. Who?

"I'll bet you don't recognize me," it said. "Why would you? You've never seen this face before. The one I had when you knew me is long gone. Rotted in a grave somewhere. But this one, well, this one I had to buy. It belonged to some homeless person. Came cheap. See, I read about you in the newspapers. How you'd been diagnosed with terminal cancer and had your body frozen so that you could be resurrected when there was a cure for it. Gave me an idea. I did the same thing. Except that I had myself downloaded from the next place, then uploaded into this body, the one you see now. Have you figured out who I am yet? Probably not. One thing you likely didn't know about me is that I was very good with computers, particularly coding. It was easy to write a little script that would corrupt your upload and delete itself once it had done what I wanted it to do. I've been working here, waiting for you for… I guess it's seven years now. Time is different in the place where you are. I died sixteen years after you did, and I've been in this body for eleven. Took me a couple years to get hired here. It's been sixty-four years since you drank your lethal concoction in Switzerland. It did take a while for technology to get to this point. But we're here! Isn't it great?!"

Grey. Who spoke? The face. FaceCopis. SpeakRubens. Something. Name? SwitzerCopis.

"Still haven't figured it out yet, have you. I'll tell you. Yes, I will. Even though your broken mind probably can't even process what I'm saying. This is called gloating. You're familiar with it. You used to do it all the time."

InGloat? Who? Who. InMind. MindRubens? WhoRubens. GloatLoan?

"It's a pretty simple concept," the face said. "Once they figured out how to download our… souls, essences, memories, whatever you want to call it, from beyond, well, it was easy to reverse the process. Download. Upload. See how it works? I created a script that corrupted the data – your data – in other words, you, during the upload process. It stopped you from being able to reinhabit your body and probably scrambled your mind. At least, I hope it did. You deserve worse, but this was the best I could do in the circumstances. Oh, there's one other thing I wanted to mention. The place where I work is very circumspect. Strict confidentiality. We never know who the subjects are that we're working on. I only knew it was you because I hacked a database and found you, so I knew when it was your turn to come back. But I had to be sure. You know how I knew it was definitely you? Your hand. It was the only part of you I could see. The rest of your miserable carcass was covered with a sheet. Just as well. I didn't want to look at your grotesque face. The hand was enough. I've never forgotten that hand. Do you remember how I stared at it as I left the boardroom after you fired me? Remember now? Probably not. I'm Jensen. You fired me. Like you fired so many other good people."

Jensen. InJensen? HandCopis. JensenRubens. Confidentiality. Fired? FiredPenfolds. No?

"That's about all the time I have left. Need to go home and get some sleep. We're uploading two more tomorrow. I'll need to be at my best. Can't have a repeat of today. People will start losing their jobs, getting fired. I know what that feels like. Don't want my coworkers to find out. So that's all. I'm done. Now you know who shafted you. Hope the rest of your life in eternity is shit. Fuckhead."

The face disappeared.

Face? InFace. FuckheadCopis. FiredFired? Who. Who? JensenFired. PenfoldsShafted. RubensDownload? Grey.

# HOW BHUTAN BECAME THE WORLD'S ONLY SUPERPOWER

*I don't know how much longer the internet's going to work, so I need to tell this story while it still does. If you're watching this video then you're most likely not one of them – the blood drinkers, exsanguinary transmogrification specialists, as I affectionately call them. Vampires for those of you who are linguistically… underdeveloped. I know, I know, maybe I shouldn't use such big words. Most people out there listening to this, if anyone* is *listening, will probably have to get a dictionary and pause this video every few moments to look up a word. But why the hell not? I spent enough time writing college research papers, learning those words, and if this is the last thing the world ever hears from me, by God I'm going to use them. So, if you don't get it, don't know what the hell I just said, then do what most everyone else does – infer. Or find a dictionary. Don't make a video of your own castigating me for using words your tiny saurian brain doesn't know. I don't care about your pejoratives or your calumny. And if I sound incensed, well, it's because I am. You should be too if you're still human. After all the world as we once knew it is gone. The dreams of the globalist one-world-government types have finally come true. Just not in the way they were hoping. It's a certainty that no one foresaw what actually* did *happen. And what, precisely, was that? I'm glad you asked!*

*I'll start from where I was at the beginning of the event – Bhutan. What? You've never heard of Bhutan? Well, let me tell you about it. It's a tiny little country stuck between India and China. Most of it is mountainous, and it's landlocked, so it's not exactly the easiest country to get to. Why was I there? The mountains. I'm a climber, have been for a number of years now. My hobby started back when I was in the Army. I'd been stationed at Fort Lewis in Washington state and had the privilege of attending a presentation by a man named Ed Viesturs. At the time he was one of the world's greatest active high-altitude mountaineers and was almost finished with what he called Endeavor 8000. There are 14 mountains in the world that are taller than 8000 meters, and he was in the middle of climbing all of them without the use of supplemental oxygen. Most climbers that attempt mountains that high, carry bottled oxygen with them because the air is so thin it's hard to breathe. Ed didn't do that. Climbing one mountain that way is achievement enough, but climbing fourteen? Incredible. His presentation inspired me to climb. I've always been drawn to mountains for some reason, and I used to stare at Mount Rainier on clear days back when I was in the Army. Even drove up to it a couple times. After seeing Ed speak, I decided I was going to climb it. So, my next leave that's what I did. Summiting was a revelation.* This *was what I was going to do when I got out of the Army. And climb I did. Denali (or Mount McKinley if you like) was crossed off the list the year after I got out, a few peaks in Colorado followed, and I briefly considered the Andes. But it was the Himalayas that really called me, like they do so many others. I wanted to bag a truly big mountain. But I didn't want to climb Everest. Too many people these days. It's like I-5 through Seattle at rush hour anymore. Atrociously crowded. Instead, I climbed Nanga Parbat, Makalu and Dhaulagiri, and those were enough. But I stayed in the region after my last expedition, eventually ending up in Bhutan. I love it here. Well, I did love it. Before the vampires showed up.*

*Just how do vampires and mountain climbing relate to each other, you might be wondering? They don't. Unless you count the fact that everything started right here in Bhutan. Yep, this tiny little country sandwiched between the giants of China and India is where it all began. A little background on the country first. At one time it was a hereditary monarchy, with an actual king. Times change and this country changed too, eventually becoming a constitutional monarchy. They have a prime minister, and elections and political parties now just like other democratic countries. Why did I stay here, of all places? I love it. The people are fantastic! And if you love mountains, you can't beat the scenery. Also, I'd gotten tired of the US. It's all commercialism and consumerism, politics and more politics, almost all of it toxic and unproductive. Don't get me wrong, I'm American through and through, always will be, but my country abandoned me sometime in the last decade or so. When I started being called a racist and a bigot because I disagreed with someone's opinion, well, I knew things weren't going… well. It was more than just that though. There were so many problems in America, most of them completely avoidable too, if people just had a smidgen of common sense. That's one thing I've discovered about my home country – common sense is a very* uncommon *commodity. So, when I found myself here, on the other side of the world, in a place where life is much simpler, I decided to stay. Never regretted it for a moment either. I miss friends and family, but I have the internet to keep in touch, although I haven't heard from any of them since everything started. I don't think the exsanguinary transmogrification specialists (From now on I'm calling them ETS. That brings back a memory – "phone home" – remember that?) had any plans to maintain the infrastructure. It'll all fail soon. The power grid, the internet – everything will be gone. And maybe me too. But back to Bhutan.*

*The country elected a prime minister a few years ago who was a bit of a megalomaniac. Erase that. Start over. He was a* big *megalomaniac. This guy actually was making plans to invade both India* and *China! Can you imagine? A country of just over 800,000 people invading* two *countries of over a billion each? That would have been like using a Kleenex to smother a forest fire. But he was undeterred. In fact, he had designs on world domination. After India and China, he was going to move on Europe and the Americas. Just before he dispatched the Bhutanese army, all 8,000 soldiers of it, the ETS showed up.*

*The first report claimed that someone who had been pronounced dead actually wasn't. It was revealed later that the person really* had *been dead but came back to... not life... animation. Because she was a vampire. Apparently, the woman lived in a very rural area and had been out foraging for mushrooms or something. Her family said she went into a cave and didn't come out. When they went in after her, she was lying on the ground dead. No one knew what happened. And as far as I know, they never did figure out what she was exposed to. Somehow, they got her to one of the few doctors in the country (Bhutan has, according to the CIA's World Factbook, 0.42 physicians per 1000 people. Look it up if you don't believe me. The website is still up as of right now.) and he verified what her family already knew – the poor woman was dead. He thought she'd had a heart attack or an aneurysm; there were no visible signs of trauma. How do I know this? The doctor was my next-door neighbor – he told me the whole story. The day she woke up he wasn't there, at work.*

*They had her in a meat locker, one of his colleagues opened the drawer for something, and she came flying out, latched onto his neck, and that was the start.*

*At first the ETS were not too different from regular people. Except for their choice of cuisine. They still had their minds, their reason, their faculties. And let me dispel one inaccuracy about vampires right now – sunlight does* NOT *kill them. They walk around in the daytime just like the rest of us. All the sun does is give them a nice tan. And no, they can't turn into bats or sprout wings and fly away, although they are preternaturally fast and strong. The prime minister saw a platinum opportunity with the advent of the ETS. He would create an army of them to use in his plans for world domination. The still-human army was able to corral a few of them, and a series of experiments were undertaken whereby a few soldiers were subjected to their fangs, who in turn became ETS themselves. And here's where it gets* really *interesting.*

*According to my neighbor, there was this scientist, Chinese guy, working secretly on some project in the hinterlands of Bhutan. The story goes that he was too far out on the loony limb even for the ChiComs. They tried to arrest him, but he escaped and ended up in my little adopted country. The prime minister heard about what he was doing and secretly supported him with both refuge from the Chinese and funding for his experiments. And just what were those experiments? Mind control. I don't really know how it all worked so don't ask, but from what my doctor friend told me, he surgically implanted a little device of his own design right onto the brain which allowed him to make the subject do whatever he wanted them to do. I'm sure you can extrapolate the implications of that all by your lonesome. With the help of his Chinese Mengele, the prime minister started implanting these devices into the brains of every newly minted exsanguinator. In a matter of a few weeks, he had an army of several thousand servile ETS ready to obey his commands.*

*But the Chinese guy made a mistake – he trusted the prime minister. In order to move the plan along more quickly, the scientist had taught some other doctors how to manufacture and implant his mind control machines. As soon as they were able to produce and implant them without him, the prime minister didn't need him anymore. He was tossed into a cage with a bunch of hungry ETS and became their midday repast. Couldn't have happened to a better guy.*

*The invasion started with India. The ETS were sent out in small groups of five and ten. They'd go into a town or village, change a bunch of people, and another group, the planters as they were known, and who had also had their brains rewired, would come behind them with mobile surgeries and cases full of the devices. Those groups would implant the machines in the newly changed ETS, and the cycle repeated. They got so good at it, and so good at hiding what they were doing (it's easy to keep things quiet when everyone who knows anything is prevented from talking by the machine controlling their brain) that by the time the Indian government found out what was going on, the prime minister had an army in the tens of millions. And when I say they found out, what I mean is they figured out something fishy was happening, but not exactly what. The prime minister was truly brilliant in this aspect of his plan: he used his power of control to make his army act normal. They were instructed to go about their daily lives as if nothing had happened, which greatly assisted in the subterfuge that was playing out all over the country. They even figured out how to get people changed and planted in just over an hour. The whole thing was industrial in scale and exceptionally well-executed. I say that as a former Army officer with a Master's degree in Project Management who knows a thing or seven about planning and executing operations. It really was a first-class op, no matter how nefarious.*

*Within a month India belonged to Bhutan. Next were Bangladesh and Burma, followed by the rest of Southeast Asia – Laos, Cambodia, Thailand and Vietnam. The prime minister took some time to consolidate his conquests – one week to be exact – before he made his move on China. I have no idea how the actual mechanism for controlling implanted ETS worked, or how it could control so many, but it did. Beijing never had a clue what was coming for it. In a little over a month the picture of Chairman Mao above one of the gates into the Forbidden City was taken down. And that was the first clue that the rest of the world had that something strange was happening. The news media went nuts over the act. It was the end of Communism! Freedom for China! An end to industrial espionage! The West has finally won! Only none of that was really true, except for the part about the end of Communism. Everyone wondered how Communism could have ended so unexpectedly, and with such minimal fanfare. Pundits around the world were flummoxed that their International Studies degrees and foreign policy experience as bureaucrats in some overseas mission or NGO had failed them so badly in predicting this momentous development in world affairs. Although they never said that out loud on any of the news talk shows they appeared on. You had to read between the lines to figure that part out. But it wasn't hard. For all their "expertise" most of them aren't very bright. And they're almost always wrong in their prognostications.*

*So, while Europe and North America rejoiced in their perceived victory over the evils of Communism (and it* was *an evil ideology) the prime minister sent his army into Russia and the 'stans. You know the countries: Afghanistan, Tajikistan, Turkmenistan, Uzbekistan. They fell quickly and quietly. Two months after knocking off China, the prime minister was on the threshold of Europe. But things were starting to happen. Isolated incidents were popping up. It seems that a few of his ETS had ceased to obey commands. It was only a few out of, at this point, billions, but something was awry. The prime minister brushed them off as anomalies, but my doctor friend wasn't so sure. I should tell you more about him. He was the number two man in the whole operation. That's where my information comes from. The prime minister, after dispatching the Chinese scientist, had put him in charge. He only told me all this after the fact, when he and his family were about to run for their lives. But more on that later.*

*When the prime minister did finally invade Europe, he did it with gusto. Swarms of his ETS flooded into the former Soviet Bloc countries, rampaged right through them and on to the English Channel and the Mediterranean. A separate army departed from St. Petersburg, Russia, and stormed Finland, Sweden, and lastly Norway. He took North Africa in a week but ignored the rest of the continent except the countries of South Africa, Namibia and Botswana. Apparently, his wife loved diamonds and he wanted to have an unlimited supply of them. DeBeers entire available inventory (and the inventories of several other extraction companies) were packed up and shipped to Bhutan where the prime minister's wife could choose her sparklies at her leisure. She was like Imelda Marcos but with jewelry.*

*The invasion of the Americas started with airplanes. ETS were loaded up on anything that flew and sent to the New World. Ports in both North and South America were taken over by advance operatives, and then the invasion really began. Cargo ships laden with containers full of ETS docked at every major port and disgorged their ravenous cargo.*

*And that's when he lost control. Maybe it was just because they'd been cooped up in conexes for weeks, or maybe it was something else. Whatever it was they went on a rampage. Hordes of ETS roamed the streets slaughtering indiscriminately. The authorities were powerless to stop it, and within a month both continents were wastelands. The same thing began to happen in India and China. Why did they start to go crazy, you ask? The answer is surprisingly simple – there was no food source left. Everyone had already been changed. So, the ETS began turning on each other. Ragged body parts littered the streets of every town and city as they went berserk and tore each other to ribbons in their hunger. At least, that's what I* think *happened. The carnage was real enough. The reason – that's my hypothesis.*

*My doctor friend had a different opinion. He thought that something went wrong with the mind control device. Maybe he's right, but I think that as time went on, ETS became more and more governed by their hunger, and their humanity, or what was left of it, faded, leaving them effectively not much more than zombies with a thirst for blood. And they are* much *faster than zombies. Don't ever try to outrun one. They'll catch you in moments. You have a better chance trying to fight them. More on that later though.*

*After the Americas were turned into a soupy mess of shredded bodies and ETS insane with hunger, the contagion, as it were, finally arrived in Bhutan. I'd missed most of the events because I'd been out in the mountains. Climbing in Bhutan is prohibited because of the spiritual significance the mountains have for the local people. The highest unclimbed peak in the world, Gangkar Puensum at 7,570 meters lies within Bhutan's borders. I thought about mounting a solo expedition and climbing it regardless of the law, but this is my home now and Western notions of being the first to do something have very little import here. Besides, I'd have probably been thrown in jail if they caught me. And logistically it was just too much. I'd have had to be there acclimating for a month or two, which means supplies and provisions for that long, which means porters. Someone would have figured out what I was up to, and the authorities would have paid me a visit before I even got base camp set up. I also have no desire to flaunt the customs and beliefs of the citizens of my adopted country. It's theirs, after all – not mine. It doesn't ultimately matter though. It's a beautiful mountain, and I hiked in to look at it and dream while the world was falling apart behind me. It was early spring when the first victim of the ETS, the woman in the cave, perished only to be reborn in an image of hell, and I was just leaving for the season. Summer is climbing time in the Himalayas, and I always took full advantage of it. There are dozens of small towns and villages throughout the country, and I'd hike from one to another, stopping here and there to camp in the wilderness, and generally enjoying the incredible scenery. I experienced my first inclination that something was wrong when I was heading back to the capital, Thimphu, where I make my home now. Well, where I* used *to make my home.*

*I was passing through a small village yet some distance from the city when I ran across a little boy and girl sitting on the edge of the road crying. They didn't speak English, and my Dzonghka isn't great, but I managed to figure out that there was something wrong with their parents. Poor kids weren't any older than seven or eight. I got them to lead me to their small house, which wasn't far from where I found them, and there just inside the front door were the bodies of their mother and father. I couldn't see anything obviously wrong with them, no knife sticking out of a chest or anything like that, they were just… dead. That alone was strange to me, but what was stranger was the utter absence of people in the village. Those kids were the only living humans there. At a guess I'd say maybe forty or fifty people lived in that place, based on the number of homes I counted, and every one of them was devoid of life. I couldn't just leave the kids there, so I told them as best I could that I'd take them to the next town, and we'd try to get help. But they wouldn't leave. I don't know if it was because I was a stranger, and obviously a foreigner too, or if they didn't understand what I was saying. Maybe a little of both. Well, I couldn't stay there with them, had to get help somehow, so I left them crying in front of their house and jogged off down the road, hoping that the next town would have a phone or a radio.*

*I hadn't gone more than a hundred yards when I heard screaming from behind me. I looked back just in time to see the little girl (the little boy was gone) get dragged into the house. Just before she disappeared, I saw a hand on her shoulder. My Army training kicked in and I sprinted back, got there in seconds, but I was too late. The mother had her mouth against the little girl's neck, and I could already tell she was dead. The little boy was laying on the ground next to his father. The mother had already finished with him. I just reacted. My fist shot out and connected with the mother's cheekbone. It was enough to get her to disengage from the girl's neck. When her head pulled back, I saw the strangest sight I'd ever seen. She had two extra teeth between the upper canines and the lateral incisors. They were about three inches long and narrow as needles. And they were nearly transparent. I could tell they were hollow because there was blood inside them, like milkshake inside a straw. The woman stared at me with more malice, more malevolence than I ever thought a human face could exhibit. Then she came at me. Good God she was fast! Before I knew it, I was struggling to keep those needle teeth away from* my *neck. There was nothing I could do for the kids, and I was in fight mode. I kicked her legs out from under her, and we both went to the ground. I'm good on the ground, one of the best in my old Army outfit, but this… creature, man, she was* strong*! We wrestled for what seemed like an hour, but was probably only a minute or two, when I was finally able to get hold of a piece of firewood that was next to their fireplace and bashed her in the head with it. It stunned her for a second, and that gave me the opening I needed. I smashed that monster's skull to pulp.*

*After I caught my breath, I looked closer at what was left of the woman's head. One of the needle teeth had broken off, and I picked it up for a closer look. It was as hard as a tooth, just much smaller and very slender. Other than that it was a pretty ordinary object. By that I mean it didn't suddenly become animate and try to stick me. It just sat there in my hand. I really wanted to throw it as far away from me as I could, but reason prevailed, and I wrapped it in a small piece of cloth I found and stuffed it in my backpack. The main thought in my mind was to get this to my doctor friend, see if he could make anything of it.*

*I set a brisk pace when I left that little village. My focus was on getting back to Thimphu and reporting the insanity I'd just been a part of. I hadn't even gone a mile when I heard someone behind me. My senses were on alert now, and I spun around just in time to get knocked over by the father. He was moving so fast when he hit me, that he caromed off and landed on the side of the road about twenty feet away. That gave me time to pick up a fist sized rock from the ground, shuck my backpack, and get ready for my second fight in the last half hour.*

*He didn't stay down long; in a second, he was up and coming at me, needle teeth sparkling in dazzling sunlight. I was struck by how pretty it was that day, gorgeous even. His teeth looked like faceted diamonds when the sun hit them just right. It was beautiful and terrible at the same time.*

*He closed the distance between us in half a second. I swear I'd never seen* anyone *move that fast. It was all I could do to dodge to the side and take a swing at his head with the rock. I missed, of course. He came at me slower the next time; it was like he'd learned his lesson, which in itself was terrifying because it indicated sentience, logical thought. Or at least adaptability. Either way I had to take this guy out before he got me. I briefly considered taking him to the ground but decided against that. Staying upright gave me more options to get away, if the need arose. It didn't.*

*He came at me again and I dodged left, back right and spun around him like a football running back avoiding a tackle, bringing my arm around with the rock in one smooth motion. It connected with the back of his head and dropped him like… well, like a rock. I didn't stand there looking at him like the moronic victim in some horror movie, waiting to see if the bad guy is going to get up. Nope, not this kid. I dove on that motherfucker and bashed his head in just like I had the mother. He didn't get up. And here's one other thing I should tell you about ETS that isn't like the movies – you don't need to drive a wooden stake through their hearts to kill them. Just bash their heads in, like I did. Now granted, that's not exactly easy to do, but it works. They also don't miraculously heal like nothing ever happened. When they're dead, they're dead. Simple as that.*

*It took me three days to get back to Thimphu. By then I'd seen a number of deserted villages and small towns, but no more ETS. That was strange too. Where had they all gone? Thimphu gave me that answer.*

*The capital city lies in a valley that runs roughly north to south. I was coming in from the north and decided not to follow the main streets, keeping to the side roads as much as possible. Thimphu was a ghost town just like every other populated area I'd been through since finding the boy and girl. Until I got near to the center of town. There's a big soccer field close to the Wang Chhu river (sometimes referred to as the Raidāk), and it was overflowing with people. I hadn't seen so many humans in one place since that Guns N' Roses concert. But what really struck me were the stage that had been set up at one end of the field and the massive video screen above it. There were a host of faces on that screen, each in its own little box like a video conference, and I was surprised to see that I recognized some of them. They were world leaders – prime ministers and presidents, heads of state. The US president was in a box way down in the left-hand bottom corner. She looked heavily medicated. Her eyes were droopy, mouth slack with just a tiny sliver of drool at the corner. In other words, she looked like Nancy Pelosi. One of the faces was speaking, the words translated into Dzonghka, which if you didn't already know is the official language of Bhutan, in subtitles at the bottom of the screen. It was a man, French I could tell (French is such a distinctive language), and he had his hand in the air like he was reciting an oath. When he spoke (his words were relayed to the crowd through an array of PA speakers) I was only partially stunned to see that he had little needle teeth like those two people I'd killed back in that village. I've no idea who he was - president, prime minister - whatever France has, but he didn't speak long. The screen blacked out and an image of the Bhutanese prime minister appeared. He was standing at a podium on the front of the stage and clapping, smiling while he did. I was too far away to see him clearly with the naked eye, but I didn't need to. When the prime minister was done clapping and smiling, he gestured to someone I couldn't see, and the grid of faces reappeared. I did a quick count and came up with 186. There are only 195 countries in the world, according to a website I checked just before recording this. It's kind of amazing that the internet still works, so long after everything went down. But like I said earlier, who knows for how much longer?*

*The next person to speak was a relatively young woman who, based on her accent, was probably from Australia or New Zealand. I never could tell those accents apart. Anyway, here's what she said, as close to verbatim as I can recall it:* "Oh, mighty prime minister, you who have given us such gifts, it is to you we the people of Australia [*I got my answer on that at least]* pledge ourselves, our will, our country, and our power that you should be able to smite your enemies wherever in the world you find them. We are yours to command."

*I'm not one to just randomly use profanity. I think it cheapens language and provides an easy way out when trying to convey something one doesn't readily have better words for. But all I could think at that moment was:* WHAT THE FUCK?!?!?!

*The recitals went on, in I don't know how many languages. Never did hear the American president say a word. She must have done before I got there. But if her face was on that screen, well, I could imagine what she said. The last one to speak was some douchebag from Canada with slicked back hair like a cheap Gavin Newsome. Or was Gavin Newsome a cheap version of this guy? Who knows? Maybe they went to the same hairstylist. He spoke in both French and English, and the words were the same as the Australian broad. Nearly every country in the world had pledged itself to tiny little Bhutan! How the hell had this happened? I'd seen the needle teeth in all of their mouths as they spoke, so I assumed that had something to do with it, but what? How had this all happened in the few short months I'd been wandering the wilderness?*

*I didn't want to be there anymore and was about to leave when the prime minister began speaking to his people. The faces on the video screen watched raptly, as if their deity had just descended from the clouds and bestowed upon them everything they'd ever wanted. I couldn't understand what he said, but the crowd roared when he was finished. So did the faces. The racket out of the PA system was deafening, and I covered my ears. It was time to go now; the crowd was dispersing, and while I was confident in my ability to take out one or two, there was no way I could fight thousands.*

*I suddenly wanted very badly to be home. My house was small, just two bedrooms with a living room/kitchen combo and a bathroom, but it was all I needed. More than enough actually. I mean, it wasn't like I ever entertained guests or had visitors in from outside the country. Nope, I liked my solitude, thank you very much. Most residential dwellings in Thimphu are multi-story apartments. But my place and the doctor's were among the few homes that Westerners would consider single-family.*

*It was easy to get back to my house. The streets were deserted with everyone being at the oath swearing, or whatever that was, and I got home relatively quickly. All the windows had wooden shutters, which were all still closed, so I just opened the door and walked in. Nothing appeared to have been touched. I opened my laptop and started looking at news websites. Every one of them had some permutation of the same headline: Bhutan's prime minister was king of the world. There was nothing about needle teeth or why everyone (except me and those two kids) seemed to have them, and I looked hard. Not a word. I was just about to close the laptop and try to figure out what to do next when there was a soft knock on my door, followed by the doctor whispering my name. A kitchen knife was the closest weapon easily to hand, so I picked it up and opened the door a crack. I made him show me his teeth; they were normal, and I let him in. First, he said how thankful he was that I was still alive, then proceeded to tell me exactly how little Bhutan had become the only superpower in the world. It took him two hours to finish the story. I was thankful that although he was from Bhutan, he'd been raised mostly in the States, went to med school there, and returned home to help his people. He spoke English like a native Texan, which was where he'd spent his youth. You already know the most important parts of the story he told me. Now I need to fill you in on what happened after he and I parted company.*

*It was just getting dark when I heard the tromping outside. One of the wooden shutters on my windows had a decent sized crack in it, and I watched through that little slit as hordes of ETS went marching past my house. None of them even looked at it. But they* did *look at the doctor's place. At least a hundred of them broke off and surrounded it. He'd told me just before leaving that he was taking his wife and son and heading for the hills. I was debating whether or not to follow him but decided to wait a day or two and see what happened. I couldn't tell you whether he left right after talking to me or sometime later, but when the ETS breached his house, they came out with nothing. I was thankful for that. He was a good guy, his wife was a sweetheart, and his son cute as a bug in a rug. The ETS stood around staring at the sky for a few moments (I suspect they were probably receiving orders through the devices on their brains), then the entire hoard spread out and started off into the hills. The doctor was obviously important to the prime minister; he was sending a few of his minions to, presumably, find the guy. I don't know which way he went or where he ended up. My last vision of that day, other than falling asleep in my little bed, was of the backs of all those ETS disappearing into the trees that lined the sloping hills which ran down into the valley.*

*The next morning, I decided it was time to go. I'd slept surprisingly well, considering what I'd learned and seen the day before. But then again, I'd been tired. I kept up a double-time pace on the way back to Thimphu, and it had taken a toll on me. After all, I'm not 19 anymore like I was when I first joined the Army.*

*Back then I was in such good shape I could have double-timed for a week and still been ready to charge into hell, guns blazing. Age slows everyone eventually.*

*I took my time packing what I thought I'd need to survive in the wild for an as yet undetermined length of time. Then I sat and waited for nightfall. Nothing happened throughout the day – no hordes of ETS, no knocks on my door, not even any screams from an unfortunate soul caught by those monsters. I'd decided to head south, out of the mountains towards India, down to where the ground is more fertile for crops. Eating is pretty important to me, and while I'm capable enough in the wilderness, I had a suspicion it was going to be a long time before this was over. Being able to grow my own food seemed like a pretty good idea. I briefly considered trying to find a canoe or boat and take the river south but decided against that plan. If the ETS were as smart as they seemed, it was entirely possible they'd have a net, or some other kind of trap strung across the river. And of course there are rapids. I'm not a professional kayaker. It was entirely plausible that I'd end up drowned and washed up on a sandbar somewhere if I tried that. No, being on land gave me far more opportunities to escape or fight than being confined to a boat, no matter how much faster the water route would have been. I could always look for a boat further downstream.*

*I left in the dark and went straight into the trees, mindful of being quiet. It was raining lightly, and I was glad I'd brought a poncho. I hadn't gone more than fifty yards when I found the first dead ETS. They'd been savagely mutilated. The first thing I thought of was bears. But it could have been a Snow Leopard or Tibetan Wolf, although it was rare to see them around people, except in remote areas. And there had to have been a lot of them to inflict the carnage I was looking at. Best I could tell at least twenty ETS had been torn apart. Fortunately, the corpses didn't stink yet.*

*I skirted the abattoir and kept going. Nothing else of note happened that night or the next. I really wished I had a gun, preferably an AK-47. They're easy to operate, ultra-reliable, and ammo is plentiful around the world. Even searched a couple isolated homes I ran across, but no such luck. Guns are legal but strictly regulated in Bhutan. Although I don't think AK's are legal there. Still, it wasn't outside the boundaries of the possible to find an illicit one in somebody's house. Anything's possible, right? I mean hell, an army of vampires took over the world! You really gonna say something is impossible?*

*My third night out I was looking for a place to camp when I heard movement somewhere ahead of me. I stopped and hid behind a thick shrub and peered through the branches to see what it was. A few moments later three ETS emerged out of the breaking dawn. Oh, I travel only at night. As far as I know the ETS' vision is still the same as it was before they were changed. Smell too. In fact, other than strength and speed, not to mention the needle teeth, they're not much different from normal humans. No preternatural abilities that I know of, no sleeping in coffins during the day, just a thirst for blood. These three were coming toward me slowly, as if they were looking for something. All of a sudden, one of them turns on the other two and starts rending at them with her hands and teeth. The utter savagery of the act shocked me. I'm sure Dahmer would have been grotesquely proud. She ripped them apart before they knew what hit them, then she ran off back the way they'd just come. I took that moment to look at something I'd been wanting to see since the doctor told me about it – the mind control device. She'd torn the top of the skull right off one of them, miraculously leaving the brain intact, and I stared at it. Nothing. I found a stick and poked around until I got the brain to pop out of the skull, like exceedingly gelatinous chili from a tin can. And there it was, on the back of the brain. It looked like a small silver starfish with eight wiry arms. I was struck by the (somewhat morbid) thought that if this thing was scaled up in size, it might make a pretty Christmas tree ornament. One of the arms hooked into the Cerebellum, the others to different areas, including the brain stem. I picked it off with the stick and watched it fall harmlessly to the pine needle-covered forest floor. It seemed so innocuous, so benign. But this was the thing that allowed the prime minister to do what he'd done. It was amazing. And sort of anti-climactic. I don't know what I expected – flashing red lights, an evil-looking logo or something. Certainly not what I actually found. I left it and the bodies and wandered off to find a good place to sleep the coming day away.*

*It took days, but I finally got down out of the mountains and into flatter land. I'd been staying mostly away from roads, preferring not to have an unpleasant encounter with a horde of ETS, so I don't really know when I left Bhutan and entered India. The first inkling that I had was a sign for Darjeeling that I glimpsed when I darted across a road. It had been days since I'd seen anything alive other than animals, and I was beginning to wonder what was ahead of me. Honestly, I was getting really tired of walking and was beginning to think about acquiring a car or a motorbike, of which there are legions here, and to hell with staying off the road. I'd somehow gotten it into my head that I wanted to be near the sea. There was no practical reason for it; it was just a desire. Maybe more like an obsession. In leaving Bhutan for India, my main focus had been getting to a place where food was more plentiful, more easily grown or acquired. I could subsist on bananas and mangoes for the rest of my life if need be. And speaking of food, I'd found plenty of it on my way south. Every time I searched an abandoned house I found something to eat. Hunger, fortunately, was not a problem. I still wanted an AK though. In one place I'd searched I found a very old and rusty rifle of some kind. I'm a military guy and even I couldn't tell what it was. The thing looked like it had last been used in like 1900. Maybe it had. It was a bolt action job, but even with my knowledge of firearms, I couldn't get it to work. And there was no ammo for it that I could find, so it was basically a club anyway. I threw it away in frustration. There's no explanation for why I wanted a gun so badly. So far, I'd only had need for one once, when I found the kids and their parents, and I came out of that alright. I don't know. Maybe I just felt defenseless. But I couldn't shake the nagging desire. So, I was elated when I found a small police station in a little town I passed through. That place was as empty as every other town I'd been in since leaving Thimphu. I had no fear or anxiety about running into ETS; they were all somewhere else.*

*The police station was intact, undisturbed, like everyone had just gotten up and walked out one day without touching anything. It didn't take me long to find the armory, and - voila! – an AK! Several actually. I only wanted one. And there was plenty of ammo. I checked all the rifles and took the one that seemed to function the smoothest, looked to be the most well-maintained. There were even a number of semi-automatic pistols. I took one of those too. Immediately I felt better – complete, protected. That AK and the pistol wouldn't help me if a couple hundred ETS got me cornered somewhere, but at least I'd be able to take a few with me before I checked out. Now that I had guns, I decided I was done walking. There was a little motor scooter in front of the police station, keys in it, and I cranked it over. It didn't start right away, and I was just looking around for a gas can and something to siphon a bit of fuel from when six ETS came screaming around a building running straight at me. I was so surprised I almost dropped the AK when I tried to get it off my shoulder where I'd slung it. They were four buildings away from me, but as fast as they are, I barely had time to raise the rifle, sight in on the closest one and touch off a round. It hit the thing in the throat and threw it backwards onto the ground. Then the weirdest thing happened. The other five ETS stopped running. Just flat quit moving. They were looking at me with almost nonchalant expressions, almost as if they didn't care that I was even there. Then, very slowly, they turned back toward their fallen comrade who was choking and gargling on the ground. The ETS moved into a circle around the guy and looked down at him, just stared. I fired up the bike again and was about to drive away when the five of them dove on their buddy and started tearing him apart with their needle teeth and bare hands. That was it for me – I boogied.*

*The next several days were chaos. It seemed I'd found where many of the ETS had gone. As I rode down the road on my commandeered motorbike, I saw ragged bodies and ETS rending yet more everywhere I looked. The entire region was a charnel house. I kept the throttle on the little bike wide open, always watching the fuel gauge, which to my good fortune was in proper working order, and when the tank started to run low, I began hunting for a place to acquire more fuel. It wasn't hard. This part of India was relatively well-populated, based on how many houses and towns I saw. There were a number of gas stations and other vehicles from which I was able to keep the tank full.*

*I'd been motoring for about a week when I saw the first sign for Kolkata. Why the hell not? Let's go see what the big city looks like. As long as it didn't drop me into a modern version of the infamously eponymous Black Hole, I figured I could handle myself. The monsoon season in India runs from June to September, and I was thankful that it was over. Riding all that way in a driving rainstorm would not have been pleasant. Fortunately, I'd been hiking in Bhutan for almost all of it. Although I did still get wet a few times. One thing I should mention before I forget is how fast the ETS actually are. The little bike has a speedometer, in kilometers per hour of course, and I was able to get a pretty good reading on them more than once. They would see or hear the bike, come running out after me and sprint like demons to catch up. The bike topped out at 75kph, which is about 46mph, and those suckers could run every bit of 70kph. Not even a world class track athlete on meth could hope to challenge that speed. The little bike pulled away from them, albeit slowly, and I was lucky that the roads were clear when I was chased. If I'd had to negotiate around stalled or wrecked vehicles, they probably would have had me. The ETS all gave up when they saw they weren't going to be successful in their pursuit.*

*Kolkata is huge. I'd barely gotten to the outskirts when I saw how bad it was. ETS were everywhere, running crazily around looking for someone to kill. And they were finding them too. I have no idea if any of the victims were still human, or if they'd been changed, never got close enough to see, but it was incredibly vicious. I stayed in the outskirts for a few days, in a small little house on a patch of land a few acres in size and waited for things to die down. I'd go out cautiously, look around, and go back to the little house. Eventually the savagery seemed to be over, and I motored on into town. The streets were awash in the dead. I would have bet good money that every inhabitant of the city had been victimized. The smell was overpowering. I only saw a couple ETS, and they weren't close. But they were running in circles like they'd gone insane. Based on the carnage, I'm thinking that's exactly what happened. The question was why. I mentioned this earlier, but what I think happened is that they simply ran out of food. The prime minister turned the entire world's population into ETS, which meant there were no regular people left for them to feed on. They started to go insane with hunger and turned on each other. I think it's that simple.*

*It took me three days to get through the city and out the other side. I had to walk the bike for large sections of it lest I take a spill riding over the dead. Besides, it seemed disrespectful to just drive over them like they were a roadkill opossum. Kolkata isn't far from the coast, and I made it to the sea without any problems. I ended up at a place called Mandarmani Beach, even found a nice resort to stay in. It was as pretty as the Caribbean or the South Pacific – warm water, soft sand, bright sun – and lots of food. There were coconuts and other fruit all over the place. This, I figured, was as good a place as any to ride out the end of the world, if that's what I'd been living through, and better than many. There didn't seem to be any ETS here, which made me happy, but I didn't let down my guard. There was lots of food in the resort kitchen, and I ate better than I had in quite some time. The first night I slept in a second-floor room with the door braced by big pieces of furniture I had to muscle across it. If the ETS showed up and wanted to get in, I could either shoot them or climb down from the balcony to the ground and get away. But I wasn't too worried about it. The only signs of life I'd seen since getting here were me and a few uninterested animals. That was another strange thing – the ETS never seemed to attack animals. You may or may not know this, but cows are sacred to many in India, and in places they roam the streets freely. I never once saw a dead one, although I passed several living specimens. I guess their thirst was for human blood, not bovine.*

*The next morning, I started exploring the place. One of the first things I found was a big conference room complete with computers and still-working internet. I got online and started checking news. There was nothing new; it was all from weeks in the past. The not knowing is the worst. We've become so accustomed to instant information in the modern age that the abrupt loss of it is disorienting. I was just about to shut off the computer and go see what else I could find when an email icon lit up. This was something. It was not my email address; whoever had used this machine had added an app to their desktop. Fortunately it had not, for some strange reason, required a password. I opened it and found an email with no subject line and no text from an address I didn't recognize, but it did have a video file attached. Hesitantly, I opened it and was shocked to see the prime minister of Bhutan. Tears were streaming down his face. He started speaking, but I couldn't understand the words, and there were no subtitles. The man talked for about three minutes, then the video cut from him to what looked like drone footage shot above London. The city was desolate, bodies everywhere, just like Kolkata. Then Paris came on screen. Same thing. A host of great cities around the world followed. I recognized Washington DC, Tokyo, Rio, Moscow, many, many cities. They were all filled with the dead. The video cut back to the prime minister. He was sobbing and seemed to be praying. Then suddenly he stopped, stared straight into the camera, raised a pistol to his head and fired. I closed the video player and went outside for a breath of fresh air.*

*It's been two months since that happened. I keep thinking about trying to get a language translation program to run that video through and see if I can figure out exactly what he said. But then I ask myself why. I think in the end he was taking responsibility for his actions, actions that led to the demise of humanity. At least, that's what I prefer to believe. I still haven't seen a single exsanguinary transmogrification specialist since getting here. Haven't seen a real human either. Maybe there are still some left, people like me who were out in the wilderness when it all went to hell in a slop bucket. Or maybe they were at sea on a ship somewhere. Or in Antarctica climbing the Vinson Massif. I don't know and may* never *know. But this place is nice, the water is warm, and the mangoes are ripe.*

# THE LONG HEAVY SIGH

*"It was more than the human heart could bear: to fall beneath the beloved ax – then to have to justify its wisdom.*
*But that is the price a man pays for entrusting his God-given soul to human dogma."*

*Alexander Solzhenitsyn, The Gulag Archipelago Volume Two, page 327*

The man in the rumpled suit jacket pointed to a squiggly red line on a map projected onto the screen at the front of the lecture hall. "The most recent models indicate that there will be another massive earthquake, of catastrophic proportions, along this fault within two months. It's a certainty." Gasps echoed around the room. These words, coming from this man, were as grave, as profound, as anything ever uttered. By anyone. Anywhere. Ever. If he said an earthquake was going to happen, then it would. The audience in the lecture hall wasn't comprised of just students at this prestigious university – there were also government officials, elected representatives, and more than a few members of the media. The man, a professor of Economic Equity and Communal Partiality, had written extensively on myriad topics, but this was his first foray into plate tectonics. The fact that he'd never taken a Geology class, or for that matter an Economics or Community Organization class, in his life was either ignored by or completely lost on the audience. His curriculum vitae didn't matter. What did matter was his earnestness, his charisma, his ability to enthrall an audience. He had appeared as an "expert" on innumerable television programs, documentaries, panel discussions, and newscasts over his career, and had opined on topics as varied as geopolitics, history, finance, horticulture and quilting. Every focus group and analytic confirmed what most already knew – he was considered believable, trustworthy, even likeable. And that's why they'd chosen him to deliver this particular address. A crisis had to be created, a warning sent, and they needed the best to deliver it.

"He did what we told him to," said the septuagenarian woman in the grey pantsuit.

"Yes, he did," said the octogenarian man in the blue pinstriped suit.

"We'll start the evacuation immediately," the woman said with a smile. The man smiled back and the two shook hands. A young man turned off the video monitor in the soundproof room and followed the two elderly people out into the hallway. Staffers bustled about carrying folders full of papers, laptop computers, and cups of steaming beverages emblazoned with a nationwide coffee shop chain's logo. The old people talked quietly between themselves as the young man followed them down the hall. He touched the screen of his smart phone a few times, then pressed it to his ear and waited. Someone answered. "We're ready," he said. The voice on the other end muttered an acknowledgment and the line went dead.

The two old people walked into a room filled with yet more people, most of *them* old too, and took their places at a large conference table. A sixtyish man with distinguished silver patches of hair at his temples sat at its head. The door closed behind them and the man spoke. "Is it done?" The woman nodded. "Then I'm activating the Emergency Powers Act and initiating an evacuation. Schedule the press conference for this afternoon."

An hour later the sixtyish man was standing at a podium in front of a room full of reporters and cameras. He shuffled some papers, cleared his throat, and looked up at his audience. It still amazed him that these people hung on his every word. He could invite almost every one of them to dinner, tell them that the third course of the evening would be sauteed dog shit with demi-glacé and roasted rat tails, and they'd show up with napkins tucked in their collars and drool dripping from their mouths. There were only one or two individuals in the room where he was about to give a speech who would dare to question his choice of entrees for the hypothetical repast, and those people would not be called on to ask questions today. This was too important for them to voice their contrarian views.

"Ladies and gentlemen," he began. "A short time ago one of this nation's most respected scientists issued perhaps the most dire warning we've ever heard."

The forty-something man watching the press conference from the living room of his ostentatious house scoffed at the distinguished man speaking to the nation. "Fuckin liar," he muttered. "They've been predicting earthquakes here since they invented the seismograph. And they're *never* right. Why in the fuck should we believe them now?" His next-door neighbor, a luminary in the entertainment industry, sat in a recliner on the other side of the room nursing a bottle of very expensive imported German beer.

"They know! I'm telling you - they know! Science has improved tremendously since then. This time they're right!"

"Are you serious?"

"How can you *not* believe them? Didn't you see the clip they played of that professor? That guy knows his stuff! The guy on tv said he's an expert!"

"Do you have any idea what *that professor's* area of expertise is?"

The entertainment man shook his head.

"He got his degree from a college that doesn't exist anymore. It went bankrupt over thirty years ago. And he only got an Associate's, not even a Bachelor's, let alone a Ph. D. In Lavatory Science, of all things."

The entertainment guy looked at his host blankly. "What does that mean?" he asked in a small, confused voice.

"It means he studied shitters and figured out the optimum ergonomic distance from the floor for the toilet paper holder. Or how many paper towel dispensers a bathroom needs based on how many stalls or urinals it has."

"How do *you* know?" he asked defensively. People like him didn't enjoy having their sacred cows slaughtered for porterhouses and New York strips.

"I fuckin researched him. You ever do that? Research things? Learn for yourself instead of just believing whatever they tell you on the Godbox?"

The entertainment man drank his beer to the bottom, then stood gingerly from his chair. "I think I have a massage now. Or no, maybe it's my therapist. Actually, I think it's my dog's therapist appointment. Or maybe it's my dog's massage. I can't remember. I'll have to ask one of my assistants. Anyway, I have to go. I have people waiting for me at my house."

The forty-something man sighed, a quiet, lost sound. "Yeah, ok. See you later." He liked the entertainment man, but his ignorance was... insufferable sometimes. It was rare for people in this community to act neighborly, but he'd met the entertainment guy a few years ago when he'd bought this place, and they'd struck up a friendship through the massive hedge that separated their properties. Privacy was of paramount importance in this neighborhood, but this home had been vacant for nearly a year before he bought it, and the hedge had been neglected to the point that much of it had died, leaving a few windows of bare branches through which he and the entertainment guy had begun chatting. They had much in common, including their love of exotic beers, and much *not* in common, like their views on politicians and current events. The forty-something man had grown up in a small town in the southern part of the country. He'd excelled in mathematics and science in school, and at the age of twenty-three had invented a highly reliable and efficient electric motor that was now widely used in kitchen appliances around the world. It had made him very wealthy, and when he'd come to this part of the country on a business trip some years back, he'd liked it so much he decided to buy a house here. A few years of searching had paid off when his real estate agent had found this place. Two years' worth of renovations later, it was home.

He watched the entertainment guy walk out his back door, down the hill to the beach, and out of sight around the end of the hedge. The man on the screen was still talking about the imminent earthquake and how destructive it was going to be. He took a draught from his own beer and focused his attention on the speech.

"And now, my fellow citizens, comes the part I really…" he paused, dropping his eyes to the podium in front of him.

"It's all bullshit, all for show," the forty-something man said to the empty room. "Here comes the hammer." The man on the screen raised his eyes. They were shiny, wet, as if he was about to cry. "Phony bastard."

"I have no choice but to declare an imminent emergency. We must act now in order to save lives. To that end I have, using the authority granted me by this office, activated the Emergency Powers Act. Effective immediately all residents of the exclusion zone have twenty-four hours to evacuate. I cannot stress enough that this needs to be an *orderly* evacuation. Our military has been put on domestic alert and will assist in maintaining law and order throughout these proceedings. Anyone caught looting or otherwise impeding the evacuation, or the efforts of our military and law enforcement officials, will be arrested and subject to prosecution by tribunal under the EPA. And I caution those who would take advantage of this extremely serious situation – if you do not comply with the orders of the authorities, the use of deadly force has been authorized."

"You cock reaming, shithole fucking, sonofawhore!" the forty-something man screamed. "You just declared fucking martial law! In my town! Fuck you and all your sycophantic turd sucking acolytes!" He threw his empty beer bottle across the room and was richly rewarded when it smashed into the screen directly on the speaker's face.

The evacuation was not orderly. He'd gone over to the entertainment guy's house about an hour after throwing his beer bottle at the screen and found that his neighbor had not heard the news. He'd been too busy getting waxed and cupped. These vanity treatments had never made much sense to him. Being oneself, as one was created, was the only way to live, as far as he was concerned. But the entertainment guy had appearances to keep up, facades to maintain, and people in his industry expected… modifications. He didn't blame the guy for doing what he did, just found it very wasteful, distasteful, and ultimately useless. Age came for everyone sooner or later, no matter how many Botox treatments, Kale juice cocktails, and personal trainer sessions you had. Why not just embrace it gracefully, take pride in your hard-won experience and wisdom instead of trying to hide it behind a Potemkin Village of expensive therapies designed to regress your appearance to a youth that had deserted you forever? Whatever.

The neighbor was incredulous when he told him the news. "How can they do this?!" he whined. "I have an important production meeting tomorrow. I can't evacuate!"

"Turn on the news and see for yourself."

The entertainment guy dismissed the pair of spray-tan-tinted young men who'd been working on him and touched a screen on a tablet device. An entire wall flashed to life, and he scrolled through a menu on the tablet until he found the option he wanted. The heavily made-up face of a young woman appeared on the wall. Over her right shoulder was a small window playing video of absolute chaos in the big city a few miles south of where they were. People were looting stores, fires were burning, and soldiers were rounding up the miscreants and herding them into vans or shooting them outright. Bodies could be seen lying in the streets among the flaming cars and fluttering debris. It looked to the forty-something man like any other riot he'd ever seen on the news. Except that this one was going to suck him into its vortex. It seemed impossible; these things happened to other people, not to him. He'd bought this house in this spot because he wanted to be away from places like that, places where riots happened, where crime was a daily and unwelcome companion, where poverty and destitution were nearly virtues. This was his haven from all that, and those bastards in the capitol had just taken it away from him. He sighed, a long and weary exhalation filled with resignation. Throwing beer bottles at the screen wasn't going to make the situation go away.

"We need to leave soon. Before it gets like that here. Get some things together; you can ride with me." Both men were single, childless, and had no one else to be responsible for. If he thought his neighbor could handle himself, he'd have left him on his own. But for all his money and influence in his industry, the guy was shockingly clueless about most of the things normal people took for granted. He even hired someone to run his dishwasher once a week.

"But my Maybach?! What's going to happen to it?! And my Rolls Phantom II?! Its irreplaceable!"

"We'll take my Range Rover. We may need it if things are bad on the way. It'll go off-road much better that your... Maybach. Now come on."

"Off-road? Where are we going?" the entertainment guy asked just as the young woman on the screen returned from a commercial break. One of the news correspondents was interviewing a man on a street somewhere. Fires burned behind them, three wrecked cars were being spray-painted by a group of teenagers, and just beyond that tableau, a group of adult men were punching and kicking someone lying on the ground. The body jerked and vibrated with the force of the blows. "It's like I said," the interviewee said into the microphone. "They gotta get everybody outta here. The earthquake is about to happen, and they can't just let people die for nothing." The person on the ground had managed to get up and was running from the group of men who'd been pounding away moments before. One of them drew a handgun from somewhere and fired. The running figure pitched face first to the asphalt and lay still. "And there you have it," the news correspondent said. "The authorities are in control and are doing this to save the lives of everyone in the evacuation zone." A group of soldiers came into view just behind the correspondent and began firing automatic weapons at the group of men. The one with the gun spun around, raising his pistol as he did, and was immediately cut down by a barrage of bullets. "And now back to you in the newsroom," he said.

"You believe that? The forty-something man said. The entertainment guy stared at the screen with an unreadable expression.

"The special effects they used are terrible. I have people who could have made that look far more realistic. I'll have to make some calls."

"That was *live tv!* You think that was *fake?!*" The entertainment guy didn't respond because the heavily made-up news anchor came back on the screen that doubled as his wall.

"There is breaking news at this hour. We've just received this release from the authorities in charge of the evacuation. It reads: 'All citizens of the designated area are instructed to immediately make their way east. Further instructions will be provided at checkpoints along major roads and thoroughfares. Military patrols, assisted by civilian law enforcement agencies, will be conducting house to house inspections to ensure full compliance with this directive. Failure to obey will result in arrest and prosecution. We urge everyone to comply with the authorities and to remain calm during this crisis. More information on where evacuees should go will be forthcoming.' And that's all. We pray for everyone out there to remain safe and to evacuate the area as quickly and calmly as possible. Our newsroom has contacted the authorities for an update on when people may be allowed to return to their homes, but as of this moment we've not received a response to that inquiry. We'll be back in a few moments, and you won't want to miss this – a prominent starlet has been arrested on drunk driving and cocaine possession charges. Find out who when we return."

"Had enough yet?" he asked the entertainment guy.

"I know who that is!" he said triumphantly, obviously more concerned about the incarcerated starlet than the evacuation. "She was-"

He cut the man off. "I don't give a fuck. We have to go. Now! Get your shit together. I'll be in your driveway in five minutes. If you're not out in six, I'm leaving without you." The entertainment guy nodded.

He got in the Range Rover five minutes and thirty-nine seconds later. They pulled out of the driveway onto their quiet residential street, and were soon on the freeway a half mile from their houses. It was jammed with cars heading north. Another freeway branched off of this one a few miles away that led east. He'd put a case of bottled water and a few snacks in the car, and the entertainment guy helped himself to some beef jerky and an Evian. As his neighbor guzzled happily, he berated himself for having bought that particular brand of water. It was nothing but expensive, pretentious shit. Water was fucking water, no matter how much it cost. He should have filled up a milk jug from the kitchen faucet. This guy wouldn't have known the difference. They rode in silence for several minutes as they watched other cars swerve and jockey for position on the crowded freeway. Horns blared, epithets were hurled, and middle fingers stood at attention as everyone tried to get ahead of everyone else.

"You know this is just a bunch of shit right?" he asked.

"What do you mean?" the entertainment guy replied.

"I mean this is a hoax. They're up to something. They can't tell you whether or not it's going to rain in the next two days with any accuracy. You really think they can predict a cataclysmic earthquake two months ahead of time?"

"The authorities know what they're doing," he replied. "They wouldn't tell us to evacuate if there wasn't a real risk."

He sighed, a heavy, disappointed sound. Some people just couldn't reason for themselves. Or listen to reason from others.

"So, you actually have faith that they're doing this in the interest of safety? Of the public good? Out of some sense of altruism? Those fucks don't do anything that doesn't directly benefit them. It's a sucker's game, Three Card Monte."

"No, they wouldn't do that. They care about the people. I know some of them and they're true humanists."

"Oh yeah? How much were they worth before they got powerful? And how much are they worth now? Ever wonder how someone can get to one of those positions and become a multi-millionaire on a public servant salary? Hmm?"

"They made smart business decisions. That's all. Everyone uses their position to make their own lives better."

"Believe that if you want to. They sold us down the river and over the waterfall."

The entertainment guy looked at him with sympathy, as if he was so delusional that the only thing he deserved was pity. "I think I'm going to take a nap. Wake me up when we get there."

He sighed, a low defeated sound. Maybe it was best if the guy just slept until they got to… wherever they were going. East of here were the coastal mountains, beyond them was the interior, a flat, hot, dusty place. He didn't like it there, which is why he'd bought his house overlooking the ocean. Waterfront property – it was always in style, always in demand. Hell, the place had appreciated in value by over six hundred percent since he'd bought it. He never planned to sell, but if he did, it would bring him a very tidy ROI.

They finally made it to the exit and onto the eastbound freeway. The traffic was lighter here; many of the other cars had continued north, and for that he was thankful. He'd almost been hit by panicked drivers a half dozen times in less than an hour. The entertainment guy was snoring softly in the passenger seat, and he turned on the radio to have some background noise. It was tuned to a talk radio station on the AM band, and some kind of panel discussion was taking place. He hated panel discussions. Most of the time they devolved into shouting matches where no one could hear, let alone understand, anyone else. He preferred either monologues, or discussions between two or at the most three people. Whoever these clowns were, they were obviously on different sides of the current issue.

"It's unconscionable making citizens of this country evacuate under threat of being *shot!*" a man said.

"No – it's in the public interest! We have to get everyone out of there before the quake hits!" a woman responded.

"People should be allowed to choose whether or not they want to stay," said another woman. "They're being told to leave their homes, or the military will arrest them."

"But something has to be done! The threat is real and it's not going away! We could have prevented this if we'd just had stricter residential zoning laws. People are packed into these urban areas like grains of rice in a jar. *That's* unconscionable!"

"It's a crock! They don't have the authority to do this!" the man retorted. "They passed some law when no one was looking and gave themselves 'emergency powers that allowed them to turn this country into a banana republic!"

"They did it to protect people! You just can't trust them to do the right thing! People are so stubborn!"

"And what exactly *is* the right thing? Forcing someone to leave their home or you're going to shoot them is *right?!"*

"No one said they were going to shoot them if they didn't leave."

"The people have been told to comply with the authorities' edicts. Failure to do so is punishable by imprisonment or, and I quote, 'the use of lethal force is authorized'. So, by very definition, not complying with an order to leave your home could lead to you being shot!"

"They wouldn't do that unless those people were threatening them. This country is so gun crazy! How many people are meeting the soldiers, who are trying to help them, at their door holding an AR-15?!"

"There aren't even any urban legends about that, let alone any verified incidents."

"But it could happen!"

"And the earthquake could *not* happen!"

"But the scientists say it will!"

"Science also once said that smoking is good for you and that the earth is flat! It's been wrong countless times throughout history!"

"But it's not this time!"

"How do you *know*?"

"Because that professor was on the news. I heard him say it!"

"So, *he* can't be wrong?"

It was all too much; he turned the radio to a smooth jazz station. People were so attached to their opinions that they refused to even consider one that was contrary to theirs. The arrogance was appalling. And disheartening. He remembered a time, and maybe his memory was flawed, but it seemed that when he was young that people could agree to disagree. Now they had to destroy each other. And civilized debate? That was deader than Elvis. Even universities, once the bastions of free speech in the enlightened Western world, were actively practicing censorship, silencing the voices that adhered to positions counter to their dogma. Or maybe people had just always been people. Maybe arrogance had always existed. Maybe there had always been censorship. Maybe it was just this age, with its instantaneous forms of communication and the vast public forums that were now available that gave the most extreme among the populace a sense of importance and legitimacy regardless of the validity of their views. Maybe he just didn't remember clearly. Or maybe, in spite of his doubts, he was right.

They drove through the mountains and descended the pass on their eastern slopes. He grimaced as the flat land of the interior spread out before them. It was brown, dead and dusty, just like the last time he'd seen it. The line of vehicles in front of him slowed to a crawl, and an hour later he saw why. A host of dark green military trucks lined the road ahead of them. The entertainment guy woke up and stretched his jaw in a massive yawn. "Cupping always makes me sleepy," he mumbled.

"And it makes you look like you got attacked by a rabid octopus," the forty-something man muttered.

"What did you say?"

He ignored him. "There's a checkpoint ahead. Military. Could get interesting." The entertainment guy sat up in the passenger seat and peered through the windshield.

"There are a lot of soldiers up there," he said. "They'll tell us what to do. They'll make sure we're safe."

"We'll see," he replied. It took another two hours before they got within a quarter mile of the checkpoint. The gas gauge showed that he had just under a quarter tank. They were going to have to find fuel soon, or they'd be walking. It was hot outside, and he'd had the air conditioning on since they left, but it increased the engine's fuel consumption rate by a pretty significant percentage, and he turned it off to save what they had. A touch of a button rolled down the window and let in a blast of hot air. The entertainment guy looked at him but didn't say anything. The road was flat here, with fallow farmland on either side, and their view of the roadblock was obscured by all the vehicles in front of them. They sat in the Rover, sweating in the heat and breathing the exhaust fumes of all the other cars, when a popping sound rang out.

"What was that?" the entertainment guy asked.

"Sounded like gunshots," the forty-something man replied as he sat up in his seat. More popping echoed across the road. Suddenly the roar of engines drowned out every other noise, and clouds of dust rose from near the checkpoint. "Put your seatbelt on," he said. The sun glinted off something ahead, and he watched as a car pulled out of the line and sped off across a field. It found a ditch or depression of some kind and ground to a halt. Three people got out of it and began running away from the road. The two occupants of the Range Rover watched in horror as several camouflage-clad soldiers raced after them, shouting commands that were nothing but gibberish in all the sudden noise. Four of them stopped running, dropped to one knee, raised their rifles, and fired. The three running people all fell.

That was all he needed to see. He spun the wheel to the left and hammered the throttle. The Range Rover jumped into motion. They bounced over the median, across the opposite lanes of the freeway, and out into a plowed field. Low rows of mounded dirt ran perpendicular to the freeway, and he followed their path, trying hard to keep the tires on top of the little hills. The Rover fought him as he tried to keep it from getting high-centered; the tires wanted to slide off the dirt mounds and into the troughs between them. On the far side of the field, probably a half mile away, was a lone farmhouse. A barn and a few other smaller structures stood a short distance from it. He had no illusions of being able to hide there; the dust cloud from the Range Rover would lead the military right to them, but if there was a paved road, maybe he could get far enough away that they could find a place to hide.

They were about halfway to the farmhouse when something exploded a few yards to their right. Dirt flew into the sky and peppered them both through the open passenger side window. "What was that?!" the entertainment guy screeched.

The forty-something man had seen enough war movies to know that the soldiers were firing more than just bullets now. "Some kind of artillery, mortar or something," he said and pushed the gas pedal to the floor. The Rover bounced and jolted through the field as more explosions crashed all around them. He looked in the rearview mirror, and through the dust cast up by the Rover's tires, saw other vehicles following him. Several were burning, and one pickup truck exploded in a gout of flame and smoke as the military scored a direct hit. The farmhouse was rapidly approaching, and he was thankful he'd been the first one to drive out this way; the cloud of dust the Rover was creating behind them must surely have made it almost impossible for anyone following to see where they were going. More explosions ripped through the field, and one blasted the barn to bits.

He spun the wheel at the edge of the field and was suddenly driving across a dead lawn. The brown grass crunched under the tires. A wooden fence ran across their path a few yards ahead, and he drove through it; the dry wood splintered with the force of the Rover's impact. Just beyond the fence was what he'd hoped for – a paved road that led away from the military. Another explosion echoed to their right and the farmhouse exploded in a fiery blast. The tires squealed in protest as they made contact with the cracked asphalt, in seconds they were hurtling down the road at over a hundred miles per hour.

"Slow down!" the entertainment guy wailed.

"I'll slow down when we're away from *them*," he spat. His passenger's eyes were wide with fright.

"They just wanted us to stop," he said over the roar of the wind rushing through the open windows and the screaming engine.

"Is that *really* what you think?!" he asked, "that they fired those bombs, or whatever they were, in order to get us to *stop*?!"

"You heard the news! If we just cooperated, we'd be fine."

"Yeah. The Jews in Eastern Europe said the same thing in the 1930's and 40's."

"What's *that* supposed to mean?"

"It means you don't know what the fuck you're talking about!"

"I do so!"

"The fuck you do!"

"Stop this car and let me out! I can't ride another minute with you!"

The forty-something man looked at his passenger. The entertainment guy's eyes were utterly sincere. He meant it. He'd rather walk in this heat or get blown up or shot by the military than have his precious beliefs questioned.

"Whatever you say." He slowed the Range Rover to a stop and watched the entertainment guy get out. "Good luck," he said as he sped away. He looked in the rearview mirror and the last image he had was of the idiot looking around frantically for somewhere to go.

Three days later he was in the basement of a two-story cinderblock building a hundred miles north of where everything had gone wrong. He'd run across a small, abandoned hamlet a short distance from where he'd dropped off the idiot, and in a shed behind a ramshackle house, he'd found four five-gallon gas cans full of precious fuel. It had gotten him this far, but he'd eventually run out of gas and hadn't been able to find more. A battered mountain bike ride later, here he was, hiding in a basement like a rat. He'd passed scores of burned-out vehicles and countless bodies on the way. This entire region had turned into a war zone, and he was caught in the middle of it. His water had run out the day before, and he'd had to leave most of the food in the Range Rover; it was too heavy to carry. Hunger was becoming a problem. There was nothing in this building to eat, and he'd searched a couple other places without luck. Sooner or later, he was going to have to emerge from this hole and find food. He waited until night to come out.

The little town consisted of maybe twenty buildings total, with most of them being houses, and the majority either in utter disrepair, or with for sale signs on the lawns. He looked through six or seven but didn't find anything edible. His hand was on the knob of the next house when a voice shouted at him from across the street. "Stop! Hands up!" He froze on the porch, frantically trying to decide whether to run or fight, when the sound of running boots met his ears. This was it – he was caught. A moment later he was slammed to the ground, and handcuffs were roughly and tightly applied to his wrists. Hands pulled him up, and a hood was jammed over his head. He was partly carried, partly dragged, away from the house and thrown into something he thought was a van or truck. A metal door closed behind him with a clang, and the vehicle began moving.

"What did you do to get caught?" a voice asked. It was a woman. Her voice was rough and scratchy, like she smoked too many cigarettes.

"I was just looking for something to eat," he replied as he struggled to get to his knees amid the rocking and swaying of the vehicle.

"Hmmph," the woman said. A jolt knocked him over, he hit his head on something hard, and everything went black.

He woke up to bright light. As he slowly opened his eyes, he heard the sounds of many people around him. Voices were speaking and screaming, wailing and cursing. He rolled onto his side and made it to his hands and knees. His stomach convulsed and he vomited on the ground. Someone kicked his leg, but he ignored it and tried to stand. Everything hurt, especially his head, and the light made that worse. Squinting, he managed to stand shakily and looked around. He was outside in a wide-open area. There were people everywhere, walking around dazedly, staring into the distance, and even two men fighting on the ground a short distance away. No one paid any attention to them. As his eyes adjusted to the brightness, he saw a massive chain link fence topped with razor wire – no, there were *two* massive fences running parallel to each other, one about fifteen feet beyond the first. His eyes followed the fence line, and he quickly realized he was in a huge open-air prison. The fences described a rectangularly shaped border nearly a quarter mile long. There were no buildings inside it, only hordes of people. Outside the fence, perhaps thirty yards away, was a row of large camouflage-colored military tents. Soldiers milled around them, and more stood guard along the outer perimeter of the fence or looked down on the prison from tall watch towers at each corner. A large gate, guarded from the outside by yet more soldiers, stood just to the side of the tents. As he watched a truck backed up to the gate and a group of soldiers with rifles at the ready rushed over. One of them opened the gate while another opened the back of the truck. Several people got out, their heads covered by black hoods and their hands cuffed behind their backs. Other soldiers removed the bags and cuffs as the rest forced them through the gate at gunpoint. A small group of five or six prisoners rushed at the soldiers as soon as the last new arrival was through the gate. A barrage of gunfire dropped them all, and several rounds impacted upon others who'd not taken part in the escape attempt. A soldier emerged from one of the tents with a bullhorn. He put it to his mouth and began speaking. "Any further attempts at escape or insurrection will be met with deadly force," he intoned. "Obey our commands, remain calm and everything will be fine. You'll be reunited with your loved ones shortly."

"Bullshit!" a man screamed in response. Other voices rose to join his in protest, but the soldiers ignored the cries as they dragged the bodies of the dead out of the prison and closed the gate.

The forty-something man suddenly realized he had to pee. He stopped an older man who was shuffling slowly and distractedly past and asked him where the lavatory was.

"There isn't one," the man replied blankly. "All we have is an open latrine, just a pit they dug in the ground. There aren't even walls separating men and women."

This was not possible! Not in this country! He pushed past the man and made his way through the crowd, his head still pounding. Something crusty tugged at his skin, and he raised his hand to wipe it away. It came back covered in small flakes of dried blood. He'd been knocked out in the truck, then just thrown in here and left to rot with everyone else. How the fuck could this happen?!

The crowd parted in front of him a few paces ahead, and he suddenly realized why - he'd found the latrine, and the stench was so intense that no one wanted to get near it. The old man had been right too. Men, women and children of all ages stood and squatted next to and above what was only a long ditch in the ground as they relieved their bladders and bowels in front of everyone. More than one person was openly weeping. There were no seats to sit on, or even any toilet paper. He wondered what the professor with the Associate's degree in Lavatory Science would think of this arrangement. A very old woman tottered over to the latrine and stared at it. Then she silently turned and walked away. He was disgusted to see her skirts start to darken as she chose to release her bladder in her clothing rather than subject herself to the humiliation of the open pit latrine. He had no such qualms, and boldly walked to the edge of the ditch, held his breath, and released a long stream into the morass below. Finished, he found his way to the edge of the fence where there were fewer people and sat down in the dirt.

A few minutes of observation showed him what appeared to be people from every race and social stratum there was. A man and woman in expensively tailored clothes huddled together a short distance away, while a young man covered in the sores and scabs characteristic of a chronic drug user eyed their jewelry hungrily. He sighed, a sound of despair and resignation. It had happened here. Everyone had said it never would, that it couldn't. They'd been wrong. Just like most people who say that things can't happen are wrong.

He fell asleep in the hot sun, only waking when a change in the temperature made him chilly. As he woke, groggy from sleep, he saw a series of large spotlights on tall poles flare to life, bathing the prison in sterile white light. Shadows flickered as people moved through the beams, and the sound of sobbing reached his ears. He had no tears to cry, only anger to release.

A noise from the area of the gate summoned his attention, and he stood to get a better look. A large group of prisoners had gathered and were shouting at the soldiers. Threats, epithets, and entreaties alike rang out in the rapidly cooling night air. No one in the prison had even been given a blanket. A young mother with two small children a short distance away from him had pulled her shivering progeny in close to her and was speaking soothingly to the obviously frightened kids. The voices at the gate grew louder, more demanding, and soon people were shaking the fence and throwing whatever they could find over the tall structure toward the soldiers. He looked toward the tents and saw the same man who'd come out earlier with the bullhorn emerge again. The soldier looked toward the gate and raised his hand in a signal to the other troops there. They reacted immediately. One of them opened the gate, while behind him at least thirty aimed their rifles at the crowd of prisoners as yet more soldiers poured into the prison. They withdrew collapsible batons like the police used from pouches on their belts, and waded into the group of protesting prisoners, swinging their clubs indiscriminately. The dull thunk of metal on bone reverberated throughout the prison, and the crowd quickly dissipated. The soldiers walked out and closed the gate behind them, leaving a score or more of battered bodies behind. Many were writhing in pain, some were screaming, and some were eerily still and silent. The forty-something man closed his eyes and wrapped his head in his hands. The children with the young woman were wailing as she tried vainly to comfort them.

He must have drifted off again, because the next thing he remembered was waking up to dull light as the sun began to rise across the flat expanse of the wide valley. He was desperately thirsty, his stomach rumbled with hunger, and he wondered if they'd be given water and breakfast, but up to this point the only thing he'd seen the soldiers give the prisoners was a good beating. Or a bullet. He stood and stretched, thankful to find that his head didn't hurt nearly as much as it had yesterday. A look through the fence showed him the coastal mountains many miles away from the prison. To think he'd just driven through them a few days ago, a free man in an expensive Range Rover, only to end up here, was nearly impossible to reconcile. How had it all come to this? Earthquakes, evacuations, and prisons? Had he suddenly been transported through time and space to Poland circa 1942? Or the Soviet Union circa 1937? Or maybe Cuba circa 1960. Might as well have been. He was about to go find the latrine for the second time when a familiar voice spoke behind him. "Didn't think I'd see you again," the entertainment guy said. He turned and found himself facing his former neighbor and travel companion.

"I didn't think so either." The entertainment guy's hair was matted with blood, and he had a generous shiner under his left eye. "What happened to you?" he asked.

"After you dropped me off, the soldiers found me. I tried to tell them I didn't have anything to do with you and it wasn't my idea to run, but they hit me with their rifles. Then I was here. Been here almost a week."

"Don't they feed us?" he asked as his stomach rumbled for the ninth time in the last ten minutes.

"Every couple days they show up with a big water tank on a trailer and cases of those army ration things in the little bags. They're not too bad. Haven't had any in a day or two, so we should be getting something today or tomorrow."

"And you're ok with that?"

"With what?"

"You just said they give us food and water every couple *days*. That doesn't bother you? You don't think we should get food and water *every* day?"

"They feed us when they can. The authorities have… really important things to do. We should support them and not make trouble. We'll get food when they have time to give it to us."

Did he actually just hear him say that? What happened to his Rolls? The one he didn't want to leave behind when they evacuated? Suddenly forgot about it in his delusional desire to acquiesce to what was clearly a horrific civil and human rights violation? Was he really so wedded to his ideology that he couldn't see what was going on right in front of him, hell, that *he himself* had become a *victim* of? "I'll be right back, gotta take a leak," he said gruffly. The entertainment guy nodded and watched him walk off.

As he approached the latrine, his throat parched and bladder nearly bursting, he saw the old woman who'd pissed herself the day before. She was squatting over edge of the ditch, but her old legs were trembling as they tried to hold her in one position. She swayed and shook as she tried vainly to hold still long enough to handle her business. It was like watching a tower of Jell-O try to stay still while on a boat in rough water. Suddenly her legs gave out, and she toppled over backward into the latrine. A couple people shouted, some turned to look, but only the forty-something man ran to help. By the time he reached the ditch, the woman was gone, sunk beneath the surface of the stinking filth. There was nothing he could do.

He stalked away from the latrine, glaring at everyone around him, and proceeded to piss on the chain link fence. A soldier with a rifle stood outside and watched him impassively. "You like that?" he yelled to the man. "Wanna come closer? I'll piss on your boots you fascist fuck!" His water drained, his anger momentarily vented but not even close to gone, he walked back to the entertainment guy.

"Took you long enough," his old neighbor said. "Get lost or something?"

"Or something." He regarded the man for a long moment. "So have you changed your mind?" he asked finally.

"About what?"

"About your precious authorities. About the reasons they put us in here."

"We're here because we didn't obey their commands."

He suddenly wanted nothing more than to pound this idiot's head to a pulp. "You're telling me that after all this, after getting your head bashed in by rifle butts, after getting thrown in prison, that it's *your* fault? It's *their* fault?' he asked pointing to the small children with the young mother.

"Of course, it is. All we had to do was what they told us to, and we'd have been fine. They had to do this, build this place. None of these people can be trusted to do what's right. You heard them – there is an emergency and we had to evacuate. Thousands would have died if we'd stayed where we were. They know things we don't, which is why we had to listen to them."

"Trusted to do what's right?! Do you even *hear* yourself?! Do you realize where you *are?!* You did the *right* thing and look at you – stuck in here with the rest of us. And you're ok with that?!"

"I didn't... I mean, I couldn't... *you* drove away from the checkpoint! I was just a passenger. It's not my fault – it's *yours*!"

He almost punched him, was just balling up his fist to do that very thing, when a loud sound interrupted him. It sounded like feedback from a microphone at a rock concert. Neither of them had noticed in the midst of their argument, but a series of loudspeakers had been set up outside the fence, and they now blasted out the sound of someone speaking. "My fellow citizens," a man's voice intoned. They both turned toward the speakers and listened. "As of this moment the evacuation of the exclusion zone is going according to our plan. Most of the areas within the zone are clear, the residents having been moved to safer places around the country. I assure you – all are being well cared for. We have several units of the military right now distributing food, blankets, and other humanitarian supplies to all of them. Additionally, private citizens have donated their precious resources and time to help those whose lives have been so dramatically impacted by these events. Our deepest gratitude goes out to them, as do our deepest sympathies to those unfortunate evacuees who've had to endure so much hardship. We will have further updates in the coming days, but please be assured that the danger is not yet over. Just moments ago, I received an update from our chief scientist who assures me that this devastating, calamitous earthquake could happen at *any* moment. We simply *must* be prepared for it. Our brave soldiers and law enforcement personnel are nearly finished clearing the final towns within the exclusion zone, and those efforts are expected to be concluded by tomorrow at the latest. Be brave, my countrymen and women, the worst will soon be behind us, and our lives can return to normal. Thank you and goodnight."

He turned to the entertainment guy. "Alright, you heard him. Still believe that horseshit about all this being for our own safety?"

"Of course! You heard what he said. It's almost over, they've nearly got everyone out, but the danger's still there. The scientists said so."

"How can you *possibly* believe that?! From in *here*?! Are you fucking *blind*?!"

"I used to like you," the entertainment guy said with more heat than he'd ever heard from the man before, "but I don't think I can stand you anymore. You're just as bad as all those racists, transphobes and bigots who voted for… *that man* a few years ago. You saw what *he* did to the country. If you're just too stupid to understand that this is all for the best, then you're more of a moron than I ever -" The forty-something man's fist connected with the side of the entertainment guy's head right on his shiner, and he crumpled to the ground without another word. A new commotion was happening at the gate, and he spun around to see what it was. It looked like almost the entire prison population was rushing the soldiers. Just as he realized what was happening, rifle shots accompanied by the low chugging of machine guns split the air. Bodies began falling all around, and stray rounds kicked up little clouds from the dusty ground. He glanced toward the young woman and her kids and was shocked to see her lying on her back, a hole in her forehead and a huge pool of blood growing around her. Next to her body was that of what looked like her youngest, a little boy probably no older than two. A large red stain graced the front of his Spider Man jumper. The other child, a little girl maybe a year or two older, was unharmed and kneeling next to her dead mother and brother, tears spilling down her cheeks and a wail emanating from her small mouth as she shook her mother's lifeless arm in a desperate attempt to wake her. He snapped at the sight. There was nothing left to do.

The gate was maybe two hundred yards away, and he dashed toward it, nothing in his mind except getting his hands on the throat of one of those soldiers and squeezing until the life left him a camouflage-clothed corpse. About halfway across the prison, a bullet hit his left shoulder, spinning him around and dropping him to the ground. It didn't hurt, just felt more like a very strong punch, and he was quickly up and moving again. Another round grazed his right shin, and that stung, but it only made him run faster. Just as he neared the back of the thinning crowd, many of whom had succeeded in bringing the inside fence down, two more bullets hit him in the chest, and he slumped to the ground. His shoulder suddenly hurt, and he raised his hand to feel the wounds. It came away covered in blood. Breath was very difficult to find, and his chest heaved as blood filled his lungs and choked off his respiration. He was on his back, looking at the sky, and watched mesmerized as a bird floated high above on some unseen thermal updraft. It wheeled and spun, dove and soared as people struggled and died on the ground far below it. As the bird flew out of his field of vision, his eyes closed, and he saw the beach outside his house just as the sun sank into the ocean like a round, fiery ship torpedoed by a stealthy submarine. It was the most gorgeous sight he could ever remember seeing. He sighed for the last time, a long, heavy sound, full of… ending.

"Is it finished?" the septuagenarian woman in the grey pantsuit asked.

"Yep," said the octogenarian man in the rumpled blue pinstripe suit. "Should be good to go."

"I'll let him know," she said and walked out of the office. When she was back in her own office, she opened a drawer in her desk that was secured by a digital combination lock that also required thumbprint identification and extracted the only contents – a cell phone. She unlocked it using a six-digit code and touched the screen. A phone number appeared, and she pressed send. Someone answered on the second ring.

"Yes?" a distinguished voice said.

"It's done. You can cancel the alert."

"Understood." The line went dead.

In another office in another building, a sixtyish man picked up a phone on his desk and dialed a number. A voice with a foreign accent answered on the third ring. "Yes?" it said.

"Things will be moving again soon. Watch my press conference in a few minutes."

"Understood," the voice said.

Twenty minutes later the sixtyish man was behind a lectern in a room full of people holding cameras, notebooks, and digital recorders. Their glowing eyes slathered him in love and adoration as he shuffled some papers and looked up.

"My fellow citizens," he began. "Our top scientists have just informed me that a sizeable earthquake has just occurred in the exclusion zone. It was not as catastrophic as our models initially suggested, but damage to property in the area is considerable. We will have crews on the ground soon in order to determine whether or not it's safe to return. This process could take several weeks, even months, as we inspect buildings and infrastructure. Please be patient and know that we are doing all we can to ensure the safety and comfort of everyone." He stopped speaking and waited.

This was the signal for questions from the audience. Several of them were openly weeping in relief, and he called on a young man in the front row. "Yes?" he asked. The young man stood.

"Sir, I just wanted to say thank you. Your guidance and leadership through this crisis have been... incomparable. The people of this nation, and the entire world, are in your debt." A lone tear spilled down the young man's cheek as he began clapping. The room erupted in applause and cheers. All but three of the people in the audience were standing and cheering as if the man before them was a rock star. Or a god. He basked in the adoration, and only after nearly a full minute did he raise his hands for quiet.

"Our friends from across the Pacific have made the deposits to the offshore accounts," the septuagenarian woman said. "Did you get yours?"

The octogenarian man nodded. "And I checked on *his* too. It's all there. Where are you going to live after they build their *'business park'*?"

"I have my eye on a couple properties up the coast," she replied. "There is a pair of houses I've seen from my yacht that I really like. Only thing is there's an enormous hedge between them. I think I'll hire a bulldozer to just level them both and build one big place. It won't be a problem now that we've passed Rebuilding and Reconstruction Act. My foundation was granted exclusive rights to ten thousand acres of my choosing, provided I don't try to take what was already promised to our friends across the ocean.

The exclusion zone idea was brilliant. We were able to get everyone out and keep them out. Wish we'd thought of that sooner. I'm nearly too old to enjoy the fruits of our labors!"

The octogenarian smiled. "I know exactly what you mean," he chuckled.

*Author's Note for The Long Heavy Sigh:*

*Thanks must be given to Ray Profitt for providing me with the title to this story.*

# CRYPTOZOOLOGY

"Ha ha! The little freak pissed himself!" said the kid in the jean jacket about the small boy cowering in the corner. "I'll bet he pisses the bed too!" He looked quickly to either side just to make sure the two boys with him were displaying appropriate levels of both derision for the victim and mirth at his predicament. Being a bully wasn't much fun if your efforts went unrecognized and unappreciated. He didn't have anything to worry about; Stevie and Brock were laughing and pointing at the small boy with the wet patch on the front of his jeans. Just like they should be. The boy was staring up at his tormentors from where he squatted in the corner; his eyes were wide and glistened with fear and nascent tears. But there was something else in them that Dylan couldn't quite identify, something other than fear, an emotion so heavily veiled that it was barely perceptible, felt more than seen. His young saurian mind bounced off the potential revelation like a rubber ball tossed onto a glass-topped table.

"I think he's gonna shit himself next!" Brock said in a mocking and cruel tone.

"If he does, I'm gonna beat his ass," Stevie added.

"Don't get any shit on your hands!" Brock laughed, delighted at his own wit.

"Shut the fuck up or I'll make *you* piss your pants," Dylan said to both of his henchmen. Stevie and Brock instantly fell silent. Neither one had ever directly challenged Dylan physically. In fact, no one at their school had. The general of their little army had been talking big and tough since… well, since any of them could remember. And he *was* bigger than most kids, which meant that he was probably stronger, which meant that he would probably win in a fight against anyone who tested him. At least, that's what their seventh-grade logic told them would happen. It was simple, really. Bigger and stronger equaled winner. They had not yet discovered that traits like speed, agility, guile, and skill could (and often did) win the day against larger and more physically powerful opponents. That was a lesson for later in life. Right now, all that mattered was who was bigger and stronger, and more importantly, how others perceived his supposed strength. Nearly to a student every kid at Wilkeson Middle School in Washington state feared Dylan. And he liked it that way.

The small boy was one of their favorite targets and had been since the four of them began attending Rocky River Elementary school together. The tormenting and bullying had started when Arturas Miskinis first began school in the second grade. Now, five long years later, it continued in middle school.

His family was from a small town in central Lithuania called Baisogala. Arturas was born in 1983, and had grown up speaking his native Lithuanian, and at the instruction of his mother, English. She'd worked for the government as an interpreter, having learned English herself from her own mother who'd originally hailed from Scotland. His father was a mechanic on a local farm who could fix almost anything and loved nothing more than refurbishing old farm equipment and buildings. He'd taught his son from a young age to be inquisitive about everything, to not be afraid to wonder how things worked or ask why they'd been built the way they had. Arturas was fascinated by machines and structures and spent hours with his father as he tinkered with engines or built fences and chicken coops on the farms that hired him. Arturas had one older brother and one younger sister, neither of whom had the slightest interest in machines or construction. His brother was fascinated with the violin, while his sister preferred to learn sewing tricks from her mother who moonlighted as a seamstress. The entire family had grown up under communism when Lithuania had been a vassal state of the USSR. Arturas' mother was fond of telling them stories her own mother had told her about what life was like in the West.

His grandmother had come to Europe from Glasgow in late 1945 to work as a nurse in Berlin. This was during the reconstruction of Europe after World War II ended. It was there she'd met his grandfather, a former Soviet soldier who'd been conscripted into the military, and who'd also been among the first to enter Berlin where he'd been wounded by an artillery shell. Somehow, he'd ended up in an Allied hospital, even though the British and Americans didn't reach Berlin until after the Soviets. They'd been smitten with each other from the first moment, even though neither spoke the other's language. By the time he finally recovered, they'd learned enough to communicate, and he'd told Arturas' grandmother that he wanted to return to

Lithuania, even though it would have been a simple thing to move west and remain free. His small country was already a part of the USSR, but she agreed to go with him and sent a letter to her family back in Scotland informing them of her decision. They lived a quiet but mostly happy life in Baisogala and raised four children, one of whom would go on to become Arturas' mother.

His father had become disillusioned with Communism after seeing firsthand how people suffered under it, and after being told many stories by his wife's mother of how bountiful and free the countries of the West were. Arturas' parents spent many nights debating whether and how to escape their country. Life behind the Iron Curtain was difficult for those without political connections, and most at least pondered leaving, even if they had no means to carry out their plans. Arturas' parents, after watching the entire harvest of a neighbor's farm be confiscated and publicly burned for failing to produce the required quota, decided they'd seen enough and that it was time to leave. In 1987 they began to slowly sell off their possessions so as not to attract too much attention, and when they felt they had enough money, left their bucolic hometown one dark Spring night and made their way to the Baltic coast. When they finally arrived at the sea, in a town called Palanga, Arturas' father met a man who owned a boat and with whom he'd already made arrangements, and two nights later they put to sea from a small harbor north of the town.

Arturas was as excited as he'd ever been. Up to that point he'd only ever seen boats on television or in books, and his keen inquisitive mind, encouraged and molded his father, analyzed the shape of the hull, the design and sound of the engine, and he watched how the captain guided the boat through and over the large waves that rolled across the sea. Their destination was the Swedish island of Gotland, which lay some two hundred and sixty miles to the north. His father had told them how dangerous the trip could be. The Baltic was not a body of water to be trifled with; it had claimed countless vessels over the centuries. But bad weather and rough seas weren't the only risks. There were also the military patrols. The key to escaping the oppression and misery that defined the Soviet Union and Eastern Europe at that time was evading the guards and soldiers whose primary purpose was not to keep invaders *out*, but to keep the citizens *in*. The man Arturas' father had hired claimed to have contacts in the maritime forces who would, for the right price, look the other way as his small boat sailed for Sweden. They had to leave that night, regardless of the weather, or another bribe would have to be paid. The family couldn't afford to pay twice, so at the urging of the captain, they boarded the boat and watched the shoreline of their homeland disappear into the darkness behind them. The weather was bad, the seas rough, and everyone except Arturas and the captain ended up seasick. But they made it across the Baltic alive.

The captain was a fine pilot and conducted them safely to Gotland where he put in at a secluded harbor on the southern side of the island. Some people met them there who spoke Lithuanian with a strange accent that made Arturas stare in fascination until his mother addressed them in English, which they all spoke. Later she explained to him that they were members of an anti-Soviet resistance group who helped people like themselves escape the horrors and deprivations of Communism for a much better life in

Europe or North America. After many weeks and months shuttling around Sweden, they finally received asylum in the United States, and in May of 1988, they boarded a plane in Stockholm and flew to New York.

Arturas was amazed at the sights and sounds of America. It was like nothing he'd ever dreamed of. The grocery stores alone made him gape in awe at the plethora of products available to consumers. They had no family in their new country, but his father had heard of a group of Lithuanians who'd settled in Washington State, and who welcomed expatriates from the homeland, and two days after arriving in New York, the entire family was on a Greyhound bus headed across the country. It was on that trip that Arturas tried his first Big Mac, his first Pepsi, his first Hostess Cupcake, and it was also when he realized that he never wanted to return to Lithuania. America was his home now, in all its vastness, beauty, complexity, chaos, and bounty, and it was here where he would make his life and fortune.

His father had been wrong about the Lithuanian community in Washington. Their bus trip ended in Seattle on a warm June day, and when he discovered that what he'd been told was inaccurate, he'd taken his wife aside and asked her what they should do. Their money was nearly gone, the only possessions they had were in four battered suitcases, and they had no home, no support group. His father had been given a small brochure by some faceless government bureaucrat that featured a list of phone numbers that immigrants could call if they needed help, and his mother extracted it from her purse without a word, found a pay phone at the bus station, and dialed the first number she saw. After many minutes and a number of transfers, she finally reached someone who put her in touch with a local charity that helped refugees like themselves, and three hours later a big Plymouth Gran Fury pulled up to the curb, and a smiling woman beckoned to them. They piled into the car, and she drove them south out of Seattle, finally arriving in the small farming town of Enumclaw. For the next five months they lived together in a single-wide mobile home on a large farm at the edge of town. Arturas' father quickly went to work repairing equipment, just like he had back in Lithuania, while his mother, himself and his siblings all did odd jobs around the farm. Eventually they saved enough money to buy a small house of their own a short distance away in the town of Wilkeson where Arturas started school.

He'd loved it at first. His grasp of English was excellent thanks to his mother's teachings, and he absorbed every lesson eagerly. Arturas excelled in academics, and it was obvious to anyone that he was by far the smartest student in the class. He'd been in school for less than a month when he met Dylan for the first time.

It was recess and everyone was out on the playground. Arturas hadn't made any friends yet, preferring to spend his free time reading and studying. His mother and father had told him about universities and how they taught so much more than the lower-level schools, and Arturas was determined to attend one. He'd learned a bit about engineering from his teacher during a lesson on hydroelectric dams, and the topic had fascinated him. The library in his school was small but it had several years' worth of Popular Mechanics magazines and a book about road construction, and he devoured all of it. The day they met Arturas was sitting alone on a bench near the basketball court when a very big kid and two others walked up to him. A copy of National Geographic was open on his lap, and he was reading about textile manufacturing in India. He didn't notice the other boys until a hand slapped the magazine off his lap and onto the ground.

"Whatcha readin'?" Dylan drawled.

Arturas looked up with a quizzical frown. He didn't understand what was happening, why this boy had just knocked his magazine to the ground. Instead of responding he bent forward to pick it up. Dylan kicked it away, the pages ruffling and tearing from the impact of his tennis shoe. The other two boys laughed. "What a dickhead," one of them said. "Fuckin' readin'!"

Arturas looked at the boys in confusion. What did they want from him? He opened his mouth to ask them, but Dylan was faster. He spit right in Arturas' face. "Try readin' that you fuck!" he said. The three boys walked away laughing. Arturas was shocked. He'd never experienced anything remotely like what had just happened. For several long minutes he sat perfectly still on the bench while Dylan's saliva dripped from his left cheek. At last, he stood, picked up the magazine, and went to the bathroom to wash his face.

Three days later they found him as he walked home. Ordinarily Arturas stayed after school for an hour or two in the library to read. But that day his mother had told him to come straight home. It was his sister's birthday, and she was cooking a big dinner to celebrate. So, Arturas left the school when all the other kids did. It was not a long distance to his house, only about six blocks, but part of the route led him down a dirt path through a section of woods.

Dylan and the others were waiting.

They were sitting on a big pile of rocks that had been dumped there at the completion of some construction project, and Arturas didn't notice them until they'd hopped down and surrounded him. His mind was on the Space Shuttle and a film they'd watched at school about the program that birthed it and the tragic Challenger disaster. Before he knew what was happening, Dylan was standing in front of him.

"Where you goin' fucktard?" he asked derisively. Brock seemed to like that pejorative if his cackles of laughter were an indication.

Arturas looked at Dylan with much the same confusion he had the first time the boy had accosted him. "Home," he said softly.

"I don't think so," Dylan replied. "Least not til I'm done with ya."

"What do you-" Arturas' question was cut off by Dylan's open-handed slap across his face. Tears sprang to the boy's eyes and his hand flew to his cheek.

"Don't ever fuckin' talk when I'm talkin'! Get it?!" Arturas was too stunned to nod. "I asked you if you fuckin' get it?!" Dylan screamed. The woods were thick here, the houses not close. In later years development would see this patch of forest cleared and houses built, but in early 1989 it was still dense woodland. Voices did not carry far through the trees. No help would be coming.

Arturas tried to run past Dylan, but the larger boy stuck out his arm like a professional wrestler, and the much smaller boy was knocked to the ground. He landed on his backpack, and his breath went out of him with a whoosh. "Grab his arms," Dylan said to his lackeys. Brock and Stevie each did as he bade them, and hoisted Arturas up. The small boy was gasping as he tried to breathe and cry at the same time.

"Awww look at the little crybaby!" Stevie said derisively. "Want us to call your mommy for you?"

Stevie had no idea how much Arturas actually did want his mother at that moment. He couldn't understand why they were doing this. What had he done to them? What did they want? It would be years before he came to understand that bullies don't need a reason, only a target.

Dylan nodded to his friends, and they dragged Arturas to a large evergreen tree and held him fast against the trunk by his arms. Their leader stood in front of the terrified Lithuanian boy and leered at him. "Think you can just come over here from wherever the fuck country and do whatever you want, huh commie?" he spat. Arturas was crying openly now, his tears wet the front of his shirt and splashed on his thrift store Adidas. His arms were really beginning to hurt. Stevie and Brock each had one and were pulling them backward around the trunk of the tree to keep Arturas in place. Dylan smacked him again. "I asked you a fuckin' question commie!" he yelled in Arturas' face. Spittle flew from his mouth and spattered on the small boy's skin. Arturas struggled against the hands holding his arms, which only served to infuriate Dylan even more. The bigger boy began to rain blows, punches, into Arturas' torso. His already labored breathing became gasps, inhalations that brought him no oxygen. He felt himself getting weaker, his vision darkened, and he blacked out.

"Oh fuck!" Brock said, releasing Artruas' arm as the small body of their victim went limp and slid down the trunk of the tree. "You fuckin' killed him," he breathed, his eyes wide.

"No, I didn't," Dylan replied. "He's still breathin'. Look." Arturas' chest was rising and falling in fits and starts as his lungs tried to reinflate, his diaphragm to operate normally. Somewhere not too distant a car horn honked. Brock shook his head at the sound as if clearing cobwebs. "I gotta go," he said quickly. "My mom's waiting for me." He didn't look for approval from Dylan but instead dashed off down the path.

"I got chores to do," Stevie added as he watched Brock disappear into the trees. "My dad'll beat my ass if they aren't done before he gets home." Dylan just looked at the other boy, who also ran off down the path before he could be told not to leave. Arturas was stirring on the ground, his breathing more measured and even as his body corrected the wrongs that had been done to it. Dylan looked down at him, smiled and walked nonchalantly away.

The bruised and beaten little boy walked slowly through the woods, his tears finished for the moment, and was relieved when he emerged from the trees to see only an empty street and not his tormentors waiting for him again. The two blocks from that point to the small house he shared with his family seemed to take forever. His ribs ached where the big kid had pummeled him, and his face stung from the slaps. And he was filthy. What was he going to tell his mother? His father was still off at work, but mother would see him the moment he walked in the door. She would definitely question him. What would he tell her?

He opened the screen door slowly and turned the knob on the big wooden door with trepidation. It swung wide without a sound. One thing his father hated was squeaky hinges, and he was liberal in his application of lubricant to every door on everything they owned. Arturas was thankful for his father's diligence. He was able to slip into the house without anyone hearing him. His mother was humming along with a radio in the kitchen as he entered the living room. Arturas' room was down a hall to the left, while the kitchen was straight ahead and to the right. If he was lucky, he'd get into the hallway before his mother knew he was there. He walked as softly as he could, and once he was safely in the hall, just a few steps from his room, he called out to his mother. "Hi mom!"

"Hello little squirrel!" came her reply. He sometimes hated her pet name for him, but today it was more than welcome. It felt like a warm blanket on a cold day, like ice on bruises.

"I'm going to take a shower." That was unusual. He would have to think fast.

"A shower?" she replied with more than a little disbelief. "Why are you taking a shower?"

"I was playing with some other kids on the way home and got dirty."

"Oh." His mother's voice was flat, uncomprehending. This was most out of character for her son. "Playing. Ok, sweetie. I have some cake beaters for you when you're done." Arturas could always be counted on to lick the bowl and the beaters from the mixer when his mother baked something. Before he could reply to her, the squeaky, yet somehow beautiful sounds of his brother practicing the violin erupted from the room next to his. He mumbled something just loud enough so that she could hear but not understand, then rushed into his room and closed the door. Arturas quickly shed his filthy clothes, gathered up clean ones, and dashed across the hall to the bathroom. His ribs were bruised and aching, but somehow the slaps had not left any marks on his face. Several minutes later he was dressed and in the kitchen enjoying the residue of his sister's birthday cake as he used a spatula to scrape it out of a Pyrex bowl.

The reign of terror continued through elementary school, only relenting when summer vacation arrived. Dylan and his little gang didn't find Arturas every day, and some days they did but inexplicably left him alone. And sometimes they found another kid to abuse and harass. Arturas was glad for the respites, and also sad for the other victims. Things never went beyond threats, a few punches, and some generic insults until that day in seventh grade.

By that time Arturas had been placed in classes for gifted children. He still loved school and learning but had come to fear Dylan and his cronies so much that he often feigned illness in order to stay home. His mother couldn't understand how her healthy happy child had suddenly become sickly. She blamed it on the awful processed food Americans ate and asked her husband to get more meat and fresh vegetables from the farms where he worked.

Arturas never did tell his parents, or anyone else, about the bullying. One thing he'd learned from a very young age growing up under Communism was that you don't talk. There were informants everywhere in the old USSR, but those people talked to the authorities primarily out of an instinct for self-preservation. Most of them had been accused or denounced by someone for some amorphous crime and ratted on others in order to save themselves a ten-year prison sentence in Gulag. Or worse.

Arturas' parents had told him from the earliest time he could remember that ratting could get someone killed. And the authorities were going to do what they wanted to you anyway, so better to remain silent and spare everyone you could. He'd carried that lesson throughout his life, and it was the reason he never told anyone about Dylan and his gang.

The day everything changed had started like any other day. Middle school was different from elementary. Instead of being in a single classroom with a single teacher presiding over all the lessons, a student had multiple classes, each with a different instructor, and in different rooms. Arturas welcomed the change. He was no longer forced to sit in the same room for an entire day with Dylan or the others. And since he was in advanced classes, he rarely saw them at all, except in the hallways where they were usually too busy accosting the girls or seeking out fresh victims for their cruel punishments. But that day they found *him.* He'd gone to the bathroom after lunch and was walking toward the room where his next class would be held when, seemingly out of nowhere, Dylan was in front of him.

"Thought I'd forgotten about you, huh?" he asked with that same cold and mirthless smile he'd exhibited since second grade. The sound of shoes squeaking on highly polished floor tiles caused Arturas to look over his shoulder. Too late. Here came Brock and Stevie. "Get him!" Dylan said. Stevie and Brock grabbed Arturas before he could run, and Dylan opened a door Arturas had passed countless times but never paid any attention to. Now he saw it was a janitor's supply room. Brock and Stevie flung Arturas into the small space and all three followed him in.

"Yeah, I've been thinking about you for a while now," Dylan said. "We haven't had fun in a long time. Have to change that." He'd grown since the last time Arturas had seen him up close. The lead bully was now about six feet tall and had to weigh nearly two hundred pounds. Arturas was a little over five two and only about a hundred and thirty pounds. Even one-on-one he was not a physical match for Dylan. With two additional bullies aligned against him and only one door, which they were blocking, the situation was hopeless.

They pushed him into the far corner of the room and stood shoulder-to-shoulder in front of him, forming, for their diminutive victim, an impenetrable wall.

"I wanna show you something," Dylan said quietly. There was a peculiar light in his eyes, one that Arturas had never seen there before. He'd always looked both angry and gleeful when engaging in his favorite pastime, but now Dylan's expression was something worse. The only adjectives that fit were: menacing, sinister, evil.

Dylan reached slowly behind his back and withdrew a long hunting knife. Arturas could see that the handle was made of antler or bone, the blade of polished stainless steel. He took a step closer to the small boy, the knife held up between them. Dylan lowered the blade until it was at Arturas' waist. Using the tip he lifted the boy's shirt a little, just until a small sliver of skin was revealed. He smiled at him, the grin showing too many teeth, too much enjoyment. Too much malevolence. "I could stab you," he said quietly. "You'd die here. No one would find you. No one would help. Your guts would fall out all over the floor. You'd look like one of the deer my dad shoots during hunting season. Maybe we could hang you up in the garage like he does to them." Dylan moved the tip of the knife forward until it made contact with Arturas' flesh. The point was sharp and dug in a little, causing a small but sharp flash of pain. A drop of blood emerged around the tip.

Arturas felt his bladder let go. There was nothing he could do about it; it just happened without warning and completely outside of his control. Dylan, disgusted, stepped back. "What the fuck?" he exclaimed.

Arturas ignored the three boys. His back slid down the wall until he was squatting in the corner. His wet pants, which had been warm, nearly hot when his bladder had voided, were rapidly cooling and would soon be cold. And wet. And smelling of urine. At that moment he didn't care. The only thoughts in his mind were an image of himself slumped down in this very corner, his viscera arrayed around and across his legs, and of Dylan's face being smashed by a sledgehammer. That last thought was strange, foreign. He'd had any number of visions of his own death, of pain and suffering, of humiliation. It's what often happens to people who've been victimized repeatedly. But this other thought, the sledgehammer, that was something new. Revenge. That's what it was. Arturas had never contemplated revenge against any of these three, but he was now, and it was fueling something inside him, an intense desire to live that he couldn't explain or quantify.

The boys were saying something about shit, but Arturas didn't care. He stared up at them as ever more graphic and violent images flooded his mind, each more gruesome and extreme than the next. That his own mind could conjure such images was itself a shock. Combined with everything he'd just experienced, it was unprecedented in his young life. Revelatory.

The three bullies took a last look at him and left the storeroom. Arturas stayed where he was for several more minutes until he was sure fifth period had started, then he quietly but quickly made his way to the boys' locker room and rinsed his pants and underwear in one of the showers. If anyone asked, he'd just say he spilled something on his pants and washed them off. Let everyone think what they want. And as for the wet pants – they'd dry; water would surrender to heat. But the fire in his mind and heart wouldn't be put out by anything.

Arturas had never been a particularly adventuresome boy, but that summer he discovered that he enjoyed long walks in the woods. His hometown of Wilkeson was situated very near to Mt. Rainier National Park, and there were trails everywhere. Walking alone in the woods stimulated something in him, some primal instinct. His mind was still as incisive and inquisitive as it had ever been; the depredations and torments of Dylan et al. had not dimmed or stunted it. And he found that not only did he very much enjoy the solitude of the woods, but that he did some of his best thinking when he was out on a trail somewhere, away from people and civilization. His favorite pastime soon became as simple as taking a book or two, a couple bottles of water and some snacks, and heading out into the forest. His mother did not understand the sudden change in her son, but she was happy to see him finally enjoying something other than learning. Children, she believed, should study hard, yes, but they should also play hard. Explore. Venture out. Find the boundaries of their capabilities and push beyond them. His father, by this time, had started his own mechanical repair business and was too busy with work to notice what his son was doing all day during the summer. His siblings were busy with their own lives and friends, leaving Arturas alone to pursue his solitary walks at his leisure.

June turned into July, July into August, and soon September and the start of school would be upon him again. As much as he loved learning, he did not relish the thought of returning to school for another year. Arturas' knowledge and abilities academically had outpaced even his closest intellectual rivals, and school had become boring.

Arturas left the house early one late August morning, and got on his bike, determined to find a new trail. He rode toward the mountain, through the small town of Carbonado, and crossed the Carbon River via the Fairfax Bridge. The road ran steadily uphill since he was in the foothills of the Cascade mountains, and Arturas' legs were soon burning with the effort of pedaling.

He'd been biking for what seemed like hours when fatigue dictated that he stop for a rest. Arturas sat down on a large rock on the side of the road and watched a few solitary cars drive by on their way to Mowich Lake or some camping spot further up the road. He was just about to get on his bike and keep pedaling when he saw something glinting through the trees to his right. Leaving his bike concealed behind the rock, he walked into the trees to investigate. As he entered the forest proper, Arturas thought he was on an old trail. It was heavily overgrown, but it was just possible to make out what looked like a rut in the forest floor running away from the paved road behind him. The glint he'd seen was just a clear beer bottle someone had thrown away. Arturas picked it up and placed it at the edge of the trees next to the road, intending on picking it up on the way back to dispose of properly. He detested littering. It was to him the laziest, most careless, and slovenly human activity of all.

The path he'd found, and it was definitely a path he could now see, even though it hadn't been used in what looked like many years, intrigued him, and he followed it deeper into the forest. The sun was bright overhead; its rays penetrated the canopy above creating a shattered array of golden yellow light that splashed the forest floor and created beautiful contrasts of brightness and shadow. A panoply of natural colors that always enchanted Arturas pleased his eyes. The walking was moderate through the overgrowth, and he wondered how far the path went. On his wrist was a beat-up Timex watch his father had given him for his birthday a few years ago, and when he'd entered the forest it had been 9:21 am. It now read 11:53. Two and a half hours he'd been walking, and it felt like ten minutes. Arturas didn't want to be out here all day, but this overgrown path had captured his fancy, and he was determined to see its end. He looked at his watch again – 12:19. If he didn't reach the end of the trail by 2:00, he would turn back.

At 1:48 he found the building.

It didn't look like a building at first, just an overgrown hill, and he would have kept walking right on past it if a hint of grey hadn't shown through the trees and underbrush. The path kept going, but Arturas stopped to get a better look at… whatever *it* was. He couldn't tell from where he stood. The object was too far away, too hidden behind vegetation. Getting to it would be difficult; he could tell that easily enough. But there was something there, the suggestion of a shape, and he couldn't stop himself from investigating.

Arturas snapped a branch on a nearby tree and left it hanging, still attached, as a marker to find his way back, then plunged into the forest, snapping additional branches as he went. The shape of the building resolved itself, and he soon realized he was standing in front of a relatively large structure. Arturas had learned about the history of this area in school, but he'd never heard mention of this building. The only thing like it was an old coal works that had been abandoned for almost a century. But that building was not *this* building. No, this building was entirely different from that one, or any of the other left-over mining equipment and structures from when this area had been a coal-generating hub in the latter part of the nineteenth, and early part of the twentieth centuries.

Arturas stepped around a big cedar and found himself looking at a metal door set into a cube-shaped block of stone-like material. It was not made of individual blocks, but was strangely seamless as if the stone had been liquified and poured into a single mold like concrete. The rest of the building spread out to either side, made entirely of the same material and shaped much like a box. He couldn't tell how far back it went into the forest, but it was big. The roof was flat and overgrown with vegetation, and since it was only a single story would be almost impossible to spot from the air.

The door was closed and when he tugged on the handle, it didn't budge. That was too bad. He very much wanted to see what was inside. Arturas stood still and silent for several moments, pondering the building and how to get in, when an idea occurred to him. He quickly climbed a tree that rose very close to the wall of the building and jumped off onto the roof. It was covered in the detritus of the forest – leaves, moss, dead branches, pine needles and cones, and was very spongy to walk on. Shrubs, weeds and other plants grew in the natural compost, and even a few trees had sprouted. Arturas was looking for an air vent or skylight, but he could see right away that he would find neither. Still, he decided to walk the roof for a bit just to see if he could tell how big the building was. He counted his paces as he walked, and even with a few detours around vegetation that was too large to step over, he counted two hundred and seventy-eight paces. Arturas' stride was short, just a little over two feet, and some quick arithmetic told him he was standing on a roof that was about six hundred and forty feet long, and about half that wide. As he'd suspected – it was a big building.

Defeated in his quest for an alternate entrance, Arturas began walking back toward the path. The day was growing late, and he needed to be out of the woods and back on the paved road before the sun fell too far down the western sky. He was nearly back to the tree he'd climbed to get to the roof when he heard the crunching of footsteps in the forest. Instinct caused him to drop to his stomach. Arturas was fortunate in his involuntary hiding place because he was screened in front by several juvenile examples of salal.

Something was moving through the trees on the ground just in front of the door. Due to the angle of his view and the roof obstructing much of it, all Arturas could see was a head, but that was enough. The head was huge and bulbous. Pale yellowish skin mottled with brown spots covered the skull and dull red eyes stared out from under a heavy brow. The mouth was wide but closed, and there was only a hint of a nose and no ears at all, only small holes on either side of the head. It was hard to tell from his vantage point, but the head seemed to be much higher from the ground than it should have been, as if the body below it was much taller than an average human. The head disappeared as it reached the door, and Arturas flinched when he heard a metallic screech as the door opened. He waited, unconsciously holding his breath, for the sound of the door closing, which never came. Arturas crept forward slowly like an assassin approaching a target and peered over the edge. He could just see the top edge of the door; it was definitely open. What the hell had just happened? Arturas was not fond of using profanity, even mild versions. He wasn't offended by it; his father used it all the time and it didn't bother him in the slightest. He just found it to be the second most lazy thing humans did. Take the time to learn a few words instead of always relying on cursing to express yourself. But no matter how much he distracted himself with digressions into the practical applications of profanity, the question remained unanswered: what had he just seen?

Arturas' inquisitive and keen intellect had served him well academically, if not so effectively socially, and right now it was spinning like a uranium enrichment centrifuge. The presence, the *existence,* of that... creature, did not compute. It was an impossibility. Nothing like it existed anywhere outside the realms of science fiction and fantasy, neither of which held much appeal to Arturas. He much preferred tangible facts, logic, proof, over the musings of imagination. Nothing he'd ever learned had indicated that an animal or ethnic group of humans possessed an appearance and size even remotely close to what he'd just seen. This most peculiar situation required further investigation. Arturas wasn't afraid; his curiosity completely overwhelmed any sense of danger or self-preservation that others might have felt in the same circumstance, and he quickly rose from his hiding place and made his way down the tree to the ground.

The passageway beyond the open door was lit only by small slits a few inches from the floor which emitted a yellowish light. They were spaced evenly along both walls at intervals of what Arturas estimated to be about fifteen feet. The lights stretched off into the darkness, disappearing at what he thought was probably a turn in the passage. Arturas took three hesitant steps in and paused to listen. The only sound was the breeze rustling the forest foliage behind him. He looked at his watch again; it read 2:02. He'd found this building at 1:48, which meant that only fourteen minutes had passed. Strange that such a profound event could happen in such a short space of time. And there were yet more revelations ahead of him, if the dark passageway was in fact a path toward further discoveries, as he suspected it to be.

Arturas took several more steps, his confidence growing the further in he went, until he was walking comfortably, if slowly, down the gloomy hall. The door behind him remained open and he glanced back at it just as he reached the corner where the passage turned. The trees outside were dappled in diffused sunlight – a vibrant and lively green where it touched their limbs, and dark, nearly black, where they were submerged in shade. Arturas thought that he might be looking at one of the most beautiful scenes that Nature had ever created. His mind was, by its innate composition and his father's influence, a math and science-focused organ. But his mother had tried to teach him to look around, to find the beauty in the world, even in the bleakest and most sere of environments. It was a lesson he sometimes forgot, but on this day, it overwhelmed even his strongest inclination – curiosity. He stared for what felt like minutes as the shadows crept across the tree limbs, chased into hiding by the sunlight, until with a sigh he turned back to the unexplored realm before him.

Arturas graduated from high school two years early and immediately started college. He graduated from M.I.T. in six years with doctorates in applied mathematics and physics. His advisors called him one of the most gifted students they'd ever had. Job offers poured in from everywhere – the military (the navy wanted him to work on their nuclear reactors), academia (no fewer than twenty-three elite universities wanted to add him to their faculties), private industry (he had offers in aviation, mineral extraction, car manufacturing, pharmaceuticals, and anything General Electric was into – which pretty much meant everything), but he chose instead to work for NASA where he helped design more efficient fuel systems for rockets. He enjoyed it for a time, but eventually his curious nature pulled him in a different direction, and he left NASA for a position with Raytheon where he worked on ultra-secret government projects for the Department of Defense. But even that kind of work left him feeling less than fulfilled, and after three years he departed for a position with a financial firm on Wall Street. But Arturas didn't like New York city, and when his employer refused to let him work remotely, he quit that job too. He'd made a lot of money and knew enough about the markets to make more if he wanted to, and instead of going right back to work, he took six months off and traveled the world, living out of a backpack and sleeping wherever he could find a hostel. He sojourned all over Europe, and even ventured to places that were once trapped behind the now vanished and not lamented Iron Curtain.

Toward the end of his odyssey, Arturas made his way to Lithuania and his old hometown of Baisogala. His memories of that time were blurry, fuzzy, but some things were as he remembered. The house where he'd lived was still there, albeit unoccupied and decrepit. When he'd told his mother he was going back to the old country, she'd asked him to look in on a few people, friends of hers she hadn't seen or heard from since their escape so many years before. Arturas still spoke Lithuanian very well; his mother insisted on speaking to him in their native tongue much as she had insisted he learn English when he was a child, and communicating with the locals was simple enough. Except that he couldn't find any of the people his mother wanted him to. They had all died or moved away when Communism had finally been flushed into the septic tank of history where it belonged.

Other than a few familiar places and his family's old house, Baisogala did not have much that interested Arturas, and he spent only a day wandering the small town and talking to the people who remained. About an hour before sunset, he left the small café where he'd had dinner and began walking north. The land here was relatively flat, the walking easy, and he watched the sky turn pink, crimson and purple as night approached. This area was pastoral, agrarian, and dotted with farms and other small towns like the one he'd just left, and Arturas was not afraid of being forced to sleep outdoors with only his backpack for a pillow. He'd done it several times already on this journey and was prepared to do it again, should the need arise.

Dark had truly fallen when the chugging old flatbed truck crept slowly up a low hill he'd just crested. He turned and looked at the wheezing machine. Studebaker. Probably one the US had sent the Soviets back in World War Two. Many people didn't know that the US had sent the Soviets shiploads of supplies through the Lend Lease program during that hideous conflict, among which were a large number of trucks like the one coming up the small hill behind him. The Studebakers had proven reliable and rugged, and apparently at least one was still in service all these years later. The dim headlights lit the cracked asphalt around Arturas as he waited for the truck to pass. But instead of driving by, it slowed to a stop, and a voice raspy from age and too many cigarettes spoke in Lithuanian from the darkened cab.

"Do you want a ride?"

"Sure," Arturas replied and opened the creaky and rusty passenger door. "Thank you for stopping. I was going to look for a good place to sleep soon."

"You can sleep in my barn," the voice said. It was a man's voice, and in the faint glow from the dashboard, he could just make out wrinkles and a bulbous nose below extremely bushy eyebrows. "I'm Henrikas," the man said as he extended a huge hand. Arturas took it and nearly winced in pain as the driver squeezed his own much smaller appendage. The man laughed as he sensed Arturas' discomfort. "My father always told me to look a man in the eye and give a strong handshake," he said rather smugly.

"That's... good advice," Arturas said as he quietly massaged his squished hand.

"Where you going?"

"I don't know yet. Just north for now. Maybe to the Baltic," he said.

"Hmmph. A wanderer like those kids from Europe and America who come over here to get *culture,*" he said derisively as he put the truck in gear and eased out the clutch. The old Studebaker jerked forward and began rolling down the far side of the gentle hill.

"Not really," Arturas replied.

"Well then what are you? You speak our language at least." the older man asked testily.

"I'm from here. From Baisogala. My family left when I was very young. I came back... I don't know why I came back. Just to see it again, I suppose."

"Well," the man said grudgingly, "at least you're one of us. Mostly."

Arturas wasn't sure whether that meant he'd been accepted or just tolerated, so he kept his mouth shut and watched the dark landscape roll by out the windows. They drove on in silence for a time until at last the man slowed the truck and turned into a darkened road lined on either side by fields filled with a crop Arturas couldn't identify. The truck stopped in an open area in the middle of several buildings; the air was redolent of freshly turned earth and animal manure, and Arturas not surprised to discover they were at a farm. "You sleep in there," the man said as he pointed toward a large barn. "Don't burn it down smoking your marijuana, and don't leave it a mess. My wife will give you breakfast in the morning, then I'll drive you to Šiauliai. I have to go there tomorrow anyway, so you'll come with me. Be up and ready by daybreak." The man turned and stalked into his house leaving Arturas to stare at his back. It had been very kind of him to stop and pick up a stranger, but his attitude since had been rude to bordering on hostile. Perplexed, he turned toward the building where he would spend the night.

The barn was just a barn, full of hay, tack, and tools much like the ones Arturas had seen on the farms where his father had worked. There was no bed, but he found a corner, piled up some loose straw, and was asleep in minutes.

He woke, groggy from sleep, sometime in the small hours. Something had woken him, but he didn't know what. A dream? Maybe. He rarely remembered his dreams. A sound? If so, he couldn't recall it, and his heart wasn't pounding, so it hadn't startled him. Whatever it was, it made him intensely curious. Arturas rose from the straw pile and walked to the door of the barn. Outside it was still dark, but there was one solitary dim light coming from the house Henrikas had entered. He watched for a few silent moments, then took a few hesitant steps into the courtyard between the buildings. The Studebaker was parked a few paces away, a now silent hulk of antique machinery, and somewhere in the distance a dog barked. Arturas walked slowly along the perimeter of the courtyard, peering into outbuildings and finding nothing unusual until he finally came to the house where Henrikas, and presumably his family, lived. The light he'd seen upon first emerging from the barn was completely obscured by hideously hued orange and brown drapes. He stepped close to the window and listened. It was impossible to see anything through the gag-inducing curtains or tell what room the light was coming from. There were some faint noises coming from inside, but Arturas couldn't tell what the sounds were. Maybe it was a tv left on while Henrikas or someone else slept in an easy chair in front of it. Maybe one of the residents liked to stay up at night and clean house or something. He couldn't even tell if the sounds were coming from the room on the other side of the curtain, or from somewhere else in the house.

Arturas crept slowly along the wall listening intently. He felt slightly ashamed of himself for prying into the business of these people, but the feeling he'd awakened with and the accompanying curiosity, were still there, and had even grown stronger. Something was, maybe not wrong, but off here, strange, if his instincts were correct, and like finding the end of a trail, he was obstinate about discovering what it was.

He reached the front door, which was on the far side of the house, and found it slightly ajar. Growing up in a rural area like he had in America, it was not at all unusual for people to leave their homes and cars unlocked. But it *was* unusual to leave a door open like that. Maybe there were young children here, and one of them hadn't closed the door all the way upon coming inside. That was certainly plausible, but it didn't feel right; it was too innocuous, too easy an answer. He gently pushed the door open with one hand while keeping most of his body out of the doorway and looked inside. It was just a living room. The light he'd seen from outside was coming from a different room in the house. There was just enough illumination to discern stout but worn furniture scattered around the room in places where you would expect to see it. The one conspicuous absence was a television.

Arturas heard the sounds again, coming from deeper in the house. They had a sharper quality now, and there was something else, a lower sound that had been completely masked by the curtains and walls. Something in it sounded miserable, anguished. But maybe that was just the feeling that had spurred him to enter this house in the first place running roughshod over his perception.

The light that he'd seen from outside was leaking into a short hallway through a crack between the bottom of the door and the carpeted floor. He could just see enough of the hallway from where he stood in the living room to note that the hallway boasted four doors, two on either side. Arturas slid quietly along until the sliver of light showed him the tips of his worn hiking boots. The sounds had stopped; he hadn't heard them since entering the house. Arturas didn't know what to do. Should he open the door slowly? Break it down? Wait in the hall for something to happen? He had already invaded someone's home. Might as well go all the way. He raised his leg to kick the door when it suddenly opened.

The room beyond was just a room – four walls, a closet and a window. It was the occupants that made him nearly faint. He'd been a boy the last time he saw one of these things. Strange. He hadn't thought of that day in years – of the huge head with yellowish skin and red eyes, and of the door in that building the creature had left open, and that he'd walked through. Had he really done that? It was so faint, so indistinct in his memory that it was hard to even be sure. Arturas had learned how fallible memory was, how two people could remember the same event in such drastically different ways. His memory of the creature was absolutely correct, spot on. But his memory of that building, and what had happened inside it, that was the hazy part.

The thing stood in the open doorway, its red eyes flat and dull as it regarded the interloper. Beyond it were two other creatures, one smaller than the other, but obviously of the same… Species? Genus? As this one. None of the three was as tall as the one he'd seen as a boy, but they were still much bigger than he, even the small one; Arturas had never been big as a child, and he was small as a man, standing only about five six and weighing in at just over one hundred and fifty pounds. The smallest of the three creatures was easily two hundred fifty and at least six feet tall. The largest one was over seven and had to weigh near four hundred. Their bodies were unclothed, the skin the same color as the heads. They had two arms and legs, like humans, but there were no obvious features to indicate gender; their torsos and groins were as flat as a Ken doll.

They regarded each other for several tense moments, then the huge creature opened its wide mouth, revealing two rows of startlingly human-like teeth. A snarl escaped from its throat, a low, menacing sound. The two creatures behind it stepped closer to the doorway, and Arturas could just see a strange grey disc about two feet in diameter in the middle of the floor. He stared at the bigger of the three for a tense moment, then bolted for the living room, not waiting to see if it was following or not. Arturas burst from the still open front door and dashed toward the barn. He had to get away from this farm but not without his backpack; his entire life was in it.

The barn was still dark, but his eyes had adjusted enough that he was able to find the backpack quickly, sling it on and turn back to the door he'd come in by. It was blocked by one of the creatures. The thing advanced toward him slowly, the dull red eyes not so dull now but shining forth with something Arturas equated to malevolence. The look on Dylan's face the day in the storeroom burst out of his memory accompanied by both the terror of the experience, and the intense desire to live it had fostered. His analytical mind couldn't help but ponder this latest memory, another one he hadn't thought about in years. Why were these things suddenly coming back to him here, now? Was it a response to stress? Was it that simple?

Arturas forced the memories away and focused on his current situation. There had to be another way out. He looked around frantically. There! On the opposite side of the barn was a small window. If he could get to it, smash the pane and get through, he'd be on the far side of the barn from the creatures. Plan in place Arturas snatched a pitchfork that was hanging on a hook on the wall next to where he stood and ran toward the window. He didn't wait to see what the creature was doing. The pitchfork smashed the glass easily, and in moments he'd knocked out all the loose shards, leaving a clear path through the wall. Arturas wasted no time diving through. The ground rose toward him quickly, and he tucked himself into a ball, somersaulting across the dirt to absorb the impact of his crash landing. He was limber and bounced up quickly, already running as he did. Ahead of him were dark fields, dark trees, a dark sky. Behind him was… What? Pain? Torture? Death? Something worse than all three? He didn't know and didn't care. Those menacing red eyes were enough impetus. To be away from here was all that mattered. Terror and desire for life, he thought as he ran.

The former could petrify to immovability, the latter inspire to seemingly unattainable summits.

Arturas ran through the fields, between raised rows of unknown crops, their leaves patiently waiting for the morning sun so they could resume their doomed-to-end-up-in-someone's-dinner lives. The fields flew by in the dark, trees stretched gnarled limbs toward the sky beseechingly, and the air was crisp and moist. He'd never been drawn towards sports or physically demanding activities, other than the leisurely bike rides or walks in the woods, but Arturas was in shape, didn't smoke, and fueled by the fear of the creatures behind him, could have given a professional marathon runner a contest on that night. His sense of direction had always been relatively accurate, and he'd been following a roughly northern heading since leaving the farm. There was a larger town in that direction. What had the farmer called it? Šiauliai. That was it. He remembered the name from his youth, although if he'd ever actually been there, that memory was gone. It didn't matter. He needed to get to that town, then out of this country and back to America, or, rather, the US. After all, Canadians were just as much Americans as someone born and raised in Indiana was, or someone from Nicaragua or Tierra del Fuego. The continents those places were part of were in fact named North and South *America*. So, didn't that by definition make every resident of either continent American? Strange that his mind should wander to such trivial subjects. What would a shrink say about it? Probably some psycho-babble-bullshit about how the mind was protecting itself from stressors by turning its thoughts to things more... palatable than being ripped to pieces by creatures from... somewhere.

Where *had* they come from anyway? And where was the farmer? Had they… eaten him?

Lights in a house a couple fields away distracted Arturas and he stumbled on something, falling flat on his face and getting a mouthful of dirt in the process. He pushed himself up, spitting out the dirt as he did so, and looked behind him. The night was quiet and still, the only sounds a breeze rustling foliage somewhere nearby, and the various insects that came out after sunset to do their insecty things. No creatures anywhere to be seen. Arturas finished clearing his mouth the best he could, the remaining dirt gritty on his teeth, and stood. His breath came in gasps, and he was terribly thirsty, but alive and intact. He'd take that in exchange for a mouthful of dirt anytime. Walking instead of running, Arturas started off across the field toward the lights. It was another farm, and this time there were actual people up and about. Three men were working on a tractor engine underneath a pole-mounted sodium vapor lamp. Beyond them the sky was lighter than it had been. Dawn was coming. Which meant it was later, or earlier, depending on one's perspective, than he'd thought it was. He didn't try to hide but called out to the men when he was about a hundred yards away. One of them turned and stared at the dirty, sweating, and disheveled man who was walking toward them across a field of what Arturas thought were probably sugar beets.

"What are you doing out there?" asked one man who was significantly older than the others.

Arturas hadn't thought to concoct a story to explain his appearance, and he'd never been much good at lying, so he just told them the truth. "I've been running from a… creature. It has red eyes and a huge head."

The men shared a look; something like fear or apprehension crossed their faces, then suddenly disappeared as each mastered his emotions. "Hurry, over here," the older man said beckoning to Arturas with his left hand. His right was gone, leaving only a stump a few inches above where a wrist should have been. All three men ushered Arturas into a small building with a roof and no walls that was occupied by large bales of hay. "Now what's all this?" the older man asked. Being among them now, Arturas could see that they all resembled one another. The older man was surely the father of these two younger men. "You're running from… a creature?" the father asked. Arturas nodded. "And you said it has red eyes and a huge head?" He nodded again.

"Velnias," one of the sons said quietly. The father shot him a sharp look and the young man dropped his eyes.

"Who is Velnias?" Arturas asked.

"Just a story parents tell their children to make them behave," the father said tersely with admonishing looks to both younger men this time.

"It's not a story!" the other son interjected. "Steponas and me saw him! You never did believe us! Now here's proof – he saw him too!"

"Shut your mouth boy!" the father spat. His son glared back at him with undisguised anger and a flushed face.

"Look, I don't want to start a fight, but I know what I saw," Arturas said quickly before fists could be formed from unclenched hands. "All I really want now is a drink of water and to get to Šiauliai. I'll walk if I have to, but I'm not staying here."

The father sighed. "We will give you water. Then one of my sons will drive you to Šiauliai. It is not a long drive; you will be there by daybreak." Arturas noticed the sky had lightened considerably over the last few minutes. The sun would be up over the horizon soon. Somehow the banishment of night by dawn's edict didn't assuage the anxiety he felt about the creatures. It seemed as if they were just around the corner, waiting to pounce on him the moment he was alone again. "Get him some water," the father said to the son whose name had been revealed as Steponas. "You go get the car warmed up," he ordered the other. "I want you on the road in five minutes." Steponas left and came back with a blue plastic cup and a glass pitcher full of water which he handed to Arturas. After several deep draughts he refilled the glass, took a few more sips and looked around. The father hadn't spoken again but had instead been staring off toward the south with an unreadable expression on his face. Just as Arturas finished a second glass of water, a newer Fiat pulled up and the other son leaned over to open the passenger door. "Get in," he said. Arturas thanked the father who grunted in response, then turned to Steponas and thanked him as well. The younger man smiled and shook his hand, then gestured to the waiting car.

They were on the road in moments and hurtling north at a speed Arturas wasn't sure was entirely safe. He hadn't learned the other son's name, the one who was driving, and decided to just ask.

"Jonas," the young man replied. They were approximately the same age, Arturas thought. "Did you really see Velnias?" he asked excitedly.

"I don't know what I saw," Arturas replied tiredly. Now that he was out of danger and no longer running, the fatigue of having only slept a few hours, combined with intense fear and his adrenaline-fueled exertions through the rapidly disappearing night, left him feeling exhausted. "It was... something."

"I think you saw Velnias!" Jonas said. "My brother and I saw him, when we were little boys. My father says he doesn't believe us, but I think he saw him too. I think Velnias took his hand, he never told us how he lost it, and he's afraid. That's why he won't let us talk about him."

"I saw three of them," Arturas said tiredly.

"Three?" Jonas asked incredulously. "How is this possible? There is only *one* Velnias!"

"Who the hell is Velnias anyway?" Arturas asked.

Jonas glanced at his passenger as the car nearly skidded around a corner and said quietly, "The devil."

Two days later Arturas' plane landed in New York. He had a layover in the airport before his next flight, which took him to Pittsburgh, then on to Seattle where he disembarked. A not-very-quick trip to the car rental counter (the attendant was a disinterested young man with more metal in his face than a steel mill made in a day) later he was crawling down I-5 with the rest of the early Thursday afternoon rush hour traffic. He'd called ahead; mother was expecting him at the house in Wilkeson. They'd agreed not to tell his father in order to have the visit be a surprise, and as he exited I-5 and dropped down the hill on Highway 18 into Auburn, he wondered what the old man had been up to the last couple years. He'd retired from working on other people's farms, and according to mother spent most of his time tinkering with his own inventions in their small garage. Arturas had offered to pay to build him a shop in the backyard, but his father refused. He was a stubborn man, well set in his ways, and mother didn't seem to mind him taking over the garage.

Arturas' father was heartily surprised when his son walked through the front door, and practically dragged him by the arm into the garage to show him his latest invention. It was some kind of contraption that when perfected, his father said, would locate and remove nails and screws from lumber. Arturas didn't see how it would do that; the thing was only about the size of a deck of cards, but who knew, maybe old pop was onto something.

Two days after getting home, Arturas had visited everyone who needed visiting, told his parents all about his travel exploits (except for the bit about the farmer, the creatures, and his nighttime flight through the countryside of Lithuania), and decided to do what he'd really come here for. He was up early that morning and left the house before either of his parents were awake. The drive to the start of the path was much shorter than his bike ride all those years ago had been. There was nowhere to park near where he remembered finding that faint path, and he had to leave the car at turnout nearly a mile beyond it. The walk back was pleasant, the air clean and crisp, but his heart was performing calisthenics in his chest.

It took him longer than he wanted to find the spot. Much had changed since the days of his youth, and the overgrown path had only gotten more overgrown in the years since he'd last trod it. Once he did find it, following it was relatively easy. The faint rut was still there, and he followed it toward what he knew lay at the end.

And after a walk that took over an hour, but which felt like ten minutes, there it was – the strange, lonely building he'd found so many years ago. It was even harder to see now, the trees and shrubs of the forest having grown yet larger and more dense since his last visit, but the outline was there if you knew where to look. The form of the structure resolved itself further as he approached, bushwhacking his way off the path and through the undergrowth, and he was mildly surprised to find the door open. Was he expected? A sound from behind caused him to spin, his heart suddenly trying to jackhammer its way through his ribcage. He was shocked at what he saw. A figure stood on the path facing him from about twenty yards away. It was dressed in normal clothes – jeans, a t-shirt and light jacket, topped by a baseball cap that bore the logo of some sports team or other. But it was the face that shook Arturas. He was looking at Dylan.

"Remember me?" his old tormentor asked acidly. Arturas hadn't thought of him since that flash of the bully's face back in Lithuania, but seeing him again, now, brought all those old memories and feelings back as vividly as if he'd just experienced them an hour ago. He couldn't speak for a moment, so he nodded instead. "Still a fuckin' coward aren't ya?" Dylan asked derisively, mockingly. Arturas remembered that day in the supply room, how Dylan had pressed the point of his knife to flesh, drawing a small spot of blood. And he remembered the rest. His wet pants, how he'd washed them as best he could in the locker room shower and how he'd worn them wet throughout his classes that day until they'd dried. He also remembered the thoughts he'd had – thoughts of revenge, of Dylan's battered and broken body lying on the ground before him, the torments the sadist had visited on himself, and others forever ceased by Arturas' hand. Those thoughts had sparked something in him, that determination and desire for life that he'd carried with him since. It had spurred him on to high academic achievement, to excel in science and in the various vocations he'd pursued, but it had never led him to that deep place within him where the images of a dead Dylan secretly and quietly resided. No, he'd never acted on those impulses for revenge; his intellect and logical acumen told him that nothing good would come from it, that he'd probably end up in prison, which, for a small boy like him, would be worse than anything Dylan had ever done. "You gonna say something or just stand there staring?" Dylan's voice brought Arturas back to the moment. His eyes refocused, and he met the bully's gaze directly.

How in the hell had Dylan found him here? How had he known Arturas was even back in town? The entire situation was absurd. He hadn't told anyone about the building or the creature, yet here his childhood tormentor was, standing in front of it and waiting to pick up where they'd left off. No, not this time. That desire, the fire, was still there, maybe more intense than it had ever been, fueled as it was by the sight of his old enemy. This time he would not wet his pants. This time he would fight if it came to that. And one of them would lose. Definitively.

"Haven't you grown up yet?" he asked quietly.

Dylan snorted a laugh. "I grew up a long time ago," he said in a low tone.

"Apparently not, since you're still as much of a dick as you used to be."

"Well don't you have a smart mouth now," Dylan replied. The challenge in his voice was unmistakable. "You were more respectful when we were kids."

"Yeah?" Arturas asked. "Well, I'm not a kid anymore. And I'm not scared of you. *Dylan*." He nearly spat the name. It seemed to please his old enemy because his mouth broke into a wide grin.

"Sounds like you wanna fight. Think you can take me?" Dylan had been big when they were kids, and time had only filled out that large frame with what looked to be mostly muscle behind a generous pot belly. Arturas couldn't have bested him when they were kids, but they weren't kids anymore. Dylan reached behind his back and pulled out a large knife. "Know what this is?" he asked as Arturas' eyes lingered on the blade. "It's a Ka-Bar. This one was my old man's, got it when he was in the Marines." Dylan's eyes glowed almost lovingly as they ran up and down the length of the knife. "He's dead now so it's mine," he said in a voice utterly devoid of emotion. How could he talk about his own father that way? Maybe there was something Arturas didn't know about Dylan's relationship with his father, and maybe it was something bad. "He said he killed some guy with it in 'Nam." He stared silently at nothing for several long seconds, then raised his eyes to Arturas' and spoke. "*I* killed someone with it," he said quietly. "Wanna know who?" Arturas felt sweat break out on his brow. Despite telling Dylan he wasn't afraid, the truth was that the appearance of the knife had caused his old fear to resurface. He was fairly certain he could outrun Dylan on clear ground, but in this forest, if he tripped and fell it was over. And where could he run? Dylan was standing on the only path he knew of. He could easily get lost out here in the woods if he didn't follow that very path back to the road. Arturas was confident in his sense of direction, but even seasoned woodsmen with all the appropriate kit got lost and died in forests. There was really only one place he *could* go.

"Don't you wanna know who I killed?" Dylan asked again. There was a whiny quality in his voice this time, as if Arturas' lack of interest in the victims' identity had caused Dylan some consternation. "Well, I'm gonna tell you anyway. I actually killed *two* people – my ex old lady, and…" He paused for dramatic effect. Arturas was incredulous. Dylan was acting like he was about to reveal the winner of a sweepstakes contest instead of the name of some person he'd murdered. It was surreal.

"Stevie!" he exclaimed triumphantly. "Little fucker thought he could rip me off in a poker game. Heh heh heh! He took a swim down the Carbon River after I stuck this in him." There was a madness in Dylan's eyes that had been there when they were kids, but which had blossomed fully in the years since. Arturas was sickened by it. "I won't tell you about my old lady. That shit's private. But I am gonna go for the hat trick. Or what do they say at the horse races? Yeah, the trifecta!" Dylan started toward Arturas, apparently finished with talking, and that was all the motivation the smaller man needed to turn and run toward the foliage-draped building behind him.

He reached the door in seconds and was elated that it was open and that the small light-emitting slits along the bottom of the wall were still emitting light. Arturas dashed along the hall and skidded around the corner at the far end. The hallway led a short distance to another door. His memory of this part of the building was very hazy, but he seemed to remember touching the door the last time he was here. There was no choice this time; he could hear Dylan pounding along behind him. The big man with the knife would catch him in a moment if he didn't get that door open.

There was something familiar about this door, but he couldn't quite figure out why. It was grey, almost the color of Navy ships. Was that it? Arturas' hands made contact with the door, and he felt something akin to an electric shock course through his body. The sensation was jarring and unpleasant but only lasted a moment as the door swung away from him on its own, breaking the contact with his palms. He couldn't tell what was beyond; the space revealed by the now open door was the purest black he'd ever seen. Arturas stepped over the threshold and suddenly felt himself floating as if he were weightless. He scrabbled around, trying to get his sneakers to find purchase on the floor, but there was no floor. His arms spun as if he were swimming, and he thought he could sense movement, propulsion, like his efforts were actually carrying him away from the open door behind him. A look over his shoulder showed him nothing; the blackness was complete. Nor was there any sound. If Dylan had come in here after him, he wouldn't know until the man grabbed him. It was like he'd been suddenly dumped into one of those sensory deprivation tanks. He'd never understood the reason for getting into one of those. Sure, he'd read about them and how they were supposed to be great for all sorts of ailments of the body and mind, but he'd never seen the point. If your problem was mental, go see a shrink or figure it out yourself. If it was physical, either go see a doc or just deal with it. The so-called naturopathic and alternative remedies always seemed to Arturas like so much snake oil. Might as well believe you could spin straw into gold for all the good they did.

He swam forward in the nothingness. It was impossible now that he'd been here for a few moments to tell whether or not he was even moving. The sense of propulsion that he'd had was gone, replaced by a feeling of stillness. Were his arms and legs still moving? Had he become completely inert? Frozen? And where was Dylan? Maybe he'd reached the threshold of the strange electric door and lost his courage, abandoned his quest for the trifecta. Arturas wished he could remember what had happened to him when he'd been here before. Had he made it to this place? How had he gotten out? There was no direction here, no reference point, no dim silhouette of the door to guide him back to his world. Who had built this place? And what was its purpose? There was some kind of force in operation here that he'd never encountered in all of his studies, all of his schooling. It was beyond modern science's ability to explain what he was at this moment experiencing. The intellectual part of him was fascinated by it and wanted to collect as much empirical evidence as possible, while his baser instincts screamed at him about self-preservation and begged him to find a way out.

Arturas completely lost track of time. He could have been here an hour or a decade. It reminded him of a short story he'd read several years back; he thought it was by Stephen King. The basic premise was that teleportation had been invented, but those wishing to travel by that method had to be put to sleep before departing. A curious kid stayed awake because, well, because he was curious, and when he reached his destination, he'd gone insane but said something like, 'it's eternity in there.' The implication was that teleportation took the person to some other dimension or something, and if you weren't asleep, you just floated along in nothingness for 'eternity' until you finally emerged at your destination, by which time you'd lost your mind. Had he found that story's real life analogue? Arturas didn't want to find out. He redoubled his efforts to swim through the black nothingness and even called out to anyone (or any*thing*) that might be near. There was no response. He began to panic then, his baser instincts to overwhelm the logical, rational parts of his mind. He was going to end up like that kid in the story – insane. It was a certainty that he knew in his bones. Did he even have bones here? Everything was gone – his body, the outside world, all that was left was his mind, and it was rapidly breaking, deteriorating like tissue in the washing machine. Arturas screamed then. Whether it was out loud or only in his mind was immaterial, didn't matter. The expulsion of the fear and terror he'd been feeling was like opening the pressure relief valve on a hot water heater – it prevented the thing from blowing up, but probably hadn't resolved the underlying problem that had created the condition in the first place.

Arturas drifted. His mind was quiet after the scream, his thoughts muted and flowing slowly, like quality Maple syrup. Dylan didn't exist anymore than he himself did. Consciousness was the only reality, and even that might have been nothing more than a remnant of something larger, a fragment of an unknowable imagination cast into the nothingness.

When the change came Arturas thought he was dreaming. The first thing he noticed was a very dim glow. He had no idea if it was in front of him or behind him; his mind could see in three hundred and sixty degrees. Arturas watched impassively as the glow intensified until it resolved itself into a single white rope of light stretching into the eternal blackness. Both ends were lost to distance, but Arturas' curiosity returned, and he stretched a hand (or maybe a thought) toward it. When his appendage made contact, he again felt that electric shock like when he'd touched the door to this place but magnified exponentially. The force of it knocked him out of his lethargy and filled his being with an energy and vitality unprecedented in human experience. It suddenly felt as if everything science had posited, dreamed of, was possible. All the knowledge of the known and unknown universe was here in this cord of light. All experience, all imagination, all intellect, available to him. The feeling threatened to overwhelm him, to scourge the part of him that was Arturas, leaving behind only a shell that would be filled with this incalculable volume of knowledge and possibility. Then a voice spoke to him from somewhere in the maelstrom of information.

"Welcome back," it said in a calm and pleasant tone. "It's been a long time since you were here."

"Who are you?" he asked.

"You already know that," it said. The voice was androgynous but not robotic or emotionless. He found it somehow soothing and trusted it immediately.

"We've met before, haven't we?" he asked, already knowing the answer to the question.

"Of course. When you were here as a child, and not so long ago on the other side of the world. You thought we were monsters then."

"But you're not."

"Well, to some we are. But no, we don't consider ourselves monsters." This line of conversation brought back memories of Dylan, and before Arturas could ask, the voice spoke again. "Don't worry. We've taken care of *him*."

"What did you do?"

The voice chuckled in mild amusement. "Have you ever heard what would happen if you fell into a black hole? Spaghettification? Something like that is happening to him, although it is much less pleasant and will last longer than the milliseconds it would take for a black hole to annihilate you."

"What-" Arturas began before the voice cut him off.

"He's gone forever. That's all you need to know. The universe will be a better place without him. And speaking of the universe, we have something to show you. Hold tight to the string."

Arturas understood that by string the voice meant the rope of white light that had appeared in this void. He thought he already had a hold of it, but as the first sensation of movement began to manifest, he felt it slip. His hand (or mind) clamped down harder on the light, and he was suddenly dragged away at an impossible speed.

Lights began to flash by, dots of color, stretched and warped by the speed of his movement exploded into and out of his field of vision. There were thousands upon thousands of them. "What am I seeing?" he asked.

"The universe," the voice replied.

It was impossible to even begin to fathom what he was seeing, even with his expanded consciousness. This was the universe? He was flying through it, holding on to, as the voice had called it, a string of light? How was this even possible? Technology beyond anything conceived on

Earth, that was how. That vast repository of knowledge was still there, and Arturas instinctively understood how this was happening, the physics behind it, and realized he could create a device that would do the same thing, if he could acquire the same fuel source that powered this one. The construction would be a fairly simple matter. "No," the voice said, "building a string machine is not why you're here."

The being could read his thoughts. That too was eminently possible. He could build a machine for that as easily as he could the string machine. But that knowledge also told him he was there for a different purpose, and it had nothing to do with building machines. He was unsurprised when the pace of his passage began to slow; of course there was a destination. When he finally stopped, he was looking at one of the most incredible sights he'd ever seen.

He was in the center of what appeared to be a nebula. Massive clouds of vividly colored dust and gas swirled and billowed around brightly shining stars. No, not stars, they were planets that were orbiting a trifecta (there was that word again) of stars – two small yellow ones and one large orange one spun around each other and were in turn circled by a dozen planets. Small dots flitted between the planets like bees moving among flowers, and Arturas realized he was looking at ships that were using interplanetary space like a kind of celestial highway. "This is our home," the voice said. "But you knew that already."

"I did," Arturas replied. There was one question that none of the knowledge he'd so effortlessly (amazingly!) accessed could answer though. "Why am I here?"

"Have you ever heard of the Loch Ness Monster?" the voice asked.

Arturas was utterly confused. The voice was asking him about, of all things, the Loch Ness fucking monster? Of course he'd heard of that mythical creature. And there were stories of other things like it throughout the world – Chupacabra, Sasquatch. Velnias. "Yes," he said, waiting for elaboration and wishing it would hurry up and arrive.

"We are it. And everything else like it. Some on your world have taken to calling the study of these creatures Cryptozoology. We think it an apt name."

The knowledge was fading; answers he'd had moments ago were gone, comprehensions of possibility had disappeared. Arturas felt a little panicked, but the voice spoke again in a soothing tone.

"If we had allowed you to keep what you learned, it would have driven you mad within moments of your return to your world."

"So, I'm not on Earth anymore?"

"No. And you haven't been since you opened that door."

"The door. It reminded me of something. I didn't remember what. Now I do. It's the same color as that disc on the floor in that house where I saw three of you."

"Yes," the voice replied. "It's one of our methods of traveling. Think of it like the teleport room in Star Trek."

Arturas, the knowledge of the universe nearly gone, pondered this development, and decided not to question it further. His thoughts turned to the building in the woods and to asking questions his interlocutor might actually answer.

"What is that building anyway, and why is there a path to it?"

"There was once a homestead in that area, and the people who lived there had horses. The passage of the horses and people created the path. As for the building, we built it some years ago. It's a portal between our worlds – yours and ours. We allow only a very few to find it."

"How... *why* – did you... create – or whatever you did – the Loch Ness Monster?"

The voice paused for a long time. Arturas was beginning to wonder if he'd offended it, if maybe the conversation was over, and he would be left floating here all alone until the end of time. When it finally spoke, its voice was subdued, quieter, and there was a melancholy in it that had not been there before.

"You are losing your belief in something beyond your limited sight. We are speaking of humans as a species. There was a time in your short history when you believed in something greater than yourselves. Your culture has become so corroded and corrupted that you've nearly lost the ability to be mystified, entranced, enraptured, amazed, except by small and largely insignificant things. We have tried, for your sake, to reintroduce some of that mystery. Without it, you will decline and eventually disappear. Sadly, we seem to be failing in our efforts. Our own ethos prevents us from more direct interference in your affairs, so we try to influence them indirectly. Allowing some of you to catch glimpses of creatures unknown to your science is one of the ways we've chosen to try to keep what little real belief you have left, alive. This is also why we allowed your mind to absorb all that knowledge – so that you can see what is truly possible. People like you are the dreamers and creators, the designers and builders. If your species is to be saved, it is others like you who will be instrumental in that effort."

Arturas realized that all that knowledge, all that experience, was gone. He felt a small pang of loss but understood that to have held on to all of it, or even a portion, would have burned his mind to cinders. No storage medium yet devised by humans, nor a human mind itself, could contain that much information. Perhaps at some point in the future someone would discover what these beings obviously had and invent just such a device, but that day was far in the future.

"What do you want from us?" Arturas asked.

"Nothing. We just want to prevent you from destroying yourselves. We've seen this scenario countless times. A society is born, evolves, develops some technology, abandons the values that led it to prosperity, and ultimately destroys itself in an avaricious quest for gain. It is a pattern that is sadly predictable. The only remedy we've ever found that can hope to prevent it is a belief in something beyond the immediate. We are not trying to be what you would call gods, or to force you into believing in monsters or the supernatural. We are just trying to nudge you off the path you're currently on and onto one that might provide a means forward for your species that does not result in your utter destruction."

Arturas understood. He watched the spacecraft fly from planet to planet and marveled at the technology that allowed them to achieve such a feat. There were still two questions he hadn't gotten answers to yet. "Did you bring me here on purpose? When I was little?" he asked.

"We did. You possess a rare combination of intellect and appreciation for mysteries beyond science. These traits were identified in you, and we nudged you, just like we are trying to nudge your whole planet." It didn't matter how they'd accomplished that, but he felt incredibly privileged to have been chosen for this experience and was intensely thankful to his parents for instilling in him the values that they had.

"And what about that farmer in Lithuania? Was he… one of you?"

The voice laughed. "No. Think of him as a sort of… bodyguard for those of us you met in that house. And by the way, they were simply surprised that you were there; they wouldn't have hurt you. But we understand how you got scared and ran. People in Lithuania have been catching glimpses of us for centuries. The name Velnias was given to one of ours."

"But that means devil."

"A malevolent force is as easy to believe in as a compassionate, magnanimous one, perhaps easier. And if it assists us in our endeavors, then we are comfortable with it." The voice was silent for a moment. Arturas watched a massive cloud of pink and green cosmic dust envelop two planets and billow toward a third. It reminded him of a pyroclastic flow hurtling down the side of a volcano, and he thought it may have been the most exquisitely beautiful sight he'd ever seen. Somewhere beyond it two spiral galaxies spun lazily, and the white string lanced out between them. "Our time is at an end. We have to return you to your world. When you are back it will be as if you'd never left – no time will have passed. Hold tight."

Arturas gripped the string again and felt the now familiar sensation of electricity jolt him as he began sliding along the white light. The two galaxies flashed by, and soon he was hurtling through the universe at a speed far beyond that of light. He wished he understood how travel at that speed was possible. Hadn't he just had an idea about that a moment ago?

Arturas woke up on a comfortable bed of moss in a forest somewhere. He looked up into the trees and was delighted to see birds darting around, their songs providing a beautiful soundtrack to his interrupted repose. Moving seemed unnecessary so he lay still for several minutes breathing the fresh, moist air, and watching the birds. But he couldn't stay there forever. His mother and father were probably waiting for him. They'd said something about a pork roast for dinner, and Arturas realized how hungry he was. His mother made a gravy from pork roast that he swore would make her a millionaire if she could bottle and sell it. His mouth watered a little at the thought, and he pushed himself up from the soft green moss. There was someone else here, and the sight of another person startled him. He nearly ran but stopped when he realized there was something familiar about the body lying on the ground about twenty feet from where he'd been. He knew this person.

Arturas walked slowly over to the form. It was a man, and a big one, lying on his side facing away from Arturas, so he had to walk to the far side to see his face. And he was right – he did know him. He knelt down and shook the shoulder of the sleeping man. "Hey! Wake up!" The man shuddered and opened his eyes.

"What's going on?" he asked groggily.

"We fell asleep. Gotta get up and out of the woods before it gets dark."

"Ok," the man said as he stood shakily. He shook his head to clear the cobwebs then smiled at Arturas. "Weird. I've never fallen asleep in the woods before. Stevie is gonna give me shit for years! Don't tell him."

"I won't," Arturas laughed. "Now come on. My mom's making pork roast with that gravy you like."

"Should we call Brock and ask him to come?"

"Sure. He's always welcome at my mom's house. You know he was her favorite of all my friends."

The big man feigned a hurt look. "And I thought I was her favorite because of my name."

"Just because she likes *Bob* Dylan, doesn't mean she likes you!" Arturas said.

The men laughed aloud as they walked through the woods toward home.

# PERFECT

The times were perfect, people were perfect, the climate was perfect, food was perfect, interpersonal interactions were perfect, housing was perfect, transportation was perfect, power generation was perfect, medicine was perfect, human reproduction was perfect, government was perfect, the world was perfect. Everything was… perfect.

The nineteenth, twentieth and twenty-first centuries boasted the most consequential industrial, technical, political and social developments humanity had ever witnessed. Other events throughout history – the invention of the wheel, ancient Greek philosophy, the Roman Empire, Top Ramen™ – contributed in their own unique ways to the world of A.D 2107. The world in that year had been made whole, complete, the visions and dreams of miserable, tormented centuries past were at last fulfilled, made real, made perfect.

Hello! I'm so happy to meet you! When I learned you were coming for a tour, I couldn't wait for you to arrive. Please feel welcome. There is nothing to worry about here; everything is provided for. Hungry? Take a mag-walk to the nearest provisioning nexus or prov-nex as we call them. What's that? You don't know what a mag-walk is? Well, let me tell you about them. Once you ride one, you'll never want to actually walk again. Mag-walk is short for magnetic walkway. See that path over there? The grey one that's hovering above the ground? It's like a conveyor belt, except that it operates on an electro-magnetic field. You stand on it and it transports you to wherever you wish to go. The corinim– What? I didn't? I'm so sorry; I'll explain now. The corinim, as the device is known, is actually called a Cortex Interface Implant. It was developed in the early twenty-first century by some of the true visionaries of that time. The goal was to allow humes with disabilities– What's that? A hume is short for human. We don't call each other people anymore. That word was deemed exclusionary, colonial, and racist. And it hurt feelings. It was decided long ago that positive feelings, and being protected from stimuli that caused negative feelings, were as essential as shelter and sustenance, so we are all humes now. But back to the corinim.

In the previous age, before our advances in medicine, spinal cord injuries and diseases like ALS were debilitating and often left the afflicted unable to move or speak. Corinims were invented to provide those unfortunate humes with a means to communicate and express themselves. Self-expression is at the core of our value system. If a hume does not have the ability to speak, then social enclosure is the result. Social enclosure? That's when a hume cannot freely express. Being enclosed is worse than death. The corinim can do so many things. The hume's thoughts are translated into audible words which are broadcast through a speaker. In some cases corinims have been able to restore mobility – actually make humes walk again. Our scientists and researchers are still studying and improving them. They've done such great things for humes. We can discuss these things in more detail later. Right now, I'd like to take you to a prov-nex – you're going to love them. Right this way – we'll take the mag-walk.

I'm sure you noticed when you stepped on that your shoes stuck to the surface? That's because the mag-walks are made of a material, please don't ask me what it is, I don't know, that somehow interacts with the magnetic field that moves these plates we're standing on and keeps you stuck to this spot. It also keeps it suspended above the ground as you saw earlier. Trying to take a step while the mag-walk is in motion could cause an accident. Someone could fall. Humes could be injured. We don't believe in allowing humes to make decisions that could not only lead to harm, but also cause others to be inconvenienced by their selfishness and poor choices. How do I mean that? Let's say someone wanted to run on the mag-walk and fell, injured themself and someone else. We would have to help them. Other humes would need to assist them in getting medical treatment. Hume health professionals would have to stop the important research they are conducting in order to repair the damaged bodies. The entire affair would be a tremendous inconvenience to everyone involved. It was deemed selfish and egocentric to permit activities that could lead to injury or premature discorporation. Ha ha ha! Yes, I know, I've seen a few documentaries; there are a number of them in the archives. To think that humes actually used to climb mountains, even sheer cliffs, with no safety equipment other than a bag of chalk. And jumping out of aircraft with little more than a bed sheet strapped to one's back? Simply extraordinary. Such activities have been prohibited for decades. No hume here would remotely consider engaging in such absurdities. What's that? It could be considered a form of expression? Personal freedom? Climbing a mountain? I'm not sure I understand what you mean… Well, yes… I suppose that is… umm… I don't…

We're almost there.

I know. I'm hungry too. Famished actually! You can get anything you want in the prov-nex – they're simply marvelous. One of our favorite dishes is twice baked roaches. What kind do we use? Generally, the Brown-Hooded Cockroach, Cryptocercus punctulatus, is served, but once in a while we get a delicacy – the Smoky Brown Cockroach, Periplaneta fuliginosa. It depends on the farms and how their production numbers are. And you must try the maggot salad with cattle tick and bedbug croutons. Absolutely divine! Oh, you can get a number of things. Alkaline water is always available of course due to its positive health benefits, but I'd suggest that you also try the earthworm milk. It's full of protein. Our sustenance substances are scientifically formulated to provide the perfect balance of nutrition, vitamins and minerals.

I'm sorry, could you repeat the question? Oh yes, we take our health very seriously here. It's one of the most important aspects of our daily lives. Our society is based almost entirely on health and safety;

nearly everything is geared toward providing and perpetuating them both. There was so much needless self-indulgence in previous eras. Tobacco, alcohol, a variety of drugs, sugary food and drink, and a general societal acceptance of unhealthy behaviors and unsafe lifestyles. We've changed all that. I have to lower my voice here; not everyone knows this next part. Have you ever heard of Pepsi, Frito-Lay or Hostess? No? They're brands that were owned by what were known as corporations – commercial entities that existed to provide goods and services to humes on a for-profit basis. Unbelievable isn't it? The notion of profits? Completely unnecessary today, and utterly alien to our society. Those three corporations, and others like them, including what were known as fast food restaurants, contributed disproportionately to the health crises of the last era. But the worst were those firearms and gasoline-powered car manufacturers. I simply cannot understand how they were allowed to continue making such hideously unsafe devices. Insanity. Our antiquities chroniclers have documented how destructive and deadly such corporations and the products they produced were to the previous society. They no longer exist of course, and will never be allowed to exist again. They're simply too dangerous to the health of humes. A philosophy concerning these types of organizations was even created and adopted by our society. The brilliant antiquities chroniclers even gave it a name – enterprise existentialism. Its premise is really quite simple. Health and safety is at the absolute center of everything instead of profits. An unhealthy and unsafe society cannot survive – or be allowed to exist. The one exception to this philosophy our civilization allows is in medicine.

There were once corporations called pharmaceutical companies. They produced an array of compounds in a variety of forms that were intended to treat a plethora of ailments, many of them brought about by the products and lifestyles created and championed by those corporations I mentioned earlier, and others like them. The pharmaceutical companies were driven by profit too, but their products were altruistically intentioned, so when the social realignment happened, they were absorbed and reorganized into the entities they are now. Without them cancer and diabetes would still be raging. Look around. Do you see any sick humes? There aren't any. Everyone is healthy and happy. Oh no! Please, don't look-

I'm so sorry you had to witness that. What happened? The hume you watched fall was deactivated. No, I... wasn't going to tell you about this. It really is unfortunate you had to witness it. Yes, of course I will. You deserve an explanation after seeing that. Humes can occasionally be deemed... defective. When that happens the corinim serves... another purpose. It deactivates them. No, no, it's very humane. There is no pain at all. The hume just stops. The collection crew is arriving now. They will dispose of the bio waste, or the husk as we refer to it. That's a rather strange question. No, we do not bury them. Each husk is... processed. Perhaps recycled is a better word. We have facilities for this. It's a rather... distasteful topic. Perhaps you'd like to discuss something less.. moribund?

Now that is an excellent question! Why *is* everything grey? Because colors are racist, sexist, ableist, ageist, and exclusionary, and like the words person or people, they hurt feelings. Think of how many words and phrases of the old language had their roots in racism. Whiteout, blackout, brownout. blackboard, whiteboard. Red herring. Brown sugar. Green with envy. Having the blues. Yellow-bellied. Blueblood. White as snow. Black as night. In the red. In the black. Red tape. Paint the town red. Red-handed. Brown eye. All of these things were ethnically and racially offensive. There were many others. Also, I'd appreciate it if you didn't mention what I just said. Some humes are still very sensitive to those words and phrases, and it's illegal to hurt feelings. So, to answer your question, everything is grey because it is the least offensive color we could find. Grey doesn't hurt feelings. So that's why all our buildings are grey, our clothes, this mag-walk, even the food, which you'll soon see at the prov-nex. We should be there soon.

Don't try to move at the next junction. The plates we're on will separate from this mag-walk when we reach the right pathway. You'll see. They just split off from the one we're on and join another. The invention is ingenious. I admit that I don't know how it works. The science behind it, the engineering, is beyond me. But I do love mag-walks. They're so much better than those horrid cars humes used to drive. And that brings me to my next point – energy.

Have you heard about energy and how the methods we use to generate it have changed here over time? That's good. Then you know that the previous era relied almost exclusively on what were known as fossil fuels. They were incredibly damaging to everything – humes, trees, even pizza. Yes, I know it sounds strange, and we don't eat pizza here because it's unhealthy, but it's true. Pizza became so popular that humes of the past had it delivered to their enviro-doms, of course they weren't called that back then, they were known as apartments or houses. The humes that delivered the pizzas used vehicles that burned fossil fuels, which of course were horrible, terrible and bad. But the worst thing was the particulate matter from the burned fossil fuels that landed on the pizzas. They called it exhaust back then. The antiquities chroniclers have documented countless instances of disease and death resulting specifically from this phenomenon. What's that? You know something about pizza? Yes, please tell me – I'd like to know. They were delivered in... boxes? That were kept inside large insulating pouches to maintain their temperature? Wait, what are you saying? That the particulate matter could not have settled on the pizza? That's impossible. The chroniclers have said so. I think you've gotten some bad information. It is indisputable fact that countless thousands of people died from contaminated pizza.

But I've digressed from our original topic. We were discussing energy, yes? So, we've established that old forms of energy were... very bad. We use the sea now. Yes, the sea. Massive machines were installed underwater many years ago. As the currents move, they cause the machines to spin, which generates electricity. I'm sorry, I don't understand the question. Sea life? Fish and whales? Yes, I've heard of them. We have fossil records of these creatures, but they went extinct millions of years ago. The only life found in the sea now is plants. Oh, and a few microbes. You don't think what part is correct? You believe that fish and whales existed as recently as a few hundred years ago? I admit that I'm skeptical of this. Our chroniclers tell us differently, and they are very learned. Alright, yes, back to the machines. We have so many of these machines in the oceans now that they generate too much electricity. We can't even use it all. Isn't that incredible? And all we had to do was put them underwater. The oceans weren't doing anything for us anyway – why not use them? The simplicity of it is... genius. There are so many smart people working to create a better life and world for all of us. We are truly fortunate to live here, in this time.

Ah, here we are – the prov-nex. Help yourself. Oh, what a treat - there are two choices today! They must have known you'd be here. I think you've impressed someone! Maggot salad in the blue bowl, Brown-Hooded Cockroach soufflé in the red. After we eat, I'll show you the enviro-doms.

You didn't finish your salad. I don't want to lecture, but I should tell you, simply as part of the tour you understand, that waste is strongly discouraged here. What you didn't eat will be recycled for others to consume, but there is something else I should mention. Many maggots gave their lives to make that salad. We honor their sacrifice by consuming their bodies so that we may live in health and harmony. Hmm? Yes, that is similar to the notions some primitive cultures had regarding food. They believed that all life possessed some sort of essence, force, a soul, they sometimes called it.

Even animals and insects! Can you imagine? We do not believe in such superstitious things, but we do honor the sacrifices of the insects. They die so that we may live.

We're here. Just before you, are the enviro-doms. Yes, it is a big building. It can house over a million humes quite comfortably. It is comprised of individual nodes, rooms really. Each node is enough for a single hume. Follow me, I'll show you one.

As you can see everything a hume needs is here. This panel on the floor slides back to reveal a sleep mat. They're quite comfortable and were designed for maximum spinal health. You can try it if you like. That panel in the wall conceals both sink and toilet. The funnel you see is not mounted to the wall. It has a retractable hose attached to it. All one must do is pull it out in order to use it. What does it do? It evacuates all biological waste from the hume who lives here. I'm sure you can work out how to operate it without an explanation. A sanitizing solution is passed through it automatically after each use, and that same tube dispenses water for all the hume's needs. No, no, it's perfectly safe. Our engineers tested the system rigorously before it was accepted for general use in the enviro-doms. That little flap next to it opens to reveal a tray where the enviro-dom receives orders sent to the prov-nex. One can get a salad or a souffle delivered right to their enviro-dom. Not unlike those pizzas we talked about earlier! Except that our fare is far healthier. How big? The entire node is three meters square. Yes, our engineers planned for everything when they designed these spaces. How much more does a hume need? There is a place to sleep, bodily functions and nutrition have been addressed, and if you touch that spot on the wall there, a small table and chair fold out. Go ahead, try it. Isn't that something? The material is made of nano tubes, which makes it strong enough to withstand the weight of a hume sitting on it while also being thin enough to fold into the wall without having to increase that wall's thickness to accommodate the device. It's really revolutionary, just like so many other things here. Oh, no. Humes are not allowed to cohabitate. There is no need. Procreation has been addressed. We have no fear of the population ever declining or growing to an unsustainable number. A steady population has been maintained for decades under the wisdom of our leaders. How does procreation work? Let's go to the progeny center, and I'll explain on the mag-walk. There's nothing else to see here in the enviro-doms. If you've seen one, you've seen them all.

So, as I was saying, procreation is an industrial process. Each hume's complete genetic code is stored in a database. When it is determined that a new hume needs to be created to fill a role in our society, the codes of males and females are compared, and a match is made. The entire process, from conception to life, takes only three months, and is performed entirely within an automated factory. No humes needed to make more humes. This is such an extraordinary society!

Here's the factory. As you can see through the window it's like a laboratory but without the scientists and technicians. The robots in there do everything. The process has been so refined and perfected over time that all variables have been planned for and eliminated. There is no need for humes to be involved at all in procreation. Why are there such large windows on this facility? Transparency. Our leaders want everyone to know exactly what's happening everywhere. They have no secrets from us. Did you notice that it was the same at the prov-nex? If I were to take you to one of the factories where our food is created, you'd see the same thing – glass walls and complete transparency regarding the process. No secrets at all. There's not much more to see here. Shall we move on to our leaders? Alright.

The mag-walk ride will take a bit longer this time. We have to go quite a distance from here. Why is that? The Civilizational Directorate, that's what our leadership body is called, prefers to have their headquarters out in an isolated area. There are many distractions here, and they've found it preferable to minimize them. Their business is so very important. They can't allow their attention to be diverted from ensuring a better life and planet for all humes.

Yes, it is a very beautiful day. Every day is beautiful here. I'm sorry? What? Snow? I'm not familiar with the word. Frozen water? Falling from the sky? Forgive me, but that's... absurd. And I think likely impossible. The weather is the same every day. Always sunny and seventy-three degrees Fahrenheit. It has never been different. The chroniclers told us so. No. They have records going back to the early twentieth century. Rain? I don't know that word either. Well, the plants receive their water from humes whose job it is to give it to them, and much of that is automated. Climate? I don't really know what you're talking about, but we don't discuss the weather here. There is no need. It never changes.

In fact, I think this is the first time in my life that I've ever discussed the weather, and I'm afraid I only know what I told you, nothing more.

Would you like to discuss anything else? It is a fairly long mag-walk ride until we reach our destination. You'll get to see all the fields of grass here in our community. No, all the trees were eradicated decades ago. They were a safety issue. Yes, trees were unsafe. Leaves on the ground created slippery conditions that could have led to falls. And of course there was always the possibility that a branch could break, fall off and hit someone. There haven't been any trees anywhere in the world in a very long time. Grass is slippery too? I wouldn't know. Humes are not allowed to walk on grass. Our passing could damage it, spoil its natural beauty. We have the mag-walks and constructed pathways. There is no reason for a hume to ever touch grass.

What about transportation? You'd like to discuss that? Certainly. There isn't much need for it anymore. You've seen how many humes the enviro-doms can house. Our communities have been very well planned by our wise leaders. No one wants for anything. As long as there is a prov-nex close by, which there always is, then our needs are met. Vacations? To other parts of the world? No. Humes do not engage in such extraneous and destructive behavior. There are mag-walks that connect each region of the world, and which even cross the seas, but they are not used except for scientists and technicians, those who have reason to travel to another region. A hume, once generated, will live its life entirely within the confines of the community in which its assigned enviro-dom is located. I didn't?

Terribly sorry, I thought I had. Yes, humes are assigned to an enviro-dom. No, they do not have a choice. Each hume is genetically engineered, I believe I mentioned this process earlier, to perform a specific task within our society. That task, whatever it may be, dictates which enviro-dom a hume is assigned to. But that does not really have anything to do with transportation. My apologies for going off-topic.

There was something else you wanted to discuss, I believe? Ah yes, medicine. Our learned and brilliant scientists have been able to modify the hume genome so that there are no longer any diseases. The chroniclers teach us that in previous eras, disease killed randomly and indiscriminately. Our technologies have stopped that, putting an end to needless tragedy. We require very little in the way of medical care. Of course, once in a great while someone falls down or cuts their finger through some negligent action, but those injuries are usually superficial and are dealt with swiftly. Why does everyone look so young? Because we're healthy. It's that simple. The prov-nex gives us the nutrition we need, the enviro-doms ensure we get enough rest and shelter. I forgot to mention this when we were there, but every night at ten the lights turn off automatically, and they come back on again at six in the morning. Our perfect eight hours of sleep is planned for us. All we have to do is lay down on the floor, which if you remember also serves as a sleeping mat. They're quite comfortable, and falling asleep is very easy. A mild sedative in gaseous form is pumped through the ventilation system each night beginning at nine-thirty. By the time the lights go off at ten, most of us are on our mats and asleep. So, as you can see, our health is paramount in the thoughts of our leaders. They truly care about us. Isn't it wonderful to be so well cared for? To have nothing to worry about, nothing to fear? I think it is. Our minds are free to focus on the tasks we are assigned, to do our part for the greater good of society. I feel truly sorry for the humes who lived before, all the horrors they had to endure. It must have been excruciating to be required to plan one's own life. And the food they ate... I'd rather not contemplate it. Primitive. Utterly barbaric.

Elderly? I don't know this word. Aged? Old? The question, I must admit, has confused me. There is nothing like this elderly here. A hume's duration is preplanned by the progeny center. At a specified time the corinim will deactivate the hume. This generally happens when one has begun to devour more resources than it produces. Would you repeat that? Fabian? Social-ism? These are not words I am familiar with. Are you sure they're real? Perhaps I will petition the chroniclers for an explanation when the tour is completed.

We're getting close now. See that building up ahead? That's it. That's where the Civilizational Directorate live and work. No, we are not allowed inside. Their tasks are too delicate and complex for them to let just anyone enter their enviro-dom. Oh yes, I agree – it is a marvelously beautiful building, and so very different from our enviro-doms. Why would humes not be allowed to live there? That building is reserved for the wise leaders and thinkers of the Civilizational Directorate. They need such a building, such an environment, for the monumental task of overseeing and managing our society. No, I do not question it. They deserve to live in such a place for how difficult and tedious their lives must be. So how will we speak to them? There is a place a short distance from the building where humes gather when summoned, and where we can commune with the leaders. There it is. You can just see it there, that round spot without grass. No, it's just small rocks. I believe it was once called gravel.

And here we are. Just follow me up this path. And please don't step on the grass. It has been carefully engineered and cultivated by experts to achieve and retain this vibrant green color. I believe I mentioned this earlier when we were discussing trees. There can also be severe... consequences for straying from the path. Oh good. I was hoping you'd understand. This way. It's not far.

Thank you for remaining off the grass. It truly humbles us that you've accepted our customs so readily. Now if you'll direct your attention towards the leaders' enviro-dom, an image of a white flame surrounded by a gold circle will appear in the air. That is the signal the leaders are listening. Oh, I almost forgot to mention something. You will not hear the leaders' voices. They do not actually speak directly to us. We pose our questions or make our statements, and an emissary of theirs will respond in due course. You find this strange? Why would it be strange? The Civilizational Directorate are so busy with maintaining our society and constantly striving for ways to improve it that they simply don't have time to interact directly with humes. Why would they summon us if they aren't going to speak? I hadn't thought of it that way before. I suppose it might seem strange to you. Societal harmony is extremely important. The leaders pay very close attention to the mood of the humes, and if they sense something amiss, then we are summoned here individually or in groups to air our grievances, should there be any. I honestly don't know why anyone would have anything to complain about. We have everything we need here. This truly is a perfect society, a perfect life.

I will wait here for you. Why? Only one hume, well, excuse me, you're not actually a hume, but one... individual, at a time, is all that's allowed to make a statement to the leaders unless a group of humes has been summoned.

What do you mean? Groups of leaders in other societies have specific names and titles? Yes, our chroniclers have mentioned them. I remember the names congress and parliament, president and minister. Our leaders felt that these titles created distance between them and the humes. They did not want to be perceived as being aloof, apart. So, they disposed of titles in favor of being called the Civilizational Directorate. A stroke of genius, really. Humes are completely loyal to our leaders. And why wouldn't we be? Look what they've created for us. It's paradise. I'll be here when you're finished.

How was it? Oh, that's good. I'm very glad to hear that it went well. You should have a visit from an emissary with their response by the time we're back at the enviro-dom. Yes, we need to stay off the grass on the way back as well. Thank you for your understanding.

Careful there – watch your step. Good. You're on the mag-walk safely. I will have to report that. The mag-walk should be completely level with the ground. That was at least three millimeters difference in height between the ground and the surface of the mag-walk. Unacceptable. It's a dangerous tripping hazard. I will report it the moment we're back at the enviro-dom.

And here we are. I trust you've enjoyed the tour? Thank you, I did as well. You are most welcome. If you have another few moments, the emissary should be arriving momentarily. No, it isn't a hume. It will come by autonomous drone. I didn't? Oh, I'm so sorry for the oversight. Yes, drones are used extensively here. Most are microscopic so that they don't disturb the eye or create distractions. Only a few, like the emissaries, are large enough to actually see without a magnification device. The Civilizational Directorate employs them to watch us and make sure we're safe. It's how they judge the overall mood of our society and keep abreast of developments, although there is never much to report since our society is already so well-developed. I'm sure I've said this before, but their main purpose is to ensure the health and safety of humes, and they are an essential tool to ensure those things.

Ah, here it comes now. Just take the cylinder. Inside it you will find their wisdom. No, it is for you only. Hmm? I have no idea what's inside. Yes, you may take it with you when you leave. Consider it a gift from us. No, thank you for being such gracious visitors. We look forward to hearing from you. All the best.

"What does it say" the woman asked.

He scanned the note again, a slight frown creasing his brow. "It says if we try to buy that planet, that they'll mobilize for war," the man replied. Outside the huge window stars sped by as the craft arrowed through space toward their home world.

"Are they serious? Do they know what we could do to them? And their… humes are so docile they wouldn't know what to do in a fight."

"Obviously they *don't* know. I mean, it *has* been centuries since our ancestors left there. They probably don't even remember what happened."

"I strongly doubt they do," the woman said. "Almost everything about their history has been erased. They've tried to create some sort of utopia or something. It was sickening listening to that… tour guide. She didn't even know how ignorant she was, how brainwashed. I wanted to show her exactly how their 'leaders' lived, but I doubt she would have believed me. Probably would have thought our surveillance recordings of them and their… bacchanalia were fake. And can you believe that shield they put around the planet to regulate the climate? They really have no clue how much harm it's done, how many mines they had to build for the materials, how many species of animals and plants they eradicated."

"But it keeps the temperature at a steady seventy-three degrees Fahrenheit," he replied, his voice both mimicking and mocking their tour guide. The man paused a moment, his gaze rested unfocused on something out in space beyond the window, then he sighed in resignation. "People believe what they want to believe, what they're *told* to believe. That place lost the ability to think critically a long time ago."

"So, should we buy it? They're not asking very much. The comps in other parts of the galaxy are far more expensive, but it is our home world, even in that condition."

The man sat back in his seat and stared out the window as a nebula flashed by. He'd always liked nebulae. They were among the most impressive sights in the universe.

"There's another planet in NGC 4594 that I'd like to look at."

"That watery place with all the mountains poking out of the sea?" the woman replied skeptically.

"Yeah, that one. I think the kids would love it. It would actually be a nice vacation planet for the family."

"But what about Earth? Are we going to do something about it?"

The man sighed. "I suppose we should. It's sad to see our planet of origin in such a state." The woman stared silently at the man. "Ok, we'll buy it. You're right about the price. Can't pass it up for what the current owners are asking, although they sure could have done a much better job of maintaining the place. I'll talk to Pete when we get home. He knows someone with Universal Exterminators. We'll have the planet fumigated, have the trees replanted, get those stupid machines out of the oceans so the fish and whales can come back, and in a few centuries the place will be as good as new."

"And we'll get rid of those hideous enviro-dom things? And bring back cows so we can have steak for dinner?"

"Of course. We'll put it back the way it was – full remodel."

"Oh, you're the best," the woman said as a broad smile lit up her face.

# APOCALYPSE FOOTBALL

Author's Note: This story is a sequel to another story called Apocalypse Pancakes which can be found in my first short story collection, French Press Sludge.

*May 19, 2026*

*Well, that didn't fucking last long. The place I'd thought was the closest thing to Utopia the earth has ever seen? Yeah, not so much. I barely got away from there alive. In truth, I'm not really sure how I did it, so I won't explain it right now. I'll think about it, process it, then write it down in this asinine journal I'm keeping that no one will ever read. For now, let's talk about other things.*

*It's been forty-six years and one day since Mt. St. Helens in Washington state erupted for the first time. Most people only know about that first eruption, but it actually spewed its ash load into the air several more times after that. I was not alive the first time it blew, but I remember something about it in the news sometime after the new millennium. It was spewing again or something. Why am I talking about a volcano? Because that farm place erupted like one. Fuck. And I wasn't going to talk about it until later. Fine. Alright. My brain wants to spew the story like St. Helens did her ash? Ok then, let's play. But let me finish my St. Helens thought first. You might have noticed that each of these entries is dated. How do I know what the date is? Answer: I don't for sure. I know what year it is and it's not hard to divine what month it is by paying attention to the weather, but the actual date is sort of arbitrary. I met a guy some time back who claimed he'd been keeping track of the date since the shit storm started. I suppose it was his way of staying connected to the world that used to be. His cheese had slid quite a ways off his cracker, and I couldn't really blame him. (Don't judge! How would YOU handle it if everything you'd ever known was suddenly turned upside down and given a good shake, like a kid tossing a dirty pair of jeans for loose change to buy candy with? Not too well is my guess.) Anywho. I found a little spiral notebook, you know – the kind nerds keep in their breast pockets behind the row of pens and pencils - and wrote the date in it. Been using it as my informal calendar ever since. And why did I bring up Mt. St. Helens in the first place? Because I saw a poster of it on the wall of a house I slept in last night and when I read the caption on it, I realized the anniversary of its eruption was yesterday. No reason other than that.*

*Ok, pleasantries are finished. On to the meat of the conversation. What the hell happened to Utopia? Fucked up people, that's what. It's really that simple. The place was incredible when I first got there. What did I call it? Let me look back at that entry. Found it. Here's how I described it: "It's as civilized a place as I could have hoped." And it was initially. But after I'd been there a week or so, the cracks started to show, the mold started to grow.*

*It was little things at first. I'd be walking somewhere and catch someone looking at me. They'd look away quickly when I met their gaze. You learn to look for little things like that, small signals, when your life could depend on them. There are enough bad (or maybe just desperate) people around that you have to be constantly vigilant. It becomes a habit after a while, and I hadn't been there long enough to have lost my hyperawareness when I started seeing things. What else did I see? I'm a light sleeper and I'd hear people shuffling around in the dark outside the small cabin where I slept with three other single guys. Or I'd see someone duck behind a building when they noticed me coming. Individually these events didn't mean much. Collectively they made the hair on the back of my neck stand up. Something was most definitely NOT RIGHT here.*

*No one threatened me directly at first, they just acted… weird. So, one night I decided to sneak out of the little house I shared with the other guys and go see what was what. The whole farm was asleep. They had sentries at intervals along the walls, but nothing dramatic ever happened, and no alarm was ever raised in my time there. I prowled the fucking camp from one end to another and didn't see shit. I'd just said fuck it and was heading back to bed when I heard a creaking sound somewhere off to my left. There were several buildings in that direction, most of which were for families, but there didn't seem to be anyone around, so I cruised on over that way. That's when I saw the doors open. They were metal, bolted to a robust concrete frame that was flush with the ground, and presumably led to a set of stairs. I'd seen them before, even asked someone about them once, and had been told it was the entrance to a utility vault left over from before. And that there was nothing down there. I hadn't given it a second thought and had forgotten about the doors until the moment I heard them open.*

*Light spilled from the opening, and I watched as a stream of people emerged. None of them spoke and all were wearing dark clothing. I was fucking lucky no one saw me. There was just time for me to dive behind a water storage tank next to one of the houses when the first people came out. A couple walked past me, and I could clearly see their faces. Their eyes were vacant, dead, staring.*

*And there was something wet on their chins. It was too dark to see, but I had my suspicions. It was hard to tell how many came out of those doors, certainly not the whole population of the farm, but I guessed about half.*

*I waited where I was until they were all gone, then waited a little while longer. The doors were still open, and I walked up as quietly as I could to take a look. I'd been right about the stairs. A nondescript concrete stairway led down into the earth. It reminded me of a storm cellar you might see in a movie about tornados or some shit. No sound from below, but there was light down there, dim, like from a lantern placed a long distance away. I went down slowly, listening hard. At the bottom there was… of course you guessed it – a concrete hallway stretching away from me. About fifty yards from where I stood, the hall turned to the right, and hanging on a wall in the corner was a lantern. At least I knew where the light was coming from. There were no pipes or conduits in the passageway, just plain old grey concrete, boring as hell, but oh-so-strong. It was strange to me that the doors had been left open. Last one out turn off the lights, close the doors, and all that jazz apparently didn't register with these people. Or there was still someone (or more than one someone) down here. That's what got my heart pounding – not being alone. I didn't have a weapon with me, just my fists, and I'd never been particularly good with them. Fuck it. I'd lived this long after all the shit the world had put me through. If it was my time to go, then that was it and I'd say fuck this place on the way out.*

*I peeked around the corner and found a door looking back at me. It was just an ordinary metal door, nothing special, and it was ajar. I put my eye to the gap and… I don't want to tell the rest right now. Maybe tomorrow.*

*May 29, 2026*

*It's taken me this long to... I guess process is as good a word as any - what I saw. That's what I was going to do originally before writing anything down, but my brain decided it wanted to vomit up this emesis of a story anyway, so that's why I wrote the entry before this one. Who knows why the mind works the way it does. Steven Pinker claimed to know, even wrote a book called 'How the Mind Works'. Maybe he knows more than I do. Probably he does. Did. No idea if he's alive right now or not. What-the-fuck-ever. You really want to know what I saw, you sick fuckers? Can't wait to hear the gory details, like this is some kind of tabloid? Just salivating over what comes next in this sordid tale, aren't you? Ok, here you go. I saw kids. Three of them. Oldest probably no more than eight or nine. They'd been hung upside down from the ceiling. Throats cut. A big metal wash tub sat on the floor below them. They'd used it to catch the blood. There was still quite a lot in it. Fuck. I feel sick thinking about it. Gonna take five. Or more.*

*June 3, 2026*

*They'd been drinking the blood. Like vampires. That's what I'd seen on the chins of those people who'd walked past me in the dark before I went down into the concrete tunnel. Blood. Like they're fucking Count Dracula or some shit. Psychos!*

*Come to find out Dorothy – remember her? She's the leader of this little cult I'm telling you about – thought she was some kind of Aztec priestess or some shit. The kids were a sacrifice to some god or another. Probably one she made up. She thought killing them and drinking their blood would magically bestow fecundity on her people and farm. She was quite wrong. What it did is contribute directly to its destruction. Remember those guys*

*I told you about? The ones I roomed with? They were all in their beds asleep when I snuck out that night, so I knew none of them were involved in the hideous things the others were doing. The next morning I told them what I'd seen. They didn't believe me at first, but after a few times through the story, they started to come around. That night we all snuck out and I took them down to that room. We'd secured a few weapons though – two pistols and all of us had knives. I took my knife from the kitchen, didn't ask where the others got their weapons, not my business. Point was we had them if we needed them.*

*The bodies of the kids were gone along with the tub, but there were still blood splatters all over the place. One of the guys said he'd been a cop, detective, and that he'd seen enough blood spatter at crime scenes to know he was looking at the real deal. Question was – how could they believe me and my story? Maybe they used this room to slaughter pigs or something. I had no proof. Then we heard doors open. We'd closed them on our way in, now someone was opening them again, coming our way. The slaughtering room provided nowhere to hide; it was completely empty, except for a couple of eyebolts embedded in the ceiling, so we took positions on either side of the door and stayed as quiet as we could. A few moments later Dorothy and some guy I'd never seen before walked in. They had a kid with them, little girl. She was gagged and her hands were tied behind her back. The guy was carrying the tub. Dorothy was saying something to him about the will of the deity, or some such horseshit, when the guy saw us. He dropped the tub. It made a huge clang sound. And he reached for something behind his back. One of the guys knifed him in the chest. Must have hit a sensitive spot cause the douche dropped like, well like the tub. Except all he did was groan. No clang from him. Dorothy was surprised to see us. The cop tried to question her, but all she wanted to do was mumble some… prayer. Incantation.*

*Charm. Magic spell or whatever-the-fuck. It was not in English, and she wouldn't answer any of the questions the cop was asking, so he untied the little girl and used the cord to tie Dorothy's hands behind her back. She kept muttering her gibberish as we led her out of the room and back to the surface. I wanted to just bash her head in and be done with her, but the cop talked me out of it. He said we needed to find out what was happening here and try to stop it. I guess he was right in his own way. But I wanted to just kill them all. Anyone who can hurt kids does not deserve to live. Period.*

*One thing just occurred to me that I hadn't thought of before. The guy who knifed Dorothy's henchman: he did it so fast – almost immediately, and without hesitation. We've all had to do… distasteful things since the shitshow started. Have we really come to this? Can we really kill so quickly, so nonchalantly? Dorothy and her twisted followers are a whole separate case study for some future shrink to examine. I'm talking about the average person. Was our humanity all just an illusion? A social construct? A set of norms forced on us by parents and teachers, peers and elders, governments and leaders, laws and their attendant punishments? Are we no better than hyenas fighting over the scraps left by lions? Is there anything left of what we used to call civil society? Or did the civil society even exist? Street gangs killed each other over petty disputes and perceived slights. Serial killers stalked and murdered their victims. Domestic disputes turned violent with one spouse slaying another. Wackos walked into schools and shot the places up. Those things don't really happen now because there is no society left. I wonder if what I saw that guy do is something that everyone from before was capable of but just didn't realize it. Or maybe they just repressed that part of themselves because of the constraints that civil society placed on them. Who the fuck knows? Alright, back to the story.*

*We got to the top of the stairs before we met anyone else. And who we met was everyone. That is, all of Dorothy's minions. They were waiting for us. Well, probably not for us, but for her and her now dead henchman to come back out of their concrete cave. There was definitely surprise when they saw her with us. She screamed at them, in English this time, to kill us all. And damned if they didn't try. The whole group rushed us. The guys with pistols started firing at the mob, but that didn't stop them. Out of the corner of my eye I saw the little girl run, and I took off after her. There's no shame in running when you're hopelessly outnumbered. It's about living, not keeping your precious pride intact. Hell, even the US Army ran from the Germans during the opening hours of the Battle of the Bulge. They got themselves squared away eventually, and ended up kicking some Nazi ass, but initially many of them ran just like I did that night.*

*I followed the girl. Don't know why. It seemed like I needed to. But I lost her in the darkness. Haven't seen her since. That's another thing that sucks about this horseshit world. Before, you could use technology to find someone you'd lost contact with. Social media allowed you to find damn near anyone, anywhere. Not anymore. To this moment I have no idea if that little girl is alive or dead. That really fucking sucks. I'll wonder about her until my last day.*

*People who hadn't been at the concrete cave were coming out of their houses, bleary eyed and confused. The gunshots woke them right up, and pretty soon everyone was running and screaming all over the place. (I remember writing before about how these were such good people. Fuck, was I ever wrong.) Somehow, I found myself in front of a building I'd never been in before. The door was open, and I went inside. Don't know what I was looking for, just wanted to be away from the chaos. They were all killing each other by this point. I'd passed several bodies. Didn't look too closely. Why bother? I didn't make any friends there, just acquaintances, so there wasn't anyone I was trying to find or hoping would live through the shitstorm that had just started. And I've seen enough dead bodies in this lifetime. There really is no need to examine more of them.*

*The building was, incredibly, the armory. Or what was left of it. The place had been ransacked and most of the guns were gone, but I did find my old AR-15, for a wonder. And there was still, for some bizarre reason, plenty of ammo. I found a backpack someone had tossed in a corner, dumped out the dirty old clothes that were in it, and tossed in as much AR ammo as I felt I could carry. Next stop was my old bunkhouse to get the rest of my stuff, especially my seeds. I'd already decided to keep heading south like I'd been before I found this place, and I'd need my seeds to start my own farm somewhere else.*

*There were lots of gunshots outside now. Screams. Groans. War. I was never in the service, don't know at all what war between armies is like and don't claim to. But this was definitely a variety of war. I ran out of the armory and toward my old bunkhouse. Fires had broken out in a few spots and the flames provided a hellish light by which I could see the carnage. Dead and injured were all over the place. People were running everywhere, shooting, hiding, screaming. Dying. Fucking horrible. We'd truly devolved into animals. Just like we've probably always been. Maybe I just sort of answered my own question from a couple pages ago.*

*I found my bunkhouse. It was on fire. The front door was open. I think every door in every building on this entire farm was open by now. Everyone had more important things to do than close them. My seeds were pretty important to me, so I ran inside. Fortunately, the place wasn't completely engulfed. My bunk was on the far wall opposite the fire. The smoke stung my eyes and burned my lungs, but I found my seeds in my pack under the bed. I grabbed it and turned to run back out just as the fucking ceiling collapsed in front of me. I guess the fire had done more damage to the building than I'd at first thought. There was no window behind me, just a wall. One thing I've always wondered about in movies and tv is why don't more people try to kick out a wall when they're trapped? They always look for doors, windows. Like water they search for the path of least resistance. Why, oh Lord, why?! Most times it's just drywall, insulation, and plywood or OSB that constitutes a wall. Those things are relatively easy to break. The smoke was getting bad, but it was either kick out the wall, run through the flames, which were really raging now, or just wait there and die. I decided that I wasn't going to die that day. I kicked and tore at the drywall until I'd opened a hole between the studs that was big enough for me to fit through, then I kicked on the exterior sheeting until it splintered. The heat was getting really intense when I finally broke through. Just as I scrambled out the rest of the ceiling collapsed. I'd made it by seconds. Inches. Like in a baseball game.*

*My hand is getting tired of writing. Should I wrap this up for tonight? No, I'll get through the next little bit, leave the story in a better place than it is right now.*

*The farm had a wall around it. Remember me describing it? It's made of whatever materials the inhabitants could scavenge. I don't want to call them people anymore. Almost called them monsters. But inhabitants works, I suppose. The wall wasn't far from my bunkhouse, maybe fifty yards or so. Problem was that there was a big group of people between me and it. They were all fighting each other – women attacking men with garden rakes, elderly men attacking young women with their bare hands – it was pandemonium. I can take care of myself, wouldn't have made it as long as I have if I couldn't, but part of that can be chalked up to, like the old Kenny Rogers song said, "You got to know when to hold 'em, know when to fold 'em, know when to walk away, and know when to run." Believe me: I know when the time is right for each one of those actions. The situation before me was not one I cared to interject myself into, so I took the last of Kenny's options and ran the other way.*

*I dodged around buildings, jumped over bodies, and had no idea whether they were living or not, and didn't care. All that mattered was being out of that level of hell. Dante would have had some things to say about what went on that night, believe you me. The wall was further away in the direction I was running. That was fine, as long as I didn't run into any hostiles. And I didn't. Until I got to the damned wall. And who did I find? Of course. Dorothy. She'd gathered four of her followers that were still alive, and they were trying to use a wheelbarrow and a couple of pallets to make a platform they could stand on to reach the top of the wall and pull themselves up and over. Idiot that I am I'd thought I was home free and ran right into them. Dorothy looked surprised to see me at first, then she recognized me and started screeching in that hideous other language. It reminded me of the movie Invasion of the Body Snatchers, the one with Donald Sutherland from the 70's or early 80's, whenever it was. Ever see it? Those who had been snatched would screech something awful at those who hadn't. She was doing that but in her own way. One of her goons slid over the wall just as she opened her ghastly mouth, so that was one I didn't have to contend with. But there were still three more. And Dorothy herself.*

*My rifle was in my right hand, a round racked in the chamber, and I raised it to fire just as the first goon started toward me. A touch of the trigger and the rifle barked, the goon fell. But the others were on me before I could pivot to engage them. I was just too close. I'd come around the corner of a building too fast, thinking I was clear, and blundered right into them. Fucking idiot. I'll never make that mistake again.*

*The goons tackled me, and I would have lost my rifle except for the strap attached to it, which I'd slung around my right shoulder. But I did lose my grip on it when my back slammed into the ground. The goons started wailing on me. (I have to digress just a moment to address something that has bothered me for a long time. Wailing, as I just used it, is slang for beat-the-shit-out-of. I've seen it spelled "whaling" various places in print, and I don't like it. Spelling it that way makes me think of Moby Dick, or some show on Discovery Channel about Humpbacks bubble feeding. It does not make me envision fisticuffs. Wailing, on the other hand, makes me thing of crying hysterically, which is what that spelling of the word actually means. So wailing, to me, seems closer in overall feel to the slang term than whaling. After all, if you get wailed on long enough, you may just end up wailing in pain. I feel much better now. Sorry for the long interlude.)*

*So, there I am, on my back, wind knocked out of me, and two goons pounding my ribs with their fists. Neither one went for a headshot; I'm still puzzled as to why. They may have won if they'd gone for the head. (Oh, come on now. Was there really that much suspense to all this? I'm writing it aren't I? Ergo I won. Or at least lived. Surely you figured* that *out, right?) Could have knocked me out, and that would have been game fucking over – no more lives left, do not repeat level eighteen. Had to throw in a video game reference. It's been too long since I've been able to veg out on a PlayStation or Xbox game.*

*No breath and ribs getting beaten to mush. Bad situation. Then I remembered the knife. You remember it too, don't you? I told you about it earlier. It's the one I took from the kitchen when my bunkhouse roomies and I first went down into that abattoir. What I didn't tell you is that it's just a little thing. Yep, present tense; I still have it. The blade is only three or four inches long, certainly not a match for that giant Bowie-type knife Stallone brandished to such exquisite perfection in the second Rambo movie. (Damn I've written a lot tonight. Should I leave you right on the edge of this heart-stopping cliffhanger? Fuck yes! I'm tired and my hand hurts. Sweet dreams.)*

*June 19, 2026*

*Ha ha! Made you wait! Well, made myself wait actually. You, future reader, only had to move on to the next paragraph. Lucky fucking you. It's been an eventful... how long? Fifteen? Sixteen days? Something like that since I last wrote in this ragged old journal. I found a bicycle in some house that, incredibly, had two good tires. Since I was still heading south, I rode it until the rear tire blew. Made great time. I'm somewhere in east-central Arkansas. It's nice here. Maybe this is where I'll stay. Although I have been thinking about Georgia and Florida lately. Used to watch a little golf on tv, and The Masters tournament was always my favorite. Augusta National was on my bucket list of places to visit, so maybe I'll make my way there. The course will be totally overgrown by now, but it would still be pretty cool to actually be there. And Florida. Why there? I don't know. Read somewhere that it's the flattest state in the country, so walking would be much easier than going up and down all these hills I've been contending with since the shitstorm. I think maybe it's the water. It's tropical so gets lots of rain, which means I won't really have to worry much about drought. And I could swim in the Gulf of Mexico. That water is so warm you can stay in it all day. Or so I've heard. I'm sure I can find a place with good enough soil to grow my plants. And I can always fish. The stocks will have rebounded nicely now that no one is overfishing the waters anymore. Everything is going back to the way it was before humans. I sometimes wonder what the world will look like in a hundred years. A thousand. Will people have repopulated the planet? Rebuilt? Made the same stupid mistakes as before? My guess is yes. Sadly.*

*Ok. Time to tell you, like Paul Harvey used to say, the rest of the story.*

*There I am on my back, on the ground, ribs getting pummeled like Glass Joe in Mike Tyson's Punchout. (For those of you upon whom that reference is lost, it's about a video game. Glass Joe was the first boxer you had to beat in order to advance and eventually fight Iron Mike himself. Joe was easy. The other opponents got progressively harder. I actually beat the whole game once, including Mike. True story.) My knife was tucked under my belt in the front of my pants. I'd almost put it behind me, on my back, and am I ever glad I didn't. It probably would have stabbed me when I fell, for one, and been impossible to get to while the goons were beating on me, for two. I was able to get a hold of it with my left hand and immediately shoved it into the armpit of Goon # 1 who was on my left side. He gasped and stopped hitting me long enough for me to shift the knife to my other hand and slash Goon # 2 across the face. I felt the blade pass right through his eyeball. He screeched louder than Dorothy and rolled away from me, holding his face. Goon # 1 had his left hand pressed to the wound up under his right arm. Blood was pouring across his fingers and spattering on the ground. It was dark, nighttime. How could I see all this? Dorothy had been thoughtful enough to bring two lanterns with her. They were both on the ground, one on either side of the wheelbarrow. Probably so they could see better as they tried to escape the hellhole they'd created.*

*Goon # 3, he was on the other side of the wall, remember? Well, he was pounding and hollering from over there, but the only response he was getting was Dorothy's caterwauling and the screaming of Goon # 2. I stabbed him in the neck in order to shut him up. It hurt to sit up; my ribs were in bad shape. But in situations like that if you quit, you're dead. Instead of me it was Goon # 2 who ended up dead. I'd hit whichever major blood vessel runs up the left side of the neck. Carotid? Jugular? Fucked if I know. He bled out in a very short time. Goon # 1 was looking pretty pale in the light from the lanterns. He was sitting up, holding his armpit, and with a very vacant look in his eyes. I figured he was about done for, so I left him alone to die in peace and got up to deal with Dorothy. I'd had entirely enough of her fucking screeching and was going to end it. Except that she decided to run. The crazy bitch jumped up on the stack of pallets that was precariously balanced on the wheelbarrow, and promptly upset the whole thing. She crashed down next to the wall with a thud and clatter of wood. I wasn't about to leave her alive to gather up some more goons and chase me all over creation. Besides, she needed to pay for what she'd done to those kids. Who made me judge, jury and executioner, you ask?* I *fucking did. Elected my goddamn self. In the world as its currently constituted you handle your own business, and that bitch had become mine.*

*She was trying to get up, but the stack of pallets had pinned her legs. The screeching had stopped though, so I was happy about that at least. I stared at her from three steps away. She stared back, saw the bloody knife in my hand and her two goons I'd vanquished. Goon # 3 had fallen strangely silent. I only realized that fact later, after everything was over. She opened her mouth slightly then closed it. I took a step toward her and that appalling mouth opened again. This time she spoke. The twat actually begged for her life! Can you believe it? After everything she'd done? "Don't kill me, please! It wasn't my fault! You don't understand! They made me do it!" and all that jazz. I'm sure you can imagine it. I didn't answer, just took another step toward her, going for the kill. Her right hand was in plain view. It was on the ground at her side. I didn't think to look for her left hand, and that little oversight almost killed me. A board on one of the pallets had broken loose when the stack fell over, and she'd managed to get hold of it. One end had four nails sticking out of it where it had once been anchored to the rest of the structure. Dorothy tried to hit me in the head with it. I'm lucky I'm fast and that she was a bit slow, because I was just able to dodge it. I reacted instinctively, kicked out at her arm and was rewarded with a sickening, yet most gratifying, crack as some bone broke. She screeched again, but I didn't give her time to keep it up. I picked up her erstwhile murder weapon and hit her in the head with it. The nails all penetrated her skull. She shut up instantly and went rigid. I have no idea if she died right then or after I cut her throat like she'd done to who knows how many kids. The cut bled a lot, so maybe she was still alive. I don't care. Her death has not cost me a minute of sleep since. Both goons were dead now, and I was more than ready to be away from this place, so I righted the wheelbarrow, restacked some of the pallets and climbed up to have a look over the fence. My rifle was ready just in case Goon # 3 was lurking around trying to get the drop on me. But he was down on his back with a small gang of The Fucking Dead chewing on him. Nothing to see here. Move along. Just zombies feasting. I rolled the wheelbarrow down the wall a ways and checked again. No Fucking Dead. So over I went and off into the dark. Found a house a few miles from the farm and went to sleep. Now here I am. More to come tomorrow. Or the next day. Or whenever I fucking feel like writing in this goddamn journal again.*

*June 24, 2026*

*Took a few days off from writing, as you should be able to tell by the dates. Do you even pay attention to them? They are a timeline of my life and story, but does it mean anything to you? Do they register? Do the gaps of days between them make you wonder what I did during those times? Should I even bother continuing to date the entries? Yeah, I suppose I will. There might be some future academic reader of this little tome who actually is interested in the dates and how they relate to the events I've been chronicling. There is another reason I date the entries though. It helps me track the passage of time. When your days amount to little more than scavenging for food, keeping clear of The Fucking Dead, and trying to find a place to sleep where* they *won't find* you, *well… the days sort of all blur together. One season blends into another, and pretty soon you have no idea how long you've been living this way. That's how it was before I started this journal. Now I feel more… what's the word? Grounded? Maybe. Tethered. That's better. I feel tethered to life a little more than I did before I started writing things down. It also gives me a purpose other than survival. Once in a while I run into someone who has no purpose at all. They're just existing from one day to the next. No goal. No destination. They just wander, scavenge, shit, and sleep. Hell, they might as well be The Fucking Dead themselves. I won't be one of them. Some day in the future The Fucking Dead will all be gone, rotted and their bones scattered. When that happens people will begin to rebuild, if there are any people left. I plan to live as long as I can, so who knows – maybe I'll be one of the lucky ones to come out the other end of this zombie-infested colon of a world.*

*Just reread some earlier entries, and I realized there were a few things I didn't tell you. That is, things that happened after I killed Dorothy and escaped from her personal insane asylum. I told you about the bike, but there were a few other things that happened that I forgot to mention. I did say it had been an eventful period.*

*Three days or so after I got out of that madhouse, I found a fantastic cache of canned food. Ran across what looked like a cattle ranch and poked around for a while. There was no one there alive, just a few skeletons. No need to go into details. I'll just say that some people were unable to deal with the world as it is now and chose to check out of this mortal hotel early. (Just made that one up. I like it better than 'mortal coil'. Might use it again sometime.) So, I'm rummaging through things, cabinets, closets, wherever I get a notion to look, and I accidentally bumped into a grandfather clock. Something thumped inside it, which of course made me look. It was full of good stuff! Chili! Peaches! Green beans! Fruit cocktail! Dinty Moore Beef Stew! I had a right feast that night! My stomach was so full I fell asleep almost immediately. Didn't even try to hide. I hadn't seen any Fucking Dead since the farm, so figured I'd be ok for one night. That's breaking my own rule about always being as safe as possible, but what the fuck? It's mine. I'll break it whenever I want.*

*Left the next morning with all my limbs and digits intact. No Fucking Dead found me so quit yer bellyachin' about safety. I don't want to hear it. It's my shitty little life and I'll live it or die however the fuck I want.*

*Ok, moving on.*

*I took as much of that canned food as I could carry, which was all of it. You crazy? You think I'd leave even a* single *can behind? No fuckin' way! Food like that is like… food to the starving. When you don't have any, it's all you think about. Piss on gold or jewels, mansions or fancy cars, women (or men if that's the way you roll), or anything else you can imagine or desire. Food is all that matters when you're hungry. Just ask anyone who spent time in the Soviet Gulag or Nazi concentration camps. Don't believe me? Read Primo Levi or Solzhenitsyn. They're both well-known; they won't be hard to find.*

*Three days after I left that old ranch, I ate the last can of food. It was mandarin oranges. They were SO good! That's another reason I'm going to Florida. Guess I just decided that right now. Oranges. I love them. Florida is famous for its oranges. So, I'm going to Florida. There. All done. Decision made, destination set.*

*I rode and rode, over hill and dale, for nigh upon half a fortnight ere I encountered what could surely have proved my undoing. (Couldn't resist waxing poetic [or maybe archaic, you decide] for a moment. Sorry. No, not sorry. That was kinda fun to write.) Translation of previous passage: I rode that damned bike for a week without seeing shit until the day I ran across one of the strangest sights I've ever seen. I tried to stick to the larger roads – highways, freeways, and the like – back roads are too narrow, the vegetation too close to the pavement. It's easier to ambush someone on those kinds of roads. The highways were more open, wider, even though they have their own dangers. It's a calculated risk, just like everything else in life.*

*I reached one of those big cloverleaf interchanges that are so common on interstates, and down on the ground under one of the overpasses was a crowd of people. It was a big group; I guessed there had to be over five hundred people there. That was more than the farm – by a lot. What the hell was this? I could hear sounds – cheers, yells, epithets, but had no idea what it was all about. An offramp led down to the crowd, and I rode slowly toward them. A couple people at the back noticed me but didn't do anything. There didn't seem to be any threat, so I kept approaching. Eventually I reached them. There was an older cat, probably in his sixties with long white hair and beard who was a little apart from the main group. They were all gathered around something I couldn't see, so I asked the guy what was happening. You know what he told me? A fucking football game! I was a fan of the NFL before, not a superfan who had to watch every game of every team, wear the jersey, paint the house in the team colors and all that, but I liked it. I won't tell you which team(s) I was a supporter of though. If you, future reader, were a fan of one of my team('s) arch-enemies, then I don't want you to get your panties all in a twist and quit reading this. I don't know why I care about that, but I do. I'm weird, I guess. Gimme a fucking break already.*

*I didn't ask the dude to go into details because I wanted to see this myself. The crowd was stacked up ten deep, so I walked my bike around until I found a little pile of dirt I could climb to get a better look. Sure as shit there was a game of sorts going on. Someone had set up a chain-link fence in a roughly oval pattern. It was about thirty yards long by about twenty wide and inside it were a bunch of The Fucking Dead! They were all wearing football helmets and wandering toward one end of the "field". I hadn't seen it before but there was a small wooden tower across from me, about ten feet tall and with a little platform on top. Two men were up there sitting on folding chairs, and each had a little plastic bucket in front of him. One would reach in and pull out something, then toss it to the zombies in the pen below. They would knock each other over trying to get to it. Eventually one of them would get the object and... of course you guessed right – start eating it. Those guys were throwing meat of some kind to the Fucking Dead. I don't want to know where they got it.*

*I quit watching the "game" and started watching the crowd. The people were gambling on the event. I saw all kinds of things change hands as bets were won and lost. I don't know what they were betting on, or even what the rules of the game were. Some girl came up to me and asked if I wanted to wager my bike against her three rounds of .38 Special ammo. I said no. She walked away pissed off. Fuck her. I don't have a .38. Why would I want her shitty little bullets? Besides, my bike is worth way more than three rounds. Offer a hundred and we might start a conversation.*

*One of the Fucking Dead was chewing vigorously on a piece of meat it had acquired, and the rest were pawing at it, trying to take away the morsel, when someone at the opposite end of the field screamed. I looked in that direction and was, not shocked, nothing shocks me anymore, but as surprised as I probably could have been, to see three big men open a little gate in the fence and shove a woman into the pen with the zombies. She was screaming and crying about something, I couldn't understand her words over the crowd. The guys on the platform each threw a piece of meat in her direction; one of them hit her in the side of the head. The crowd went crazy, cheering like they'd just watched a touchdown pass in overtime. The Fucking Dead started converging on her, and she ran along the fence to get away. That worked for a moment, until they'd found the meat the guys threw and devoured it. Then they came at her. The meat had left a smear of blood on her face, and they must have smelled it because they were coming for her. It was weird to see them with football helmets on. I forgot to mention – the little bars across the front (What are they called? Faceguards?) were gone, so there was nothing impeding their ravenous teeth. She ran this way and that, trying to escape, but there was nowhere to go. If she got too close to the fence or tried to climb it, someone would show her a knife or sharpened stick, and she'd move away. Damned if she did, damned if she didn't. The crowd was in ecstasy. I was sickened. That woman had survived who knew what, and was going to meet her end like this? Purposely thrown to The Fucking Dead?*

*I'd seen enough. The capacity for cruelty and callousness exhibited by my fellow "humans" still has the ability to repel me.*

*Think I'm going to stop there. I'll tell you the rest later.*

*July 21, 2026*

*I'm in Georgia now. Got across Mississippi and Alabama over the last few weeks. How did I do that so quickly? I found another bike. This one lasted me until the tiny little town of Pansey, Alabama on US-84. I've decided to live on the west coast of Florida, and there's one simple reason for that. I want to watch the sun set into the sea. It seems wrong to me to see it come up out of the ocean like you would on the east coast. Maybe I'll find a nice beach somewhere around Tampa or Sarasota. How do I know the geography of Florida? I read a map dummy. Try it sometime, you might learn something. That reminds me. There was a girl I went to high school with who could not point to our hometown on a map. She had no idea where we lived. That type of ignorance always bothered me. And it made me wonder. Was that a failing of our education system, the parents, or the student? My guess is it was an amalgam of all three. Still bothered me though. Hell, it bothers me now. The problem with ignorance is that most do not really know how ignorant they actually are until that very ignorance is pointed out to them. And just so we are quite clear, there is a difference between ignorance and stupidity. Ignorance is simply the absence of knowledge. Stupidity comes in two forms: believing your abilities are greater than they are and being utterly unable to learn from your mistakes.*

*I left off last time by telling you about the zombie football game and the lady they threw into that pen with The Fucking Dead. Ok, we'll pick up the story from there.*

*I didn't want to watch that woman's end. Why? What was the point? She'd never done anything bad to me, and I don't find it entertaining to watch someone die. Haven't we all seen enough death? Are we all so debased and dehumanized now that we can actually turn someone's last moments into a sporting event? A spectacle? Apparently we are. So that's why I left. Got on my bike and rode away. I don't know how that all came to be – the pen, the zombies, the helmets, the crowd. The whole thing is still a mystery to me. I can surmise that some enterprising individual found a way to support him or herself by creating the whole thing, profiting from death, but I don't know for sure. If that's how it all came about, then good for that person. And I hope they burn in hell. We should be banding together against The Fucking Dead, not feeding each other to them. I did say it was an eventful period, didn't I?*

*Not much happened after I left the "game". I just rode and rode. Finding food was fairly simple. There were lots of farms along my route, and while they hadn't been tended since before, there were still a lot of things growing wild. My menu was strictly vegetarian, but that's fine. I like vegetables and fruits. I'm a botanist, remember? Plants are sort of my thing. Saw a few deer and other animals, but I left them alone. FedEx Steve (sure hope he's doing well and finds his family) taught me a bit about how to dress wild game, and I will no doubt use those skills in the future, but for the moment I had enough food. Besides, animals are as much fun to watch as they are delicious to eat. Once I've established myself on the west coast of Florida, I might set up a little place where I can process any game I kill. If I was to kill a deer right now, I'd spend most of my next two or three days cutting and drying or smoking it. I'm not willing to do that right now since I'm kind of in a hurry to get to Florida. Since when was I in a hurry? Since getting away from the farm, I guess. That place, what I saw there, is still with me. I think about it more than I'd like to admit. Somewhere in the back of my mind I've been telling myself to get as far away from that accursed place as I can. And I have. It's far beyond the horizon now. Florida is ahead.*

*Look forward, never back.*

# PLUGGED

"Is there *anything* that's not racist these days?" the woman asked. Blank stares and closed mouths offered no answer. She surveyed the other people in the living room of the upscale house. They were women just like her. Most of them were mothers. All of them loved to do what they were doing right that moment – sitting around in their little group, sipping chardonnay, and gossiping about everything. Except things that really mattered. They were pretentious and well-to-do but not as ghastly as those hideous harpies on the 'reality' tv shows about housewives. There was a good deal of narcissism in this room, but it was not at an All-Star level.

Karen realized a moment too late that she'd crossed over an undefined but gargantuan imaginary line by asking her question. It wasn't a line really; it was more like the Demilitarized Zone separating North and South Korea. She'd just walked right into the minefield. Snipers were watching her through their scopes, adjusting for elevation and windage, and artillery pieces were zeroing in the range.

The other women in the room were doing one of two things: looking directly at Karen with undisguised horror, or pointedly looking away from her while desperately pretending not to have heard the question she'd just posed. One did not talk about such things here. It was strictly verboten. Like yelling 'fire' in a crowded theater, or 'bomb' in an airport security line. Someone chuckled softly, nervously, then tried to turn it into a polite cough. The attempt was unsuccessful. Everyone knew it was a ploy to cover up yet another major social gaffe. One did not laugh about such things here. That too was strictly prohibido. Like laughing at someone's kid who'd fallen flat on his face (unhurt, mind you!) while trying to show off for his friends, or maybe discovering a nugget of humor in the jokes of a particularly off-color comedian. There were rules that governed gatherings of this variety. Unwritten. Unspoken. As stout as a bank vault door and locked up securely inside. Karen had, in a few seconds, cracked the vault, stolen the contents, and murdered the security guards and tellers on the way out. She may even have kicked a puppy. Hard. But she'd left the bank management team intact, and they were silently expressing their extreme disapproval.

"I think Tristan is almost done with soccer practice," a woman named Trinity said as she stood to leave.

"My mother is texting me," someone else intoned. "Looks like her water heater isn't working."

In moments the party was over as the women collected their things and departed. In mere moments Karen was left alone with the owner of the house, a woman named Lila.

"I can't believe I forgot," the hostess said, "Evan needs me to meet him somewhere this afternoon. I have to go. I'm sorry," she said placatingly but with more anxious urgency than she probably intended. Karen took the hint and left with a wave and a promise to get in touch soon. The moment the door closed on her Subaru Outback, she burst into tears. It took her fifteen minutes to get herself under control enough to drive away. She never heard from any of the other women ever again.

"Look at this shit," the teenaged boy said as he stared at his phone. "It's a whole fucking gang. They're beating that guy's ass. What the fuck?"

"You can't fight them one on one. They all jump in every time," another kid said.

"The enemy of my enemy is my friend," said yet another.

"What the fuck does that mean?" asked the first boy.

"I don't know. Heard it in history class the other day."

The man in the car was thinking and talking to himself as he drove down the freeway.

*Fuck that stupid teacher bitch. Trying to teach* my *kid to judge people based only on race? No fuckin' way. I'll yank her out of that class before I let her finish that assignment. What kind of psycho would even think of having kids do that anyway? Tell them to go out in the halls and look at the groups of kids exclusively by race, figure out which are the most oppressed and which are the most privileged, then write a report about it? Making sure to explain what, specifically, each student is going to do to be more inclusive in the future? What kind of shit is this? Somehow I don't think MLK would approve. Wasn't he the one who talked about judging people based on character and not skin color? I think so. Doesn't really matter who said it – they were right. This shit is fucking ridiculous. And this is an assignment in a* Health *class?*

*What happened to learning about cells and the digestive system? Shit like that? They throw that out to make room for all this woke bullshit? I'm calling the goddam principal the minute I get to the office. My daughter is* not *going to be taking that class or doing that assignment. I might even file a formal complaint against that retarded fucking health teacher. Stupid bitch.*

"Did you kids hear that the Polish army is going to buy ten thousand septic tanks?"

Four sets of puzzled eyes stared back at the old man. A small boy of perhaps eight years shook his head.

"As soon as they learn to drive them, they're going to invade Russia."

One of the children, a girl of fourteen, smiled slightly. Or maybe it was more of a grimace. The expressions of the others didn't change.

"You know that's kinda racist, right grandpa?" the girl said.

"Racist, shmacist," the old man replied. "It's funny. Imagine driving a septic tank to invade a country! Like it was a Sherman or something."

"It's not funny to make fun of other people," the girl admonished.

"Yes, it is," her grandfather said. "You kids today have all gotten too soft. What's that word they use? Snowflake. That's it. We all should be able to laugh at jokes, even at jokes that are about us. And that's what I just told you – a joke. I have nothing against the Polish people, and they certainly aren't any dumber than anyone else. It's a joke. Nothing more."

"But," the girl said, "my teacher told our class that things like that are microagressions, and that they hurt people's feelings."

The old man grunted. "Some people *need* their feelings hurt," he muttered.

*Project Manager wanted. Pay DOE. Minimum Requirements: bachelor's degree in related field or equivalent practical experience. We are an all-inclusive company, BIPOC and DEI friendly. Those from privileged and elevated backgrounds are discouraged from applying.*

"I'll tell you exactly why you're racist," the woman said to her audience. "Every one of you in this room has been prejudiced since before you were conceived. It's in your DNA. You can't help it. You were all literally made that way."

The audience in the barn at the abandoned lodge was raptly listening to this woman speak. Each person had paid north of twenty-thousand dollars to attend this seminar. But not one of them had questioned why an event like this was being held in such a dilapidated building. It was enough that they were there, in the presence of the august and learned speaker. Many of them began crying when they learned they'd been racists since before their own conception. Tissues were liberally applied to dripping eyes and runny noses. Others, not crying, stared at the floor in shame.

"But there is something you can do." That perked up the audience. Sniffles replaced sobs, heads looked up from shoe-gazing to reengage with the speaker. This was new. Maybe there was hope for them, a way to get rid of their innate racism.

"You all received a welcome bag when you registered. No doubt some of you have already noticed a strange item and a tube of epoxy inside it?" Heads nodded around the room.

"You'll learn what to do with them soon enough. But first I'm going to tell you why they're in there." Expectant, hopeful gazes, some bordering on fanaticism, waited anxiously for the next pronouncement from the sage at the front of the room.

"Everything you do is racist. Everything! Even defecating." Some of the hopeful expressions changed to puzzled frowns.

"You heard me correctly. Taking a shit is racist. You all know that shit is brown right?" Heads nodded in acknowledgement. "So you expelling it from your asses and flushing it down the toilet is the absolute most racist thing you can do. That turd you just shat out is representative of every oppressed brown person all around the world. If you were truly not racist, you'd scoop that turd right out of your toilet bowl and show it the love you've never shown to any brown person ever in your miserable lives." The weeping had begun again in earnest. Nearly the entire audience was sobbing in torment at this most horrific of transgressions. How could they all have been so blind? It was unconscionable. Unforgivable.

"There is only one way for you to all get absolution for this sin, and it's going to be a group effort. You will have to help each other." Heads bobbed furiously as this lifeline splashed down just within their reach. "Every one of you stand up and drop your pants. Underwear too." The audience looked around in confusion. Was she serious?

"I'm one hundred percent serious," the sage intoned in an imperious voice. "Do it now."

The attendees stood and did as she bade them.

"Alright. Now take out the epoxy and that other little thing. Do any of you know what it is?"

A woman three rows from the front cautiously raised her hand. The sage gestured for her to speak. "I think it's a… butt plug. Right?"

The sage nodded. "That's exactly what it is. Now here's where you're going to help each other. Take the cap off the epoxy and squirt it all over the plug. Now, one person bend over. For the person standing, I want you to shove that plug right up the other person's ass. That's it. Make sure you put more epoxy around the outside. I don't want a single one of those plugs coming out."

A man in the front row raised his hand hesitantly. The sage graced him with her gaze and nodded. "I'm a doctor. This isn't going to be very… healthy… for us."

"And how healthy do you think it was for all those poor brown turds you flushed? How do you think they felt being shat out your ass and just abandoned to drown in the sewer?"

"Well, I see what you're saying, but…"

"No. There are no buts. Except all yours being plugged. That's it. Your racism ends today."

"Can you believe this shit?" a policeman said to one of his colleagues. They were at a decrepit lodge in a remote part of their state. Some hunters had come through the property, which had been abandoned for years, and discovered a terrible scene. At least forty people, dead in a rundown barn.

"No, I can't. Coroner says he's never seen anything like it. It reminded him of Jonestown. He suspects they all died from perforated colons based on the fact that every one of them plugged their asses shut."

"Any idea why?"

"Not yet. Some kind of cult or something is what everyone's thinking so far."

"What a bunch of fucking morons."

*Sowers, Mark [@MarkSowersBooks].* "Posting this for a story I'm writing so I can cite it. In MLA format even. If you're a good and decent person, we'll probably get along. If you're an as*ho*e, we probably won't." *X, 17 February, 2024,*

https://twitter.com/MarkSowersBooks/status/1759011878498705707

# ABOUT THE AUTHOR

Mark grew up in Tacoma, Washington, and currently lives in Wasilla, Alaska. When he was very young he lived for two years in a suburb of Athens, Greece. This experience to this day shapes and informs his perspective on other cultures. After spending much of his twenties working various labor and construction related jobs, he decided it was time to get an education.

He began attending Tacoma Community College, where he received an Associates in Arts and Sciences in 2005. Mark, with an ever-persistent desire to improve himself and challenge himself to reach his goals, decided to continue his education and enrolled at the University of Alaska, Southeast (UAS). Obtaining a Bachelor's degree had been a personal goal for many years, and in 2013, he achieved it graduating magna cum laude from UAS with a Bachelor of Arts, Social Science. He majored in History and minored in Economics and Political Science.

In between college endeavors Mark met his amazing wife Marcy and they moved to Juneau, AK and married in 2009. They have raised three incredible children, Jade, Iris and Harold. The couple eventually moved to Wasilla. They now have a grandson, Levi Henry, also known as Henle, who has the most infectious smile and has them both wrapped around his little finger. They have a German Shepherd who entertains them on a regular basis. The couple loves moose watching, gardening and enjoying Marcy's culinary delights, always created with much love.

He enjoys music and has been an avid musician since he started playing guitar at age 12. Mark is a talented musician who is mostly self-taught. After guitar he took on the challenge of teaching himself drums and bass guitar. Mark has been in several bands throughout his life. He and his wife dream of creating an incredible jam space for Mark to pursue his love of music.

A short time after graduation he landed a job working in the Arctic oilfields of Kuparuk which is west of Prudhoe Bay. With the catastrophic effects of COVID19 and the oil price depression Mark was let go from his position on the north slope. However, during that time Mark was able to see some things most people never get to see such as arctic foxes, herds of caribou, brown bear roaming the tundra (he did not get to see a polar bear), but unfortunately did see the thick, black swarms of mosquitos in summer. Mosquitos are affectionately known as the Alaska state bird. Mark worked long hours, twelve-hour days for fourteen days straight. He commuted to and from work to and from Kuparuk on a flight that took an hour and forty minutes by jet (in state)!

This schedule, while rigorous allowed him to pursue another goal - writing.

During Covid-19 quarantine Mark completed the second in the series The Blackfire Chronicles, Volume 2 which is close to publication! He is currently working on Volume 3 along with several other exciting works. A new job allows Mark to work closer to home and his schedule provides him more time to pursue his writing career. In summer, when he is not helping his wife in the garden he is writing or mowing the lawn, (which is so big it takes 8+ hours on a riding mower!) he is finishing other books, short story collections, editing and writing. Ultimately, he would love to retire to spend his days at his true passion, writing! Your support reading his books, writing reviews are what can help him get there!

# WORD OF THANKS

Thank you, dear reader, for
reading, *Fractum Ostium*.

Please take a minute to leave a review for this book on Amazon and Goodreads. All feedback and reviews are helpful for authors.

Mark hopes you have enjoyed this book as much as he did writing it. He is working diligently at creating, he can often be found writing at his desk. Follow him as an author on Amazon to make sure you are notified of his latest publications. Mark works hard to reply to all reader emails. His blog page has an email form you can use to write to him. You can also follow Mark:

On X, @MarkSowersBooks

on Minds, @MarkSowersAuthor

his blog at: http://www.marksowersbooks.com

# BOOKS BY THE AUTHOR

## The Blackfire Chronicles Series Overview

The Blackfire - that mysterious and gigantic wheel of black flame spinning in the southern sky has been an enigma for thousands of turnings. What is it? Who created it and why? Magic – it once existed, but no longer. Where did it go? Will it return someday? Revan and Arval – two young men, slaves, who seek to escape their tormentors, the brutal and vile Nojii. How will they win their freedom? What will they discover when they finally escape, and where will fate lead them? Will secrets and knowledge, long hidden and lost, be revealed and understood?

### *The Blackfire Chronicles, Volume 1*

From the depths of a pit in a barren desert rises an enormous stone box. Slaves toil in the broiling heat, digging out the mysterious object which has no door, no windows, no features of any kind. Revan has spent nearly his entire life here. He has only vague and indistinct memories of a time before he dug for his life. Unseen and unknown to him, above the rim of the pit and far to the south, looms the Blackfire – a gigantic rotating wheel of black flames that obscures and dominates the entirety of the southern sky. Red and gold lightning flash threateningly and ominously in its fringes. Can Revan escape the pit, find his freedom, and discover the secrets of the Blackfire?

***The Blackfire Chronicles, Volume 2***

In the aftermath of the violence in Kessar, Arval learns what it means to disobey the Jix. Revan reaches Enrat and resumes his search for the documents that may help answer some of his many questions. Kanar passes through the Blackfire with the mysterious cowled man. What does he find on the other side, and will it help him in his mission for revenge on the Nojii? New characters, new places, and new adventures are waiting inside The Blackfire Chronicles, Volume 2.

***The Blackfire Chronicles, Volume 3***

Two Kryxaal found, two more hidden somewhere in the world and the Blackfire spins more ferociously, yet with more ominous mystery than anyone in The Three Kingdoms can remember. What happened to Otarab when he fell from the steep and slick steps down the wall of Enrat's promontory? Kanar and Savasta begin to make their way back to the Blackfire to pass through it on a mysterious mission from Ul'll Uhas. Arval, with the help of Miladwin, discovered just what Revan's white tunnels look like, but found something more than he was expecting when he finally entered them for himself. And Revan last saw Queen Andissa with an arrow in her back as she fell from the ramp of light that had saved their lives. Answers, new revelations, new places, new creatures, and new characters are waiting in The Blackfire Chronicles Volume 3.

### *Enders & Associates*

Adrian Blake just knows things, which for a time made him one of the FBI's most successful investigators. Some might call him psychic, but whatever his power is, it couldn't prevent the tragedy that changed his life forever. When his mother passes away unexpectedly several years later, Adrian's life is upended when he learns that he has inherited a silver mine. Researching the mine and how it came to belong to his mother reveals an ancestor he hadn't known existed - the enigmatic Bertram Fields. Who exactly was he? When Adrian travels to the small town of Boot Mesa, Arizona to find out, he discovers that strange and terrible things have been happening there for many years. Was his family somehow involved in the mysterious deaths and disappearances? Adrian, with the help of park ranger Mandy Moretti and his old FBI colleague Pete Sparks, will soon find the answers to his questions – and they are far from what he expected.

### *Society's House of Intractable Tension*

Bryce Ingman doesn't know anything different. His entire life has been spent under the steel-shod boot of oppression. In this, the Federated Territories of North America, freedom and self-determination are forgotten notions from a dusty past. But there are those who still remember. Follow along as Bryce discovers what it means to be free, how absurd and self-aggrandizing tyrannical governments actually are, and how much politicians and the institutions they create deserve to be ridiculed. At turns poignant, tragic, sarcastic, parodical, and philosophical, Society's House of Intractable Tension is cautionary tale of what has been and what could yet be if certain elements in society aren't opposed by those who believe in true freedom.

### *French Press Sludge*

French Press Sludge - like the residue left at the bottom of a cup, these are stories author Mark Sowers wrote between working on his full-length novels. Sometimes a tale only needs a few thousand words to be told completely, sometimes it takes tens of thousands. These are the leftovers, the ideas that didn't demand a full-length novel, but that in many ways are just as impactful. From the social commentary of Halftime, to the absurd tragi-comedy of Stoner Ghosts, to the anger, despair and destitution of Apocalypse Pancakes and Never in Blue Genes, this collection of stories follows a disparate and entertaining cast of characters as they navigate through worlds dystopian, apocalyptic, true-to-life, and post-life.

# REVIEWS

**5.0 out of 5 stars AWESTRUCK**

Mark Sowers stuck a bullseye on his first entry into a genre I rarely find engaging. I was captivated by the striking cover art, and absorbed in the creative realm Mark lays out in a manner befitting the best authors established in the field. His ability to capture the settings and characters had me feeling as though I was going along on the adventure with them. Names of characters and places were congruent, dialogue coherent, and pacing captivating. I await the rest of the volumes as I also have had the privilege of reading some of Mark's short stories. Mark Sowers is a gifted author whose career I will follow as closely as I am following Revan and Arval. I hope to see this series on video some day, although seeing it my mind's eye already is as satisfying as any written tale can be to a reader. A must read for those who love adventures of epic scale.

-Amazon Review for ***The Blackfire Chroniclies, Volume 1*** by Philip Blagg

**5.0 out of 5 stars A New Author to Watch in the Fantasy Genre**
With his first book, Mark Sowers has established himself as an author to watch. New authors seem to pop up all the time in this genre, many never to be heard from again after a book or two. Others seem to have that indefinable "something" from their very first chapter. Mr. Sowers, in my opinion, definitely belongs in the latter category. The eye-catching cover and intriguing story description caught my interest and compelled me to hit the purchase button and within a couple of chapters, I was glad I did!

Mark has done an amazing job of creating an immersive world, filled with fascinating locations and peoples. In Revan and Arval, he's brought to life a pair of characters the reader comes to care about, root for, commiserate with, feel their pain, thirst, fear and wonder as they travel on their quest across strange new lands. Several times during the course of the book, I had to stop and shake my head in amazement that I was reading the work of a first time author and not a seasoned pro. This book definitely left me with a desire to see what awaits our heroes next and I'll be anxiously waiting to hit that Purchase button on Book 2 of The Blackfire Chronicles!

-Amazon Review for **The Blackfire Chronicles, Volume 1** by Bob L.

**5.0 out of 5 stars**
Mark continues to delight my mind as I ponder the predicaments his characters endure in so many

imaginative scenarios. His sharp insights regarding the social milieu we share piques my curiosity as to how we relate to one another at this challenging time in the world. Mark's sense of humor is as keen as his sense of irony. His characters' dialogue is authentic in its alternating crudeness or compassion. I eagerly await the next journey on the pages of Mark's excellent and growing body of work.

-Amazon Review for ***French Press Sludge*** by Philip Blagg

**5.0 out of 5 stars Couldn't put it down.**
This story is fast-paced and continues to pull you farther and farther into the story as you read.

Mark tells an interesting story and does it very well.

-Amazon Review for ***Enders & Associates*** by Mike Lupro

**5.0 out of 5 stars Great read**
A very enjoyable book to read I didn't want it to end. I kept looking at how many pages I had left,So Mark needs to get busy writing Volume 3

-Amazon Review for ***The Blackfire Chronicles, Volume 2*** by Howie

**4.0 out of 5 stars Fantastic sequel!**
I'm waiting on pins and needles for the third book! These are so hard to put down and stop reading, but I need to go to work... AWW!

-Amazon Review for ***The Blackfire Chronicles, Volume 2*** by Joyce Baker

**5.0 out of 5 stars Enders**

Enjoyed reading this book and would recommend to others who enjoy a good suspense novel. The writer is very creative with his mix of mystery, suspense and a little bit of the supernatural to keep it exciting.

-Amazon Review for ***Enders & Associates*** by Carol

**5.0 out of 5 stars The saga continues!**

I appreciate this exciting journey as Mark presents it through his creative imagination. What really helps me enjoy it more fully is his manner of referring to aspects of the story that I have a tendency to lose the thread of in other books.
Without being redundant, Mark reminds the reader of details regarding characters, location, and events in a way that expands the understanding of the current state of the

adventure we share. It continues to grow in fascinating ways. Where to next?

-Amazon Review for ***The Blackfire Chronicles, Volume 3*** by Philip Blagg

Made in the USA
Columbia, SC
31 October 2024